The Drop Pot Man

K Saunders

For Gary

Thank you for all your
insightful comments when
g was writing this book.
Keith

For Maureen Devlin… we miss you.

Part One

Somewhere in the West Country of England:
Just before the Ban on Hunting with Dogs.

What has he seen? He's crouching. Now he's on his knees. He's moving his hand. The dog has dropped to the ground. That lurcher of his is well trained. I think I can see something to their right. Yes, at the edge of that hollow... so that's what he's looking at.

The fox has a narrow face and no cheek ruffs. It's the vixen. She seems intent, despite the erect ears and quick movements of her eyes, looking everywhere apart from at the two – no, three – rabbits, at the bottom of the shallow hollow.

The vixen has started to chase her tail, snapping at the white tip of her brush. Then – as if stung by a bee – she's bucked up into the air. Now she's rolling slowly, over and over – the deep russet brown of her upper fur, changing to the white of her under parts and then back again. What the hell is she doing? Of course! This is Fox Charming. I've seen it once before, a long time ago. The fox is acting out a performance to try and mesmerise the rabbits. It's working. They are spell-bound and not moving. The vixen is rolling closer... and closer. She suddenly lunges and snaps: a little early. Spell broken, the rabbits dive into the burrow.

The fox is stretching as if it was all of no consequence. Now she's off, heading across the field at the edge of the wood, probably in search of lesser prey in the sparse downland hedgerows. He's got to his feet and is brushing some leaves from his trousers. A snap of the fingers and the huge brindled lurcher has come to heel... and within seconds they've disappeared into the trees.

I can't see them, but I know they will be moving silently along *the path that is difficult to distinguish from the rest of the woodland floor covering of thick layers of leaf litter and beech mast. It is beautiful that wood. The pale green leaves of spring are turning into a darker canopy, but it is still light enough for the towering trees to create a soaring, cathedral-like, image.*

They will soon be in sight again… Yes; there they are, just inside the trees on the right hand side of the narrow wood. He'll leave the dog now. Yes, it's down on its haunches. He's going on alone, picking his way through the bracken growing at the edge of the trees. He must be able to smell the musty-sweet fox urine before he even sees the fox earth. It's lucky that the earth is right on the edge of the trees. I can see everything from here. He's approaching slowly – strange, there is really no reason too. He must know that the four fox cubs – there were five until recently – will be underground. It will be some time before that vixen with the distinctively deep russet fur will be returning from her scavenging.

He'll go through the routine now. Yes, he's moving the large stone on the top of the earth to one side to uncover the old burrow. Now for the brace of rabbits he has in the poacher's pocket sewn into his combat jacket. They will have blood stains on the back of their necks where they had been caught in the lurcher's jaws. Down the hole they go and now he'll replace the covering stone. Then he'll inspect the fox-hole: the sole entrance to the earth. It is only about eighteen inches high, quite small for a fox-hole, but ideal. It will be easy to block when the time is right.

All done.

He's retracing his footsteps. He re-joins the dog. They disappear from view. It will be a minute or so before they will come out of the wood where they had entered it.

The last of the purple light of dawn is disappearing. It looks like it will be a beautiful day…

There they are. He's stopped and he's unfastening his jacket. I know why, it's what he always does about now. He's going to have a smoke. Yes, he's taking out a tin from an inside pocket and begins to roll a cigarette. That tobacco, almost certainly contraband, would have come from that decrepit back street pub, The White Dog, which is, ironically, only a hundred yards from the old harbour-side Customs and Excise Office – now closed.

Drawing heavily on the roll-up, he's looking around at this great sweep of chalk downland: this sparse landscape where things stand out; the creamy line of the rough flinty track, where his old van is tucked into a field gate; the line of pylons striding out of view, and the white of an old chalk pit that contrasts sharply with the dark shadows of the solitary field barn. And to here, where sheep graze below the three tumuli, the ancient burial mounds which even after three thousand years still form clear bumps on the skyline.

He can't see me with the naked eye… I can see him as if he was yards away.

He's looking up to the sky: he must be listening to the high calling skylarks and at the same time he's stretching out his arms….

Perfect.

A Crucifixion.

Elevation drop correct… windage calculated… dead centred in the scope crosshairs… breath in… gentle… gentle trigger squeeze…

'Agur Aio!!'

Strange, just for the second between the moment the bullet hit him and he fell to the ground, there seemed to be complete silence.

And now you can't hear the call of the skylarks or the bleating of the sheep… for the howling, and howling, of a dog.

1

The truth is that if Graham Styles hadn't slit that postman's throat with a Stanley knife, then Clare Morell wouldn't be here now, in a small nick out in the sticks, waiting to be told she'd been side lined… yet again.

Detective Superintendent Paul Simmonds was staring out of the window at the gates of the police station courtyard. It looked like he was expecting something to happen: an unlikely event. She remembered someone saying that the heavy reinforced gates, built over a hundred years ago in anticipation of riots by farm workers, had only been closed once – fifteen years ago, just before a Poll Tax rally.

She coughed – twice.

'No, I'm afraid not this time, Clare,' he said, as he half-turned from the window. 'I'm going to ask Mike Crick to take charge of this one – yes, yes – I know you had a lot of experience in your last force, but this particular shooting, it's a countryside matter, there's probably no great mystery and Mike's local, he knows the area like the back of his hand.'

'Are you sure, sir?'

Detective Superintendent Paul Simmonds nodded. 'Right, we'll leave it there for now.'

'Yes, sir.'

'Perhaps next time.'

Yes, next time, next time there's something like a messy domestic.

Detective Inspector Clare Morell left the office – and

slammed the door behind her. The frosted panes rattled. She knew that Simmonds would expect her to close the door in something of a huff, so made sure that she used rather more force than he would have been anticipating. Right, she thought, in for a penny, in for a pound. One, two – she pushed on the handle and put her head round the edge of the door.

'Oh, sorry about that, sir – I don't know my own strength sometime.' Her false smile became genuine when she realised that she'd caught him perfectly mid-curse. She stayed just long enough to have the satisfaction of waiting until the corners of his fly-catching mouth, slowly and awkwardly, curved up into a cadaverous smile. Paul Simmonds with his deathly pale complexion, long face and bald head, had been called Yorick when he was a young copper in Stratford-on-Avon. The name had followed him around.

'A fellow of infinite jest, of most excellent fancy… my arse,' she muttered as she walked down the corridor. This had been the third time recently that she'd been angry with Simmonds and she knew from the last couple of occasions there was no point trying to get him to change his mind. Though, there was one thing about him that she was grateful for. In the few months she'd been here, he'd never said anything about why she'd moved sideways – most would say backwards – from Greater Manchester Police to down here. Especially, when there'd been a DCI job at GMP on the cards: a proper front-line, dirty hands promotion. She'd turned down back room and liaison promotion offers in the past.

Clare then went the long way round to the car park to get something from her car that she didn't need. The last thing she wanted to see was an older, but far less experienced, smug looking Detective Inspector Mike Crick coming out of Simmonds's office.

'This won't take long,' said Mike Crick, holding up a folder. 'The dead man's name was Dean Galpin. He was local, from Undermoigne, aged twenty two. He lived with his mother. She didn't know when he went out. The body was discovered on the edge of Full Moon Copse by someone taking a dog for a morning walk, who heard Galpin's own dog howling long before they saw the body. The lurcher had–'

'A lurcher? So, we know what young Galpin was up to, don't we?' interrupted Detective Sergeant Andy Melbury. Melbury, a big, heavy man who looked, even in plain clothes, every inch a policeman, spoke slowly in the distinct soft rolling tones of the local accent.

'Well, you and I know, Andy. I don't know about anyone else,' agreed Crick, looking at the other three people in the room.

'Was he out poaching?' asked PC Karen Garland, one of the two women in the room.

'Course he was, Karen,' answered Crick – who was the only person in the room who'd not registered the gentle sarcasm in her tone. 'He was, with others. I'd put my bottom dollar on some of them being out "lamping" and he got hit with a stray shot by accident and the others buggered-off when they realised he was dead.'

Crick paused for a moment. He was obviously enjoying the experience: a new experience. He had only recently been promoted, very late in a long career in his local force. A second bonus was the fact that the station's detective chief inspector was on long-term sickness leave. Also, as Mike Crick had a reputation of having a very low opinion of women police officers in general, it was a well known fact that he had little regard for the woman DI who 'has only been here two minutes'.

'Oh, I suppose I'd better explain "lamping" to our city folk,' said Crick, looking towards Clare Morell and the young

14

man sitting next to her. 'It's exactly what it says on the tin. It's shooting in the dark with lights.'

Clare, who had been out 'lamping' for foxes on her uncle's farm in the Lakes – said nothing.

'It's strange though, Mike. Poachers with lurchers don't need guns. If night time hunting they need powerful lights like laser spotlights, as the dogs are sight-hounds – but no light was found,' said Melbury, as he scratched his chin and swung back on his chair. It creaked. 'He might have been hit by a fluke shot from someone. Remember me telling you about my cousin getting a .22 bullet through her kitchen window?'

'The Kenwood Chef copped it, apparently,' whispered the young man sitting next to Clare. She glanced at him. Detective Constable Matt Johns looked as if he should still be wisecracking from the back of a classroom, rather than sitting in a CID incident room.

'Right, now who's carrying out the PM?' Crick, who ignoring completely Melbury's remarks, then answered his own question by looking in the folder he was holding,

Clare, her head buzzing with what the detective sergeant had said, was watching Crick carefully.

Hmm… he's hesitating.

'Well, Andy, you and me will go and have a word with Sir Alan Vine. Full Moon Copse is on the Winterstone estate and Sir Alan usually knows what's going on, on his land.'

'What about the post-mortem info?' asked Melbury.

Crick wiped his forehead with the back of his hand. A heavy, red-faced overweight man, who smoked, drank and ate too much, Crick looked as if he would not make great demands on the police pension fund. He pushed the folder, slowly, reluctantly, across the desk towards Clare and Johns. 'Perhaps you and Wonder Boy here can go and check up on things at the morgue?'

Clare nodded: Crick, as always, was reluctant to use her name.

'Well, come on, Andy! Oh, and Karen, you put things together here, and let me know if anything new comes in. OK?'

'Yes, Inspector.'

Crick and Melbury left the office. Clare picked up and opened the folder. A Doctor Nick Howarth was in charge of the post-mortem. Matt Johns went over and sat on the edge of the young woman PC's desk.

'Karen, what's all this Sir Alan business?'

She stroked back the pony-tail of her auburn hair, as she looked up. 'Oh, it just gives Cricky a chance to put on his green wellies and his Barbour jacket and go to the big house to see his lord and her ladyship and tug his fore-thingy.'

'Tug his fore… lock,' said Johns, playing her game.

'If you say so, Matt.'

Clare looked up from the folder and smiled: she liked these two. She tapped an open page, 'Karen?'

'Yes, boss?'

'What's the history between Inspector Crick and Dr Nick Howarth?'

'It's funny you should say that. Dr Howarth got really annoyed with Inspector Crick in a case some time ago and complained to the Super. It was about the inspector just barging into the morgue and being off-hand or something. That's probably why he passed it on it to you.'

'Yes, I thought it was something like that. Thanks, Karen,' said Clare as, with her finger on the open folder, she picked up the telephone.

Just at that moment Crick burst back into the office and grabbed something off a desk. 'You lot still here, chop-chop,' he snapped as he left.

Johns picked up a newspaper, turned to the crossword

and took out a pen. 'Four letter word… starts with a T… ends with a T as well.'

By the time Clare came out into the station yard, Johns was already waiting for her in his car: a clean little Peugeot. With his boyish face and short blond hair he looked no older than some of the joy-riders she'd seen being dragged into police stations. She smiled at the thought.

The young detective constable looked at her quizzically, 'What?'

'Nothing, Matt.'

Johns turned out of the station and onto the main road leading into the town from the north, a road that in a few weeks would be jammed with cars full of tired holidaymakers and stroppy are-we-there-yet kids. Clare had noticed that Johns, unlike other times, said very little when he was behind the wheel. DC Matt Johns had only been stationed here for about four months. Barely two months less than herself. Clare liked working with him: firstly, he was bright; secondly, there was no chance of anyone mistaking him for the inspector, and thirdly… she decided to put the third reason on hold.

They were passing the old part of the College, where neatly cut lawns set the elegant group of buildings off a little from the road, when Clare looked at her watch. 'Matt, pull in at the back of M&S. By the time we've seen Dr Howarth, we'll be starving.'

'I'll say,' said Johns as he turned at the roundabout onto the esplanade.

For anyone unfamiliar with the town, the sea front makes a sudden appearance when driving in from the north. One minute, the road is lined by fine, huge houses, now converted into hotels, guest houses or flats – then suddenly there's the elegant curve of one of the finest esplanades in the country:

four narrow strips as one, of seafront buildings, road, promenade, and sand, that front the sea.

Johns pointed to the statue of Queen Victoria. She looked rather less severe than usual, due to the addition of an empty Kentucky Fried Chicken bucket perched on her bonnet.

'Suits her better than a traffic cone, boss?

'Definitely,' replied Clare – thinking that HM would most certainly 'not be amused'.

They drove to the far end of the esplanade where the main shopping street backed onto the sea and parked on the yellow lines opposite the rear entrance of Marks and Spencer.

'What do you want, Matt?'

'Err… err… err.'

Clare held out a ten-pound note. 'Right, you go instead. I'll have a pasta salad with light dressing, one of those "Good for You" jobs and a bottle of water.'

'Boss, you can't be watching your weight! You're just about the only woman in the station who doesn't have to. Most of them would scratch each other's eyes out to have your–'

'Out!'

'And your–'

'Out!' she laughed as she pushed him.

Johns stopped just before he entered the store. His broad smile changed to one of mock horror as he pointed down the sea front to where the formidable figure of the traffic warden, known locally as Eva Braun – after her penchant for wearing jack boots – was picking her relentless way along the line of parked cars. Clare slid across onto the driver's seat and twirled a finger, indicating that, if necessary, she would drive down to the roundabout and back. Unlike some she had worked with, DI Morell liked to stay as anonymous as possible: no pulling rank, plain clothes, in her book, meant plain clothes.

While keeping an eye on Eva Braun's progress, she thought about what Johns had said. Yes, she was lucky. She ate healthily (most of the time) and exercised by choice and not of necessity. Nearly five foot nine and never been over nine stones (well nearly) in her life, now seemed to be pay-back time for being a stick-insect when young. It was a family thing. Her father was tall and still slim and she, so she had been told, was like her mother. The mother she had never known, who had died giving birth to her. It was uncanny how that photograph she had of her mother sitting on a bicycle looked exactly like photos of her in university when her hair was long: unlike now. She looked up at the rear view mirror and ran a hand over her short jet black hair. Her mother and her. Her dad had often said that she had her mother's eyes. The strange grey eyes were a family feature from her mother's side. There was an old wives' tale, that some of the women would inherit 'the sight' and could tell fortunes. Her grandmother, she had been told, was one of these. There is one more family trait. The embarrassment of being accused of being underage in pubs when she was twenty is proving beneficial at thirty five.

Then she thought about her father again. It was only a few hours drive back home to that northern borderland where the flat plains of Cheshire meet the slopes of the Pennines. Clare had little trace of a northern accent. Her father, in contrast, had never lost his Cumbrian tones. She hadn't seen him, for what, four months? This was about the longest period ever. Her 'gap year', as such – some of which she couldn't remember, and some of what she could remember, she wished she could forget – was about the same length of time.

Dad and her…

They'd had their fair share of, 'You're not going out dressed like that!' and 'What time do you call this?'

Clare caught her smile in the rear-view mirror. Yes, it was

always worse if both happened on the same night. But they only seriously fell out once… and how. She got a first in English and was offered a chance to do a doctorate. He told just about everybody. Then she told him what she was going to do.

One copper's enough in this family he muttered, and didn't speak another word to her for two days. It was assumed that she was just following in his footsteps, but that was not true. Only she knew the real reason why she joined the police… and it made her shudder every time she thought about it.

There would be no need for her to move the car. The traffic warden and a motorist were having an altercation. It looked rather one sided. A very small man being harangued by a large woman against a backcloth of promenade, sand and sea: like an old seaside postcard come to life.

Clare slid across into the passenger seat.

'I wouldn't like to be in his trousers,' said Johns as he got in the car. He passed Clare a carrier bag and her change. 'Cheers. I'll pay for the next lot – and I'll throw in a yoghurt.'

She noticed that the carrier bag, in addition to the pasta salad and water, contained a prawn sandwich, a small packet of low-fat crisps and a can of diet coke.

Well, that makes a change from the pie and chips of old!

Johns turned round in the road and drove back down the sea front. From this direction the rump of the pier looks a little longer and the fine-spire church near to the be-decked Queen Victoria, makes a dramatic full-stop to the esplanade. Johns turned away from the sea to where the surprisingly large nature reserve stretches virtually into the heart of the town. They were going to a low – almost camouflaged – building, just the other side of the tongue of open water and the fringing reed beds with their scattered patches of scrubby bush.

The morgue.

2

The secretary knocked on the door and entered. 'It's Detective Inspector Morell.'

'Detective Inspector Morell, come in. I'm Nick Howarth,' said a tall, gangling, middle aged man, who had got to his feet and was walking towards them, smiling.

'Dr Howarth,' Clare shook hands: a handshake, considering his occupation, which was reassuringly warm.

'Thank you for phoning. It is very much appreciated. Some of your colleagues just roll-up and expect me to drop everything.'

'This is DC Johns,' Clare said quickly, anxious to curtail Johns's widening smile at the dig at Crick.

'How do you do, sir.'

Howarth gestured them towards the two chairs on the opposite side of his desk to his own.

'Amazing view,' said Clare, looking out over the reed beds which almost came up to the huge low office window, and onto the open water beyond.

'Yes, you can see why I sit with my back to it; otherwise I wouldn't get much work done. Funny though, although it may seem a strange location for this place when you consider that over there,' he pointed in the direction of the old harbour, 'was where it was thought that the Black Death entered the country in 1348, then perhaps not.'

Just then some birds flitted in the reeds nearby.

'I really should take more interest in ornithology – I

suppose they are some species of warbler.'

'I think they're Sedge Warblers, sir. Reed Warblers don't have those eye-stripes.'

'I'm impressed, Detective Constable.' Howarth looked over the top of his spectacles. 'Everything is ready downstairs. Shall we go and have a look at him?'

Howarth nodded to the white coated assistant who carefully removed the sheet covering the corpse and then paused for a moment or so… 'Dean Galpin, aged twenty two. An uncle did the I.D. There is, as you can see, a single bullet entry. He would have died instantly. The entry was almost perfectly to the centre of the heart. If it was an accident then it could not have more unfortunate. If it was a deliberate shot, then it could not have been more precise. Apart from the bullet wound, there is, as you can see, a puncture wound high up on the left thigh. That is a few weeks old. It looks as if it was inflicted by a stiletto type blade.'

They were looking down at the body of a young man: tall, good-looking, muscular, and well endowed. Howarth and Clare were standing alongside each other. Johns was opposite.

'Apart from that, is there anything else unusual here?' asked Clare.

'You must be joking, boss,' muttered Johns.

Clare, fighting back embarrassment, glared across at him. There really was something special about Clare Morell's eyes; the strange grey eyes. They could disarm or attract, or as Johns had just discovered to his cost, and more than one scally confirm, be capable of freezing (as her old desk sergeant had once said) a boiling kettle at ten paces.

'Now, the bullet – that is interesting.'

Clare appreciated that Howarth had chosen to ignore

Johns's aside. 'Dr Howarth, just before that, when do you think he was shot?'

'Probably, no more than three hours before he was found.'

'So, it would have been light by then?'

'Definitely.'

So, it was nothing to do with 'lamping'. Crick was completely wrong on that score!

'Now, about this bullet, it's only just gone over to Forensics – I don't know who deals with your ballistics these days,' Howarth continued. 'If it's not a shotgun in the countryside, it's usually a point two-two.'

Clare nodded. She'd seen bullet wounds before and had noticed that this entry hole looked large.

'What is your opinion?' Clare asked cautiously. She had a hunch that Howarth knew more, but was not sure if he should say. Easy does it. She glanced at Johns who correctly understood that he was not to open his mouth.

Howarth hesitated and then opened the file he had brought with him from his office. 'Well, I have worked for other… other people, as well as your lot.' He took out several scans from the file. 'These are exactly to scale. There is no doubt that it's 7.62 by 51mm ammunition, but it's not exactly like any I've seen before. I'm not sure I can tell you any more than that.'

'But, off the record… you know who can?' chanced Clare quietly. She held his eye and after a moment or so he reached slowly for the telephone.

There was the scrunch of cellophane wrapping as Matt Johns screwed up the M & S carrier bag and dropped it in the refuse bin before returning to the bench near to the RSPB Information Centre where Clare was sitting. Their game resumed immediately.

'And that?' said Clare, pointing at a duck about thirty yards into the lake.

'Pochard.'

'Right, clever clogs – and those?' she nodded towards some small birds on the edge of the bush scrub.

'Chiffchaffs. My father is a keen birdwatcher; he used to take me with him.'

There was the sudden 'beep-beep' to their right. Alerted by his bite-alarm an angler jumped out from under his huge green umbrella and grabbed one of his two rods from its rest – and then cursed.

'He struck too soon – should have let a run develop,' observed Clare. 'Hmm, I wonder what the carp take here.'

'You mean bait? They use worms I suppose.'

'No, not worms, maggots or luncheon meat: too many eels. He's probably using high protein baits, there's all sorts of flavours – passion fruit's good – or what anglers call particles, anything from chick peas to adukis, black-eyes, bolottis or–'

'How do you know all that, boss?'

'My father is a keen angler – work the rest out yourself, detective.' Clare looked at her watch and got to her feet. 'Right, it's time we joined the army.'

Howarth's phone call had been to an army camp that was about fifteen miles away.

They had been driving along a flat-bottomed open valley where a line of willows traced the course of a clear chalk stream: a valley surrounded by a patchwork of woodland, pasture and dense hedgerows. Then suddenly it changed and Clare, as she looked at a landscape of stunted pine, bracken, and gorse scrub, interspersed with bare patches of almost white sands and gravels… felt as if she was in a foreign land.

'I've never been this way before,' she said. 'It's a very strange area.'

'Yes, boss. I come this way sometimes. DS Melbury told me there are lots of stories about this heathland. The wildlife's interesting too; there are sand lizards here and smooth snakes as well as adders. You alright, you seemed to shiver then?'

'It's nothing,' lied Clare.

As they passed under the shoulder of a low gravel ridge and into the shadows cast by a huge dark brake of gorse and bracken, she got the feeling that there was something not welcoming about this landscape, and it wasn't just the mention of snakes that made her feel like this… though that didn't help. A few minutes later, in an area of thick pines – just after they had turned off the road onto a track heavily signposted 'Ministry Of Defence. No Unauthorised Entry.' – two armed soldiers appeared from nowhere and indicated for them to stop. There was a crunch of gravel as Johns braked.

Clare held her warrant card up to the window. 'DI Morell.' She raised her voice. 'DI Morell and DC Johns, we are expected.'

One of the soldiers approached, 'Sorry about this – new procedures. Would you get out, please?' He checked their ID's then looked at the inside of the car and the boot, before opening up a telescopic handle with a mirror attached. After slowly walking around the vehicle looking underneath, he signalled to the other soldier who had remained further up the track who waved back before talking into his radio.

'Sorry again, ma'am. Drive up to the gate now please.'

'I understand – this day and age,' smiled Clare. 'Who meets us when we get through?'

'That will be the Duty Warrant Officer.'

They got back in the car and drove up the track.

'New procedures?'

'I'm guessing, Matt, but stopping people when they do not

expect it rather than at the check point are new procedures learnt in Iraq and Afghanistan.'

By the time they had reached the gate in the high fence, the soldier who had spoken into his radio was already there, with two other armed sentries. The gate opened and they were waved through.

'This must be him,' said Johns, as they noticed a figure walking down the steps of a large wooden building which blended almost seamlessly with the pines.

They got out of the car.

'Good afternoon, Warrant Officer,' said Clare to the short thickset soldier, who looked as if he had very little time left to serve. He seemed both surprised and pleased that he had been addressed by rank.

They were led along a narrow corridor, their shoes sounding on the wooden floor. Johns muttered something about scout huts. When Clare had asked who would meet them, it was not by chance. It was routine to her: the answer sometimes reveals if the visit has been discussed – it also reduces the chance of being surprised.

The soldier knocked on an unmarked door, opened it, gestured them in and immediately, Detective Inspector Clare Morell, the same Detective Inspector Clare Morell who likes to stay in control, found herself in danger of losing her composure… for the second time in a day.

Captain Guy Lovat was looking at the bullet scans from Howarth. 'Very interesting – rather special – and definitely not the sort of thing I'd expect anyone to get shot with in a countryside accident.'

He smiled across his desk at Clare – again.

She was having trouble concentrating. When she was young she'd had a poster of Gericault's portrait of Lord Byron on her bedroom wall for years. The poet is shown resting his face on a hand. The picture has come to life. The original was said to be 'mad, bad and dangerous to know'. As far as this doppelganger was concerned, she didn't know about the first two – but would put money on the third.

The army captain, Lord Byron Two, reached down into a drawer, took out a box which he placed on his desk top. It contained a variety of bullets.

'Those look real,' said Johns, as he leant forward and looked down.

'That's because they are. I don't know how much you know about these, because of your weapons training, these–'

'Assume we know nothing,' interrupted Clare.

She watched carefully as he selected some bullets and put them into two groups. His hands – no ring – were very sunburnt. He probably didn't get that on a holiday beach, she thought. In fact he looked as if he'd only just got back from *somewhere*: deeply tanned and surprisingly in need of a haircut. It was wavy and chestnut – just like the original had.

'Now, these little jobs,' he said as he slowly fingered one of the two groups of bullets. 'These are what we would expect in the countryside. They are all compliant with Firearms Licence – General Pest Control.'

'The DEFRA licence?'

'Precisely, Detective Inspector,' he agreed, pushing back a lock of hair as he looked up. He then began selecting individual bullets. 'Firstly, these little jobs. This .22 is for rabbits, this .223 for foxes, and these expanding or hollow-nosed fellows are 2.34's for deer stalking, such as this Hornadays and–'

'What about the second group of bullets?' interrupted Clare.

And stop smiling at me.

'They're mainly Yankee Gung-ho's – everything from

these Winchester 257's up to this 350 Remington Magnum. It is possible, that some,' he pointed as he spoke. 'Like these 36, 38 and 357's, you could find in rifle clubs – but of course everything has changed.'

Clare and Johns nodded. In the last few years, a massacre in a small English town and then one in a Scottish school had led to tight restrictions on private gun ownership. He selected two large bullets out of the box and stood them upright on the table.

'Bingo,' said Johns.

'Nearly, but not quite. As you can see they are the size of the bullet in question. They are 7.62 by 51mm. This is military ammo. The one on the right is a NATO German made copper plated steel, and the other a US made NATO copper full metal jacket job.'

He picked up two more and held them out across his desk. 'Now these two, like the one in these photos, are real specialist kit: specialist in both manufacture and use. These two are not from the same maker and the one in the photos is different again. The generic term is Match Ammo. They are very high quality, very accurate and can be used at greater range than the NATO ones. Well, it's easier to show you.' He gestured towards the window at the end of the office.

Clare and Johns stood either side of Lovat, looking out onto a vast area of open heath, with few pines, gorse restricted to patchy breaks, and stretches of sands and gravel, white in the late afternoon sun. A series of targets disappeared into the distance.

'The nearest one is at 600 metres, the next 800. That's about the max with NATO ammo. Above that you run into all sorts of problems, such as barrel-mirage and…' Lovat fell silent for a moment, as if to check his enthusiasm.

'That seems too far. Can you really be accurate at that distance?'

'Yes, Detective Constable, with skill and good scopes.'

Clare turned to look at Lovat. 'How far can you fire with Match ammo?'

'The next marker is at 1000 metres, the last one at 1200, but the best Match jobs would go further. In fact, accurate enough to hit a target, not much more than a foot square, at a mile. It is also usually the case that the weapon concerned would be modified – have a fibre glass receiver, for example – and be finely tuned. It's interesting that the bullet has a code on it. Look.' He bent his head close towards her, as he pointed out some markings on the scan he was holding.

'That means you can find out where it comes from?' Clare said.

'Possibly – I'll keep you informed.'

As he drove back, Johns was unusually talkative, 'He was something else, wasn't he? Handsome Captain Guy! Ten to one he's from an unbroken line of Galloping Majors going back to heaven knows when. Brave to a man I bet!'

Clare had been preoccupied. 'What?'

'The Handsome Captain, boss.'

'Oh, he's not my type.'

'No, you're right there.' Johns began laughing.

Clare looked at him quizzically. Why is young Matt being so aggressive – that's not like him? Her brain had been buzzing with enough questions since they'd left, without any more. What the hell is going on here? Why was Lovat so cooperative? He's not just army is he? Had Howarth been instructed to facilitate the contact? Do they, whoever they are, just want us to do a lot of the investigating work for them before we get Special Branch, or more likely still, one of the Funny Brigades, sniffing around?

Johns sensed her mood, 'It's all a bit weird if it was an

accident. Who the hell was firing at what, with a gun like that? If it was deliberate, it makes you wonder what Galpin was in to, doesn't it, boss? No one's going to do that sort of job on him because of poaching rabbits, that's for sure… or the killer thought he was someone else. Perhaps the poor bastard copped someone else's bullet. Someone important.'

Clare turned her head and smiled. Johns's usual wisecracking was a useful cover for his razor-sharp perception. It was very handy in their job. People are suspicious of cops who appear to be logging every word and action. Her neck felt tense. She relaxed as best she could into the car seat, and closed her eyes.

Clare, feeling a headache coming on, unfastened the brass catch and pushed up the lower sash of the window. It moved easily, though its fine glazing bars and elegant staff beading were over two hundred years old: a testimony to the long abandoned practice of seasoning wood for five years before use. She leaned on the sill and took a deep breath of early evening air. It didn't smell of the sea. At this time, at sunset, air tended to funnel offshore. The only sound she could hear was the gentle percussion of halyards catching on mast heads. Standing on tip-toe she could just see them far below her, protruding – like a chorus line of Chinese wind-chimes – above the jumble of roofs of the old buildings that clustered around the harbour. Resting back on her feet again, she looked across the town that bent around the sweep of the bay and watched as the headlands down the coast darkened into silhouette.

A few months earlier, as the estate agent's voice droned on and on, she had looked out of this window for the first time and, completely out of character, without taking time to consider all the facts, had said 'I'll take it.'. And, within a few weeks, she had moved into No 3 of the twelve flats converted from a derelict red brick building originally constructed to house cavalry officers in a different jittery age when, worried about Napoleon, anxious eyes watched the Channel.

The flat had not been cheap, but she had bought her Edwardian semi in South Manchester when the local newsagent was lucky to shift a handful of the Guardian in a week. The high street then had no trendy boutiques selling exclusive original designs, no funky urban emporiums or delis, unlike now – and there wasn't even a single wine bar. However, she sold the house the week City Life nominated the local George and Dragon – where you would be lucky to get a packet of crisps a few years earlier – as the best gastro-pub in Manchester.

Clare closed the window and went looking for the paracetamol. She couldn't stop the question racing around her head.

Why the hell use, what looks like a highly sophisticated contract hit man, to kill a local poacher?

3

Clare walked down the steps of the flats to the sound of the reassuringly heavy clunk of the entrance door closing behind her. She crossed the small square – once used by horses, but now by another form of horsepower – towards a small blue Peugeot. The passenger door opened as she approached.

'Good morning, boss. Are we going to Full Moon Copse first?

Clare got in the car. 'Yes, Matt. Let's go and see for ourselves.'

Matt Johns drove out of the town on the road that lead to the north: a ribbon of 1930's redbrick suburbia at first, that suddenly narrowed as it passed through a village of stone cottages huddled around a spring at the base of the chalk escarpment. He changed down rapidly through the gears as he climbed up to the great tract of downland that curves like a protective wall around the coastal plain. They turned off onto a straight track of bare chalk and flints: a once very important ridgeway route, a sort of iron-age M1, and later a drovers' road. Johns drove slowly over the rutted surface, muttering.

'What's that, Matt?'

'Those joy-riding 4x4's are chewing this up.'

About a mile down the track they pulled up alongside a police van and a patrol car.

'There doesn't look to be many still here,' Clare observed as she got out of the car. As they walked up to Full Moon

Copse, DS Andy Melbury emerged from behind some bushes at the edge of the trees.

Johns cupped his hands around his mouth and shouted. 'Hello, sarge! Is your bladder playing you up? Understandable at your age I suppose.'

Melbury walked slowly down towards them. 'This one's a cheeky young bugger,' he said, pointing at Johns. 'I don't know why you put up with him.'

'Yes, Andy, you're right. I'm thinking of giving him a free transfer to Traffic. How are things here anyway?'

'The Scene of Crime lads and lasses gave the taped area a good going-over yesterday but found nothing and uniforms looked around the fields,' he swept his arm in a semi-circle behind him as they walked up to the wood. 'They drew a blank as well. DI Crick thinks there's no point in doing any more, for at the most, finding an empty shell case. I'm expecting a call to pack up things soon.'

They walked up to the taped-off area. The two policemen on duty looked bored stiff.

'How far out did the uniforms cover?'

'They went out to that hedge right across the dip, Matt,' explained Melbury. He pointed to a hedge line about half-a-mile away. It was easy, in this downland landscape of large open fields and sparse cover, to identify the long straight hedgerow in question. Then Melbury's phone rang and he walked away from them to answer it.

'Nice and convenient boundary for them to stop at,' said Johns. Clare noticed that he was looking at a hill in the distance which had three small bumps on the top.

'It could have been fired from anywhere around here even though there's not a lot of cover. Surely up on that hill's too far.'

'No, boss, it's 1,200 metres away – well 1,220 to be precise – I've checked. According to what the handsome captain told us, it's within range and a great viewpoint. Do you think it's worth a look?'

Clare nodded and called out to Melbury who was talking to one of the policemen. 'See you later at the station, Andy. We'll just have a tootle around and get the lie of the land.'

Melbury waved an acknowledgement and Clare and Johns walked back to the car, turned off the old drovers' road and drove onto a narrow rutted farm track. Johns pulled up by a stile but then had difficulty parking without obstructing the track. When they got out of the car, Clare stopped to fasten a shoelace. 'You go on, Matt.'

Johns crossed the stile and began walking up the steep slope of sheep-grazed grass: so short that it looked as if it had been carefully mown. The top of the hill, apart from the three small burial mounds, levelled out. Clare caught him up and they looked across to Full Moon Copse: the taped-off area was clearly visible.

'It seems such a distance.' There was doubt in Clare's voice.

'Hell of a view. You're not likely to be surprised up here.'

Clare nodded in agreement as she turned south, away from where the downland changed into a wide vale of trees and fields, to the slopes leading to the coast. The sea on the south coast always seemed so blue to her. The noise of an engine interrupted her thoughts. A Land Rover appeared from the other side of the hill, drove towards them and stopped about thirty yards away. A man got out and banged the side of the vehicle. Two dogs jumped out from the back and then the man, with the dogs at heel, began walking towards Clare and Johns in that easy, ranging stride of a man born in the countryside.

'Good morning. You're a bit far away from that shooting accident aren't you?'

'Are we that obvious?' Clare called back – not unfriendly

– to the man. As he approached she could see he looked to be in his mid-thirties.

'I'm afraid so, officer,' he said with a smile.

'Well, we are barely dressed for a country walk. We'd be more at home in a high street, stuck in the window of Next,' muttered Johns.

'Hello, I'm Josh Legge – shepherd of this parish.'

'DI Morell. This is DC Johns. There's a great view from here of the whole area.'

'Yes, Detective Inspector, there's not a better one. It was an Armada beacon site after all.'

Of the two dogs, the Border Collie, stayed glued to the shepherd's heel, but the other – a massive white coated dog with a bear-like head – came up to Clare and nuzzled her hand.

'Good grief, you're honoured.'

'What's his name?' inquired Clare, as she stroked under the dog's chin.

'Paulo.'

'Ah! Is he one of those Italian sheepdogs? I don't know the name,' suggested Clare.

'Yes, he's a Mareema, as puppies they're raised with the lambs. This one stays here most of the time and guards the flock. He's like a big sheep with teeth. The breed evolved from the Abruzzese… the wolf-slayers,' explained Legge.

'Do you have trouble with foxes?' asked Clare.

'No, not really, we got him because of the problem of stray dogs, mainly those of the damn New Age Travellers on the ridgeway. They are not like the Romany family who have come there every summer since the year dot, who know how to look after their dogs. Are you going to the top of the hill?'

Clare nodded and they began to walk the short distance to the three burial mounds where several large tan-faced sheep were grazing.

Clare turned towards Legge. 'Are these Dorset Horns?'

She noticed the look of surprise on his handsome weather-beaten face. 'Nearly, they're Horn Crosses. Though we barn-lamb these twice a year as well. When they are brought out to the hill, the foxes usually only go for the weak lambs. Dogs are indiscriminate.'

'They lamb twice a year?' asked Johns.

'Isn't it the only breed that does?'

'Yes. Well, Detective Inspector, you seem to know a little more about sheep than the average copper.'

Clare laughed. 'Not much really, though I should – considering I spent many school holidays on my uncle's farm. He told me a little about your local breeds when he knew I was coming down here. His farm, the farm he and my father grew up on, is very different from this. He runs Herdwicks.'

'The Lakes?'

Clare nodded. 'Oh, did you know Dean Galpin?'

'Yes… I've seen him around.' Legge hesitated. Clare had caught him completely off-guard.

'There's something over there!' said Johns, pointing to an old stone gatepost.

'Well, whatever it is, it wasn't there two days ago,' added Legge.

Clare reached for her mobile.

'I'll take some photos.' Johns jogged ahead – his cell phone already in his hand.

'Don't go to close, Matt,' warned Clare.

'No, boss.'

Clare quickly phoned through the location and instigated a scene of crime alert then turned to Legge. 'I'd be grateful if you did not say anything about this. It may be nothing. Here's my card. How do we contact you, if we want to speak to you again?'

Clare noticed there was a rueful smile on the shepherd's

face. Yes, he knew damn well she was going to contact him again. He surprised her by taking his own card out of one of the many pockets in his gilet. 'Mobile and e-mail on as well,' he shrugged. 'Modern farming – there's a lap-top in the Land Rover.'

Clare and Legge caught up with Johns and moved close enough to the gatepost to see clearly what was on it.

'Doesn't make a lot of sense, does it?' said Josh Legge.

4

PC Karen Garland finished shuffling the papers she was holding and looked across at Andy Melbury. The detective sergeant was tapping a pen on his desk top.

'Crick's late,' he said with a nod towards the old mahogany wall clock.

'Anyone like another coffee?' asked Karen. Melbury declined the offer, as did the other two people who were in the room. DC Matt Johns was sitting at his computer and Clare Morell was looking over his shoulder at the screen. She had just taken a phone call from the Scene of Crime officers, to say they had run a fine-tooth comb over the short downland grass of Chalcombe Bumps and had found nothing at all – apart from 'sheep shit'. Clare and Johns were looking at a photo of the large stone gatepost on the Bumps. There was yellow writing on it.

'It's so neat,' observed Clare.

On the gatepost was written:

$$SWELLS$$
$$6F + \frac{1}{2} C \ (50L)$$
$$O$$

Johns nodded. 'SOCO say it was done with a fine-head spray not a spray can. It could be from a spray gun used by model makers.'

'It makes no sense, Matt. It might have nothing to do with the shooting, but I have a feeling about it. The SWELLS could refer to the Bumps – the burial mounds – but we've no idea what the equation means.'

'Yes, boss. And I think that thing at the bottom looks a bit big for a nought – it could be a capital O.'

Just at that moment there was the sound of approaching footsteps in the corridor. Detective Inspector Mike Crick was about to make his entrance.

'Right, let's get on with it,' he snapped, as he closed the door behind him. He threw his jacket onto a chair and loosened his tie. It seemed an inadequate safety–valve. With his red face and the buttons straining against an over-tight blue poplin shirt, it appeared as if he was in imminent danger of exploding. 'I saw Sir Alan Vine at Winterstone House yesterday. He was a bit shocked. He thinks the same as I do, that Dean Galpin was hit by a stray shot by a poacher taking a pot at a deer. Sir Alan knew Galpin because the lad did odd jobs at the Winterstone Stables – that's Lady Charlotte's business – and at the Borne Hunt kennels. For those new to the area,' said Crick, emphasising his last statement, 'the hunt kennels are on the Winterstone Estate. Sir Alan said that Galpin had permission to be at Full Moon Copse–'

'I don't get that,' interrupted Andy Melbury. 'Even if Galpin did odd jobs, the Vines have always jumped on any poaching. It makes no bloody sense that.'

Crick shrugged his shoulders. There was a moment or so of uneasy silence.

Karen Garland held up a sheet of paper, 'Sir, I think this is complete now.' She began to read from it quickly. 'Dean Galpin was bound over to keep the peace for a year after attacking a hunt saboteur's van, also he's been convicted of kicking and beating a League Against Cruel Sports official – he got 140 community hours and £100 costs for that. Then other complaints after three hunt saboteurs ended up in hospital and when he was accused of threatening an anti-hunt supporter at his house – but, as often the way in these anti-hunting cases, as there are no independent witnesses, they are either for or–'

'That'll do, Karen.' Crick said dismissively.

Clare glared at Crick. Almost everything about him annoyed her, but nothing more so than the manner in which he dealt with policewomen. She herself was unique. Crick had never been in a situation before where there was a female officer of not only equal rank but also, although younger, of wider experience. His way of dealing with the situation was to ignore her as much as he could. She had been very patient. She had tried to be friendly, tried to show that she was no threat, tried to…

Cricks own impatience was showing. 'None of this has anything to do with the shooting. It was a single fluke shot to the heart. I also spoke to his mother. She doesn't know if he was with anyone, or what time he went out. '

'But whatever time that was.' Clare spoke slowly. 'He was almost certainly shot when it was light. Dr Howarth concluded –'

Crick banged his hand down onto a desk top. 'Which brings us to that fiasco? What a waste of men and money – dragging SOCO out to the Bumps like that! As if anyone could shoot that distance anyway and it was probably some kids that sprayed that nonsense on the fucking gatepost!'

Clare was surprised that Crick was looking straight at her. He was smirking, inviting a response.

He got one.

'I disagree, Mike, on both counts. A message has been left. It needs deciphering. And about that bullet – anyone shooting deer uses a 2.34. The one that killed Galpin was a 7.62 by 51 mill, but not a standard NATO copper plated or full-metal job. The bolt-action rifle used to fire it probably has a fibreglass seated receiver and top of the range optics and has been fine-tuned by a professional. When we get the full ballistics report it will state that the bullet is specialist kit. It's Match ammo. It can kill at 1,500 metres. The distance between Full Moon Copse and Chalcombe Bumps is 1,220 metres.'

Crick, even more disturbingly red faced than usual, was staring at her in disbelief. He seemed completely at a loss as to how to react. There was a long pause before he spoke. 'That's all fucking rubbish! – I'm going to the bog.'

He slammed the door as he left.

Clare's hands were hurting. It was only now that she realised she had been digging her fingernails into her palms. No one spoke as she left the office though she could feel their eyes glued on her. She walked purposefully down the corridor and turned… into the men's toilets. DI Mike Crick, who was the only one in there, was, to say the least, surprised to see her walking towards him.

'Look, you fat twat –'

Clare was gripping the edge of the wash basin, looking at herself in the mirror. What the hell had she been doing back there, spouting on like a page of Gun Nut Cases Weekly, to say nothing of the small matter of going into the men's bog and not just yelling at him but –

Oh, fuck, fuck!

There was a touch on her shoulder which made her jerk – she hadn't heard anyone come into the women's washroom.

'You look like shit, boss,' said Karen Garland taking her arm. 'Come down here.'

She led Clare along the line of cubicles. The last cubicle door was different from the others in that there were many marks and dents halfway down. Karen leaned forward and pointed to two circles drawn in red marker pen at the centre of the dents.

'We have to keep re-drawing those.'

'What are they?'

'Testicles.'

'Whose?'

Karen shrugged.

Ten minutes later, in the corridor outside the canteen, two policewomen were getting very frustrated with PC Garland.

'Karen, will you stop laughing and tell us!'

'Yes, what is it?'

She wiped the tears from her eyes. 'We need a new pair of bollocks in the lavs – in fact I think we need a new door.'

Clare turned away from her lounge window. She had been watching one of the old harbour's larger visitors gently ease to its moorings. If she'd bothered to go to the bookcase and look at the – as yet unopened – book she had bought from Waterstones three weeks earlier, she would have been able to identify the vessel as a rare three-mast topsail schooner. Increasing the volume of her stereo, she lifted an old flat-topped guitar from its stand, moved the capo down two frets, slipped on a thumb pick, and attempted, note for note, to echo those played by the long dead fingers of Mississippi John Hurt. He was playing *Candyman* – one of her favourite tunes. The guitar was unusual. A very rare Kalamazoo – a no-frills line Gibson made in the early 1930's to keep them going through the Depression. It was old when her father, then a young policeman in Liverpool, bought it in a rough dockside pub. On one of the only two photos surviving of bluesman Robert Johnson, he is shown holding a dead ringer of this one. Clare smiled at the thought. Her father had often said that it could be the same one. She was surprised when, six months ago, he had insisted she take it with her. 'My most precious possession – apart from you,' he used to say.

Are things that simple now?

A loud knock disturbed her thoughts and her playing. Clare, still holding the guitar, walked down her hallway and opened her front door. A woman, wearing a smart two-piece suit, and carrying a felt-tip pen in one hand and a nearly-full bottle of gin with a strip of paper stuck on it in the other, walked straight past her with barely a glance.

'Oh, God, what were you playing, *Police Dog Blues*?'

'Come in, Emma,' said Clare, looking at the back of her visitor who was already disappearing into the lounge.

'Right, we've had enough of you – Big Bill Boozy.'

'It's Big Bill Broonzy not Boozy,' protested Clare as she closed her front door. 'Except that it isn't… wasn't,' she corrected herself as the stereo fell silent.

By the time Clare walked back to her lounge, the woman, her neighbour Emma Butler, had taken two glasses out of the sideboard.

'I need a large gin and tonic, a shag, and a cigarette – in that order.'

'Well you're alright for two of them.'

'Aw, Christ – are we out of fags again?'

'Very funny.' Clare, reaching into the fridge for the tonic, watched as Emma unfastened and shook-out her blonde hair, before proceeding to pour out two very large gins, then carefully mark – and date – the remaining gin level with the pen.

'Emma, what's up with you anyway? Got a guilty conscience again? Just convinced yet another jury to let some complete sleazebag off scot-free, have we?'

'Yes, alright then, Morse – I should have done prosecuting.'

'Thank God you didn't! You'd have been getting poor

sods that were as pure as the driven snow, sent down for years.'

'I can't help it if I'm good.'

'Ruthless, more like. I couldn't believe it when you passed that guy that note just as he was about to start his summing-up!'

'What's wrong with sending a note?'

'Everything with one that says "I'm not wearing any knickers",' exclaimed Clare, miming inverted commas.

'Well, I had a weak case!'

'Exactly – and I rest my case,' said Clare, as she rummaged around in a drawer. 'What the hell did we do with the fags?'

The two women were leaning on the window sill, looking out over the town to where the esplanade street lights formed a great curve of yellow stars – mirrored by a second, more ephemeral one reflected in the bay.

The cigarette packet had been found and returned – minus two cigarettes and firmly taped-up – back to the drawer. It had been back in the drawer for some time. The gin bottle was standing on the window sill. The label had several felt-tip lines on it and the lines appeared to be progressively less precise, the nearer they were to the bottom of the bottle.

Clare turned towards her companion. She had been lucky when she'd bought her flat – it had come with a ready-made soul mate who lived next door. Emma Butler was pretty, younger looking than her thirty six years, with a retroussé nose and an innocent, slightly naive look – which professionally was one of her greatest assets. They talked about most things, though a few days ago, when Bonnie Raitt was singing, *She's scared – scared to run out of time*, they couldn't look each other in the eye.

'So,' said Clare. 'That's all the advice you can offer me in my hour of need. That's the best your brilliant legal brain – your nasty vicious mind – can come up with, is it, this so called "Emma's Law"?'

'Yes, it's infallible; it works, on all occasions – without exception.'

'Right, so when I see my governor tomorrow – to counter a complaint raised against me by a fellow officer, namely one DI Twat, your advice, to re-cap in full, is… is?'

'Screw him,' said Emma, picking up the gin bottle.

'That's it? That's Emma's Law?'

'Yes. Screw him. You're lucky. He'll make a complaint but there's no way he'll mention what you did to him. He'd be a laughing stock. Use it! Do exactly what I told you to do when you see your boss. *Exactly* what I told you. Trust me.'

Emma who'd been concentrating very hard on attempting to distribute fairly the last few drops of the gin, put the empty bottle on the sill and turned to look at Clare. 'Yes, when you've got the advantage, always take the initiative and screw them. The only critical bit – and this is critical – very critical,' she prodded Clare repeatedly in the arm to reinforce the point, 'is – is – pay attention – in the application of either of the words "figuratively" or "literally". Now I must admit I've sometimes messed up on that bit.'

'Shit!' cursed Clare as her elbows slipped off the window sill as she started laughing.

'I know,' agreed Emma – who hadn't noticed. 'Oh, by the way, are there any possibilities down at the nick, "literally" speaking? That nice young man who picks you up lots of mornings – he's very pretty.'

'Don't be stupid! I don't go in for cradle snatching.'

'Nonsense! If you were a few years younger it would be, but now that amount of age difference between you and him is perfectly acceptable. You'd have loads of Brownie points as well as getting a much needed – Hey! That's police brutality that. But it didn't really hurt… cos I'm pissed. And it's no use giving me the killer-look either, it doesn't, as you well know, work well on women.'

'Sorry,' said Clare. She picked up her glass. 'Funny you should mention him though, I'm pretty sure he's gay.'

There was a minute or so of silence with them both staring vacantly into space, before Emma broke the silence. 'You know,' she said, grasping Clare by the arm. 'Men are more trouble than they're worth. You know the last guy that dumped me accused me of hiding a packet of fish fingers in his airing cupboard – a month after we split up.'

'What did you do?'

'I hit him of course.'

'No, I mean, what did you do? Get a spare set of keys cut just before you returned his?'

'What *moi*! God, you've got a suspicious mind! You a cop or something?'

'Prawns,' said Clare who was vigorously shaking the empty gin bottle over her glass.

'What?'

'Prawns. A packet of prawns is best. It prolongs the agony. Hide a king prawn here, a king prawn there, and here… and there.'

'Why didn't I think of that?' mused Emma. 'Though, poor Richard has suffered enough. Everyone calls him Chip, now you know. And all due to a little chance remark, I kept repeating, and repeating… and repeating, in his local.'

'Chip? What's wrong with Chip?'

'Quite a lot, girl…when it's short for chipolata.'

Both the insomniac man and his dog, who were walking on the lane behind the harbour, looked high up the slope towards a lit open window, and the sound of women laughing.

5

DC Matt Johns watched Clare as she walked slowly across the old cavalry square from her flats. 'Jesus,' he muttered as she got closer. 'The Ghost of Christmas Past.'

She got in the car without a word.

Johns drove along the esplanade, occasionally glancing around at Clare who was slumped low in her seat. It was one of those special gusty mornings that occur here when a strong wind veers from the east – a wind that can swirl sand down the high street; sand that can send Barclays Bank staff outside to tape over their cash machine. It was the sort of day when unsuspecting motorists driving along the road behind the sea wall, can be startled by a windsurfer's sail overtaking them.

'Good,' said Johns, as he parked, lowering the front windows sufficient for a near-gale to blow through the car. 'I won't be long.' He crossed over the esplanade to Bellini's Café. Bellini's had been opened in the 1890's by a Giovanni Bellini, known locally as 'John', who had dragged a handcart loaded with bags of pennies to the bank as a deposit on the building. He'd raised the money using the same handcart, selling cones of ice cream in the summer and paper-twists of chips for the rest of the year.

Matt Johns pushed open the café door. The narrow, modest frontage misleads. The interior is elegant and spacious, with a fine white Carrara and black marble floor, rounded wall mirrors and original Art Deco panelling. It was still early and all the tables were empty. A tall, dark-haired man in his early forties, with strong handsome features, was standing by the espresso machine.

'Hello young, Matt,' said Giovanni 'John' Bellini – the fourth generation to bear the name.

'*Buongiorno,* John! Oh, while I remember, there's this area where huge sheepdogs come from called the Abruzzo. Where is it?'

'How the hell would I know? What do you think I am – Italian or something?'

The cafe had long been a favourite haunt of passing policemen. The coffee and tea were excellent – and the Bellinis always had their ears to the ground. Police trade had also increased since Mildred the station's tea lady had retired. She had been replaced by a shiny chrome drinks dispenser that had initially been christened R2 D2. However, after a few days of tasting its dispensed wares, a proposed name change to FU D2 received overwhelming approval.

John Bellini looked out of the window at the car. He'd seen it all before. 'The usual coffee for you and a "Special" for the lovely Inspector?'

Johns, glancing across the road, noticed that Clare had slipped even lower in her seat. 'Yes, and we'll have two extra shots… in the same cup.'

A few minutes later, as Johns, holding two drinks dispensers, was backing out of the door, Bellini called out. 'The Abruzzo is a lovely area; over a quarter of it is national park – catch a Ryan Air from Stansted to Pescara.'

Clare drank her coffee slowly and when she'd finished Johns gently prised the empty cup from her fingers. Then he pulled down the passenger visor, slid open the vanity mirror, picked her bag from the car well, and placed it on her lap. He touched her arm. 'Boss, I'm going for a pee… probably a very long pee.'

Clare opened her bag and reached for her make-up. She

caught her pale smile in the mirror. That third thing about him she'd not been sure about.

She was now.

Clare had never seen Yorick like this before. He was sitting at his desk, bolt-upright and with a face like thunder.

'What the hell do you think you were playing at?' snapped Detective Superintendent Paul Simmonds. 'Mike Crick said that you burst in on him in the bogs like a hysterical harpy. '

'That's not true, sir,' said Clare, in as clear and steady a voice as she could muster.

'What are you saying? You didn't go into the Men's?'

'No, sir, the hysterical bit. I don't do "hysterical". You must know that from my records – it's not in my nature.'

'Hmm.' Simmonds suddenly seemed a little calmer. Clare was relieved. This was the first time she had seen him angry and she'd been genuinely shaken because, even in the best of moods, his long pale face and bald head could be off-putting – now they were downright scary.

'What happened then?'

'Mike and I were having a disagreement over the Galpin case. You know how it is, sir, two officers of equal rank, having serious words over the interpretation of evidence and what procedures to follow. He stormed out of the meeting and I was furious with him for walking away, so I followed him – it just happened that he went into the Gents.'

'He said you were screaming at him.'

Clare struggled to get her breath under control. 'That's not true, sir.'

After telling Crick he was a twat, she'd also called him a fat wanker, who couldn't see the significance of anything he couldn't pour down his gullet, or smother in brown sauce and stuff into his big mouth, she'd shouted, but she hadn't screamed at him… though she did have her hands around his throat at the precise moment when he was least able to take effective evasive action. But as Emma had said, she was lucky; there was no way that Crick was going to admit that to Simmonds – or anyone else.

'I've no time for any of this nonsense.'

Thank God for that.

There was a moment of silence while the detective superintendent studied the paperwork on his desk. Clare noticed that sections had been highlighted and notes added to the margins.

'Right, this Galpin case, I've been looking at what we've got so far. Dean Galpin – local lad, did odd-job work at the stables and the Borne kennels out at Winterstone. Any trouble with the law related to hunting. Shot three days ago. No witnesses. OK, so far?'

'Yes, sir.'

'There was a lurcher with him and his jacket showed that he'd been carrying rabbits in it recently. He may, or may not, have been alone. Mike and Andy have told me that lurcher men often poach in groups, but more often for deer than rabbits. Also, Andy said that lurcher men don't usually have someone with them with a gun. Apparently they use Bowie knives to despatch deer brought down by the dogs – sounds a bit gruesome that. Galpin had a Swiss army knife on him, not a sheath knife. You accept all of that?'

Clare nodded.

Simmonds pausing for a moment to read, tapped his pen on the desk as if counting points. 'Hmm, Sir Alan Vine says that Galpin had permission to be in the woods – I'm not sure about that. It may have been the easiest thing for him to say. That wants a bit more delving. If we knew exactly what he was doing there, we'd possibly find out if anyone was with him, who may have witnessed it and simply decided that buggering-off and keeping stum was the sensible option. Now for the bullet,' he waved a sheet of paper. 'Have you seen this from Forensics? It came this morning.'

'No, sir, I was late in – something came up this morning.'

Did I really just say that?

'Fact – he was shot by a…' he looked at the sheet of paper, '7.62 bullet of much higher quality than the usual military stuff – they're following that up. That's what your army guy said?' Clare nodded. 'A bullet that is capable of being lethal over a long range. You said your source says…' he looked at another sheet of paper. '1,500 metres.'

'That's correct, sir – and that's apparently a conservative estimate.'

'Hell. I spoke to Forensics earlier after we got this thin report from them, to give them a rocket and get on to Ballistics, and in the meantime they committed themselves to the same broad conclusions. Their exact technical description was, I think I can remember it verbatim, "It looks as if it could fly for fucking miles".'

Clare smiled. Simmonds was relaxing.

'So, it could have travelled a long distance due to the fact that someone missed what they were shooting at – probably something with wings or four legs. A fluke death is possible despite the shot being right through the heart. There was a case last year in the north of the county of an accidental shooting slap-bang in the middle of some poor sod's temple at half-a-mile. And there was Melbury's cousin who got one through the kitchen window as she was baking… apparently the Kenwood Chef got shot.'

Clare smiled again. 'What are you saying here, sir?'

'Well, you've no proof at all that it was fired from Chalcombe Bumps – either at Galpin or something else. That yellow sprayed info could have nothing to do with it – unless we can make some sense of it that proves otherwise. Also, I don't see why anyone would shoot him deliberately. At the moment I tend to agree with Mike that it was accidental – probably at long range – as it was light.'

Simmonds paused for a moment. Clare nearly made a protest… but held her tongue.

'But, and I've stressed this with Mike – really stressed it,' his spoke louder and banged the desk. 'Accidental or not, this is a case of someone using an illegal, lethal – absolutely fucking lethal – weapon. Possibly it's an ex-competition job or something. Rifles are too clumsy for most criminal use, so any tracking down along those lines is probably a waste of time. It probably belongs to a gun-fanatic and I want the bastard caught quick without rumours going around that we've got a gun-nut shooting people, accidentally or not. Anyway, we find this joker and we've got the answers to all our questions. Well?'

'I think you've put your finger on it, sir.' Clare over the previous few minutes had been getting a sinking feeling, as she realised she'd done it again: that fault of hers of sometimes drastically underestimating the ability of officers senior to herself. She'd most certainly done it with Yorick.

'Are you alright, Clare? You look a bit pale – been overdoing it?'

'Yes, sir… you're right again.'

'Now, you and Mike Crick – I'm telling you what I told him. The pair of you work it out without bothering me. There's nothing wrong with disagreements as long as the job's done. But in your case, you over-stepped the mark. Don't do things again like going into the men's bog to make your case.'

'No, sir, I was out of order and I feel bad about something I called Mike.'

Right, you're started now: Emma's Law. Screw him. 'Do EXACTLY what I told you,' Emma said.

'Well, it's me I suppose; being a northerner – we say it as it is.'

'Well, what did you call him? 'asked the intrigued detective superintendent.

'Peanut dick.'

6

Clare was driving along the narrow winding road that skirted the base of the escarpment: the road that connected the hamlets that had grown along the spring-line. She was alone, apart from Elmore James, whom she was accompanying – on both vocals and one-hand air guitar – in a full volume rendition of *Dust My Broom*. The sun came out and, as she lifted a hand to lower a visor, she smiled into the interior mirror. Yes, it was turning out to be a lovely day… in more ways than one.

It had been very different the last couple of days. The atmosphere had been, to say the least, both tense and ridiculous, with Clare and Mike Crick on the one hand completely ignoring each other, while everyone else continually exchanged knowing glances. Rumours, as Clare had expected, had spread through the station. According to Karen, there were many 'tiny' variations in what she'd said actually said to Crick. Then Simmonds called for her this morning and everything changed.

There had been a string of incidents in the county involving the targeting of tradesmen's vans – most of them bearing signs that 'This Vehicle Contains No Tools' – being broken into overnight, and expensive tools and equipment stolen. It was all professionally done and the assumption was that much of the gear had been taken to order. There had been no positive leads, but it was rumoured that price lists had been spotted circulating in some of the area's dodgy pubs. It was getting out of hand. The station a few miles to the north, in the area where most of it was going on, was short of an inspector. Simmonds had spoken to Mike Crick, who'd jumped at the chance to transfer immediately under the pretence of being able to do some 'proper detective work'. So, Peanut Dick was off the scene and Clare was in charge of the Galpin inquiry.

And now – after promising herself *never* to cross Emma Butler – she was going to see the shepherd; Josh Legge.

The road narrowed and cow-parsley, which seemed in the last week or so to have exploded from under the hedgerows, brushed the side of the car. She slowed as she approached a wood. This looks like the one she'd been told about. Yes, it is. The fingerpost to Chalcombe was almost camouflaged by the trees. She turned onto a narrow lane which seemed to be running right into the hillside. You can't miss the house, he'd told her. At the other side of the narrow wood was a small group of buildings tucked into a coombe in the shadows of the downs that hemmed in the settlement on three sides. There was a small Norman church, a cluster of dwellings and an ancient stone barn with a free-standing thatched cottage adjacent. An old Land Rover was parked outside.

As she got out of the car she remembered the word 'bucolic' she had been trying to recall for the last few minutes. The cottage was lovely. Set to the side of the door, in contrast to the rough-hewn ridgeway stone of the rest of the building, was a block of dressed ashlar with the name Church Cottage carved on it. There were also two small stone figures either side of a bedroom window.

A dog barked and the door opened unexpectedly before she had chance to knock.

'They're nice aren't they?' said Josh Legge, as he noticed her looking up at the figures. 'According to family tradition they were nicked from Little St Mary's, over there, during a refurbishment in the 1880's.'

Clare laughed as she shook his hand. Legge ushered her into the cottage. The Border collie took one look at her then disappeared into another room.

'No Paulo?'

'You must be kidding – he's earning his keep.' Legge pointed towards the ceiling: an indication that the dog was up on the downs.

An old stone fireplace dominated the room. The stone lintel was covered in intricate carving. He noticed her looking at it.

'I think that was lifted from the chancel.'

'No wonder it's called Church Cottage.'

'Excuse me a second, I'll let the dog out of the back.'

While he was out of the room she looked at some of the large number of landscape sketches and watercolours hanging on the low walls: they were all signed 'J Legge'.

She liked them. The subjects were mainly of high, alpine-looking scenery and the locations named. Most were on the continent: Jungfrau, Monte Blanc, Monte Rosa… Italian Alps? Sierra de Pena… Pyrenees? But there were some British locations and Clare smiled when she spotted one that needed no introduction. 'Nice one of Great Gable,' she said, as Legge came back into the room.

'Thanks. Of course, I remember you have an uncle who farms in the Lake District.'

'Yes, quite close to there, in the Langdales. Is there any particular reason why they are mainly of mountain scenes?'

'It's probably the contrast to round here. Mountains draw me. Or rather I draw them.'

She nodded. Clare could understand this. Opposites can attract. She liked the local downland which was so different from the Pennines and the Lakes that she loved.

'They're very good.'

Legge smiled and blushed slightly. Somehow she liked that. 'Thanks, I was able to travel and paint a bit before Dad fell ill.'

She decided not to pursue that as she sat down in the only armchair and he slumped down opposite on an old sofa whose springs had long since given up the ghost. His heavy shoes made a noise as he stretched out his long legs over the stone-flagged floor then he ran a hand through a mass of brown wavy hair as he looked at her.

It needs cutting.

'Shall we go?'

'What?' she said – somewhat concerned at the question. 'Go where?'

'Well, Detective Inspector, you want to know about Dean Galpin. And the best place for that is up on the ridgeway.'

Conversation, as they climbed the steep track up the scarp, was impossible over the noise of the complaining Land Rover. The views, like being on a funicular railway, opened up quickly: the nearby fields, the tower of a church above trees, the ribbons of suburbia stretching towards the coast – and then the sea. Suddenly they crested the ridge and Clare was surprised that they were at Chalcombe Bumps. Of course, this was where this same Land Rover had appeared when she was with Johns. Then they headed downhill along a white flinty track over the huge open fields towards a dark green smudge on the landscape: Full Moon Copse.

As they were getting out of the Land Rover, Legge turned to the Border collie in the back. 'Stay'. Clare noticed, as they followed a path into the trees, that they were close to the spot where Galpin was shot. The path swung round the foundations of what must have been a substantial brick building.

'Strange. Do you know what it was?'

'Yes, American army kitchens from the war. There were masses of troops here just before D Day, all getting ready to fight for freedom. Ironic that.'

'Why ironic?'

'The GI's up here were under canvas. They were all black. The officers were all white and billeted in comfortable houses down in the villages.'

'That would be funny, if it wasn't so sad.'

'Yes. We need to be quiet now.'

Clare tried to walk lightly but seemed unable to stop crunching beech mast underfoot. She wished she'd worn trainers. Legge turned off the footpath into the bracken. She followed as quietly as she could.

What's that smell?

'Fox urine,' he whispered – reading her mind.

There were four fox cubs play-fighting outside the earth, rolling around on the bare ground just in front of a small, but clearly defined, fox-hole.

Legge came close to Clare and whispered again. 'Appearances can deceive. They can be vicious little sods; it's not uncommon for them to kill each other.'

The cubs suddenly froze, pricked-up their ears, and then, as if attached to elastic bands, shot into the fox-hole.

'They must have heard us – well more likely me,' said Clare.

'Possibly, but they usually have no fear of humans at their age. Though, if the adults catch us then they'll up-sticks and move to another earth. They often squat in old rabbit warrens. I don't know anything about the shooting of Galpin, but I know why he was here. He was fox-feeding, and he was good at it, coming here regularly without spooking them into a move. That's the key; we were quiet because I wanted you to see the cubs. It wouldn't bother me if they moved out of the wood – but it would bother the hunt.'

'He came here to feed foxes, yet he works for the hunt?'

'Yes, it does seem strange, but it's to do with the fact that foxhounds don't hunt foxes by instinct, they have to be trained.'

'That's weird; we didn't have to train our cats to kill birds.'

Legge smiled. 'I know, but with foxhounds they make sure the young dogs go cubbing in the few weeks before the start of the hunting season in October. They always need new dogs as a pack is kept young. Hounds are usually surplus to requirement when they're about six years old, they don't make good pets, so they're usually shot.'

'Yes, I knew they were put down at a certain age.'

'This wood has been used as a covert for cubbing for years by the Borne Hunt. It's small and has tidy edges.'

'Tidy edges?'

'Yes, so that on cubbing days it can be surrounded by the hunt and foot-followers, who drive back any foxes, especially cubs, trying to make a break for it after the young dogs are sent in when the cubs are above ground. The little'uns stand no chance, as the guy who has been feeding them times his moment and blocks the fox-holes. This one's easy to stop-up as it's small.'

'That's a nasty trick,' said Clare, who was also thinking of something else at the same time. Yes, that's why Sir Alan Vine knew Dean Galpin was here, and yes, he was probably on his own when he was shot.

'You're against fox-hunting?'

She nodded her head hesitantly. 'Yes… but I feel a bit hypocritical about it as I went fishing with my father, and shooting with my uncle.'

'It's nice and clear for me, like it is for a lot of sheep farmers. The hunt's a damn nuisance. If I have trouble with a fox then–'

'Hello,' said a quiet voice right behind them.

'Bloody hell, Doug!'

Clare, who had swung round, found herself looking at a small wiry man, with swarthy features, a full moustache, a battered brown hat worn at a tilt… and a very large grin: every inch a Romany. He'd popped up out of nowhere. It also seemed strangely old fashioned to Clare, the way he doffed his hat to her – then he turned to Legge. '*Sastimos*, Josh.'

'*Shanglo*,' answered Legge.

Clare looked from one to the other.

What the hell's going on here? It's bizarre. A shepherd and a gypsy speaking in tongues!

'I'm a police officer.' She immediately realised she'd said this in an unnecessary loud voice.

'I know.'

'How?'

'Josh has just told me. I think. He said "*shanglo*"… which is Romany for a big village bobby.'

Clare laughed with them.

'This is Doug Cooper – whose family have camped on the downs here every summer for generations. I've known him since I was a boy. Detective Inspector Morell.'

Clare smiled and Cooper lifted his hat again, 'It's about the Drop Pot Man, I suppose, miss.'

The Drop Pot Man?

She was completely at a loss. Josh Legge touched her arm, 'Over here.'

The three of them walked to the top of the earth and Legge removed a large stone. There was a hole underneath. 'It's an old rabbit burrow that goes straight down to the main chamber. Galpin dropped the rabbits down here that his lurcher caught.'

'It's called a drop-pot,' added Cooper. 'That's what he did, that's why we called him the Drop Pot Man when we saw him.'

'It's a good incentive for the foxes not to move burrows – like Father Christmas coming every day,' observed Clare. 'Mr Cooper, can you help me at all with anything about the shooting?'

'Well, that early morning's a mystery because there was a family celebration the night before – the daughter is going to get married.'

'I can vouch for that.'

'Josh was there as well, until he wobbled-off home across the fields, just before dawn on that quad-bike thing of his,' added Cooper, smiling at the recollection. 'There is something though. We recognise most of the people who come up with their dogs, and a couple of runners, but two or three times recently, in the very early morning, we've noticed someone different.'

'In what way?' asked Clare, desperately trying to keep her rising antennae under control.

'Well, a runner in those long tight things, dark blue, they were – like his top. Wore one of those little caps, and had a rucksack on his back. It was unusual.'

'What was it like?'

'It had yellow criss-cross laces on the back. He was quite a bit taller than me. Not as tall as Josh here.'

Clare held her hand a couple of inches above her head. 'Five foot ten… eleven?'

'Aye.'

'Thank you Mr Cooper. You've been most helpful.'

He chuckled. 'It's the first time a copper has ever said that to me.'

'Oh, can you remember when you saw him?' Clare tried to keep her voice calm.

It's got to be a lead this!

'I only saw him once – the day before the shooting. My

wife's brother saw him once last week. I must go, miss. Goodbye… *Rakli Yak*.' He smiled, touched his hat again, turned away and called out something else as he disappeared laughing into the trees. It sounded to her like 'Tea-Toe-Prada-Shock-Star'.

'What was that he called me?'

'*Rakli Yak* – It was a compliment. I think it means the Non-Roma Woman of the Eyes.'

She could feel herself blushing.

'But I've no idea what that other thing he said means.'

She wasn't sure if she believed him.

7

The Undermoigne valley, sheltered, wooded, and seemingly remote, is set just off the coast road. Driving down it, the village arrives unexpectedly; a sharp turn over an old pack-horse bridge, and then suddenly there's a long row of restored stone cottages, thatched roofed and wall-papered with Wisteria and Virginia Creeper.

'This is nice, sarge,' observed DC Johns.

'It's a bloody chocolate-box, these days, Matt. There's no real community now due to sodding incomers,' said DS Andy Melbury. 'See that?' He'd raised a hand from the steering wheel and was pointing at a fine wide-eaved Regency house, close to the church and set back from the road.

'Is that the vicarage?'

'It used to be, now it's the second home of some bugger from Twickenham – he probably owns Twickenham. The locals are priced out round here. Though they're not all second homes, some move here because they want to raise their kids away from all the drugs, sex, the clubs and the bright lights.'

'So they come here, where all the bored kids have left is sex and drugs?'

'Not quite, Matt. There's always someone who'll get them half a bottle of cheap vodka or a flagon of cider.'

At the far end of the village, Melbury turned into a cul-de-sac.

'This is a bit different,' observed Johns.

'They're from just after the war when it was the opposite of now. Council houses were built to get people to move into the villages. The Galpins live in the one at the end; well it's just Mary Galpin now – Dean's mother – though there's a married daughter nearby.'

'You know this area well?'

'I was the local uniform quite a few years ago, and I've got relatives near.'

There was an old white transit van, with a large dent on the backdoor, parked outside.

'I recognise that pile of crap from somewhere,' said Melbury.

They had barely pushed open the front gate, when three terriers appeared from the back of the house and began barking and snarling at their feet.

'Get back!' yelled Melbury at the top of his voice. It was enough to make the dogs reluctantly back away.

A man opened the front door. He was in his mid-twenties, short – only about fife foot five, or six – and of stocky build. His head was shaved and he was wearing the ubiquitous workman's uniform of boots, jeans and a heavy tartan shirt over a T-shirt. 'Hello Mr Melbury.'

'Right, lad, I think it would be wise if you got the dogs locked up first – because the next one that snaps at me, will be shitting teeth for a week.'

The man whistled and shouted at the dogs – a rag-bag of small terrier breeds – until he got them to follow him round to the back of the house.

'Who is he?' asked Johns.

'I'm trying to think. Ah, I recognise that van now. I drive past it every day.'

There was a clatter of a gate closing before the man returned.

'You live by the Co-op Stop-and-Shop, don't you?'

'Yes, in Sutton Cottages. It's Neil Frampton. I remember you Mr Melbury from when I was young.'

'This is DC Johns.'

The two young men nodded to each other.

'You better come in then.' Frampton looked around as he gestured them into the house.

A huge brindled lurcher lying in front of the sofa didn't move a muscle as they came in.

'I come in to look after the dogs. This one's pining; I can't do much with him.'

'Mary's at the daughters then is she?'

Frampton nodded.

'It must be crowded.'

Frampton nodded again.

'Has she had another kid recently?'

'No.'

'Well, bugger me! That makes a change.'

Frampton smiled and suddenly seemed more relaxed. Johns knew that he would be saying little. This was the big detective sergeant's countryman show… and he was playing it superbly.

'We were going to have a quiet word, but I won't disturb Mary at her daughters. Well, poor old Dean – these things can happen. Did you hear about my cousin from over Lane End way who nearly copped it when a .22 shell came through her kitchen window as she was baking?'

'Yes, I think I remember people talking about it in the pub. It was sometime last year wasn't it?'

'Almost a full twelve months. Direct hit on her Kenwood Chef it was… and her tight bastard of a husband still hasn't bought her a new one.'

Frampton laughed.

'Well, Neil. As you might guess we have to go through the hoops – waste of bloody time really. Now we know Dean worked at the stables out at Winterstone and for the Borne Hunt kennels next door. Seeing the dogs out there I assume he was one of the hunt terrier men. You are as well aren't you? I've seen you get terriers into that van of yours often when I drive past. You must often walk them at the same time as I'm going to work.'

'Yes, they like routine.'

'Dean was also the drop pot man at Full Moon Copse. Did you ever help him fox feeding?'

Melbury had been annoyed with himself when Clare had told him what she'd discovered from Josh Legge and Doug Cooper. He said he should have gone into the wood when he was at the scene of the shooting, as he knew about drop-potting and would have spotted what was going on.

'I know nothing about that. Anyway drop-potting's always been illegal.' Frampton's tone changed. It was defiant. He folded his arms.

'Know anyone who'd want to hurt him?' asked Melbury softly, adopting a patient blood-extracting-from-stone approach.

Frampton shook his head.

Melbury nodded to Johns. Message received. It would be alright for him to ask some questions now. As it transpired he only asked one.

'What about any of the hunt saboteurs?'

The very mention of 'hunt saboteurs' produced a remarkable transformation. 'Fucking antis! They get on my tits they do. Interfering townie bastards, don't know a lot, trying to stop us doing something we've been doing for ever.'

'Yes, alright Neil,' interrupted Melbury.

Melbury, with a sharp look at Johns – an indication that any further questions would be counterproductive – got to his feet and took a card from his pocket. 'I think that's all we need for now. Let me know if you think of anything. Give my condolences to Mary. Tell her I'll pop round when it's all settled.'

As they were getting into the car, Johns glanced at Frampton who was framed in the front door, somehow knowing that he would stay there until they drove out of sight. 'God, his mood changed then.'

'He's a terrier-man, Matt. It's his life.'

Moments later, Melbury was driving very slowly along the village street, behind a line of three women on horseback. He knew he would have to wait until the road widened by the pub before he could get past them.

'What did you mean exactly when you said it was his life?'

'Most people don't realise, Matt, that on the day of a hunt, there are two, not one, hunts going on. And both have fanatical supporters.'

'Two hunts?'

'Well, there's the lot like these three, who go tally-hoing it around with the hounds – who are wealthy, and in the main, posh. Then there's the other lot, the terrier-men like Neil Frampton who send their dogs down holes after the fox has gone to earth, who dig them out with spades. Now, they're anything but posh, or wealthy.'

'It must take hours to dig foxes out.'

'Yes, they're often at it long after these have gone home,' he pointed to the large rump of the horse in front of them. 'Fox earths are often old warrens, very complicated, and the fox will fight the terriers that can't kill them. They have to be dug out and shot, or killed with a spade: sometimes if the hounds are near they're released, though that was always illegal – officially. All a bit quicker these days though, mind. Many of the terriers have a radio transmitter fitted.'

'What, so they can give a running commentary, or call for reinforcements?'

'Very funny. No, for location.'

'Right, very hi-tech and civilised. So now, as they can be dug out quickly, the foxes don't have to wait so long to have their brains battered-in with a shovel!'

Melbury glanced across at the angry looking young detective. 'It's just the way it is, Matt, and it's successful. For every fox killed by hounds above ground, there's two killed from below ground.'

'Well, it's all going to be illegal now, sarge.'

'Illegal, yes and no, they can still use a couple of dogs to flush out foxes that are then shot, and anyway you're not going to stop any of it. Like poaching, you have to catch them at it. Keeping lurchers and terriers won't be against the law will it? How the hell have we got time to police it? Damn!'

A 4x4 was double parked outside the village pub. 'Great – now we're going to spend the best part of the next five minutes looking up a horse's arse.'

Melbury managed to get past the riders just before Undermoigne Lane joined the main coast road. 'There's no point looking for any more of Galpin's mates round here at this time of the day. But I know where we could try.'

'Where's that?

'The White Dog,' replied Melbury as he booted the accelerator.

The crowded buildings on the harbour side, especially those with first floor bay windows like bulging eyes, always give the impression that they are elbowing each other for space as they line up alongside the narrow quayside.

It was quiet, but in a month or so, any moorings not taken by local pleasure craft and fishing boats would be full, and the quaint pubs, tea rooms, gift shops and restaurants, would be crowded. They parked and Johns followed Melbury as he turned down a narrow passageway between a fishing tackle shop and a small art gallery.

The passageway led to a very different world from the quay side. The alleyways cramped between the backs of the buildings and the steep slopes overlooking the harbour had nothing to entice people into them, apart from a ship's chandler... and The White Dog.

The White Dog from the outside was deceptive: it housed a shambling warren of little bars and corners. It was one of the oldest pubs in the town and in the eighteenth century had gained a reputation for being the notorious haunt of smugglers, footpads and whores... and over the intervening centuries, absolutely nothing had changed.

'Pint of Jubilee,' ordered Melbury, who then turned to Johns.

'Oh... orange juice, please,' responded the detective constable. Johns was squinting, adjusting his eyes to the dark low-ceilinged interior.

The local Jubilee Ale, a dark, very strong, heavy brew, takes a while to pour, but for the whole time that the pump was being slowly and steadily drawn by a muscled, heavily tattooed arm – the barmaid did not say a word. Melbury led the way to a table near the corridor to the toilets.

The detective sergeant, all eyes, was silent. Johns took the hint and looked around. He noticed that two crusties, a man and a woman drinking what looked like scrumpy, were looking at him and Melbury. They passed a comment to each other.

A young man walked past.

'Chippy – ten minutes,' said Melbury quietly, just as he was raising his glass to take another sip of the stuff of legends.

Seagulls thrashed about in the water as they squawked and fought over the intermittent drip-feeding of chips coming down to them from the three men leaning on the harbour rails opposite the Fryer Tuck: a fish and chip take-away and restaurant, that was usually referred to locally by its quite spectacular spoonerism.

'Thanks, Mr Melbury, for not speaking to me in the pub,' said the young man next to the burly detective.

'That's alright, Ian. As you can guess it's about Dean. It was probably just an unfortunate accident and anyone shooting in the area is unlikely to come forward. It's just routine bollocks really, but has he upset anyone? Tried it on with someone's girlfriend or anything like that?'

Ian Cartwright gave a chuckle. 'God, Dean was a bugger for the girls! But he'd become more careful.'

'Why's that, lad?'

'Do you know Melvin Critchmay, Mr Melbury?'

'I'm not sure, but I know some Critchmays – they're all built like brick shit houses.'

'Yes, Melvin's a brick shit house alright… with double doors. A couple of years ago, Dean shagged his girlfriend.'

'Doesn't seem like a good idea,' said Johns breaking his silence.

'No, for the next couple of months Dean went limping around spouting crap that he'd been beaten up by a whole fucking army of hunt antis. Since then, as far as I know, he picked up girls – posh girls – at the stables. He never talked about it, kept his mouth shut. Is that it, Mr Melbury?'

Melbury nodded. 'Yes, thanks Ian.'

The young man tipped the remainder of his chips over the harbour side, and left to the cacophony coming up from below.

'Well, well that's interesting. But why did he co-operate so easily, sarge?'

'Young Cartwright knows I'll turn him and his car over for contraband roll-up baccy every time I see him, otherwise. The

White Dog is where a lot of it's shifted. Did you know that eighty percent of all the roll-ups in the country use smuggled tobacco?'

'That much? No, I didn't.'

'It's that last bloody government's fault. They buggered up the naval reserve and reduced the number of customs officers,' said Melbury, his face beginning to colour slightly. 'There are loads of drugs coming in as well. It's like replacing that little lad who had his finger in the dyke with a few people using plastic buckets.'

'Yes, sarge.' Johns looked at his watch. 'Time for a coffee?'

8

The window table of Bellini's Ice Cream Parlour and Cafe has a special mention in the local guide book. It has long been regarded as having one of the finest views in the town – some say in the whole area. Especially on a clear day like this one, with that particular intense light that sky has over sea.

The sea-front terraces, although in part pock-marked by unsuitable alterations, still maintain a harmony of height and form, and the esplanade with its elegant shelters – like a line of corporate umbrellas – is ideally seen like now, virtually deserted, and not, as it will be in a few weeks time, packed with holidaymakers.

But best of all, there is the great sweep of the bay, stirred by an on-shore wind that white-tips the wave crests, and then the succession of headlands, overlapping like stage scenery, fading into the distance.

Two early season tourists, open guide book in hand, were disappointed to find the prized window table occupied… by Melbury and Johns. The young detective constable, head down, was tapping into his laptop: the older detective sergeant, with that blasé disregard for the familiar, however special – was sitting with his back to the window; a mug of latte in one hand, and a large slice of the local Lardy cake in the other, studying his notebook that lay open on the table. Johns paused to take a sip from a small espresso cup.

'I don't know how you can stand that gravy browning, Matt.'

'I heard that!' shouted John Bellini. 'Leave him alone. I'm instructing him in the finer points of coffee drinking.'

Johns, who had been completely engrossed, glanced up 'What?' He looked at Melbury and then pointed at the cake. 'Do you know how many calories there are in that Lardy, sarge?'

'No. Do you know how many consonants there are in "Mind your own fucking business"?'

The sharp DC thought for a moment. 'Yes, seventeen.' He pointed to the laptop screen. 'It's interesting, this information about convictions of hunt supporters. There is the odd one like the guy who planted a nail bomb under his own vehicle to try and discredit hunt saboteurs, and a few, like Galpin, who threatened people at their home. But most, as you'd expect, is on the spot violence. Hunt saboteurs ridden into, driven into, whipped, punched and kicked, and saboteurs and vehicles attacked – even an Anglia TV man had his camera smashed – often by men with spades and iron bars. They've got to be terrier men like Frampton?'

Melbury nodded, and then looked at his watch. 'It's time we got back.'

PC Karen Garland tapped the keyboard. 'These are the Licence to Kill Game Certificate holders in the county.' She scrolled down the long list that had appeared on the screen.

Clare was sitting on the edge of the desk. 'It's like the Wild West down here.'

'Well, we're a rural area. They'll be mainly shotgun. These are the locals on the UK Shotgun Licence list.'

A second list appeared.

'See it's really the same.' Karen pointed at the screen. 'The law is very tight these days but there are other licences, now look at this one, boss.'

A much smaller list appeared on screen.

'These are the holders of 2.34 Rifle Licences. They are all on the shotgun register as well. Now, there are some posh and important people here – the sort that go deer-stalking in Scotland. They could also afford to buy a weapon like the one that was used to shoot Galpin'

Just then there was the sound of familiar voices in the corridor.

'Fatman and Bobbin are back,' said Karen.

Clare grunted. 'About time.' She barely gave Melbury and Johns time to come through the door. 'I'll expect a full report to take home with me tonight – but what's the gist of what you've found?'

'Well, our Dean was a bugger for the young women. And he didn't pick them up in that Cats Eyes Club either,' said Melbury as he grabbed a chair.

'The Cats Eyes,' spat Karen. She turned towards Clare. 'You need full body armour and a cattle probe to go into that dump.'

'Spoken like a real trooper, Karen,' said Melbury with a chuckle.

'He's avoided trouble as well, steering clear of other peoples' girlfriends after he was given a real kicking by some double-doored brick shithouse who found out that Galpin had screwed his girlfriend,' added Johns.

'Charming,' said Karen.

'Apparently he picked up young posh totty at Winterstone Stables. But he never gave any names away to his mates,' explained Melbury, swinging back on his chair. It creaked, as usual.

'Maybe because he thought some might have been jail-bait,' said Clare.

'He would have been perfectly at home in stables,' muttered Johns.

'What!' exclaimed Karen.

'Well, well,' said Melbury. 'So, our Dean was the ideal bit of rough, was he? Tall, good looking lad, who could be relied upon to keep his mouth shut, and who last, but by no means least, had–'

'Yes, alright Andy,' said Clare sharply. 'What about the lists, Karen?'

'Sir Alan Vine and Lady Charlotte are on the rifle, as well as the shotgun list.'

'So, we've a couple of reasons to get up to Winterstone, then haven't we?' Clare looked around at the nodding heads.

'Oh, and there's someone on the shotgun list that will interest us.' Karen was pointing at her screen again. 'One Mr Joshua Legge of Chalcombe. I had a word with Kevin, the local bobby, who told me that Legge has had trouble with Travellers' dogs attacking his sheep.'

'They're a pain in the arse on the downs.' Melbury spoke with some feeling. 'There are lots of them up there now. Unlike the Romanies, they let their bloody dogs roam.'

'Yes, that's what Kevin said,' agreed Karen, who then looked at her open note book. 'He also said that one day, last August, a pack of four dogs attacked Legges's sheep. Legge shot three with a shot gun and the other one was killed by a big dog he has. Kevin said that the shooting was incredible.'

Melbury let out a whistle, 'Yes, that's impressive. After one's shot the others usually scarper. Legge must then have brought down another, reloaded at a hell of a lick and somehow shot another without hitting his own dog or the sheep.'

'I've got something.' Johns tapped the keyboard of his laptop. A photograph of a dark blue rucksack appeared on screen: it had yellow criss-cross lacing on the back.

'Well done, Matt,' said Clare. 'That matches perfectly the description of the one carried by the guy the Romanies spotted in the early mornings just before the shooting.'

'It was easy to find. It's a newish model. The yellow elasticated cord was the key. This is a specialist runner's sack. You won't get them in the south. They're used by long distance trail and fell-runners. A few of the northern stockists do mail order.'

'It may be a long shot, but go through the stockists and try and get details of anyone from this area who has bought one.'

Clare smiled as she looked at each one of her team. 'Is there anything else?'

'There's someone I need to see who knows a lot about the Galpins,' said Melbury.

'And I'll start tracking down that hunt monitor and the Sabs that were assaulted by Galpin,' added Karen.

Clare got to her feet. 'Great, I'll just go and update Yorrick.' She felt good. Things were moving. It was great to be in charge and with the added bonus that that arsehole Crick was off the scene. Apart from the case, there was another matter she needed to discuss with Simmonds. He'd phoned earlier to say that Karen – who had passed her commission exam – could be transferred to CID. She was going to request that it be immediate, and hopefully when she came back to the office there would be one delighted young woman... and they'd all be going to the pub afterwards.

Every time Clare looked at Karen the following morning, she could not help smiling. 'DC' Garland was walking around with a wide grin on her face: like a cat who'd not just got the cream but one who'd cleared out the whole fridge. Karen was in *plain clothes*, but as she had her hair tied back as before and she was also wearing a dark trouser suit and white top like Clare – it looked as if she'd exchanged one uniform for another.

Clare recognised the sound of Melbury's footsteps in the corridor: he didn't do 'quiet'. The door flew open.

'Sorry I'm late. Hey! Look at you Miss Smarty, you look great!'

'Thanks, sarge.'

Melbury flopped down on his office chair: it complained. 'I've just come from my cousin's at Lane End over Overcombe way. She wasn't in last night. Anyway, she has a friend who is close to Mary Galpin – Dean's mother. Mary told her there had been trouble recently up at Winterstone. Now, listen to this. Sir Alan wanted Lady Charlotte to give Dean the sack from his stables job. She wouldn't apparently and my Lord and her Ladyship had a right set-too.'

'I know he only worked part-time at the Borne Hunt kennels, but he was the drop pot man for them. Was there any mention that Dean had been sacked by Sir Alan on that score?' asked Clare.

'No. It just seems his Lordship just wanted him away from the stables,' answered the detective sergeant. He looked round mischievously. 'It's good, isn't it?'

'How long had Dean worked at the stables?'

'About five years, Karen. It can't be anything to do with his work… or his general leg-over activities, I wouldn't have thought.'

'Isn't Lady Charlotte a bit younger than Sir Alan?'

'Now, Karen – that's a very naughty thought,' said Melbury, whose attempt at a lascivious grin reminded Clare of the Gurning (the face-pulling) competitions they held at Lakeland fairs.

Clare put both hands behind her head as she leaned back in her chair.

Lady 'Chatterley' Vine? Well, well. Winterstone Stables here we come.

'And there's something else. I found out that Galpin was

friendly with the hippies – the Travellers – and used to go to their camp. I'm damned if I know what he'd have in common with them – a lot of them are proper crusties. And also our Dean had been threatened by some Romanies who turned-up mob handed at the Travellers' camp – something about a local gypsy girl who used to go there. Anyway I think they are marrying her off and…'

Doug Cooper's daughter?

'I think I know who that is,' said Clare.

Clare and Karen were alone in the office. Something was bothering Clare. She'd decided that she would take Karen with her to Winterstone, but it was the thought of two women detectives in this area, rather than in a city, wandering around the countryside in trouser suits, trying not to draw attention, that concerned her. They might as well carry a banner.

'Karen, you're a country girl really aren't you?'

'Ooh aarh, boss.'

9

Clare was standing in front of her bedroom mirror. She had changed into a Gap T-shirt – bought at the time when a friend had commented that their shade card ranged the full gamut from light khaki to very light khaki – and had put on a pair of close-fitting jeans. She slipped on an old leather jacket she'd not worn in a while and then sat on the bed to pull on the unusual boots she'd bought in Manchester's Northern Quarter.

Her mobile rang. 'Hi, I'll be right down.' It was Karen Garland. They were going to Winterstone Stables. Clare had not phoned: an old boss had once told her to always try and catch people off-guard, even if it meant a wasted journey.

A young woman, wearing a blouson and with her jeans tucked into boots, was standing on the steps to the flats. Clare did a double-take. She'd not seen Karen with her long hair loose before, and involuntary ran her hand through her own.

Perhaps it's too short?

Karen looked her up and down. 'Nice one, boss – we'll do nicely.'

In the centre of the Old Barrack's square was a 4x4, whose colour was difficult to discern due to the fact that the bodywork appeared to have been customised with what looked like an even coating of –

'Is that shit?' pointed Clare.

'Don't ask – it's my brother's off-roader. The inside's clean.' She caught the expression on Clare's face, 'Well, clean… *ish*. I thought it would be useful if we want to cut back over the old drovers' road.'

'I'm not entirely convinced that travelling around in a four wheel cow-pat is the best way not to draw too much attention to ourselves,' grumbled Clare as she climbed in through the passenger door.

Karen avoided some road works by driving around the backwater and the reed-fringed edges of the nature reserve. These great reed beds are best seen on a windy day like this one, when they appear to be imitating the waves in the distance. Clare, looking across at the mortuary with its beautiful location, recalled the view from Dr Nick Howarth's office and mused morosely how it was wasted somewhat on the punters there. Then within a few minutes they turned onto the main road to the north and two miles later, suburban ribbon gone, and after passing along a village street in the shadow of the scarp, Karen was soon thrashing the 4x4's gearbox as they climbed the ridgeway onto the downs.

Clare smiled. This was one of the perks down here, this being driven around   as if on a touring holiday. It was so different from her last urban patch and her home. Clare had quickly got to like this landscape. Strange in a way: it was probably because of the contrast to the northern hills she loved. Chalk and Millstone Grit were chalk and cheese really. Unlike the roughhewn Pennines, this chalk downland always gave her the impression of being one of nature's more successful DIY projects, with rough edges rounded and indentations polyfillered into a land of smooth contours. She also liked the huge skies and the great cloud shadows which sweep across the landscape – changing the mood in an instant. Suddenly, after several miles, it ended abruptly where the chalk dips under the clay of a vale, a change – as if cut with a knife – to watercourses, woodland, rich loam soils… and Winterstone.

'This is a pretty place, Karen.'

'Yes, and the Vines keep it that way. It's an estate village. They own all of it and dictate what goes on – and who lives here. I know quite a bit about this area as my gran's from around here.'

Just on the edge of the village, she pulled up opposite the gates of Winterstone House and Clare found herself looking past the well-cut topiary pyramids, at a lovely Elizabethan manor house with stone mullioned windows.

'It's gorgeous. Do they open it to the public?'

'You must be kidding, boss! They're loaded with money from the village rents, the stables, and their own farmland and tenant farms, amongst other things,' said Karen as she put the 4x4 into gear.

The turning to the stables was just up the road. A lot of the parking bays were taken. Clare was impressed. They were classy stuff – mainly Kensington tractors. Winterstone Stables, the domain of Lady Charlotte Vine, looked every inch a slick organisation. The stables had been stylishly enlarged. The set-up was much larger than she had anticipated.

'Great, isn't it? It's too dear for me. I ride out at Friar Langham way,' said Karen as she parked in the large stable yard. 'The Borne Hunt kennels are round the back – Sir Alan Vine's the Master of the Hunt – and many hunt members stable their mounts here where Lady Charlotte also runs a profitable riding school.'

Clare nodded. It was, by the look of it, a *very* profitable riding school, catering for the wealthy, especially their wives… and daughters.

Two stable girls were chatting by the door of what looked like the office. One of them came over as the two policewomen were getting out. She looked at the 4x4. 'What happened to–'

'Don't ask,' answered Karen.

'Hi, is Lady Charlotte around?' asked Clare, with that practised tone in her voice that implied that she must be, at the very least, an acquaintance of the person she is inquiring about.

'She's over there.' The stable girl had turned and was pointing between two buildings towards a small paddock where a young girl on a pony was riding around in a circle. A woman, who was giving instruction in a voice that was as clear as cut-glass, stood in the centre.

The stable girl looked at her watch. 'They'll be finished in a few minutes.'

As she was walking back to her companion another girl came out of the office. Karen turned to Clare. 'I recognise her… Sarah Diment. We were in school together. She was a cow, and I once swore I would never speak to her again, as long as I lived. I don't know – the sacrifices we're prepared to make in the line of duty.'

Clare laughed. 'Yes, see what you can get from her.' Then, as Karen walked away, she concentrated on Lady Charlotte Vine. She looks about forty… ish. She was just as Clare imagined: an ex-Benendon School photo-fit. Tall, willowy, wearing a sweater – sorry, a jumper – and jodhpurs that were tight across her bony hips, tucked into long riding boots. What was that Stevie Smith poem? Something about, '*An Englishwoman so refined, with little bust and no behind* '?

About ten minutes passed, before Lady Charlotte, leading the pony which the young girl was riding, came into the yard. One of the stable girls took the reins from her, and Karen re-joined Clare as her Ladyship walked up.

Fifty…ish – there's quite a lot of grey in that blonde.

'Hello, I don't think I know you. Were we recommended?'

'Good afternoon. I'm Detective Inspector Morell. This is Detective Constable Garland.' Clare had deliberately not said Lady Vine, for fear of inviting the response of 'Call me

Charlotte' – and being put immediately on the back foot. Out of the corner of her eye she clocked Karen's smile when she'd heard herself being addressed as 'Detective'.

'Goodness me, you don't look at all like the police!' exclaimed Lady Charlotte.

The woman looked genuinely taken aback. Clare was pleased, 'I'm now in charge of the case concerning the death of Dean Galpin. And, I'm afraid we need to ask you a few more things. I'm sorry for taking up your time, but there are a few more necessary procedural hoops we have to jump through. I hope you understand.'

'Of course. It was a dreadfully unlucky mishap. Has anyone come forward yet, who was shooting in the area?' Clare shook her head. 'No, I guessed not. They often don't in these cases. I'm really not sure I can tell you any more than we told the police before – I noticed you've already spoken with the girls, Detective Constable.'

'Yes, I was in school with Sarah Diment. She never stopped talking then. It's surprising how some people change. Oh, boss, I need to pass some information to Matt. Excuse me,' said Karen. She smiled at Lady Charlotte then walked away as she took her mobile out of her pocket.

Clare turned towards the older woman. 'It's just one of the lines of inquiry we have. We must, on the off-chance that it wasn't an accidental shooting, try and find out if anyone wished Dean Galpin harm. We have reason to believe that he'll be missed by a number your riders… your female riders.'

Lady Charlotte laughed. 'Yes, you heard correctly. Dean was an extremely handsome young man.'

'And working here gave him plenty of opportunities?' pushed-on Clare.

'Of course, but if it did not affect his work, neither his, nor the private lives of others, are my concern. ' She was looking straight at Clare as she said this; her finely drawn features with her long narrow nose and thin lips, expressionless.

Well, make of that what you will, Detective Inspector Policewoman.

'What was he like?'

'He was a countryman, with a countryman's instincts. He was somewhat sly, cunning, quiet… and in his case not the sharpest knife in the box.' Lady Charlotte's words were spoken slowly and deliberately.

'Sorry about that.' Karen re-joined them just as a Land Rover swung into view. The vehicle came to a halt in the centre of the yard.

'It's my husband,' said Lady Charlotte, before calling out to the man who was getting out of the vehicle. 'It's the police, darling.'

Walking towards them was a short, slight man, probably in his late sixties, whose very white hair set-off the distinctive red patina in the jowls that heavy single-malt drinkers acquire over time. Sir Alan Vine was wearing the ubiquitous country uniform of the ex-public schoolboy – a Crombie house-tweed jacket.

'Well, hello!!' he called-out in that particular loud volume, customary to only the aristocracy and the lower-working class. To Clare – rather like Lady Vine – he was a caricature of what she'd been expecting. 'Jim Dexter was telling me some time ago he was going to appoint more women. Thank goodness he had the sense to pick pretty ones!'

Shit, he's made sure at the outset that we know he's buddies with the Chief Constable!

'Darling, this is Detective Inspector Morell, and this is Detective Constable Garland. It's about Dean Galpin.'

Clare glanced at Lady Charlotte. Yes and this one's a sharp cookie: the way she dealt with the questions about Galpin, and then she put His Lordship on guard at thirty paces – now she's got names and ranks right.

'Ah, Galpin… poor chap,' said Vine as he joined them. He was *all eyes*.

Clare blew through her teeth.

Oh, fuck, that's all we need to top it all off – it's Sir Sleezebag!

'It's some gaps we have to fill-in. Could you tell us what he was doing at Full Moon Copse?' asked Clare.

'Well, not exactly, my dear. You see he acted as a sort of gamekeeper there. He kept an eye on the place. I didn't mind if he did a bit of poaching in return.'

Clare decided to approach it head on. 'He was also the drop pot man for the Borne Hunt, as Full Moon Copse is a valued cubbing covert, is it not?' she said, looking at him intently – though it was the last thing she wanted to do. His face gave nothing away.

'You're very well informed – but drop-potting? Surely not, it's against hunt rules. I don't wish to speak ill of the dead, but Galpin, although excellent at handling dogs and doing general estate work, as well as being the handyman here, was sometimes rather over-enthusiastic in his love of the hunt. I have had serious words with him in the past when–'

'Three hunt saboteurs ended up in hospital, another one was terrorised at home, and a League Against Cruel Sports official was kicked and beaten.'

Vine's face temporarily darkened with Karen's interruption. 'Yes, Constable, but not all came to court and he'd served his punishment.'

'Some would say a hundred hours community service is barely apt,' added Clare – then wished she hadn't.

'I am doing what I can to get the magistrates to be more severe, you know.'

'Was there a disagreement recently with Galpin, serious enough for you to want to see the back of him in all his jobs, including here?' asked Clare, rather clumsily trying to drag the conversation back on track.

'Oh, Alan wouldn't interfere here.'

'I wouldn't dare!' he laughed. 'Oh, I've been wondering, it's all damn attractive, but why the mufti, especially the boots?'

'Well, it's just that we never know when we're going to walk into a messy situation.'

'What a nasty lech! I was willing my boobs to shrink back there – and that doesn't happen very often,' exclaimed Karen as she drove out of the stable yard.

'He made me creep as well.'

'You stopped him dead at the end though, boss. He really didn't like it.'

'I was a bit stupid there, in more ways than one,' said Clare, wondering if his lordship was already on the phone complaining to the Chief Constable. She should have been more diplomatic. They hadn't finished with the Vines yet, as they needed to find out, amongst other things, if Sir Sleezebag has a gun collection. 'What about the stable girls? You were convincing when you implied they knew which side their bread was buttered on.'

'Oh, Sarah Diment's still a big-mouthed cow, and the other two are as bad. They dished up more muck in five minutes than the horses manage in a week – I don't know how much is true about Dean Galpin and girls. Anyway, did you get anything from Lady Charlotte? That thing about needing to speak to Matt was a bollocks excuse – I didn't want to get caught in any cross-fire.'

Just at that moment Karen turned off the road onto a rough unmade track that led up to the old drovers' road and the whining of the engine and the rattling of bodywork, made further conversation impossible.

10

The old drovers' road, its chalk surface polished by innumerable hooves and wheels over the centuries, glistened silvery-white in the sunlight and Clare thought they were following the trail of a giant snail winding its way across the landscape. Karen, pulled up suddenly and switched off, and the sound of the engine was replaced by that of a skylark chorus from high in the huge downland sky above them.

'Anything wrong?' asked Clare.

'No, nothing.'

Clare looked at her companion. The young policewoman's eyes were twinkling. She was obviously excited about something.

'OK, Sherlock, spill the beans.'

Karen, still gripping the steering wheel with both hands, noticeably took a deep breath, as if deliberately holding herself back. She began slowly. 'One thing the stable girls let slip was that things had changed in the last month or so.'

'In what way?' Clare was now sitting alert and straight.

'Well, they said it was that Galpin wasn't bothering with girls. It was as if he was shagged-out, or something.'

'Barely surprising.'

'Yes, I know, but perhaps her Ladyship – I don't know why, it may have just happened but perhaps Sir Shit is just all eyes and is really Sir Can't-Get-It-Up. Well, he's ancient as well as fucking horrible isn't he? Let's say Lady Charlotte gets it on with Dean Galpin–'

'And insists she doesn't want to share,' completed Clare.

'Exactly, boss! Sir Alan finds out, goes mad, he wants him sacked, she refuses. So –' Karen got out of the vehicle, Clare followed suit.

'So?'

'So, very early in the morning, he drives out of the back of Winterstone and onto this track.' She was pointing far down the dipslope to the belt of woodland that marked the beginning of the vale. 'He then drove past here,' she half-turned. 'Then onto–'

'Chalcombe Bumps.' said Clare, recognising the familiar burial mounds on the skyline to the south. 'And is that Full Moon Copse to the left?'

'Yes, if you're right about Galpin being shot from up there on the Bumps, then Sir Shit would know roughly the time when he was drop-potting. He must have been lying to us that he didn't know about it. Well, he could have waited up there and shot him.'

'Why not just use a shotgun at close range? Vine could almost walk up to him. Galpin would think he was rabbit shooting or something?'

'Because his lordship is a hunter,' answered Karen, her voice raised, her body language more animated. 'He's a stalker. It's the ultimate kill – another human. Think of the satisfaction he must have got if he hated him as well, eyeing him up and things before pulling the trigger.'

Clare nodded. It was bizarre but possible. Sir Alan Vine was wealthy, he stalks deer, probably collects guns and he could have bought that special gun from someone.

'Well done, Karen.' Yes, it really was, she'd dropped lucky with Andy and Matt, and now young Miss Smarty Pants here. 'We need to follow up what Andy found out about the Romanies threatening the Travellers and Galpin. Our local shepherd might help.' Clare pointed to Chalcombe Bumps.

'Can you drive down the old track to Chalcombe?'

'Piece of piss – just as well you're not with Matt in that precious little Peugeot of his.'

'Karen, about Matt…'

'Oh, hello,' said Josh Legge, smiling at Clare, as he answered the door. The huge white Maremma sheepdog pushed his way out and moved to her side.

'He's lovely,' said Karen.

After a few seconds Clare noticed the big animal repositioning himself so the Karen could stroke him as well.

Typical male! What a bed swerver!

'Mr Legge, this is Detective Constable Garland.'

'Hello, Detective Constable Garland.'

And here's another one!

Legge, as he was gesturing them inside, pointed to the 4x4. 'Don't ask,' said Clare.

As they walked into the living room Legge turned to Karen: 'Haven't I seen you before? It's that long auburn hair of yours. I was in the Cats Eyes Club some time ago when a group of women got slung out for dancing on the tables. Pity, they were a darn sight better than the cabaret – someone said they were policewomen.'

'Of course not.' Clare glanced at Karen who was fixing Legge with a look of sheer affront.

'Oh, I'm sorry,' he muttered, colouring a little. 'Please sit down. I'll put the kettle on.'

When he had left the room, Karen whispered to Clare, 'And before you ask –*Yes* – I was there. It was Big Melanie from Witness Protection's hen night.'

Clare, at that moment, made a solemn promise to herself that if Karen and Emma were to meet – which quite possible – she was never, ever, going to go with them on a girls' night out.

'There's some nice looking stuff on the table,' observed Karen, firmly closing the topic.

They walked over and inspected two open boxes of expensive looking tableware.

'This fine-bone china's lovely,' said Clare as Legge came back into the room.

'Yes, they're a wedding present for Dora, Doug Cooper's girl. Romanies prize Royal Worcester, especially the strong coloured ones – that pattern's called Prince Regent.'

'Lucky girl!' exclaimed Karen. 'And two boxes – very generous.'

'Well, the Coopers are a very traditional family. They play things by the old book; one of these is for the husband's family.'

'A dowry? Isn't that rare?' probed Clare.

'Yes, even for the very traditional Romanies.'

'And you're helping with the dowry, as well as giving a present?' Karen had been too late to catch Clare's don't-be-too-pushy look.

'I've known the Coopers since I was a boy. I was at the daughter Dora's christening in the church here. They're devout Christians and proud people, unlike the Travellers. It's important to them to give a very generous dowry – I'm just helping out.'

'It's a funny thing, but that touches on why we're here.' Legge looked intrigued, Clare continued, 'What's the relationship between the Romanies and the Travellers?'

He sneered. 'There isn't one. They have little in common. The Travellers have few countryside skills; they let their dogs loose, and are stoned most of the time, living on benefits.'

'How self-sufficient are the Romanies?' inquired Karen.

'To a remarkable extent: they'll make use of some health and educational facilities, but little else. A lot of what they eat is from the land – landowners are glad that someone's catching rabbits and they don't mind some root crops taken for the pot. They're pony breeding brings in a bob or too and they sell traditional clothes pegs they've made at the country fairs and steam rallies – that's a laugh that is.'

'How come?' asked Clare.

'Well, they use plastic clothes pegs themselves – they get them from Pound Saver.'

Just as they were stopping laughing, Clare chose her moment. 'We'd heard a rumour that they had threatened Dean Galpin. I've got to speak to them and thought you could arrange it.'

The only thing that could be heard over the next few seconds was the ticking of the old carriage clock on the mantelpiece. Clare was looking at Legge closely. He kept pushing his long hair back with a hand, and his sharp green eyes flickered between Karen and herself. 'I haven't heard about any threats, but then I wouldn't. They keep their counsel and close ranks if there is a problem. Anyway, I doubt if they threatened him. They usually act if they think they have just cause – also they don't know one end of a gun from another.'

No, but you do.

'And did you know that Galpin used to go to the Travellers' camp?'

'No.'

Clare decided that there was nothing to be gained by probing further at the moment and instinct told her that it was a good time to leave – even though she would kill for a coffee. 'Sorry, we're going to have to skip the drink. If you could arrange a convenient time for me to talk to Doug Cooper and the others at their camp and give me a ring – that would be great. I don't want to barge in unannounced.'

A few minutes later, as they were driving away, Legge

was on the doorstep of Church Cottage shouting at the dog who was padding along behind them. Karen put her foot on the accelerator and waved out of the window just before she turned around the corner of Little St Mary's Church. 'He's a big handsome, strokeable individual that one, isn't he, boss… just like his dog.'

John Bellini scowled as a filthy 4x4 pulled up on the esplanade exactly opposite his cafe. He had a puzzled look on his face as the occupants were getting out. However, by the time the two women had reached the door, he had, white tea-towel over his arm, opened it with a flourish. 'Enter, my most beautiful customers, I recognised you even though in fantastic disguise.' Then he pointed at the 4x4.

'Don't ask,' they said simultaneously as they swept past him and headed for a corner table.

'Two special Lattes?' he called over.

They both nodded and sat down and then Karen leant across the table towards Clare. 'Boss, if the Romanies threatened Galpin, it can only be because he was up to his tricks with the daughter, can't it?'

'That's a strong possibility. Yes, they must have met at the Travellers' camp and the Coopers may be marrying her off to get her away. The wedding must have been arranged before Galpin was shot.'

'Perhaps with that dowry, she's already up-the-duff?'

'Yes, that's possible, Karen. Are you peckish?'

Karen smiled. 'Need you ask?'

'Can we have some of your cakes, John – they look nice,' called Clare.

Karen giggled. 'And his buns look alright as well.'

Clare smiled. Oh, to be young 'in maiden meditation, fancy free' – though perhaps the 'maiden' bit is stretching it, she thought, as she looked at her detective constable who half an hour after lusting over Josh Legge, was now giving her full attention to the man who was busy with their order. 'Ah, Italian men: good looking, with beautiful eyes, charming, well groomed, sharply dressed… with a disadvantage.'

'What's that, boss?'

'If you marry one, you marry his mother as well.'

'Yes, but I wonder if what they say about Italian men is true… well, you know,' mused the young woman quietly, pushing her fingers through loose hair.

Clare, deep in some memories from what seemed a thousand years ago… said nothing.

11

A harsh, discordant cawing came up from a black wheel of rooks that had suddenly formed and turned just above the tops of the dense clump of trees at the foot of the escarpment, and their agitated sound echoed around the great hollow of the coombe.

'Noisy devils!' said Emma, while Clare, concentrating on her running, merely grunted as they began to climb the track that lead to the downs nearly five hundred feet above. 'The steam engines that used to plough the fields puffed their way up here,' continued Emma, who was now a few yards ahead. 'Just like you.'

'And fuck you as well,' muttered Clare – glaring at her friend's back. However, she got her second wind and after the hard climb she was alongside Emma when they both slumped gratefully over the gate that marked the top. The two women were competitive and being sharp and bitchy with each other when out running, had somehow become as essential part of the training programme.

It was now light. When they had set off, the sea, as if backlit from below the horizon, had been an orange-white streak under a sky the colour of a giant bruise. They put themselves through two early morning hill runs a week since they had decided to compete in the local annual, tough switchback of a half marathon. It was in two months' time.

'I've been worried about you and the Vines,' said Emma eventually, as she was tightening the band that held her long blond hair in a pony-tail. 'And here's a good a place as any to tell you why.'

Clare stopped drinking out of her water bottle. 'Well?'

'Look around,'

Clare, who'd been on auto-pilot since Emma had given her a ridiculously early wake-up call, did as she was told. There was an amazing view from here. The coast, a series of headlands and bays disappearing into the distance in front of her and in the other direction a huge vale with the shadowy outline of a line of hills far to the north.

'Nearly all you can see,' said Emma, 'is owned by the Vines and two or three other families, and has been for centuries. Individually they own up to 15,000 acres, they may be Eurosceptics but they happily trouser over a million quid apiece a year in EU farming subsidies and have property portfolios elsewhere. They have power and contacts. A rural area like this is still almost feudal and they're from a class of people who can be charming and benevolent, but who can also be ruthless, vicious bastards – it's inbred. I'm not from round here, but do you know how I know this?'

'Because, you're one of them?' Clare knew Emma was from a 'small, quite well-off, county family' – though not this county. Though, saying that, her own Cheshire family, on her mother's side, were not exactly 'short of a bob or two'.

'Exactly, and as you've crossed them – be very careful,' answered Emma as she turned and set-off running along the ridgeway, causing a small flock of Jacob sheep to scatter like autumn leaves in a gale.

'Hey, slow down, boss,' complained Johns as Clare was taking the tight turns of the road up the scarp far too fast.

'Sorry, Matt.' Clare eased-off the accelerator. It was difficult to do so. Clare's early morning hill run with Emma had obviously produced a surplus of get-up-and-go, a feeling shared by her car. Her Golf GTI may be getting on a bit, but it had felt rejuvenated since she'd followed Andy Melbury's advice and 'taken it to Vic's'. Vic's Garage was a one-man backstreet operation that many of the police used. Vic, apparently, was not a diminutive of Victor, but of the mechanic's previous, ecclesiastical calling.

'Where are we meeting Shepherd Legge?' asked Johns, now more relaxed that Clare, having reached the top of the ridgeway, was now driving along the straight downland road.

'He will be at that old ruined barn. Apparently the Romany camp is not far from there.' As she turned off the main road onto the old drovers' road and began navigating around the pot-holes, Johns spoke again. 'I've been looking-up on Romanies. You know only one-percent of them still live in gypsy caravans. Vardos they're called. There's different types; Bow-Top ones and Reading ones. You know they never learned to make their own, they used *Gorgios* – that's us – as wagon builders.'

'Yes, Matt.'

'Now, the one-percent, like the Coopers, are the really traditional families. In these families it is a custom for newly-weds to live with the bride's family. You said Legge told you that the girl was moving to the groom's family. Now there's probably got to be a bloody good reason to break tradition hasn't there?'

Clare looked across at the young policeman. He was smiling; his bright blue eyes shining. 'I don't know what I'd do without you – well, you and your little friend.' She patted the lap-top Johns held on his lap.

'Hey, steady on there, boss.'

Clare looked across at the skyline of the ridgeway and recognised Drovers' Knoll. It was strange to think she was up there running just a few hours before. 'Ah, there he is.'

Legge was sitting on a quad bike where a track from Chalcombe Bumps joins the drovers' road at a disused stone barn. They pulled up alongside. Clare lowered her window. 'Good morning.'

'Morning – right, wagons roll.' Legge started his engine and moved off.

As they followed the quad bike with Legge's collie perched precariously on the bags of sheep feed piled up in the back, Johns began to hum louder and louder the theme tune of 'The Archers.'

'Shut up – that's an order.'

After half a mile or so, Legge indicated that he was stopping and pulled up alongside a hedge which, unusual for downland, was both thick and high. Clare parked up and she and Johns joined him. 'Stay,' Legge ordered the dog as he pushed open a small section of wattle fence that acted as a gate in a gap in the hedge.

Three Romany caravans, together with a few ponies and assorted dogs and chickens occupied a small field bounded by the thick embanked hedge.

'This was one of the overnight cattle holding areas used by the Welsh drovers on the long drive to London.' Legge pointed at a small pool in a corner. 'This one's even still has its dew-pond.'

'As smug as a bug in a rug,' observed Clare.

Legge pointed at the wagons. 'Those are called–'

'*Vardos* – these are bow-topped ones,' interrupted Johns.

Legge looked at him in surprise then shouted, '*Sastimos.*'

The three people sitting around a fire waved and got to their feet. The two lurchers lolling around under the wagons barely raised an eyebrow at the strangers' approach and it was left to a tiny pup, looking like a bag of rags and barking for all its might, to rush up and uphold the honour of the camp.

'Hello, miss,' said Doug Cooper as he doffed his hat. 'This is Calib Hughes, my wife's sister's husband, and my wife Lal.'

Clare stifled a frown. Hmm, men are definitely first here, even if the guy's about as close a relative as the Pope. The man, who had a beard, nodded: the woman smiled shyly.

'Would you like to see the *chiaz,* miss?'

Clare, puzzled, turned towards the woman.

'The wedding presents,' explained Legge.

'Yes, I'd love too.' Clare gave Johns a look as she turned to follow Cooper's wife who was walking to one of the wagons. Johns nodded – message received and understood. Matt will try and get something from the men.

Clare, as she climbed up the short steps into the vardo, also had a clear feeling that it had been engineered for her to be alone with Lal Cooper.

Women's business?

The inside was cosy and brightly painted. It looked like a miniature china shop. The Royal Worcester that she'd seen at Church Cottage was on display with some other pieces. There was also a blue bag on a cloth.

Money?

They sat down alongside each other on a rug covered bunk. The Romany woman was typical of many Clare had seen in the past when she had been taken by her Lakeland uncle to the annual horse fair at Appleby: swarthy with that typical nose and with her black hair pulled back – somehow they looked more Romany than the men. There was a photograph of a pretty dark haired girl who looked about sixteen. Shame how the women age, it must be the hard life, she thought. Clare pointed to the photo. 'She's lovely. Is that Dora?'

'Yes, you have daughters?'

'No, I don't have children – I'm not...' Clare felt herself, for some reason or other, blushing.

'That's a shame, such a pretty lady like you. Your eyes, miss? Do you or your women kin have the "seeing"?'

Seeing? Clare was puzzled for a moment then said, 'Fortune telling?'

'Something like.'

Clare laughed. 'Well they used to say my grandmother could–'

'Ah, so your grand-*dya* had "the seeing". Well, it seems your first daughter will be a true *dukka* and blessed with the gift. She'll have your eyes, another *Rakli-yak* – and more.'

She's smiling. She's relaxing. Keep her talking.

'Yes, I know what that means. There was another expression I remember a bit of from when Josh Legge and I met your husband; he said something to Josh that sounded like "Tea-toe-prada-shock".'

Lal Cooper let out a hoot of laughter.

'What is it?'

'Well, miss, I don't know what your word is for when a man has…' She mimed something with her hand. The something was crystal-clear and unequivocal.

'An erection,' said Clare, who was well on the way to getting a very bad feeling about this expression.

'Yes, it's something our men folk say when they see a man looking at a girl in a certain way.' She paused. Clare wished that the pause would last indefinitely. 'They say "*Te to porada shoska*", which means, "May the rest of your…?'

She's enjoying this.

'Erections,' muttered Clare.

'They say "Yes, and may the rest of your erections be like tent-poles as well." I'll get some tea.' Lal opened up a small cupboard to her side. The door made a shelf. She quickly spooned tea from an old tea-caddy into an earthenware tea pot which she took with her out of the vardo. Clare, grateful to be on her own for a moment, watched through the doorway as the woman put water into the pot from the heavy blackened kettle hanging over the open fire. The men were near the far hedge. Johns appeared to be doing the talking: he was pointing at something. Clare smiled when she realised it was a bird.

Lal came back and poured the tea.

Clare picked up Dora's photograph and looked at it.

'She's… she's a good girl, miss. She'll be wearing red for the first and last time tomorrow. You know? The boy's women-kin have checked.'

Clare was taken aback. Checked? Christ, checked that she was a virgin? And these people have lived here for centuries! What in a bubble? If that's true she couldn't have been made pregnant by Galpin.

'We'd heard that your people had threatened the dead man, Dean Galpin, about Dora. Galpin had a reputation as a womaniser and we–'

'No, miss, no! The men-folk and some kin went down to the hippy camp and told them not to let our Dora go there – the drop pot man was there with them, with them hippies, that's all, I swear.' Lal Cooper was becoming very distressed: then she began to sob.

Clare touched her arm. 'What is it, Lal?'

'It were the drugs, miss. They got her on the drugs.'

12

As Johns drove towards the heath, Clare noticed him occasionally glancing anxiously at her. She had been in a bad temper earlier. Immediately on their return from the Romany camp, she'd reported to Yorick Simmonds, who had told her, in no uncertain terms, to keep away from the Travellers' camp. He'd no need to spell it out – the local drugs squad must have it under surveillance. So, for the moment, they had no way to corroborate what the Romanies had said. And why the hell was Galpin at the camp? That question, frustratingly, would have to stay on hold as well because Clare had barely come out of Simmonds's office when she had a phone call from the army camp.

Lord Byron Two had some information for her.

The first time Clare visited the army camp, the heathland seemed, well, merely foreign to the eye. But this time, as she and Johns followed the soldier up through the ranges, there was an assault on all her northern senses. The heady smell, the prickle of heat, the way sunlight stung as it bounced off the white sands and gravels, and especially the noise – not of birds, but the 'chirp-chirp' of the large jewel-green crickets, and the relentless buzzing of bees and flies. And the great fronds of fern, which, even in the hollows where the air was heavy and still, somehow managed to be stirred by breezes only they could feel, and brushed unexpectedly across her face. Then through to colour – to brakes of yellow gorse, swathes of purple heather, and there, on the horizon, dark green clumps of stunted pine.

Clare was perspiring and she suddenly had a strong feeling of uncertainty; of wondering why she was here; of being a very long way from *home…*

'There he is, ma'am.'

Captain Guy Lovat, wearing combat fatigues and holding a rifle, turned his head and smiled as they approached. She thought he would have made a perfect Army recruiting poster… to get women, in their droves, to sign on.

'Hello, Detective Inspector Morell – DC Johns. You've come very quickly.'

'Well, you did say it was important,' answered Clare.

'Of course, would you both like to wait over there? I won't be a moment.'

He pointed to an open-sided hut with a bench in it, about thirty yards away. When they reached it Clare sat down heavily. She was relieved to be in the shade.

'Are you alright, boss?'

'Yes… just a bit hot.'

Clare was aware that Johns was still looking at her.

'You sure?'

'Yes, don't fuss,' she snapped.

One of her headaches was coming on.

'Acute Stress Reaction' had been the diagnosis. Though, as she'd been told, the headaches were, with time, decreasing in frequency, duration and severity.

Lovat was deep in conversation with the soldier who had escorted them.

'The Handsome Captain is really doing the macho bit today, isn't he? Look at him – fatigues, sleeves rolled-up showing his big muscles… and holding a big gun,' muttered

Johns.

What is it with Matt and Guy Lovat?

Lovat gave his rifle to the soldier who went back down the ranges. As the army captain walked over to them, he gave Clare a big smile.

'Presumably you've found out something about the bullet,' she said.

Lovat nodded as he sat down alongside her, 'Yes, some information came in earlier. That code number on it has been traced. It was part of a quantity of ammunition stolen, all of seven years ago. Some rifles were taken at the same time.'

'Can you tell us where from?' asked Johns.

'It was in a raid on a Spanish military depot near Pamplona.'

Clare turned her head towards him. 'Isn't that the place where they let the bulls loose in the streets?'

'Yes, and it's on the edge of the Basque country.' Johns spoke thoughtfully – almost to himself.

'Exactly, I think you're ahead of me Detective Constable. Almost certainly they were stolen by *Euskadi Ta Askatasuna*.' Lovat produced some papers from a pocket in his shirt.

'ETA,' said Johns.

Clare's head was whirling. 'Look, if this involves terrorists, why the hell are you talking to us like this?'

'Good question. We have reason to believe that although taken by ETA, they were somehow off-loaded.' He opened out the papers. 'ETA's first action was in 1961. The aim was freedom for *Euskadi*, the name for the Basque country. The political wing is *Herri Batastuna*. It has similarities here with the other side of the Irish Sea, but British Intelligence only got interested when contacts were actually made with the Real IRA – in fact it was reported that ETA even planned a bomb attack on a ferry to Plymouth at one time and–'

'Where does the bullet fit into this, Captain?' interrupted

Johns.

'Bear with me a second,' he said turning over some pages. 'If we just look at this list of incidents; the first one here was at Beasain – that was a bomb, then Barajas Airport – also a bomb, Leiza – bomb, Zaragoza – shooting, Rosas – bomb, Hernani – bomb, Madrid – bomb, Granada – shooting. They were mainly car bombs. They had enough gear, for example they nicked 18 tons of Titadine explosives in 1999.'

'What are you saying?' Clare was irritable; her headache was bad, and worsening – the throbs getting louder with each new location of Lovat's Spanish tour.

'Sorry. There is no history of them using rifles, only explosives or short range weapons for assassinations. Six rifles were taken with the ammunition: they were C-75's.'

'Which only weigh about 8 pounds, and are capable of firing over 1,500 metres,' said Johns.

'How do you know that?' asked the soldier.

'I checked up on special forces 7.62 rifles capable of firing to 1200 metres comfortably. It was the only one I could find – it's also the lightest.'

'Where did you get this information?'

'Internet: *Sniper's World*.'

'God, preserve us.' Lovat was shaking his head. 'Anyway, a couple of the rifles have come to hand – given in to the Spanish authorities. They had been used for long-range hunting in a remote part of the Pyrenees and rumour has it that that's probably where most of the others are – in the hands of traditional Basque mountain families in the area called the Urola Urhoi. The guns are a real class-act. Wealthy specialist hunters would pay a fortune for one, especially these particular ones... there is a *rumour*,' Lovat's voice lowered, more confidential in tone. He looked at Clare, expecting a response, but she was staring into space.

It was left to Johns to react. 'Rumour?'

'Yes, that one of the rifles and a quantity of ammunition had ended up in the hands of… an Englishman.'

Clare sat upright. 'An Englishman? No more than that?'

Lovat shook his head.

'Oh, on another matter, can the C-75 be modified so that it can be taken apart easily?'

Lovat looked at Johns in amazement. 'These were; removable barrel, stock, scope, and receiver.'

Johns reached in his pocket and took out a picture of a blue rucksack with yellow lacing. It had dimensions marked. 'Could it fit into that?'

Lovat took it from him 'Perfectly. How did –'

'Just a hunch,' said Johns, looking anxiously at Clare.

She was worse. First the rumour about the missing guns, and then each and every new point raised in the litany of the properties of the C-75 assault rifle, had cranked up, by a few more decibels, the volume of the drum beat between her ears. She pointed to the photo. 'As Matt, said, it's just a hunch. Someone was seen carrying one of these near the scene of the shooting.'

Lovat looked at his watch. 'Sorry, we will have to leave it there. So, our position is that it's a criminal matter of a gun finding its way into the country, and being illegally held. It's your bag. However, this conversation did not officially take place, the fewer people know the better and please keep me informed of your progress.'

Message received and understood – despite the drum accompaniment. She didn't believe him and wondered which security people were already sniffing around. Clare turned towards him and forced a smile. 'Of course, Captain. Thank you.'

The three of them walked back down to the car, and as Johns was opening the doors, Lovat turned to Clare. 'Could I have a word with you… *in private*?'

After swallowing two of the paracetamol tablets that Johns had taken out of the glove compartment, together with a long swig from the bottle of water he had in the car, Clare forced herself to speak to Yorick Simpson about this bizarre new Spanish connection… and the 'Englishman'.

At each new revelation by her, and each, ever more terse response from him, all she could see in her mind's eye was the bizarre image of the detective superintendent's long face gradually being stripped of skin and flesh… he turned into a talking skull. Mission finally accomplished, she switched-off her phone, took another draught of water, and, as Johns drove across the heath, Clare stretched out her long legs and closed her eyes on the passing landscape – this landscape she found so strangely disturbing – just where the road, conveniently and comfortingly, was entering one of the great dark blocks of conifers that fringe the heathlands. She immediately fell into a fitful sleep. A sleep disturbed firstly where the woodland changed and thinned out, where the lowering sunlight, filtering through the birches and elms, produced a strobe of flickering images. Then a series of bumps over the low humped bridges which marked each time they crossed the river that meandered over the water meadows. And each time she opened her eyes, everything was, disconcertingly so, only a slight variation from the time before. The same bump, the same 'Sorry, boss,' from Johns, the same clear fast chalk stream with its great streamers of emerald green weed and the same lines of alder and willow lining the banks. But then, as they drove over the downs, the road, the gentlest of switchbacks as it crossed the great rounded folds of the chalk lands, she slipped into a deep, undisturbed sleep, until woken by the whine of the engine and the jerk of a rapidly changing gearbox as Johns steered down the steep road from the scarp to the coastal plain.

She felt better. A lot better. But what a case! An artist-shepherd-sharpshooter, a Romany speaking tongues, a dead drop-pot man, action man soldiers, Basque terrorists, then last, but by no means least, her senior officer had appeared to have changed into a talking skull.

Then she remembered Legge's paintings of mountain landscapes! The Spanish one, what was it? The Sierra de… Sierra de Pena. Yes, that was it.

She told Johns. He stopped the car and opened his laptop.

'Yes, there we are. The Sierra de Pena. It's in the Pyrenees near Navarra. And guess where's in Navarra?

'Pamplona?'

'If the Romanies are telling the truth about the girl and the drugs, then that let's Legge off the hook, but the painting and this Englishman thing puts him back on.'

'Yes, Matt,' agreed Clare, reluctantly.

'Oh, boss – funny the "Captain" asking to speak to you *privately*,' fished Johns.

'It was just something personal, Matt… nothing important.'

13

The lower sash had been pushed fully open and Clare and Emma were leaning out of the window. At one end of the window-sill there was an open wine bottle: they'd ditched the gin and cigarettes.

The harbour was busy. A large number of visiting sailing vessels had joined the locals. An event was on – what one of their neighbours had termed a Not-So-Tall-Ships Race. Things were livening up down there. The sound of arguing and scuffling in one of the back-alleys carried up the slope to the flats.

'Press gangs are out in force,' remarked Clare.

Emma, however, had her head turned towards the stereo. 'Who's this?'

'Taj Mahal.'

'I like him.'

'That makes a change. You liking my music – you usually show your opinion by subtly turning it off.'

Emma pushed her hair back from her face. 'You know, it's funny, but in connection with work, three fit new guys have appeared from nowhere. It's like that poem. How does it go? "Bloody men are like buses. You wait for ages and as soon as one appears – lots of them pop-up all flashing their things." '

Clare laughed. 'I think it's "flashing their indicators"!'

'Mere details, girl. As we say in the trade it's the intent that counts.' Emma took a sip of wine. 'Anyway, I was wondering if you would like–'

'No.'

'No, what?'

'You know "No, what"! Stop trying to fix me up!'

'Alright then… Mother Superior.'

Emma then tried another tack. 'What about that army captain, then? How did you describe him in that understated northern way of yours?'

'I said he was one of the best looking men I've ever seen in my life. He's absolutely gorgeous.'

'Exactly.'

'Anyway… he's asked me out.' Clare spoke in the most matter-of-fact voice she could muster.

'What!'

'It's just to a regimental dinner dance thing really, at very short notice. I'm not sure I'll go.'

'What! You must go. Brilliant! Think of those dashing young men in uniform – all pert buttocks and rows of little polished buttons.'

'The trouble is,' said Clare, resting her elbows on the sill. 'I've really nothing suitable to wear and no time to go and get something.'

Emma, after wiping away an imaginary tear, suddenly looked serious. 'Turn round… and again. Right, Cinders, I'll be back in a jiff.'

Clare looked at herself in the mirror. She was wearing a straight, very unforgiving, evening dress, in the darkest of thin green velvet. She fingered the neckline.

Hmm, it was nice – not too low.

'What do you think?'

'I don't know why you're fussing about there – you've got nice boobs,' observed Emma. 'But you could do with some jewellery, something simple.'

Clare lifted a small box from the sideboard, and took out an elegant filigree silver necklace. 'This was my grandmother's.'

'Let me,' offered Emma. She stepped back after she had fastened it. 'Perfect… now shoes.'

A few minutes later Clare was still clattering around in her bedroom.

'Get a move on, Imelda Marcos!'

When Clare returned to the lounge, she had a glass of wine in one hand – from which she took a sip – and a pair of rather dusty black high heel shoes in the other.

'Whoa! They're a bit racy for you those. What are they – leftovers from your days in uniform? Mind that dress!'

Clare after spluttering on a mouthful of wine, dusted-off the shoes, put them on, and looked at herself in the mirror. She lifted up the hem of the dress a little. 'I've got some black tights.'

'Hold it there, sister,' said Emma – who dashed out of the flat again.

Clare – who'd not worn high heels for an age – barely had time to start some serious tottering-around practise, before Emma returned. 'Tights!' she snorted. 'These are what you need.' She took a pair of black hold-up stockings out of the bag she was carrying and carefully inspected them. 'There are no signs of any bloke's nail snags – so these must be new.' She looked up. Clare was standing with her hands on her hips. 'What?'

'I'm not wearing those.'

It had been good, thought Clare, as she relaxed into the BMW's comfortable seat. Guy Lovat turned and smiled at her. He'd drunk very little. She was ok… *ish*. To thwart the little wine demon, she'd played the 'I'm thirsty – I think I'd just like a slim-line tonic this time,' game, a couple of times. Everything had been great since she'd come out of the front door of the flats, which had once been cavalry officers' barracks, and walked across what had been the parade ground. It was as if two hundred years of history had peeled back in an instant. A handsome officer, wearing a short silver buttoned dark blue jacket and tailored blue trousers with a broad red stripe was waiting for her, not with a black stallion, but with rather more horsepower... a black BMW Z 3.

Guy Lovat had been attentive and charming, and a lot of the people she'd met had been really nice. What had been good, especially when talking to women officers, was the way he'd mentioned that she was a police detective inspector. It had put her on equal footing.

They were now driving down the esplanade, the town's reflections glittering in the bay.

'Fancy a breath of fresh air?'

'Yes, that would be lovely.' she replied.

He parked just before the harbour and as they started to walk away from the car he took her hand... and she moved up close to him. It was late, but as always at weekends, there were still people around. Clare felt self-conscious – she in a long evening dress, holding hands with a soldier in fancy uniform.

'He's fit!' said one of a group of girls coming towards them.

'That's a nice dress,' said another.

They walked slowly up the steps that terraced their way to the slopes above the harbour. She opened her bag and began to search for her keys as they walked across the old square towards the flats.

Clare unlocked the outer door and he pushed it open for her. As she turned she caught his arm. 'Would you like to come in for a coffee... or something?'

She was holding a near empty tumbler of whisky. The open bottle was by her feet, alongside the guitar with the metal resonator. On the coffee table by her side, there was a guitar slide, some fingerpicks, and a cigarette packet. The packet was open: there was a cigarette burning in an ashtray – alongside several cigarette ends. She hadn't thrown away the last packet.

Clare rarely drank whisky, and usually only played her second guitar – the slide guitar – when in a black mood. She leant forward and picked up the bottle. Her hand had started shaking again. The earlier guitar playing had helped... temporarily. Her mind was a turntable. She kept going over and over what happened. It was relentless – like a tread mill she couldn't get off. And after each re-play, she became, with a predictable inevitability, more miserable.

It started again:

'Would you like to come in for a coffee... or something?'

She remembered every word of his reply. *'I'm sorry, I've got to be off early in the morning. It's been wonderful, I'll be in touch.'* Then he'd pecked her on the cheek, and with a wave, was gone.

Clare hugged herself. What the hell had been going on? Guy Lovat had fancied her surely? He'd hit on her as soon as they'd met! Oh, God, was he doing an 'Officer and a Gentleman' thing, and not taking *advantage*? What advantage? She hadn't been drunk. Perhaps he thought she was a slut? There is, she convinced herself, no ambiguity here, that's what she'd done – offered it on a plate. He couldn't have taken it any other way.

She rubbed her eyes, they were sore, but not from the smoke, then she drained the glass and curved foetal-like into the corner of the sofa...

All Saints, a tall Victorian Gothic pile and St Edmund's Church, a squat Georgian basilica, face each other uneasily across the narrow harbour and both sets of bell-ringers are always prepared to sacrifice tone and timing for sheer volume in order to 'outdo the other side'. The result is that anyone in this part of the town, who is still asleep at mid-morning on a Sunday, is woken by the inevitable antiphonal bombardment taking place across the waters of the harbour.

Clare, who had somehow managed to take herself to bed after being sick, although miserable and tired, was surprised to find that she was not suffering from a particularly bad hangover. However, she soon began to feel stupid and absolutely furious with herself for over-reacting in the way she had. Perhaps he simply wanted to slow things down? Or, more likely, (he is in the army for fuck's sake!) really did have to get up early?

'Shit!' she said out loud. 'Christ, Morell, you stupid cow!' She threw back the duvet and got out of bed. And then, wearing the stockings Emma had given her – and very little else – she stepped over the green dress and tripped over one of the high heels as she was stomping out through the door. 'Fuck!'

'Fuck!' echoed the bathroom, seconds later.

Part Two

14

A beaten-up Volvo estate pulled up suddenly and a tall, slim man with long black hair got out. Struggling with a pile of papers, he back-heeled the door closed with a desert boot which appeared as old as the car, and strode up the steps leading to an impressive Victorian doorway, at the precise moment that the old college clock struck two.

A few minutes earlier the newly-appointed Vice Principal had been looking out of his office window on the top floor of the newest addition to the college – a charmless edifice with narrow energy-saving windows which, although officially called the New Block, had since his arrival, been generally referred to as Saruman's Tower.

Gerald Lowe was what might be termed a neat and tidy man… unnaturally so. Never a hair out of place, never a crease where there shouldn't be one, and always a perfect one where there should be. Rumour had it that his wife always popped him in a bottle of Dettol overnight. The first term of his appointment had seen a flurry of orders to maintenance rather than academic staff. He was pleased how his campus looked. The car park had been zoned and the new yellow lines outside the old part of the college had made such a difference. His thoughts, however, were suddenly interrupted by the sound of an exhaust that spooked a line of pigeons into taking-off from the library roof like a squadron of Spitfires. Lowe rushed first to the window and secondly back to his desk, and at the precise moment that the old college clock struck two, the Vice Principal – with a puce face, startling in the contrast between his white hair and his even whiter collar – grabbed the telephone.

Dr Rob Ellis looked in vain at his desk for a space to deposit the pile of assignments and instead settled for the furthest of the four chairs to his left. The choice was predictable, as it was the only one that didn't already have something on it. He barely had time to sit down and take his reading glasses out of the top pocket of his jacket, when there was a sharp knock on the door.

'Come in,' he shouted and an elegant, impeccably groomed woman of a 'certain age' came into the room.

'Mission Control have just rung, you're to move the Rust Bucket off the yellow lines – again.'

Ellis pushed back his black hair, which was beginning to be prematurely flecked with a little grey, and looked at her over the top of his half-moons. 'Thank you, Moneypenny.'

Gill Doyle, the Geography Department secretary, laughed as she went out and two women students passing down the corridor gave each other a *look*. There were always rumours flying around the college grapevine about this man… but annoyingly never any evidence.

The secretary started to walk to her office but then turned on her high heels and went back into Ellis's room. She pointed to the window sill just behind his chair. 'Oh, rather than leave it on that corporation tip you call a desk there's some stuff there – it's from James Travers. He called in not long ago.'

'Bix came in, how does he look?'

'All right, I suppose. He's off again, he said.'

Ellis was looking at her hard. 'You really don't like him do you?… He's had a very rough time.'

'It goes back a long way, Rob – a long way. Oh, don't forget the departmental meeting,' she said switching the topic.

'No, I won't. What time is it tomorrow?'

'It's at 3.45 *today*,' she said, shaking her head as she closed the door.

Twenty minutes later, Dr Rob Ellis phoned the police.

Ellis was looking out of the tall round-topped windows of his office in what was known as the Old College; one of a series of lovely warm-looking Victorian buildings, built in an Italianate style in the 1870's by a local architect. He watched as a car, an old black VW GTI, reversed skilfully into a tight space in the otherwise full 'Visitors' Car Park'.

A constant stream of students on their way to and from the Students' Union and the Refectory passed below his first floor window. Two Madonna look-a-likes, nineteen year old girls striving to appear like someone as old as their mothers, walked past joined at the hip: one of his students, glancing-up and seeing him, moved to the blind side of the group he was with. Ellis frowned in the knowledge that whatever assignment he was owed, was well overdue. Four Asian girls with long black hair, and as thin as laths, moved past like a tightly-packed flock of birds. And there, flitting around them, wearing a pair of jeans which looked like they had been subjected to a serious assault by Edward Scissorhands, was a good-looking fair-haired student.

Ellis laughed and then, as he returned to his desk, said to himself, 'Jonner Dawes; one of life's great optimists and self-styled God's gift to women… any God, any women.'

In the CID office, it had been a busy morning, of mixed fortune, in following up the particular anti-hunting protestors who had accused Galpin of threats or actual assault. The three who had needed hospital attention seemed to have disappeared into the ether, and the family threatened in their home, who had almost immediately afterwards moved to London, had recently, according to the Met, emigrated to Australia. That left a David Yates, the League Against Cruel Sports official, whom Galpin had been convicted of assaulting, which had resulted in that inadequate fine and community service. Yates lived in a remote cottage on the heath. He had no neighbours. The community policeman had found out from the nearest pub that he was away a lot, but apparently some locals in there thought he was due home soon.

Melbury, Johns and Karen were sitting around Clare's desk, and she was just about to sum up the morning's work… when all hell broke loose.

'Well, what's going on here?' shouted Detective Superintendent Simmonds as he walked up and down behind his desk waving a copy of The Chronicle – the local daily paper.

'We don't know, sir,' ventured Clare, grateful, as no doubt Karen, Melbury and Johns were, that Yorick had such a wide, deep desk. 'But no one here leaked a dicky-bird. Right?' She turned to the other three who, in response to her look, momentarily resembled a line of car rear-sill nodding dogs.

'What about that shepherd?'

'I've just spoken to Mr Legge, he says not,' answered Clare.

'And the SOCO's involved said they knew nothing about it, sir.' Melbury leant forward as he spoke, as if giving his detective inspector additional physical support. 'Also, I've just phoned Eddie Dodgson, the editor of the "Chronnie" – I've known him from school. Eddie says that someone, who said they were from here, phoned up the news-desk and asked if they could add another item onto our regular weekly insert which had already been sent in.'

Simmonds sat down and picked up the newspaper that was on his desk. 'So, following our requests for witnesses to come forward for various traffic accidents is this,' he read out from the newspaper. '*Finally, in connection with our enquiries concerning a serious incident, we would appreciate any information at all about the following message: 6F + 1/2 C (50L).*'

'It's all so low key, sir, just added onto our weekly piece which is always tucked away in the paper anyway. Makes you wonder why bother,' puzzled Clare.

Simmonds was now noticeably more relaxed. 'Yes, you'd hardly call it a headline would you? That's something for us to think about.' He attempted what, with a great stretch of imagination, might possibly be referred to as a smile. 'Well, for you lot to think about.'

The place after lunch was quiet. Clare was in the office waiting to hear if there had been any further leads on the newspaper leak. Melbury and Johns had gone out to Winterstone to see Sir Alan Vine again, and Karen, who had family contacts with people who used to work on the Winterstone estate, was out 'getting paid for gossiping', as she put it.

There was knock on the door and the desk sergeant came in. 'Ma'am. We've just taken this call,' he said holding up a sheet of paper. 'It was from the College. I said someone would be over right away.'

Clare looked at the nameplate on the heavy oak door – yes, right one – and then turned her head to watch the rather charming lad with torn jeans, who had chatted her up and insisted on showing her the way into the Geography Department, walking off down the corridor. He suddenly looked over his shoulder and smiled.

Oh, shit!

She knocked on the door and pushed it open without waiting for a response. Christ, what a mess! she thought. The walls were lined with overflowing bookshelves and the chairs had papers and books on them, as had the large desk that was in front of the tall, round-topped window facing the door. It took a few seconds before she noticed someone looking at her between two piles of books on the desk.

'Dr Ellis? I'm Detective Inspector Morell,' said Clare who put on a big smile as she entered the room.

'Oh, hello, I was expecting a –'

'A big chap in a uniform? I'm sorry to disappoint.'

Did I really say that? Well, that's a great start, big mouth.

'No – it's just that I spoke to one, I suppose, on the phone.'

He got to his feet. He was taller than she was expecting – perhaps his chair is low. Six foot two? But that long hair! What is it about men round here and the barbers? He came round to her side of his huge oak desk and picked up the papers and folders from the chair in front of it.

'Please take a seat,' he said and then returned to his side of the desk. He hesitated, looking for somewhere to put the papers and folders he was carrying. Clare was tempted to point to the far end of the windowsill, which, as far as she could see, was the only clear horizontal surface – apart from the floor. He decided on the floor, then slumped down in his ancient office chair and with both hands pushed back his hair from his face and looked at her.

Clare was surprised; his long black hair was flecked with a little grey but he was younger than she expected. Her age or late thirties at the most? He's a good looking bloke, she thought, apart from that long hair and those ridiculous spectacles.

'Sorry, DI… Detective Inspector Mor…?'

Slight Welsh accent?

'Morell.'

'Isn't that a mushroom?'

'No, that's M-o-r-e-l. I'm M-o-r-e-l-l.'

She gave him a *look* that was met by an unusual response. The hazel eyes that were studying her over the top of his half-moon glasses, after just a flicker of hesitation, held their own. She also got the annoying feeling that he was smiling at her – without actually smiling. 'Your… your phone call, Dr Ellis?'

From the pile of papers on his desk, he picked up a newspaper. His copy of The Chronicle was already open. He tapped the relevant column – it had been circled with a red pen – with a finger. 'It's this request for information, this *6F + 1/2 C (50L)* bit.'

'You know what it means?' asked Clare, realising immediately that she'd sounded too keen.

'Oh, yes, I think so.'

She found herself gripping the chair.

Ellis stood up. 'We need to go to the Map Room – it's right at the top.'

They left his office and she followed him along the corridor. He's a real scruffy devil, she thought. How long has he had that leather jacket and those desert boots? Desert boots! They started to walk up the three flights of steep spiral stairs, the windows carefully positioned to show a changing vista of magnificent views across the bay. Clare came to the conclusion that he wasn't going to say anything. So, it was time for page two of the fictitious 'Cop's Charm Manual'… *Small Talk.*

'This is a lovely place to work and you've got a good reputation as well. Are you independent?' she said, addressing the back of the lecturer who was taking the steps two at a time.

'In practice, though we're officially collegiate to the University.' Ellis, no more out of breath than Clare, pointed out of the window as if the mother university was just the other side of the nearest headland, and not fifty miles down the coast. 'And we're grateful for the continuing connection. The Principal – Mother Courage, bless her – fought tooth and nail to save us getting involved in any crap amalgamations closer to hand.'

'They say at the station, that your students cause very little trouble, but someone was telling me about that incident with those American sailors.'

'That was a misunderstanding,' snapped Ellis, without looking around.

What's up with misery guts?

There was no one around and Clare surprised herself by childishly pulling a face behind his back.

Andy Melbury had related to Clare the saga about a particular Saturday night a couple of years ago that, as he told it, 'occupied an important place in the battle-honours of the local police force.' According to Melbury, vastly outnumbered officers coped heroically with boat loads of sailors from a visiting US naval vessel swarming around the college campus under the misapprehension that the women's student hostel was in fact a cover for the biggest brothel this side of Bangkok.

Clare was not to know that several lecturers had been seen in a pub the night before the incident talking to some American sailors. Ellis had been one of them and for a time had been the chief suspect. However, the mischief had been caused by a Sociologist, now departed, bitter about being constantly overlooked for promotion.

As they entered the Map Room, Ellis waved an arm in the direction of the ranks of map drawers. 'This stuff isn't really my bag, this cartography, especially this history of cartography. I've been dealing with it temporarily as the cartography guy is not around at the moment. Right, C4.'

He walked over to a block of drawers marked C, opened the fourth drawer down and extracted the top two maps. They were large and looked very old. He carried them over to a huge glass mapping table. He looked at the top one, and then pushed it to one side. 'That's an eighteenth century land enclosure map, in acreage using old measurements like rods and poles.' He pulled the other one towards him. It had a Post-It sticker on it. 'Ah, this is the one. It's a survey map from the same time. Come and have a look.'

Clare walked over to the table and lowered her head to look closely at where Ellis was pointing his finger. 'Can you read the figures on this field boundary?'

'They're a bit faint, err… 2F… 3C… 8L.'

She struggled to stay calm.

'Furlongs, chains and links' said Ellis, answering her next question before she'd asked it.

'So, it relates to measurements that went out with the Ark.'

'Barely, Detective Inspector,' said Ellis. 'A cricket pitch is 22 yards, which is a chain, and horse races are in furlongs which are 220 yards. Now a link is part of a chain, full name apparently – I've been reading this up recently – is a Gunter Chain.'

Something told Clare that Ellis had definitely clocked the for-fuck's-sake-get-on-with-it look she was giving him, but he smiled and carried on… and on. 'It was named after one Reverend Edmund Gunter who invented it about 1600. It's a part decimal system: 100 links in a chain – each link is about 6.6 inches –'

'So, what about this "*6F plus 1/2 C*" business?' interrupted Clare.

He walked to the blackboard, picked up some chalk, and

wrote as he spoke. '6 furlongs is 220 yards multiplied by 6, which is 1320 yards. Half a chain is 11 yards. The total is 1331 yards. Now the 50 L in brackets in your information after the1/2C is just a clue to make sure we get it, because–'

'Because 50 links is half a chain,' said Clare, who then took a breath before proceeding. 'Now what's 1331 yards in metres?'

'1331 multiplied by 36 and divided by 39, err,' Ellis looked at the chalk in his hand. 'Maths isn't my thing either – just a jiff.'

When he returned a minute or so later clutching a calculator, Clare, chalk in hand, was looking at something she had just written on the blackboard.

'Yes, that's it: 1220 metres,' said Ellis.

15

The sun shining directly behind Paul Simmonds, cast him into silhouette. Strange, Clare hadn't noticed before that the detective superintendent's neck appeared to be almost as wide as his long narrow head – Yorick had something of the Homer Simpsons about him.

She'd gone straight to his office when she got back from the College.

He leant back in his chair. 'So, Clare, well done, you were right all along about that message sprayed on the post. Galpin was certainly deliberately shot at Full Moon Copse from Chalcombe Bumps – exactly 1220 metres away. Which means?'

'Well, sir, I think it now clarifies three things; that firstly this is now definitely a murder inquiry, secondly, we are looking for a killer who is a hell of a shot, and thirdly there is most certainly a tie-up to one of the guns that were stolen at the same time as the ammunition.'

'Ah, yes. It was to do with the range, wasn't it?'

'Yes, there's a great range of snipers rifles used by NATO and other countries that take 7.62 by 51mm ammunition,' she said as she fingered through her note book. 'Here we are; the French use the FR-F2, Belgians the 30-11, Czechs the VZ5, Germans use a WA 2000, and our lot tend to favour L42A1's. There are others but with the exception of one, they are all not accurate over 1,000 metres. The exception, which is accurate up to 1,500 metres with the type of Match ammo used to shoot

Galpin, is the C-75 used by the Spanish.'

'So, it all points to the fact that it was one of the C-75's that were stolen, which were also modified so they could be broken down.'

'Yes, sir, it could, if you remember, fit in that rucksack we were looking for. Also it's light at…' she looked at her notes. '8.14 pounds'.

'You'll have to inform your army source straight away,' he tapped the desk with his pen. 'Correction – you're unofficial army source.' Clare nodded. She was dreading the phone call to Lovat – she'd not spoken to him since that, that night…

'There's something going on here I really don't understand, sir.'

Simmonds looked at her intently. 'Go on.'

'Well, whoever leaked the information to the Chronicle, is almost certainly our killer. So he tries to make sure we've twigged what his message means. He doesn't even know we've not understood it before he gave the leak, does he? He's giving us help in case we haven't – it's very important to him… or her.'

It was Simmonds turn to nod in agreement.

Clare smoothed her hair before continuing. 'That's the problem. We're looking for the murder weapon and the one who has it hidden is encouraging us to look for it. So, if we search anyone we suspect's property, ten-to-one, it won't be there. Someone's pulling our strings. Why?'

'You're right, someone's fucking with us. Who's in the frame? We have a couple?'

'I don't know all about the Winterstone connection yet. Andy and Matt are out there trying to find out more about Sir Alan Vine's gun collection. As you know Sir Alan had a disagreement with Galpin and wanted Lady Charlotte to dismiss him. And there's that rumour that one of the stolen C-75 rifles fell into the hands of an Englishman. They're a piece of class kit – but Sir Alan could afford it.'

Simmonds nodded his head again. 'And what about that shepherd?'

'Josh Legge is a suspect. He's a crack shot, we have evidence of that from the way he killed the Travellers' dogs. He was in Europe for some time, including the Pyrenees, after the guns and ammunition were stolen, so could have picked up the gun then.'

Simmonds leaned forward and began that other annoying habit of his, of drumming on his desk top with his fingers – it was worse than his pen-tapping. 'Despite this new evidence, we're still screwed. There's no point searching Winterstone House or Legge's cottage and I can't let you go into the Travellers' camp until the Drug Squad, give us the OK. So, for the moment there is no way that you can confirm that story the gypsies told you about the girl and drugs, or if they were telling porkies and they were threatening Galpin – and Legge himself being a sort of honorary Romany, did the *business*.'

'Well, sir, that was just guessing really. They're very traditional, Galpin may have seduced the girl and '

'Legge may have helped in a sort of honour killing?'

Clare was taken aback by Simmonds choice of words. 'It's… it's all guesswork, sir.'

'Yes, we're all guessing here, but keep everything tight, only involve your three and no one else here. The whole county would go ape-shit if it got out. Think of it, "Killer on the loose! Who will be next?" Jesus! So officially it's still a tragic accident. We know they happen.'

Clare nodded.

Simmonds began to push the papers on his desk together. 'But let your army contact know.'

Lovat was the last person she wanted to speak to. 'Yes, sir,' she said quietly.

'Oh, what did you tell that Dr Ellis about the case?'

'Well he fished around after he came up with the goods, and got narked when I side-stepped everything. I told him nothing, just thanked him for his help.'

'Good,' said Simmonds, before giving, surprisingly, what as many as six out of ten observers, might recognise as a smile.

Clare smiled back and got to her feet. She was getting on well with Yorick: he stamps hard at times, but he's sharp and isn't really a miserable sod at all – just looks like one.

'The thing is Clare. Why bother leaving clues to be solved after you've already killed? I'm getting a bad feeling here.'

She nodded in agreement.

You and me, guv.

The door of her Golf GTI shut at the second time of asking. It's showing its age. Clare, looking around, noticed that no one was sitting in the elegant promenade shelter she'd parked by. She walked over and sat facing the sea. It was comforting, sitting here, partially cocooned from the outside world by a glass roof and sides. She'd read somewhere that this shelter, and the several others along the front, were all over 150 years old. The words of her grandfather conjured themselves out of the sea air*: 'They knew how to make things then'.*

Clare wiped the corner of an eye and focused down the wide sweep of the bay: past the slumped blue-grey clays of the nearest headland, appropriately named Grey Cliff, to the great cream coloured chalk cliffs further down the coast.

Then she looked at her watch. Another five minutes.

God, that Ellis was a pain in the arse! She hadn't told Yorick the half. After they left the map room Ellis had probed nonstop about the significance of the equation and didn't she think he was due an explanation. He walked with her all the way back to her car. She'd ducked, dived, avoided and lied through her teeth – everything apart from kicking him in the balls. And that came close.

Clare's hands had shaken earlier when she'd phoned Lovat. It had been an unreal stilted conversation. She told him the facts. He thanked her and said he had nothing to report from his end. And that was it. Numb after. She just felt numb.

She got to her feet. It was time to go over the road to Bellini's. There was less chance of being disturbed here than at the station. Clare had phoned Melbury to give him the information. He and Johns were coming straight from Winterstone: she'd also contacted Karen who was out in one of the villages. She knew they would be on a high when they met. There's always a lightening of mood, euphoria almost, whenever there is a breakthrough.

Karen Garland was already in the café. She was leaning on one side of the counter, John Bellini on the other. They were deep in conversation and hadn't noticed her come in.

Hmm, watch it young lady, the missus is Sicilian. We don't want you ending up in the harbour with cement in your wellies.

'Hello.'

Bellini turned, 'Oh, hello, Clare.' He flashed one of his handsome smiles.

Yes, alright, gorgeous.

'OK, Karen?'

'Hi, boss – I've left my stuff over there,' said Karen turning and pointing to a corner table. The two women ordered some coffee and then walked past the wall of Art Deco tiles and sat underneath the mirror with elegant glass corner figures that had windswept hair like Lalique car mascots. Karen lowered her voice though there was no one close. 'Well, I'd like to see Mike Crick's face when he finds out what a twat he was about the shooting.'

Just then the door opened noisily. Melbury and Johns had arrived. They waved to the two policewomen, placed their order and then walked over to the quiet corner where Clare and Karen were sitting.

'It's a funny old world, that lecturer coming up trumps,' exclaimed Melbury as he flopped down on a seat.

Johns put his laptop on a spare seat. He was frowning. 'I'm not sure – it pops-up more questions than answers, if you ask me.'

Clare smiled. Yes, must have a long chat with young Matt. 'Now, for starters, we keep completely stum about this development. Only us and the Super to know anything. OK?'

There were serious nods all round.

'Good. Is there anything new from Winterstone, Andy?'

'I was shown around the Trophy Room. Sir Alan stalks deer in Scotland, as we know. But he also goes on fairly regular trips abroad. He couldn't resist boasting about the Ibex and Chamois he's bagged. According to his Lordship it's a lot cheaper than Scotland at 1,200 euros a licence. Quite a few toffs go over together, apparently. Ask me where in particular?'

'Where in particular?' humoured Karen.

'The Pyrenees! Also, he's a gun collector – got lots of old ones. I didn't see the new jobs inside the gun safe but he could have the one we're looking for. And that rumour – well, here's one *Englishman* with a lot of money and interest.'

'What did you think, Matt?' Clare turned towards Johns.

'Oh, he wasn't there,' exclaimed Melbury. 'He was left behind with her Ladyship in the Library, impressing her no end with his bird knowledge – she's got rare prints by some artist. What was his name? John Thomas Aubergine?'

'Ha-ha. John James Audubon. She owns some amazing hand-coloured etchings from the 1830's as well as an octavo-sized edition. They are worth a fortune,' stated Johns.

'I found nothing at all, boss,' said Karen.

Clare leaned back in her chair and gestured with open

hands. 'So, it's a shame to put a dampener on it, but Dr Ellis has only really confirmed what we already knew.'

Just then John Bellini approached with a tray of coffees.

'That one has skimmed milk – as *ordered*,' he said as he put down a drink in front of Melbury.

'I didn't ask for that – and where's my Lardy cake?'

Bellini shook his head. 'Skimmed milk and no Lardy.'

Melbury frowned and then glared at him with narrowed eyes. 'My Linda's been in, hasn't she?'

Bellini nodded. 'She explained that as she'd learnt how to skin rabbits when she was growing up – what she'd do to me would be very easy if I didn't do as I was told.'

Melbury looked around the table and pointed to Bellini. 'He made a pass at my wife once!'

'We were all fifteen at the time,' answered Bellini as he turned and walked away.

16

Clare was deep in thought. It was quiet, as it had been arranged that Karen would pick up Melbury from home and then they were going to look for the elusive League Against Cruel Sports official who lived out on the heath. Johns was not in yet.

Then the CID office door flew open. It was the normally calm, unruffled desk sergeant, red-faced and breathing heavily. He shouted. 'Come and look at this, ma'am!', and disappeared out of the door again. She found him in the corridor pointing out of a long window that overlooked the main road.

'We've just had a call saying it was about the shooting and telling us to look over the road straight away!'

Clare ran to the window and looked out. 'I want that taped and secured and really done over and dusted.'

Sprayed on the bus shelter the other side of the road were the words LOOK AGAIN in large yellow letters.

'It's vital, just get it done. I'll explain later,' Clare ordered as she began to run down the corridor. 'Oh, and get onto the bus company, taxis and anyone here who might know when it was done.'

'I'm pretty sure that writing wasn't there when I came in last…' the desk sergeant said as the stairs doors slammed shut.

'Matt! Matt! Where the hell are you?' Clare shouted into her mobile as she ran across the car park yard. 'On your way in? On the top road? Good – go straight to Chalcombe Bumps, I think there's another message. See you there.'

She got in her car and started it. She began to reverse out of her parking space when a patrol car swung into the crowded yard far too fast and nearly caught the GTI's tail. 'Blind twat!' yelled Clare out of her window, adding to the already considerable lexicon of the unpopular Sergeant Tim Dodd's nicknames.

Luckily at this time of the morning, most of the traffic on the road to the north was coming into town, though Clare was held up through the village at the foot of the escarpment. But then, booting-in the accelerator, she climbed, tyres squealing, quickly up the hairpins of the chalk scarp; responded impolitely to a violent fist-shake and a variety of obscene gestures, and drove fast on the stretch of straight downland road, before burning her discs as she braked and swung off the main road. It was then the turn of the shock absorbers to go through hell as the car bounced along the old drovers' road.

Johns's blue Peugeot was parked on the track near the stile at the foot of Chalcombe Bumps. He had only just arrived. Clare spotted him on the lower slopes of the steep knoll. She parked and, crossing the stile, began to run up the footpath. 'Shit!' Slipping on some mud, she found herself on her knees. 'Damn, I should leave some trainers in the car,' she said to herself as she struggled to her feet – and a couple of sheep nearby appeared to nod in agreement.

'And I thought I was reasonably fit,' panted Johns a few minutes later when she caught up with him just before the top. They moved quickly up to the stone gate posts near to the burial mounds.

'Yes, Matt, there's something else here. Not too close.'

Sprayed on the opposite side of the post to the original message were the figures 128: they both took photos with their mobiles.

Clare caught John's arm. 'Look, Matt. I've got a strong feeling that no one's going to leave another message like this and warn us in the way they did with that writing on the bus-stop and the phone message if something isn't going to happen soon – today, this morning, any time!'

'What another shooting?'

'Maybe. You ring for SOCO's. Speak to Andy as well – Karen's with him.' Johns, phone still in hand, nodded and moved away a few yards. Clare looked at her mobile. Yorick first or Ellis? She made up her mind and then cursed under her breath when there was no answer from the Geography Department Office number he'd given her: Ellis, on principle, he'd said, refused to use a mobile phone.

Idiot.

'Matt, stay here whatever happens. I'll be in touch when I can,' shouted Clare over her shoulder.

The young policeman looked up and was about to respond but was left open mouthed as his detective inspector disappeared over the crest.

Minutes later, after slipping and falling at the same place she had on the way up and reversing the car down the narrow track to the drovers' road, Clare left a message for Simmonds who was unavailable, but then, on finding that the College number was still engaged, hit the steering wheel in frustration, spun-off a pothole and nearly ended in a ditch. However the drive into town on the main road was marginally less eventful than the outward one, until the Golf caught the kerb on the tight entrance to the College. Pulling up with a screech by the old clock-tower, Clare dashed up the steps. After taking one wrong turn down a corridor in the surprisingly empty building, she had just reached Ellis's door when –

'Excuse me.'

Clare turned. An elegantly dressed woman – stiletto heeled, and with a figure to kill for – was walking towards her, looking her up and down as she did so.

'Have you parked by the steps?'

'Yes.'

'Well I'm afraid you'll have to move your car immediately. I've just had a phone call about it.'

Bollocks, the car's only been there a minute!

Clare took out her I. D.

'Well, Constable.'

Cow.

'Detective Inspector.'

'It makes no difference I'm afraid. Also all visitors are supposed to report to my office. Gill Doyle, Department Secretary.' As she pointed up the corridor, a long, red-painted fingernail cut the air in a parabola dangerously close to Clare's face – then she turned away.

Clare, glaring at the retreating pencil-skirted rump, muttered, 'Stilt-walking bitch,' knocked on the door and went in.

Dr Rob Ellis was sitting behind the mountain of paper on his desk and the startled look on his face quickly changed to one of annoyance. 'Is this part of police training – this entering without being invited to do so.'

'Oh, I'm sorry, it's important. I've got–'

'Mud on my knees?' he said, as he looked at her over the top of his reading spectacles.

Bare hands or kick him to death?

'There's something new.' As Clare walked up to the desk she clicked open her mobile, found the photo and passed over her phone quickly. Her hands were shaking.

Ellis scratched his head. 'Hmm… '128'… and that's unusually wide at the base for a gatepost.'

What the hell's he on about?

He held the phone out to her. She, worried that her hands might still be shaking, almost snatched it back, and then became uncomfortable because of the way he was looking at her. 'Could you tell me what it means, please?' she said, then immediately wanted to kick herself for sounding so pathetic.

'Well, as I said last time, if I knew what was going on it would help and I might be more inclined to–'

Clare narrowed her eyes.

Damn, he's still got the hump for not being told everything last time.

'I'm sorry if I didn't make it clear, but it wasn't in my authority to tell you more than I did.'

He sat back in his chair and pushed the hair back off his forehead.

Oh, for fuck's sake get it cut!

'Can I see that photo again?'

Clare handed over her phone. Ellis studied it carefully for a few moments. Then he looked at her hard. She felt uncomfortable. It was unusual for someone to look at her like he was doing.

'Please it's so urgent. Would you at least come and have a look at it? It's on Chalcombe Bumps.'

Then he surprised her. Within seconds, he'd got to his feet, written the word OUT on a piece of paper which he propped precariously on the top of his desk pile, said something about most of his students being on teaching practice or work experience, and was accompanying her out through the door.

'My car's by the steps.'

'Good for you.'

He kept up with her as she moved quickly out of the building and down the steps to her car. 'Oh, do you know you've got mud on your backside as well as your–'

'Shit.'

'No, looks like mud.'

'A boot in the balls – then slow strangulation,' she muttered through clenched teeth, as she opened the door and slipped into the driver's seat.

'What?'

'Nothing – get in.'

'No.'

'Why not?' she yelled.

He pointed. 'Flat tyre.'

'Oh, fuck!' There was a loud thump as she booted the well of the car. 'I hit a kerb coming in!'

There was another thump.

'Alright, stop kicking seven bells out of your car. You'd best get out and lock up,' he said quietly.

As she was doing this, Ellis suddenly shouted, 'Hey Jacko!' and gestured to a gardener who was working on one of the flower beds. The man, who looked as if he'd spent very little of his fifty odd years indoors, came over.

'What's up, Rob?'

Ellis pointed up to the New Building tower. 'Can you keep Saruman's clamp-bearing orcs away from this car for a while?'

'Yes, no probs.'

'Cheers – my car's over there,' he pointed to the nearest car park, and as he and Clare started jogging, Ellis shouted over his shoulder. 'See you in the Albion tonight. I owe you a pint.'

The gardener laughed. 'You already do.'

A minute later they were driving out of the campus. Clare's arm was hurting after she'd had to use all her strength to yank open the Volvo's front passenger door, and despite being tall she was barely able to see out because the seat springs had collapsed that much. Then, struggling with the seat belt, she banged her shoulder on the door pillar as Ellis suddenly swung up a back lane.

'Why are we going this way?'

'One, because it's a short cut and two – give me your car keys.'

'Why?'

'Oh, for Christ's sake woman, I'm trying to help here – just give me the fucking keys!'

Surprisingly she handed them over without a word, and then nearly ended up through the windscreen as the Volvo suddenly braked to a halt. Ellis blasted the horn and lowered his window. Clare, recognising the brightly painted corrugated shed realised they were at Vic's Garage. A round faced, cheerful looking man with glasses came out. 'Wotcha Rob, Oh, hello Inspector–'

'Sorry, Vic, we've no time to chat,' said Ellis as he tossed Clare's keys to the mechanic. 'Detective Inspector Morell's Golf has a flat – it's on the college yellow lines by the steps.'

'Whooo, on the college yellow lines! That's a hanging offence. I'll pick it up straight away and drop it off at the station later,' responded the mechanic – addressing the last of his words to Ellis's waving arm and the tail-end of a fast disappearing Volvo Estate.

17

Neither Clare nor Ellis spoke a word – though even if they had it would have been drowned out by the sounds of the Volvo's complaining bodywork and engine. For most of the journey Clare was preoccupied with trying to fasten her seatbelt. She gave up when the car, quite literally, hit the drovers' road and her field of vision increased, though somewhat intermittently, as they bounced up and down over the deep ruts. Ellis clipped the bank as he swung into the short track to Chalcombe Bumps, and Clare suddenly found herself across his lap. He pulled up by Johns's Peugeot and they quickly got out and crossed the stile.

She was still flushed with embarrassment as they began to climb quickly up the steep grass covered slopes. It was still clear, although it had turned windier and colder. The wind, as typical of the approach of a cold front, had veered from the south to the south-west, and great towers of cumulonimbus clouds – like huge piles of dark cotton wool – were forming out to sea.

'Hello, boss, I couldn't contact Karen and Andy – there's no mobile reception on the heath. SOCO are coming as soon as they can.' greeted Johns, as they jogged up to him.

'SOCO?'

'Scene of crime officers, Dr Ellis – this is DC Johns.'

Ellis shook hands with Johns, and then swung round to face Clare. 'As I thought, that's not a gatepost. Well, it's been one for a long while, but it wasn't originally. It has too wide a base. And I bet there's a hole in the top as well.'

'Yes, there is Dr Ellis!' exclaimed Johns. 'What is–'

'It's Rob, and that thing,' he said, pointing at the stone post with the yellow painted message, ' – and this is something I've only found about recently – dates from the time when we were all crapping ourselves over the possibility of Napoleon invading. There were tented camps all over these downs, and a hell of a lot of defensive and other military building.'

'Like the gun fort in town and the old barracks where you live, boss.'

'Yes, but what's this got to do–'

'Please listen a minute,' interrupted Ellis, annoyingly making a habit of ignoring Clare's for-fuck's-sake-get-on-with-it look, yet again. 'This is an area where they trained military surveyors.'

'So, this is a sort of surveying post?'

'Spot on. What's your name?'

'DC Johns, sir.'

'No. What's your name?'

'Matt.'

'Right, Matt. The hole in the top would support a lamp or a theodolite spigot. They were called Ramsden posts after the name of the theodolite they used. So, ten-to-one, that figure, that 128 someone's just added, is a –'

'A bearing,' completed Johns as he began looking around. 'So there must be another bearing somewhere for this to make sense.'

Clare pulled her jacket closer around her and watched as a wide attractive smile spread across Ellis's face. 'Brilliant!' said the lecturer as he pushed wind-blown hair away from his face. 'Now, where's the other one likely to be? The tall lecturer was agitated, prowling around, looking in all directions. 'Yes, of course, it's bloody obvious. There!' He pointed at the next highest point along the ridge. It was about half a mile away.

'I know that hill, what's it called?' asked Clare.

'Drovers' Knoll, and I've just remembered I've been told there are the ruins of one of these Ramsden posts there. Right, come on, it'll be quicker on foot.' Then, to Clare's and Johns's surprise, Ellis suddenly turned and began to run down the hill. Clare, looking at the back of the fast disappearing lecturer, dithered for a moment.

'Oh, shit! Matt, you take your car to as near to that hill as possible. I'd better try and catch up with Speedy Gonzales.'

'What about–'

But she was gone, leaving Johns pointing to Full Moon Copse.

Ellis was moving fast. By the time Clare was half-way down the slope, he'd nearly reached the stile. Head down, she began tentatively to run faster but was concerned about her footing. She glanced up in time to see Ellis cross the narrow farm track where the vehicles were parked and climb over another stile.

After reaching the lane herself, and struggling up the first steep rise out of the little dry valley, Clare began to stride out along the rolling grass covered crest with the huge sea views on one side and the great folds of downland sweeping down to wooded vales on the other. The cold-front wind, which had increased further, had also, typically, veered yet again, and was now due west. It was at her back and pushing her along. It seemed to be pushing Ellis more.

'Slow down, you long-legged Welsh bastard,' she muttered.

Clare seemed to make up a little ground on him during the last steep climb up the exposed slopes of Drovers' Knoll, but by the time she'd got to the top, he was already inspecting the stump of a pillar and the pile of stones, which were all that remained of the old surveying post.

'Bollocks! There's nothing here.'

Which was really, of course, something she'd expected. 'I've got something to tell you – it's about that 1220 metres. There was a poacher and his dog, well he wasn't really a poacher, he worked for the local hunt, and the rabbits his dog caught he fed to fox cubs and…'

Just at that moment, a few large raindrops fell out of a windy but still clear sky.

Ellis didn't say anything immediately after she'd stopped talking: he pulled up the collar of his jacket and turned his back to the wind. Then he swung round. 'Why the fuck didn't you say something before?' The gale now whistling over the hill top made it necessary for him to raise his voice, though even the most cursory observation of his body-language would have come to the obvious conclusion that he would have raised his voice even if it had been flat calm.

'I'm sorry. You know I couldn't say anything when I saw you the first time. You're not police, you are assisting us in our–'

'Oh, for God's sake woman, you could have told me in the car! '

'What, speak in that rust-bucket of a hearse? My teeth would have rattled out!' Clare shouted back as she wiped a large raindrop off her cheek.

'That's stupid! Well, what about up on the Bumps then?' he shouted, looking prophet-like, as standing on the hill top with his hair streaming in the wind, he pointed back along the ridgeway.

'You didn't give me a chance. One minute you were there, then the next one you'd buggered off into the distance like Forrest Gump!'

It was at precisely that moment that the squall-line hit and the heavens opened as the mother of a cold front passed overhead, yet the whole time they were coming off the hill heading towards where they could see Johns's car, Ellis kept complaining. While they had been running to Drovers' Knoll, Johns had, with some difficulty, reversed past Ellis's Volvo to the drovers' road, driven along it down to the next farm track and had got as close as he could to the knoll. There was a barbed wire fence at the bottom of the field close to the car. Ellis held down the top-strand and Clare, rather awkwardly, got across. The wire snagged her trousers. Expensive trousers. She didn't say anything aloud but cursed continually under her breath…

Shit, fuck, bollocks, shit, fuck…

She pushed down on the strong barbed wire with both hands and Ellis, just after he had swung one leg across, made the mistake – potentially a very big mistake – of starting to sound-off again. 'You really are the most annoying woman I've –'

Right, big gob, that's quite enough for one day, thank you very much.

Ellis had halted in mid-sentence because Clare had lifted her left hand up from the fence and showed it to him. As he glanced down to her right hand, she raised her index finger from the barbed wire. 'You wouldn't dare.'

'Try me.'

There wasn't a word as Ellis, one hand clutching a wobbly fence post and another trying to hold the barbed wire, very slowly lifted his other leg across. They just glared at each other. Somewhat of an unusual experience for Clare – this glaring duel thing: very few men, were able to hold her eyes when they were switched into Attack-Mode. The lecturer looked wet through and his hair was stuck to his face like strands of tangled seaweed. It was only then that Clare, shivering, was really aware that she was soaked to the skin. Also, as they scrambled down the steep bank to the farm track, she realised that the rain had stopped as suddenly as it started and the sky had cleared.

'Shit!'

As Ellis struggled back up on his feet, she stepped behind him and looked him up and down. 'Yes – I think you're right.'

The Peugeot's door swung open and a perfectly dry Johns got out. 'I've always keep some walking stuff in the car, including OS maps and compass and I've plotted that 128. God, you both look wet–'

'I wouldn't have been if she'd told me earlier about –'

'Well, if you hadn't shot-off like a startled rabbit, then I wouldn't either!' Clare was furious with herself. Her professionalism had gone out of the window – there was something about him that set her off.

'Oh, don't be so –'

'Boss, Dr Ellis!' interrupted Johns, after a moment or two of resembling a tennis umpire with a dropped jaw. He turned and looked at the solitary wood in the distance. 'We've got to get there quick.'

A few minutes later, after parking in a wide gateway on the drovers' road, the three of them were running up the short path to Full Moon Copse. Johns glanced anxiously at the other two. During the short drive his detective inspector and the college lecturer had sat in silence. He had turned the heater on full but that had really been a gesture – they were past help. 'This is where the body was found, Dr Ellis,' he said, as they reached the open area just at the start of the trees.

'What's that over there?'

Clare looked towards where Ellis was pointing. 'Oh, it's the remains of some kitchens from when American troops camped here during the war.'

Ellis dashed ahead.

'Oh, God he's off again!' muttered Clare.

'There's something there!' shouted Ellis.

The figure 141 had been sprayed in yellow paint on the bricks of the one remaining corner of the old kitchens. A couple of minutes later they were back in the car. Clare was shivering, as was Ellis, who, sitting in the rear of the car was looking over her shoulder as Johns plotted and drew the second bearing on the OS map he was resting on the steering wheel. He'd already drawn on the first bearing from the Bumps.

The second line intersected the first exactly on the coast.

'That's where The Galleon is!' exclaimed Ellis.

'Is that the pub in a tiny cove?'

'Yes, boss.'

'I'll get the station to send a couple of squad cars there pronto.'

As Johns was pushing the map into a side pocket, he looked back at a shivering Rob Ellis and then at Clare who was struggling to get a wet mobile phone out of an even wetter pocket. 'Right, first things first – you two need to get back to town before you catch pneumonia.'

On days like this, even with storm clouds brewing in the distance, the sea below the cliffs – before the wind veers – is clear and quiet and you can hear the 'put-put' of the lobster boat and see the remains of an old wreck that looks like the picked-over carcass of a giant fish.

From the edge of this sycamore wood, high above the switch-back of the coastal footpath, I can see all the great sweep of the bay. The cliffs gradually change to the west, from creamy chalk to blue grey clay, then stop just before the curve of the town's long esplanade and the breakwaters of the old naval harbour.

And just below me is the tiny cove that was formed by a stream cutting a deep valley through the cliffs, leaving just about enough room for a few fishing boats to be pulled up on the shingle, and that narrow, straggling building of an inn.

He'll be pulling into the pub car park down there within the next few minutes; he's a creature of habit… just like the first one.

This peaceful scene is misleading: this is a landscape redolent of war. Inland, on that ridgeway skyline are the tell-tale ramparts of the hill-fort that was overrun by Vespasian's centurions and the knolls where the Armada beacons were lit. About two miles out to sea there is a patch that is different. I can see it clearly from here, it is white-tipped and disturbed and sea gulls mass over it because the swirling water drives fish to the surface: it is always so. Locals say that Neptune constantly stirs it up from the deep with his trident, and on the day when the embers of the beacons were still smouldering, several Spanish galleons, their rudders wrecked by

Neptune's stirrings, drifted aimlessly in the bay.

Then, even at this distance, the squat Napoleonic Wars fort, like a bulldog watching out to sea, remains impressively sentinel over the town. It must have provided some reassurance to the children who were threatened that if they were not being good, then the Boney Man would come and get them.

The old naval base inside the breakwaters over there is quiet now; unlike the night in August 1914 when the latest Charlie Chaplin films flickered to a stop in the picture houses, and the booing subsided when the projectionist wrote on a glass plate and a message appeared on the tiny screens – 'Return to Ship'. And although the first of the warships, like great grey ghosts, were sailing out to their battle stations in the first mists of dawn, there were so many of them that they were still leaving harbour when that esplanade down there was alive with the sounds of Punch and Judy, the hurdy-gurdy man and the horse-drawn charabancs: sounds that in the weeks to come would be in competition with those of the military bands and the newly-learnt salesman patter of the recruiting sergeants.

Over the next four years, on quiet nights, many ships slipped back into harbour with damaged cargo. In particular, the town was hospital to many Anzacs returning from Gallipoli... who wouldn't go waltzing Matilda no more.

Three decades later that great harbour was alive with men again, able bodied sons of Uncle Sam, down from their tents on the ridgeway, boarding the warships that were also taking their landing-craft. All around here there are details from the same times; I can see with the naked eye an overgrown pill-box on the under cliff, and what looks like the lower section of an old electricity pylon. It's not. It is all that remains of a radar station.

I love that ancient legend of the ridgeway. They say that to the north, where this arm of chalk meets the other downland spurs, there is a chamber deep below ground where Arthur's men sleep. King Arthur's bodyguard, giants of men who will, when summoned by Arthur's battle horn, rise just the once to save this island in time of greatest need. But perhaps they already have? Perhaps that radar station standing where a part of the self-same ridgeway drops to the sea is Arthur's battle horn, and it has already sounded, raising the few – the pilots of the Spitfires and the Hurricanes – to the Battle of Britain. Were they Arthur's men?

Is that the time? He should be here by now.

Patience.

From up here, no vessels can be seen inside the breakwaters – the naval base looks like an empty shell. The last time it bustled was when ships were being hurriedly prepared before that long journey to the South Atlantic. We are sailing, we are sailing, as someone said, to fight another bald man over a comb.

Then nothing – apart from the clatter of helicopter blades and the screech of low flying aircraft which, rather perversely, were practising over water before doing the real thing over the sands of Iraq…

Yes, there he is! Just in time, those storm clouds are getting close. He usually parks that old transit van in the far corner of the pub car park. He does. Now he'll get out quickly, to open the rear door and let his four terriers, lively and unleashed, run to the steep coastal footpath. There they go! I can only see three. Aargh, there's the other one by that tree.

There are some people coming down the path towards the pub. Let's have a closer look. There are two men and a woman. They have large rucksacks on their backs. They must be walking the long distance coastal footpath. It will be close, but the man and his dogs have already climbed to within fifty metres of my marker – that hawthorn bush.

Elevation drop fine. Windage needs adjusting half an MOA. Good. The target is nicely in the cross hairs. Hold breath. Gentle… gentle trigger squeeze.

Agur Aio.

It is strange it should be here. Here where the artefacts of war are disused and the weapons gone and all is quiet; well, with the *exception of my rifle… and this moment when the 'put-put' of the lobster boat is being drowned out by a woman's scream and the barking of dogs.*

18

Detective Sergeant Andy Melbury turned his head as there was a crunch of gravel and a familiar blue Peugeot swung into the narrow pub car park of The Galleon. As he began to walk over towards it, the doors flew open. 'Bloody hell,' he muttered to himself when he saw the state of Clare. Then a tall man with long hair, looking similarly wet through, got out of the car. 'And who's this – John the Baptist?'

A quarter of an hour earlier, at Full Moon Copse, Matt Johns had easily convinced a shivering Clare and Ellis that, as Clare had alerted the station, it was necessary to get them both back to town. He had been just about to turn up the track to Chalcombe Bumps to take Ellis back to his Volvo, when a message came through that caused him to swing back onto the drovers' road and drive fast towards the main road.

The message said that there had been an incident involving the use of a firearm at The Galleon public house.

'Alright, Andy,' shouted Clare to the approaching Melbury. 'Leave that question you're dying to ask until later. What are you doing here – and where's Karen?'

'We were going back to the station after failing to find the Scarlet Pimpernel again, you know that League Against Cruel Sports man – we'd been out of touch, there's no signal on the heath. We weren't far away from here when we heard the message.' Melbury pointed to the far end of the pub. 'Karen's got the witnesses in the snug – two men and a woman. We've only been here a few minutes.'

'Who's that uniform?' asked Clare, looking towards the far end of the car park where a police officer was talking to a short thickset man. They were standing by an old transit van. There was a lot of barking coming from inside the vehicle.

'That's Kevin – PC Hamer, the community bobby. He was already here,' answered Melbury as the policeman said something to the man, then began to walk over quickly towards them. 'And that guy he was talking to is Neil Frampton.'

'Frampton? The one you and Matt interviewed, who was looking after Galpin's dogs?'

'The same.'

PC Kevin Hamer, fresh faced and with rosy cheeks, appeared to be wearing a uniform that was a full size too large for him. He looks about twelve, thought Clare. So, that's Kevin. Where the hell's the –

'Kevin?'

'Ma'am.'

'Kevin, where's the body?' Clare was looking in all directions.

'The body, ma'am? I put it in the boot of the car.'

After he had gone round his Peugeot closing the doors, Johns's jaw-dropping morning continued as he looked across just as his detective sergeant appeared to be restraining his detective inspector from physically attacking a policeman he'd never seen before.

'In the boot? Are you mad? Forensics have to be called, nothing touched and –'

'What, for a dead terrier, ma'am?'

Clare could feel herself leaning heavier and heavier against the rear wing of Hamer's police car as she continued to stare into the open boot. She felt absolutely exhausted, chilled to the bone; aching everywhere she wasn't numb… and feeling stupid, especially feeling stupid.

Shit, what a mess.

Melbury and PC Hamer were standing either side of her. They were all looking down at a pathetic little bundle of fur, flesh, and exposed bone that was lying in a pool of blood that had gathered in a hollow of the thick plastic sheet that lined the boot of the police car.

Hamer then told them what had happened. When he had arrived he saw a man carrying the dead animal back into the car park with three other terriers barking and running around him. Hamer, a local farmer's son, who'd seen many animals shot with .22's and twelve bores, was surprised. 'It wasn't like anything I'd seen before. It was much the same as if you or I had been hit by a shell,' he'd said.

The young policeman had then convinced Frampton that it would be wise to keep the dead animal separate from the others, and while Frampton was putting his other dogs in the van – not an easy task as the dogs were agitated – Hamer placed the dead creature in the boot of his patrol car. Then he said he had a lucky break. He saw something and using his pocket knife located the bullet. He said that, from the section he'd uncovered, it looked like a military job. This had surprised him. It must have stuck in a bone junction. A large shell would have been more likely to have gone straight through something so small and could have gone anywhere; a 'needle and haystacks job, that would have been'. Also, he'd shouted to one of the pub staff to look after three walkers with rucksacks, who all appeared to be in a state of shock, until more police came.

'Excellent, Kevin,' said Clare, who was beginning to feel unwell. 'Take it to Dr Howarth at the path lab. I'll ring him.'

Clare then turned her head as she recognised a familiar voice calling to her. Karen Garland was standing in the pub doorway: a doorway with a large sun symbol carved above it. Then she felt a touch on her arm.

'I think you'd best go over and try and get warm and dry,' said Melbury gently. 'And take him with you.' He nodded towards the centre of the car park where Ellis – his jeans and jacket stuck tight to him like a second skin, and his hair looking like he was wearing a helmet – was walking up and down.

Clare looked around. 'Oh, him,' she muttered.

Then she thought, if he's like that, what must she look like, all wet through and with her short hair stuck flat on her head?

Ellis was agitated, staring at what he was holding in his hand. It was Johns's mobile phone.

'Boss, it's got to have been from up there,' shouted Johns. He was looking to the east, along the switchback of the coastal path as it followed the cliff line, pointing to where the edge of a sycamore wood crept over the skyline. 'It's comfortably within range. We need to get up there and…'

Johns's words faded as he watched a very sodden, miserable looking, college lecturer marching purposefully towards Clare.

'You should have said something earlier. Look at this – it's so bloody obvious,' said Ellis, pointing at the photo of the survey pillar on Chalcombe Bumps on Johns's mobile. 'Apart from the code which was easy enough to sort out, this circle at the bottom is too big to be the letter O. It's a symbol, a full moon symbol. Full Moon Copse?

'Well…' Clare was flustered.

'It's clear after giving you the top one, the "Swells", for Chalcombe Bumps.'

'Yes, I did get that one, Dr Ellis – I did see the burial mounds,' she answered back with as much sarcasm as she could muster.

'Burial mounds! They're tumuli! Swellings? Tumuli?

155

Tumour? – How about tumescent?'

'Yes, I understand.'

'Of course, silly me, you're bound to understand *tumescent* – you're good at big cock-ups.'

Clare could feel herself changing colour. 'You could have seen the first message on the post yourself if you'd looked instead of just shooting off to the knoll! Oh… Oh, just piss-off back to Wales! And get your hair cut!'

Ellis's body language changed completely, well, to be more precise, it was frozen in time as, for a moment or so, he appeared to be completely pole axed – but only for a moment or so. 'Ha – that's rich that is, coming from someone with a French name who looks like Joan of Arc in some kind of a butch wet T-shirt competition!'

Clare pulled her open soaking wet jacket over her equally sodden thin shirt. 'Kevin!' she shouted, as she could feel the heat emanating from her cheeks.

'Yes, ma'am.'

'Take Dr Ellis back to his car – now!'

'What about the path lab?'

'Now!!'

'Yes, ma'am.'

The police car was moving slowly along the ridgeway track. Heavy rain can make exposed chalk as slippery as ice, and potholes easily churn into a light grey mud. Strange, the vehicle was moving slowly, but sections of the landscape appeared to be moving fast – an illusion that occurs, at times like now, when scattered storm clouds trying desperately to catch up with the pack, cast great fast moving shadows over the rolling downland.

'You're steaming up a bit, sir,' said PC Hamer over the noise of the car's heating operating at full blast.

'Yes, in more ways than one, officer. What's your name?'

'PC Hamer, sir, call me Kevin… everybody else does. Where's your practice, Dr Ellis?'

'It's Rob, and I'm not a medical doctor.'

'Ah, you've got one of those PH thingies.'

'Couldn't have put it better myself, Kevin. Mine's a geography *thingy*. If I'd tried to do one into the mind-set of women detective inspectors, I'd be shovelling shit on my uncle's pig farm.'

Ellis then fell quiet and leaned forward to get closer to the heating vents. Hamer didn't say anything either. He was busy remembering what Ellis had said ready for total recall at the next community policemen's darts night.

19

For the last few minutes Melbury and Johns had been proving it is a fallacy that men gossip less than women.

'Yes, but I still think that the best bit was when she told him to piss off back to Wales and get his hair cut!' said Melbury with a chuckle. 'Though, fair play, he gave as good as he got.'

'And how, sarge! Didn't she blush? They were arguing like that at Drovers' Knoll. What worries me is that he's almost certain to raise a complaint and the boss will be in real trouble.'

'That's a point – we're here,' said Melbury as he indicated, slowed down, then turned and parked in the forecourt of the Co-op Stop-and-Shop on the main coast road at the turning to Undercombe.

Melbury and Johns were going to see Neil Frampton.

'He's definitely in this afternoon, is he?' asked Johns as he was getting out of the car.

'Yes, he said he wasn't going into work after that shock he had this morning – he'd need to settle the dogs as well.'

'Is that Frampton's van over there?' asked Johns, pointing to an old white transit van parked in front of one of the short row of cottages adjacent to the supermarket.

'Yes, and that's where he lives – Sutton Cottages,' said Melbury as he zapped the car lock.

Frampton was watching out through the front window: they didn't need to knock. There was the sound of bolts being shot before the front door opened. 'Hello, Mr Melbury.' he said quietly then nodded to Johns. There were the sounds of dogs barking. Frampton indicated over his shoulder. 'They're out at the kennel in the back – they're restless.'

'That's understandable, son. Can we come in?'

He nodded and showed them into a small front room. The furniture was old but there was a very large new looking TV and a sound system which looked expensive. Frampton seemed very nervous and edgy. There was a smell of whisky on his breath. The room stank of cigarette smoke. Johns coughed and at the same moment Frampton stubbed the roll-up he was smoking on the edge of a large full ash tray and immediately took another one out of the tin in his jeans pocket and lit up.

'Well, what do you make of all that this morning, Neil?' asked Melbury. He spoke slowly and softly.

Frampton, looking down, shook his head. He drew hard at his cigarette. His hand was shaking slightly.

'Don't know.'

'Did you see anyone?'

'No, Mr Melbury – well, some walkers that's all.'

Johns glanced at Melbury. They knew they would have to tread carefully. Melbury was to do the talking.

'How far where you behind the dog, Neil?'

They knew according to the witnesses interviewed by Karen, that Frampton was a good twenty metres or so back down the path.

'I don't know – but Flash was well ahead of me and the others.' Still with his head down, he took another pull at his cigarette.

Melbury looked at Johns. The young detective nodded. Message understood. The dog was targeted. There was no way that it was a shot at Frampton that missed and hit the dog by mistake.

'Can you think of anyone who would want to harm you, or your dogs? You know, hunt sabs, anti-hunt supporters, and the animal rights brigade?

Frampton shook his head. Unlike the last time they'd spoken to him, he didn't rise to any of this – he just stayed clammed up.

Melbury looked at Johns who nodded again. They were not going to get anywhere here.

'Well, son,' said Melbury as he got to his feet. 'We'll leave you in peace for now – you've got my number if you think of anything.'

The two policemen had barely moved a couple of yards away from the door, when they heard the sound of, not one, but two, door bolts being fastened.

'He's as jumpy as hell. We got bugger-all but at least he didn't ask us anything, which is good as we've been told to stay stum about the Galpin connection for as long as we can,' said Melbury, half to himself, as they walked away

'Yes, sarge. He may just be completely shaken up… but I'm not sure. Oh, what does he do for a living?'

'Works in the Forestry Commission saw mill on the edge of the heath and gets a bit of money from the hunt. Why?'

'Well, he can't make that much can he? It's just that he had a Bang and Olufsen sound system in there – it costs an arm and a leg. Expensive watch as well and that huge TV,' mused the young detective with a scratch on his short blond hair.

'I don't know, Matt. He could have been left a bit of money and I'm not sure if he didn't inherit his cottage, so he'd have no mortgage would he?'

'Suppose not, but it is worth checking. And those bolts on that door show that he's really edgy about something.' Johns looked at his watch. 'So, that's it for today?'

'Enough isn't it? What a bloody day!'

Night seems to fall quickly here, where the coast road swings inland of the cliffs to follow a valley at the foot of the ridgeway. The sky to the south has that particular blue it reserves for when light fades over the sea.

The small supermarket, with its bright fluorescent green Co-op sign, looks incongruous here, set alongside a single row of cottages at a road junction. Appearances, however, can deceive – passing trade is steady and the summer camping sites a bonus.

A beam of light suddenly spills out from one of the cottages as a door opens. Good, it's the one. Dogs bark and a man curses. He continues cursing, and they continue yapping, until the dogs – there are three terriers who have rushed down the short path to the gate – reluctantly go back into the house. He closes the door on them. I think I deserve a small vote of thanks from his neighbours – as from this morning, I've reduced the yapping by a quarter.

His old transit van is parked on the road under a street light. He gets in. He takes something out of his pocket and places it on the dash. Let's have a closer look through the bins. It's a tin. A tobacco tin. He takes out a roll-up and lights it. Readymade roll-ups tend to be standard – there's no tell-tale packaging that can be linked to contraband. Also, it is unlikely to be anything but tobacco, because the odds are stacked against a transit not being stopped in this area at night: the tranny being the vehicle of choice used for country house robberies and poaching – now that Cortina estates seem to have all gone to the car grave yard in the sky.

He starts the engine then looks around furtively, ironically arousing suspicion where there was none, before putting something (a pill?) in his mouth, as he drives off. He's going east, which is good. It's half a mile to the roundabout and there are no junctions before that. The transit disappears around a bend, a hundred yards up the road. This steep track opposite the cottages was a perfect viewpoint; now let the old Land Rover free-wheel down to the road...

I must get him in sight before the roundabout. There he is. Not too close. The transit turns left on it and disappears. He's going along the valley road away from the coast. Put your foot down now. Locals say that a gibbet once stood where there is now this roundabout. Good, there are his lights. There's no need to get close; I'll be able to spot him easily as he goes over that series of hump backed bridges. The valley is deep in shadows, in contrast to where the skyline of the downs is highlighted by a strip of orange sky. Someone is walking on the skyline: someone looking like a giant cut out of black paper.

Where the hell's the van?

Yes, I know where he's gone – quick, park deep under those trees past the large stone gate posts.

It's an impressive house this one: the main part is old, not quite Georgian, and not quite Victorian. It was built between the two when William IV was on the throne. There are two later wings which somehow fit well. It has been divided into a few expensive apartments. It is called Tallington House. Check. Good, there's no one around. Run on the grass to the side of the gravel drive. The transit is parked by the east wing. The lights are off but the cab lights up. He's struck a match. He gets out and walks to a side door of the house. This rhododendron bush is perfect cover. He doesn't seem to knock: there must be a buzzer. After a minute or so, the fan light above the door gives away the fact that a hall light has been switched on. He looks edgy – moving from foot to foot.

The door opens. A woman is standing in the doorway. She's

wearing a bathrobe and holding a towel. She's not pleased to see him. In fact she looks furious. She remonstrates with him but keeps her voice down. She is making a point – punctuating her words with a jabbing finger. Her long hair catches the light… long wet hair… long wet red hair. She looks around and makes to hit him. He retreats down the steps. Then she's gone and he's left facing a closed door.

And I'm left with a problem. A woman! I am not permitted to shoot a woman… not shoot.

I must use another way.

This will take a little planning…

There's a thrush whose late evening song is being disturbed by the discordant sounds of my Land Rover's engine still cooling where I've parked under these trees. I'm reminded of that poem about the aged thrush who 'flung his soul upon the growing gloom'.

A death lament?

Appropriate… but he won't need to sing it again for a few days yet.

20

Clare, having checked the papers she had in front of her, sneezed… again. She's not looked directly at anyone since she'd come into the CID office this morning, though she knew the others had been glancing at her, and each other. Oh, what a shambles yesterday had been, she thought – and it could be summed up in two words.

Rob Ellis.

No, three words. Rob Ellis Bastard.

She had been soaked through and her short hair had been plastered flat on her head when they'd had their final argument. His comment about her looking as if she was in a wet T-shirt competition had been excruciatingly embarrassing, but it was the 'butch' remark that had hurt… really hurt.

Yorick wanted to see her when she'd finished here. Ellis must have made a complaint. She had been so unprofessional but there was something about him that just wound her up. She tried not to think about it – which was difficult as she'd thought of nothing else through a largely sleepless night and had come into work in the same tortured frame of mind.

Right, get on with it, Morell.

Melbury was looking at his note book. His chair complained as he leant back on it. Karen, her hair savagely pulled back, was sitting in front of her computer. Johns, as usual, was looking at his laptop – he'd have to go into rehab if that was taken away from him. Clare carried her coffee over to the 'brewing-up' table, where with the kettle, mugs, tea, coffee and Melbury's sweeteners, there was a box of individual long-life semi-skimmed milk capsules. She opened and poured an extra one in. Andy Melbury had made her one of his 'specials' that you could have stood the spoon up in – but she was touched by the thought. She walked back to her desk and leaned against it.

'Ok, let's make a start,' she said. 'The only new thing is that Forensics have confirmed what Nick Howarth – who thankfully was more amused than annoyed about having to carry out a canine autopsy – had said last night. The bullet was from the same batch of special Match ammunition as before and had definitely been fired by the same gun that killed Dean Galpin. We'd have been surprised if it was otherwise. Let's put all the bits and pieces into some kind of order. Karen, you start with the witnesses.'

'Well, boss. Jonathan Porter, Marcus Timms, and Nicola Morley, all from Ashford in Kent, are work colleagues doing the Coastal Footpath Walk. I have all their contact details. Now, while Meg at The Galleon kept two of them happy with coffee and biscuits, I interviewed the other one at the far end of the Snug. They were all a bit shaken but the stories are the same. They were nearly at the pub–'

'What was the time exactly?' asked Johns.

Karen looked at her note book. 'Porter said he'd just checked his watch, it was just 10.20. He made a remark to the others about wondering if the pub was open for coffee. Then it happened: they all say the terrier that was shot was running about twenty yards ahead of Frampton and the other dogs. It was about fifty yards away from them, then it –' she looked at her notes. 'Nicola Morley – who was really cut up – said "It sort of flew backwards.".'

'Thanks, Karen,' said Clare. 'Conclusion?'

'Dead Eye Dick hit exactly what he was aiming at,' said

Melbury, who then swung around in his chair to check that everyone was nodding in agreement.

'Now, apart from the bullet, there is a second tie-up with the first shooting. One Neil Frampton.' said Clare, as she was scribbling a note on one of her papers. She looked up. 'Andy?'

'Neil Frampton, aged twenty five, lives at Sutton Cottages by the Co-op Stop-and-Shop on the coast road by the turning to Undermoigne where Dean Galpin was from. Now, as you know, he was at the Galpin house feeding the dogs when Matt and I went round. Frampton is an out-and-out terrier man for the Borne Hunt – Galpin, although primarily the drop pot man, also ran with the terrier men. The shootings are connected, it must be the same motive, some anti-hunt nut has –'

'Alright, Andy, let's not jump ahead.'

'There is something,'

Clare turned towards Johns, 'Yes, Matt?'

'When we were at Galpin's house, Frampton really blew his stack when I mentioned the anti-hunt brigade. His behaviour yesterday was so different, he barely said a word.'

'Well, wouldn't you be different after a shock like that?' interrupted Melbury.

'Yes, I've thought about that, but it was more somehow. He was so edgy, and the way he bolted his door... I don't know. And there's something else. How the hell can he afford that top of the range television and hi-fi system and that expensive looking watch on a forestry worker's pay?'

Clare's cop's antennae immediately registered this, in so many cases, money – a surplus, or a shortage – was the clue. 'Good, that's got to be important. We need to do some digging there.'

'I haven't found anything on records about Frampton,' said Karen. 'But I think he's lucky not to have been up in court. Kevin – PC Hamer – says that Frampton's been involved in punch ups at the hunt meetings, nothing specific… except.' She hesitated.

'Except, what, Karen?'

'Well, boss, according to Kevin, when Mr Yates, the League Against Cruel Sports guy was beaten up – rumour has it that Neil Frampton, was there. He couldn't be identified as he'd pulled a balaclava over his face.'

Melbury laughed and the others turned to look at him, He had a wicked grin. 'And you could understand what Kevin was saying?'

'Yes,' said Karen, in a puzzled tone. 'Why not?'

'Well, every time the poor lad looks at you, let alone talks to you, he's got his tongue hanging out.'

Johns smirked and Karen gave Melbury the finger.

'That will do, Andy,' said Clare. 'Now, suspects. Legge has said he was up with the sheep on the downs – no witnesses. And the Detective Super has told me that Sir Alan Vine said he was out on the estate – again no witnesses.'

As far as the Vines had been concerned, she taken Emma's advice and mentioned the fact to Simmonds that she was in a difficult position as the Vines were friends with the Chief Constable. He'd taken her point, and said that when it was in her interest to do so, she could pass the buck up.

Then Melbury, leaning forward in his chair, interrupted her thoughts. 'Well, I don't think it's Legge or Sir Alan – though it's a new one on me using a gun. It's got to be the animal rights lot. First, shoot the drop-pot man, then scare the living shit out of the terrier man. A warning to change your ways or you're dead too – and also saying, "You're dealing with a bloody crack shot here who doesn't miss what he's aiming at". That's to scare the hell out of others as well as Frampton. It's got to be.'

'It's bizarre, though.'

'Yes, Matt, but a lot of them are bloody bizarre – and mad.

Remember those idiots that dug up graves and pinched the bodies? And that lot that threatened staff in those labs?

'But hunt saboteurs are generally not like this, are they?' asked Clare.

'May be not,' continued the big detective sergeant, who was now sitting upright on the edge of his seat. 'But you only need one convert, say an ex-services guy, who becomes a fanatic.'

'If you're going down that line, sarge,' answered Johns. 'Why not a contract killer?'

'That's out of the question, Matt. And do you know why?'

'No, sarge, but since you're going to tell me anyway. Why?'

'It's because the anti-lobby couldn't afford to.' Melbury laughed. 'Now, if it was the other way round, it would not be a problem as the pro-hunting brigade could raise enough cash to have every saboteur in the country shot if they wanted to.'

'Leave it, you two,' ordered Clare. 'Next, let's deal with the message on the bus shelter over the road. Karen what have we got?'

'Well, apart from the fact that the "Look Again" message was sprayed on sometime in the night, we've got very little. There's no CCTV coverage over there and none of the taxi and bus drivers we've spoken to noticed it at all. Some of our staff saw it when they came into the station in the morning, but the night desk sergeant is positive it wasn't there when he came into work the previous evening.'

'OK, Karen. It's possible that whoever did it came down that footpath from the car park. Do we have any leads there?'

'No, boss. As you know that huge car park is dead quiet out of high season, and as it's badly lit and screened by that thick hedge–'

'It's a popular venue for couples who want somewhere to do a spot of late night car suspension testing,' interrupted

Melbury. 'That's right, Karen, isn't it?'

He gave a wicked grin.

'Yes, and a rumour spread through this place that there was some dogging going on, which of course resulted in more searchlight patrols scuttling over from here than you could shake a stick at – if you'll pardon the expression. Did you go on any, sarge?'

'No.'

Clare somehow kept her face straight at the young policewomen's retaliation.

'What about the boy racers who tear round that place when it's empty?' asked Johns.

'They won't give us the time of day. I'll have a word with Jigger Troy,' said Melbury, before going on to answer the question Clare was about to ask. 'There are several tyre dealers in the area; one's expensive, another's reasonable, two are cheap… then there's Jigger Troy.'

'How will he help?'

'Well, Matt. That's where these lads go, because, as they spend all their money on music systems that you can hear all the way from here to God knows where – they can only afford crap tyres. And as most of Troy's are on the dodgy borderline, I can call for Trading Standards to pop round a bit more often, if he doesn't ask around.'

'That's blackmail, Andy,' interrupted Clare. 'Good – see what you can find. Now, here's a bit of news from Forensics.' She held up a sheet of paper. 'Confirmation that all the messages left used the same paint. That's the two on the stone pillar at Chalcombe Bumps, the one on the old kitchens at Full Moon Copse, the bus shelter, and yesterday's at Spring Rise Wood – more of that one in a minute. Also they know something about the paint now.'

'About time,' muttered Johns.

Clare was looking at the sheet of paper. 'There were

problems isolating the pigments, and… err, let's see… '

'Sounds like excuse bollocks,' muttered Melbury.

'All the messages were formed by a fine-air craft spray,' read Clare. 'The paint had been bought in a tin and thinned down. It's a car paint. A Renault colour – there's details here.'

'I know that colour. I really fancy a Megane Coupe in yellow. It's not a naff buttercup yellow, more a–'

'Well, Karen,' interrupted Clare with a smile. 'We'll hand this over to you as our Colour Consultant. Start with the obvious, the Renault dealers, though I'm sure it's not going to be that easy.'

'Karen, does this shirt go with this jacket?'

'Piss-off, Matt.'

'Now last but not least, what about the shooting and message. Matt?'

Johns passed round photographs of a tree in Spring Rise Wood, very close to the spot where the Scene of Crime officers were convinced that the rifle was fired from. An unmistakeable symbol of a tree with a circle, as if it had a hole in it, had been sprayed in yellow paint on the trunk of the real tree. The symbol was about a foot and a half high.

Johns scratched his short blond hair and looked around apologetically. 'I haven't got a clue, but perhaps when we ask–'

'We must stop there,' said Clare sharply, as she gathered her papers and got to her feet. She nodded towards the clock. 'I have to be elsewhere.'

There was complete silence as she walked to the door. She looked back. She appreciated the way they'd joked and cheered her up… now they were all giving her a sympathetic smile. Clare felt that she was about to walk the plank and not the short corridor to Yorick's office.

'Good luck… *boss.*'

Then Clare smiled.

It was the first time Detective Sergeant Andrew Melbury had called her that.

As soon as Clare had entered Detective Superintendent Simmonds's office she knew, and was amazed, that Rob Ellis had not made a complaint. Why hadn't he? She was the professional after all… he'd just been a twat.

Yorick had listened carefully to her account of the events of the previous day and he'd praised her actions – even suggesting that with a little luck she may have had police at The Galleon before the shooting. He'd also agreed that the shooting of the dog looked like a scare action – a 'horse's head in the bed'.

Then everything changed.

'Well, there's one thing. We're lucky to have that Dr Ellis on board, he's been excellent,' he'd said, with a definite smile, as he tapped the papers on his desk. 'What does he make of that symbol on the tree?'

Clare had felt herself sinking lower and lower in her chair as he'd been speaking. 'Well, sir…' She hesitated… then stopped.

'Well, sir,' she started again. 'It's unlikely that Dr Ellis will work with me in the future, because–'

'He's off the case?'

Clare nodded.

Oh, shit!

She watched as Yorick morphed into a proper Yorick as his face drained of what little colour it had. He looked at her in disbelief. 'I don't believe this. Crick's gone and now another! What the hell did you say about this one's dick?'

'Nothing, sir!' protested Clare who, in complete contrast to him, felt the colour rush to her cheeks, as she struggled to her feet.

'Yes, go on! Get out! And get him back on this case! I don't care what you have to do – anything – even if you have to stand on your head with–'

'Yes, sir, I get the picture,' she shouted – wishing she didn't – as she reached the door.

Seconds later, Clare was standing in the corridor. Both she and the glass in the door were still shaking.

'Only three more years and two months. Only three more years and two months,' echoed Simmonds's retirement mantra around his office.

'Bollocks!' she snapped.

'Ooooh!'

She swung around. The unmistakable figure of Big Melanie from Witness Protection was walking towards her down the corridor.

'Oh, fuck off, Melanie,' snapped Clare… dicing with death.

21

Clare walked up the steep steps to a table at the top of the pub garden. She put her orange juice down, and then hesitated a moment or so before deciding to sit on the end of the bench rather than swing her legs over. She was, unusually, wearing a skirt.

She pulled up the narrow fitting cuff of her jacket to look at her watch. Good, fifteen minutes early. Then, after checking the time, she took a mirror out of her bag and checked herself. She looked OK… well, more than OK.

Butch – my arse.

Emma had made an appointment for her at the hairdresser she used and, after the initial confusion over the booked-in name of Jane Marple had been resolved, it had been fine. 'That's as big as it goes, my lovely – short of plugging you directly into the mains,' *Richard* had said when he'd finished both the styling and the hilarious account of his Spanish holiday; which had gone from bad – when his money and passport had been stolen – to worse… when his valium had gone missing. Anyway, the hair (where has all this come from?) was great. It was different; it was sort of edgy somehow.

Clare took just a sip from her glass, aware that it must last. It was a beautiful day and she began to relax a little. Now that the sun had come out it was getting hot and the thin piped-linen jacket had been a good choice. A designer job with no name: a colleague in the north had got it from a small highly-regarded garment workshop. Clare had been told that it was what the rag-trade, strangely referred to as 'cabbage'. It was one of those items skilled tailors can sell on themselves, legitimately, if they manage, by careful patterning, to cut out more garments than commissioned for in a particular batch of cloth.

However, all was not well on the sartorial front. 'Damn,' she muttered, when for the second time she tugged hard at the hem of her denim skirt. She had little choice of skirts in her wardrobe and it was a bit short.

When the hell did this last get an airing, my fourteenth birthday party?

The old pub was in a beautiful location. She thought that it was almost too perfect to be real. It was as if someone had meticulously followed the instructions given in a colouring-in book: a light greenish blue for the clear waters of the almost completely enclosed cove and a deeper blue, shading lighter towards the horizon, for the open sea. The chalk cliffs were a milky cream with yellow dots of gorse along their tops and the downland beyond was a pale green. The old stone walls of the long narrow inn, pockmarked by years of winter sea spray and rain lash, had been rendered and were a brilliant white with the tiny sash windows highlighted – like eye liner – in black. The small boats pulled up on the narrow beach nearby had been painted in primary colours.

Clare had been here before, to The Preventy. Andy Melbury had explained its name. This old pub, like many on this coast, had been a centre for smuggling and had often been raided by the forerunners of Customs and Excise – the Preventy Men.

Then something caught her eye. A yacht, sails down and coming in under power, nosed its way through the narrow gap between the two headlands at the mouth of the cove. Like a lot of vessels which use this coast, it looked just about big enough to cross the Channel, and Clare was reminded of a conversation she'd had with two of the drug squad officers who worked this area. They'd said how easy it was these days to sail in loaded up to the gunnels with 'all sorts of shit' and no one any the wiser as Customs and Excise were short staffed.

Yes, we need more Preventy Men.

Then something interrupted her thoughts: the unmistakable sound of a certain Volvo estate, coming down the lane towards the pub. The decibel levels increased dramatically for a moment or so before suddenly stopping with a clatter.

When Rob Ellis came round the end of the building from the car park, Clare raised her hand as he glanced up to the garden. He looked at his watch, and then disappeared into the pub. She wasn't sure he'd seen her but a couple of minutes later Ellis reappeared carrying a drink and began to walk up the steep steps of the pub garden. The lecturer was wearing a suit and open shirt: he appeared to have had his hair trimmed and –

Whoa! No desert boots!

Ah, yes, Ellis had suggested meeting here because he had to drive to the University afterwards for an important meeting and this place, just off the coast road, was convenient. That's it, she thought, he must be up before some kind of disciplinary committee – probably been slagging-off the Vice Chancellor or something.

Ellis put a glass of coke on the table and sat down but not directly opposite her.

'Hi.'

'Hello,' she replied quietly.

Then there was an uneasy silence which was made worse by the perception, to Clare, that time had in fact come to a complete stop. But at least she could look impassively at one

175

of the great pub views of the realm. Ellis, in contrast, could only stare at an eight foot high laurel hedge. He shifted slightly along the bench.

'Shit!' he shouted as he suddenly rose from his seat and rocked the table.

'Bollocks!' snapped Clare, as most of her orange juice spilt on the pale cream linen sleeve of her jacket.

'The bloody seat's still wet.'

'Well, it's not my fault! I didn't say to myself, I'll sit this side, so he'll sit there and get a wet arse,' spluttered Clare as she made the stain on her jacket worse by rubbing furiously at it with a handful of tissues.

The next period of silence was different to the one before. Clare spent the time glaring at the sleeve of her jacket, while Ellis, perching uncomfortably on the edge of the bench, looked as if he was suffering from constipation. Then a dog howled. 'That sounds like the Hound of the Baskervilles,' commented Clare – taking the opportunity to break the silence.

'Oh, fuck!' said Ellis, getting to his feet and without warning suddenly running off down the pub garden. He appeared to take the steps down about three at a time and disappeared around the corner of the pub.

Clare just stared open-mouthed.

Oh, God – it's Forrest Gump time again!

She was smoothing and tugging at the hem of her skirt when, moments later, Ellis reappeared… followed by a dog… a very big dog.

'What is it with the men down here with this long-hair, big-dog, thing?' she muttered.

It was only as they got closer that Clare began to realise how large the animal was. It was like Clifford the Big Red Dog, on children's TV.

'He'd have started ripping the car to shreds if I'd have left him much longer.'

She was about to say Ellis wouldn't have noticed the difference – but bit her tongue.

'He's a wolfhound.'

'Yes, I know,' answered Clare, as the magnificent, rather aloof looking animal, came up to be introduced. She stroked the back of its neck. 'What's his name?'

'Wyneb.'

'What does that mean?'

'It's "Face" in Welsh. He's got this strange mark here,' explained Ellis, pointing at a black streak below the animal's left eye.

The dog, pleasantries observed, moved a few yards away and lay down on the grass.

Ellis sat down exactly opposite her this time. 'Wyneb belongs to a friend of mine who's going away for a while and I'm dropping him off on my way over to the University, at another of her friends who's going to look after him.'

'He's a very elegant Irish Wolfhound,' said Clare who was resting her elbows on the table: she ran a hand across her hair and, unusually for her, was the first to break eye contact.

'He's not Irish, he's Welsh.'

'Oh, you know what I mean.'

He smiled. 'No, seriously, there have been Welsh wolfhounds since the year dot. Have you been to Beddgelert in Snowdonia?'

Clare thought for a moment. 'Yes, when I was a kid on a holiday in North Wales. I remember something about a dog's grave. It was sad.'

'That's it! Beddgelert means Gelert's Grave. The story is that Gelert was left by Prince Llewelyn to guard his baby son, but when the prince returned he found his son's cradle overturned and blood on the dog. He drew his sword and slew Gelert. Then he heard his unharmed baby cry and found a huge dead wolf under the table.' Ellis pushed back his – now shorter – hair off his forehead and turned to where the dog had been lying. 'Where is he?'

Clare spotted him first. She pointed to the edge of the small beach, just past the pub. 'Well, he's not killing wolves – he's down there and looking as if he's about to roger that spaniel.'

Ellis jumped to his feet; Clare grabbed her glass to save what was left of her orange juice and then burst out laughing as Ellis once more began bounding down the steps.

'Wyneb bastard! Wyneb cach!'

It took several minutes of them running up and down the beach before a cursing Ellis managed to get hold of the wolfhound's lease. Clare had, with some difficulty, composed herself by the time a flustered looking lecturer and a disgruntled dog came back up the steps. Ellis fastened the leash around a leg of the table. The dog lay down grumbling with his head under the seat.

'Christ, what a performance,' said Ellis – just before he sat down and took a swig of his coke.

'What was that you called him after Wyneb bastard – it was Wyneb something or other?'

'Wyneb cach,' whispered Ellis. 'He hates it.'

'Which means "Face something"?'

'No, it's the other way round, if I'd said Wyneb coch that would be Red face.'

'And what did you say again?'

'Wyneb cach,' whispered Ellis again with his hand over one side of his mouth.

'I'm not sure I like the sound of that last bit… no, no. Don't tell me you just called him–'

'Yep –Shit face,' said Ellis with his hand over one side of his mouth again.

'That's terrible!'

There was a moment or two of silence, then Clare lent forward over the table towards Ellis. 'Oh, Shit face,' she said with a hand over one side of her mouth.

'I beg your pardon?'

'Why do you have to say it,' she mouthed 'Shit face', 'quietly in English?'

'I would have thought that was pretty obvious really, because like all Welsh speakers he's bi-lingual… well, strictly speaking he's tri-lingual because he also speaks–'

'Dog?'

'Exactly.'

Ellis, half-turned, was looking down at the cove.

'It's beautiful and calm,' observed Clare. 'It's an off-shore wind, isn't it?'

'Yes,' he answered, without looking at her. '*Fair blows the wind for France* – I think that was in Shakespeare's Henry V.'

'No, I think it's *Fair stood…* I believe it's from a poem,' she replied. In fact she damn well knew it was from a poem but didn't want to appear a smart-arse.

Oh, what the fuck!

'Yes, I remember it now,' she said, and then recited,

'Fair stood the wind for France

When we our sails advance,

Nor now to prove our chance

Longer will tarry.'

'Who wrote that?' he asked as he turned – just as she was about to tug at her skirt again.

Oh, sod it, give up and leave it to its own devices.

'Michael Drayton, a contemporary of Shakespeare. It's called The Battle of Agincourt. The first line was also used as the title of a famous Second World War novel by HE Bates who later wrote *The Darling Buds of May* – and he nicked that one from the Bard.'

Ellis was looking at her quizzically.

'English… Lancaster.'

He raised an eyebrow.

'All right nosy. First.'

He mouthed 'wow' – and gave her another quizzical look.

'And one more question? Why a copper?'

He nodded and smiled.

'Following in father's footsteps.' She momentarily shivered, as she always did when she told that lie. Only one person knew the real reason… and that was her. Just then her phone rang: she took it out of her bag which was on the bench alongside her. She looked at it and switched it off. 'That can wait.'

Ellis reaching across the table picked it up. 'I hate these damn things – but it drives them mad I won't have one. Nobody learns from their mistakes, they don't make decisions, all they do is bloody well phone up and ask what to do and they interrupt conversations – though not in this case.' He smiled as he passed over her phone.

'Thanks… sorry, I've got to go soon.'

'Yes, I've got to make a move as well,' said Ellis: he hesitated before continuing. 'This wasn't your idea was it… this meeting?'

'No, but I'm glad I –'

'Me too, it wasn't my idea either, but I feel the same.'

'Thanks for not dropping me in it with my superiors.'

He placed both hands behind his head and stretched back. 'I wouldn't have done that, anyway it takes two to *whatever*… oh, and…'

Ellis fell silent and Clare found his sudden serious expression and the way he was looking at her, disconcerting.

'I think I've worked out what's going on here,' he said – not only breaking the silence but also causing her heart to start thumping. 'The terrier that was shot was something to do with fox hunting when they dig out the foxes. I could hear others barking in that van in the pub car park, and you said that the guy who got shot at Full Moon Copse worked for the hunt. Look, I can see why you want this kept quiet. There's a mad bastard – some animal rights fanatic – getting a kick out of leaving crazy clues around and staying one step ahead of you, before shooting dogs connected with the hunt. Only in the first case he missed the dog and hit the poor fucking poaching guy instead.' Ellis took a breath. 'So, this must not get out as it would spook everybody for miles. I'm on the right lines here aren't I?'

'Yes.'

Well, he's *sort of* on the right lines, she thought – unable to believe her luck.

'I can see why you need to catch him quick before anyone else gets hurt, so send me that new information – that tree symbol stuff. I'll get James Travers, the historian and cartographer guy, to look at it as well. And I'll make sure we keep quiet about it.'

'Thank you.'

My cup runneth over.

'But please be straight with me in future.'

'Yes, I will,' promised Clare… with her fingers crossed under the table.

Ellis got up and then dropped to one knee to unfasten the wolfhound's leash from the table. 'Oh, just one more thing,' he said looking up at her.

'What's that?'

'Do you have forms at the police station to report missing property?' he said as he got to his feet and he and the dog began walking down the steps.

What's he on about now?

'Yes, of course.'

'Then, you'd better fill one in when you get back,' he said with his head turned to look back at her.

'Why?'

'Well, Detective Inspector Clare Morell… you appear to have lost your skirt,' he answered – then laughed in response to Clare's raised finger.

22

'Still no answer from Matt,' said Clare, mobile phone in hand. She glanced at her watch. She was anxious as Rob Ellis had phoned to say that Dr James Travers had something to tell her about the tree symbol that had been left at Spring Rise Wood. 'It's unlike Matt to be late.'

Karen Garland nodded and continued watching. The two women were sitting in Clare's car in the Visitors' Car Park at the College. Karen's 'watching' had nothing remotely to do with police business. 'Oh, my, look at the bum on that good looking guy over there!'

Clare looked up. 'Which one?'

'Which one! That lad with the torn jeans of course.'

'Oh, him. Seen it last time I was here… close up,' teased Clare.

'Lucky you, boss.' Karen was concentrating hard, her brows furrowed, as if she was attempting to change her eyes into binoculars.

'Right, Karen, Matt will have to catch us up.'

When they got out of the car, the student Jonner Dawes, spotted them and rushed over to offer his escort services. For a second or so, Clare toyed with the notion of threatening to arrest him for indecent exposure, but quickly dismissed the idea on the grounds that if she did, Karen would probably slap the boy in handcuffs and frisk him down quicker than you could say 'libido'. So instead she froze him with a word and a look.

They walked up the steps and Clare, as she pushed open the entrance door, pointed to the corridor leading to the Geography Department office. 'We'd better report to Madame Whiplash, I suppose,' she muttered.

'What's that?'

'Nothing, Karen.'

Just as they were approaching the office, as if on cue, Gill Doyle, the secretary, came out into the corridor.

'Hello,' said Clare. 'We have an appoint–'

'I won't be a moment.' The secretary, moving at speed on her killer-heels, sashayed past them and disappeared around a corner.

'She's taking her time,' complained Karen, five minutes later.

It was a further minute or so before the secretary returned. Clare thought that she appeared to be wearing a fresh application of make-up. The term, war-paint, somehow seemed more appropriate.

'I know that Dr Ellis is expecting you, he told me earlier. I have a lot to do preparing for a meeting this afternoon, so if you don't mind you can find your own way.' And with that she disappeared into her office.

'Bitch,' muttered Clare.

'I don't know what you've done to her,' whispered Karen.

A minute later they were standing outside Rob Ellis's office.

No barging in. Knock. Listen.

'You're new hair's great, boss. It's got attitude. It's sort of really sharp –'

'Shush,' whispered Clare.

A muffled 'Come in' penetrated out through the heavy door.

'Oh, it's you. I'm surprised,' said Ellis, peering over the usual mound of paperwork on his desk, as they went in.

184

'Why?'

'Well – because there was a knock on the door. Anyway, you're late.'

'We were delayed at Passport Control.'

'What?'

'Your secretary, Misssss Doyle.'

'Gill does everything thoroughly.'

Clare stifled a smile.

Yes, does obstruction thoroughly, does pain in the arse thoroughly – and does bitch, absolutely fucking brilliantly thoroughly!

'Dr Ellis, this is DC Garland.'

Ellis nodded and gave Karen one of his wide attractive smiles as he got to his feet and came round from the back of his desk.

Clare was taken aback. Good grief! He was wearing that old leather jacket again but this time over a black T-shirt, some nice jeans, and a smart pair of loafers.

'Right, Dr Travers is expecting us… five minutes ago.'

As they walked towards the spiral staircase that lead up to the Cartography Room, Clare noticed that Ellis was dragging his leg.

'What happened to you?'

'I slipped as I was opening a top window in my office,' muttered the limping lecturer.

'They're really high. What were you standing on?'

Just then Karen's phone rang. 'Excuse me,' she said as she dropped back.

'I put a chair on my desk.'

'Let me get this right. You somehow managed to find room to put a chair on that desk – which has a permanent model of the Matterhorn on it, made of assorted paper – then climbed on the chair and slipped as you were reaching for the window catch.'

'I've done it before.'

'What slipped off the chair, reaching up to open the window? I'm not surprised.'

'No, you know what I mean.'

Clare began to giggle. She surprised herself. She didn't do giggling.

'What?'

'You – reaching for the sky like Icarus. It reminded me of a Carol Ann Duffy poem about Mrs Icarus being one of many women watching her fella prove he's an idiot.'

'Thanks very much… smart arse. You'd be perfect for the bloody English Department in this place,' snarled Ellis, as he hobbled along like a wounded bird.

Karen caught up with them, which was easy enough as the lecturer was making heavy-weather of the spiral staircase. 'That was Matt, boss. He's not sure he can get here.'

'Oh, one thing,' said Ellis when they reached the top corridor. 'Dr Travers has kindly decided to come in to help. He shouldn't really be here, he's been off work and…' There was something in the way Ellis left-off that made it clear to Clare that no further information on that matter would be forthcoming. 'So, take it easy,' he ordered. The last remark was accompanied by a hard look at her. A look he held until he got a response.

'Yes, Dr Ellis,' she said quietly.

As they entered the Cartography Room, the figure poring over a map on an illuminated glass table, straightened up and turned towards them.

'This is Dr James Travers – Detective Inspector Morell and…'

'DC Garland,' said Karen.

Clare looked at him. So, this is James Travers. About fifty? Five foot ten? He really looks as if he's been ill; his complexion is sallow and his clothes are hanging on him.

'Hello, Inspector, hello Constable.'

Public school accent.

'Welcome to my domain,' he said, as he waved an arm around the huge room, with its brass-handled mahogany map-drawers on three sides below soaring Venetian style windows. It was impressive. The last time Clare was here she hadn't really noticed the room – she had been concentrating completely on Ellis's interpretation of the information sprayed at Chalcombe Bumps.

He shook hands. Clare was surprised that his handshake was limp and cold. Usually people who look as tense, nervous, and on edge – grip firmly. She noticed there was something even stranger: his deep set pale blue eyes somehow seemed as if they had retreated a little into his head. He's had a nervous breakdown perhaps?

He smiled. 'Well, Detective Inspector Morell, I'll have to be careful what I call you.'

'Why?' puzzled Clare.

'Because Rob here keeps referring to you as Detective Inspector Meringue.'

Clare looked at Ellis, who, annoyingly unfazed, responded with a huge false smile and a little wave. 'Oh, he does, does he?'

Which is his bad leg?

'Excuse me,' apologised Karen after coughing.

'So, I'll show you what we've come up with,' said Travers, gesturing them towards the large illuminated map table.

When they got to the table he slid one of the maps over in front of Clare and Karen. 'This is an old First Series, 1 to 25,000 Ordnance Survey map. Now look at the symbols on the side. Anything familiar?'

'The ones at the top are,' jumped in Karen. 'Like the black square with a cross, for a church with a tower.'

'Right, now look further down the column for a similar

symbol,' he said.

'There,' pointed Clare, 'just below the triangle for a triangulation station.'

The church with a tower symbol was repeated but with a white dot in the centre, as were other symbols.

'I think that that the symbol sprayed on that tree in Spring Rise Wood, although in yellow, is the equivalent of a white dot in its centre,' said Travers quietly.

'Yes, I'm there,' said Clare, straightening up from leaning over the map. 'So we can assume that tree the symbol was left on is now a triangulation point in this game that's going on.'

'Spot on,' muttered Ellis.

Travers pushed the map away, picked up a modern OS map and unfolded it. 'Right, let's mark on the nodes that Rob has told me about.' He took a pen from his pocket and placed large dots at Chalcombe Bumps, Full Moon Copse, Spring Rise Wood, and The Galleon public house. 'Pass me that metre rule, please Rob… thanks. Now, where do we start?'

'From the Bumps to Full Moon Copse and then Spring Rise Wood to The Galleon?'

'Thanks, Inspector,' said Travers as he drew the line of the shot that killed Galpin and then the one that killed the dog.

'Then there were bearings given from the Bumps and the Copse to The Galleon,' added Clare.

She noticed that his hands were shaking slightly as he drew these two lines, and then watched in astonishment as he added two more.

'What's at this new intersection?' asked Clare anxiously, as she picked up a spare felt tip and circled where two lines crossed.

'Only an open field,' answered Travers – without looking at the map. Travers turned and smiled at her as he reached out and put his hand on the map. It was a strange smile. 'The main point is that there's possibly no need to leave further bearings on the ground at either The Galleon or at Spring Rise Wood. The next clue, if there is one, could possibly be left anywhere, or in any form, now that, whoever it is, knows that this matrix has been completed.'

Clare's mind was buzzing as she struggled to get her head around all of this.

'There's something else I spotted when I was looking at this larger scale pre-war map.' Travers picked up a map from the top of the map drawers and placed it on the table. 'Here, Inspector.'

Clare leant forward to look where Travers was pointing. 'The Sun Inn? But isn't that now called–'

'Yes, Inspector, it's the pub that's now called The Galleon.'

'There's a sun carved over the door, but I've never heard it called that,' said Karen.

'It was long before your time, Detective Constable. In 1951 navy divers practising just off the cove discovered what was believed to be a wrecked Spanish Armada galleon. There was indeed a skirmish in the bay and records indicated that at least one galleon was sunk. Well, possibly with an eye on the tourist trade, the brewery changed the long standing name of the pub from The Sun to The Galleon – shame really, as the wreck turned out to be an eighteenth century coaster.'

'Nice one, Bix.'

Ellis caught Clare's eye. 'Nickname,' he mouthed.

She responded with a sort of smile: a 'yes-I-did-actually-twig-it-was-a-nickname', sort of smile.

Bix? It was a strange name. She looked at Travers; he's really done his homework here. He'd relaxed a little.

'Oh, I think I see what Dr Travers is getting at.' Karen, as she looked up, used both hands to push back her hair from her face – an action that had the opposite effect on her breasts which pushed up towards Rob Ellis. Then they definitely encroached on his personal space as she reached across for the photocopied map. Clare glared but no one noticed. 'The copse is Full-Moon, the pub is The Sun, and the wood is Spring Rise – but what about the tumuli at Chalcombe?' the young detective said pointing to each one of the locations in turn. 'Could it have, let's say, anything to do with autumn?'

'Nice thinking,' commended Travers. Karen looked pleased. 'But I don't know – tumuli mark a burial site that was meant to be seen.'

'Symbolically, like cathedrals or temples?'

'Yes, Detective Garland. A religious symbol, just like those, which is a symbol showing the conflict between life and death: the urge to accept death, but on the other hand the urge to grasp life. Sometimes in the past this was linked up with the rite of sacrifice. A victim was slain in–'

'Aren't you getting a bit fanciful there, Dr Travers?' interrupted Clare: a finger pushed hard against her forehead in a vain attempt to cancel her rapidly emerging headache. She glanced at a suddenly very crestfallen Travers before getting down to the serious business of locking horns with Ellis's sharp hazel eyes – continuing as she did so. 'I think it might be best if we could restrict ourselves to…'

'Well, that Dr Travers came up with some good ideas there,' said Karen as they were driving back to the station. 'But he really looked as if he'd been ill; he looked as if he'd been through the wringer. Do you know anything about him? Anyway boss, I thought you were a bit rough with him up there and –'

The young policewoman closed her mouth in time… just.

Clare shook her head. That hurt. She reached over to the glove compartment and took out a paracetamol packet. It made no noise when she shook it.

'But that Dr Ellis, boss!' exclaimed Karen, rather obviously getting off the topic of Travers. 'He looked so different from when you were both soaked through at The Galleon when he looked scruffy – but really he's a proper bit of eye candy.'

Yes, missy we did notice when you nearly damn well poked his eyes out!

'And while we're on about good looking guys, there's that army captain Matt told me about. What's his name?' said Karen, who catching the look Clare had shot at her about Ellis, skipped on to the topic of another male.

'Lovat… Guy Lovat.'

'Yes, Captain Lovat. He's absolutely stunning, isn't he?'

Clare nodded.

'What a waste! Matt really hates him you know. He can't stand gay guys who go out of their way to appear straight. It's not uncommon in the army apparently… Are you alright, boss?'

23

Clare pushed open the café door and walked up to the counter. She turned and looked towards the window table where Rob Ellis was sitting. He was reading. The lecturer was wearing his old leather jacket and a battered brown hat was perched on the shoulder bag that was on the chair next to him. He'd phoned. Ellis had said he needed to speak to her.

'He's only just come in,' said John Bellini. 'He said he'd have what you usually have. Anyway where are the both of you going on to then, the Temple of Doom, or are you off looking for the Raiders of the Lost Ark?'

'Ha-ha,' muttered Clare as she started walking towards Ellis's table. He'd suggested meeting here because he was being picked up from town by a coach carrying some students he was taking out on fieldwork.

He looked up. 'Christ, you seem a bit rough – been on the sauce?'

And good morning to you as well… arsehole.

'No,' snapped Clare, as she sat down. An aunt had once said that if men had the body clocks of women, then a standard working month would only be three weeks long. 'What is it that you want to speak to me about that won't wait?'

'It's about Bix – James Travers – the way you spoke to him yesterday. He was the one remember who cracked all those symbols and co-ordinates yet you were sharp with him. Look, I don't want you upsetting him.'

The chair complained as Clare dragged it up close to the table. Yes, let men's balls shrink, really painfully, for five days a month… with some exceptions of up to a week and a half, she thought, as she looked across at Ellis. 'Travers is a grown man!'

'I know, but I need to I tell you a few things… it's delicate.'

Clare was intrigued, she calmed down, but before she could say anything, John Bellini walked over to their table. He placed their coffees in front of them – then walked away without a word. They didn't speak for a few moments.

'Bix would kill me if he knew I was talking to you about him,' said Ellis, as he paused from sipping his coffee.

'How did he get his nickname? I've only heard it once before – an uncle had some old records of a jazz trumpeter called Bix Beiderbeck.'

'I don't know. I know little about him really, but I'm pretty sure he's had it since he was a kid. I think even his family used it.' Ellis pushed his hair back with both hands. There was a small faint scar just above his left eyebrow she hadn't noticed before. He smiled as he leant forward across the table. He had nice teeth… which she had noticed before.

Needs a shave.

'Well – I'm really breaking a confidence here. He asked me not to say anything, but I've decided that there are some things you need to know…'

It was tragic. James Travers had indeed suffered a breakdown and was on a year's sabbatical. About four months earlier his partner had committed suicide. According to Ellis, although he did not really know her, she had been a lively, vivacious woman, who had changed dramatically. In fact her transformation could be traced to one particular day – the day their daughter, their only child, died. The daughter was eighteen years old.

'That's awful – I'm sorry,' said Clare, when Ellis had finished.

'So that's it,' said Ellis. 'Please don't mention this at the station – obviously people in College knew, but surprisingly it wasn't generally known. He's still as flaky as hell. He's been away for much of the time and has just come back recently. The break has probably helped to put some distance from the place while the pain's still raw.'

Clare nodded. That was something she understood. She took another sip of coffee.

'I haven't pried much,' continued Ellis. 'He's not really a friend at all, never has been, he's just a colleague I've worked closely with from time to time. He's not due to start any college work for a long while yet – but he insisted on getting involved in trying to help with this case of yours. It's helped – it's somehow shaken him out of his lethargy.'

Clare was leaning with both elbows on the table with her hands under her chin. 'Are you covering all his college work?'

'No, only some of his cartography stuff. We've had to cancel several Extra-mural courses.'

'Why's that?'

'Well, he's incredibly knowledgeable on the local history of this coast. No one else could do it. His lectures are always popular, especially along the Costa Geriatrica.' Ellis pointed west: the direction of the small seaside towns with their high population of retired people. 'I hate walking on some of those promenades down there. It can be lethal with all those near silent motability scooters coming at you from all angles – I think some of them rally drive for Age Concern.'

Just as Clare started to laugh, there was a screech of brakes as a coach pulled up outside. It was a very old coach. Even though it was at a standstill, many parts still seemed to be on the move: a loose window rattled into a blur, trim vibrated and the whole body seemed to shake.

'Oh, shit! – Twitcher's driving!'

'Twitcher? Is he a keen bird watcher?'

'No, it's a medical affliction. Don't laugh. Anyway I don't think I'll have to put up with him and his box of crap on wheels for much longer.'

'Why?'

'Well, look at it the state of it, soon the only bloody thing it will be deemed suitable for will be ferrying around large numbers of school kids twice a day.' Then he suddenly looked serious and leant forward a little, rubbing his forehead with his hand. 'I'm sorry,' he said in a low voice, 'about that crass comment I made when you came in… we guys can be complete arseholes.'

Damn this man!

But Clare, annoyed, embarrassed, and then absolutely furious with herself for being more than a little impressed… gave nothing away.

Ellis stood up, slipped his bag over his shoulder and put on his hat.

'It suits you, Indiana. Where's your whip?' she said… just for something to say.

'The whip's for special occasions, Detective Inspector – like when you get the uniform out.'

She raised a finger. That was becoming something of a habit, she realised… most people just say 'goodbye'. Then she remembered something. 'Oh, what did you say the daughter died of?'

'I didn't,' replied Ellis who walked away just as Bellini's wife – the beautiful, but sour faced, Adriana – made one of her rare excursions from the kitchens. 'Ciao bella, Signora Bellini!' he called out cheekily, as he doffed his hat. Adriana smiled and then laughed out loud; Clare had never seen her do either before. Then Ellis pushed open the door and left to a chorus of catcalls from the male students on the bus. Clare glanced through the café window. The girls, unlike the boys, were hard eyed and silent. She immediately looked down and began to root in her handbag… to try and make life more difficult for them.

24

Clare looked across at Johns. It was about the only time he was quiet, when he was driving. They were following PC Kevin Hamer's patrol car. Apparently the place where the Scarlet Pimpernel lived was very remote. Andy Melbury had christened David Yates that after several frustrating attempts to find him. They needed to speak to him because he was the League Against Cruel Sports official who had been kicked and beaten by Dean Galpin. Yates lived in a remote part of the heath, with no telephone, or near neighbours, and he appeared to be away from the area for most of the time. Hopefully, this time lucky – Yates had eventually responded to the note that Hamer had pushed under his door and had promised that he would be home today.

The minor road they were on, which had threaded its way through a maze of small fields with high secretive hedge rows, straightened, as rather like entering a green tunnel, it passed under a canopy of woodland: a woodland drive that a little earlier in the year is one of sensory extremes when there is a soothing eyewash of an undercover of bluebells – while at the same time the nostrils are assaulted by the pungent smell of wild garlic funnelling in through the car's air vents.

Clare spotted a cottage. It was almost invisible even though it was not far from the road. It brought back memories: The Children of the New Forest. Memories. Memories of snuggling down in bed reading late. Memories of her father catching her and scolding her gently – though all

197

the time she knew he was proud how well she was doing in school.

The wood darkened as it changed to conifers, and then suddenly there was light and the opening up of horizons.

They were on the heath.

They passed an M.O.D sign. The army camp was only about three miles away. One Captain Lovat had not been in contact recently – presumably he'd heard nothing new from Spain about the rifle and the ammunition. Guy Lovat. Damn him. He'd used her. The irony of the term – most certainly not in a biblical sense – as he'd used her to cover up the fact that he was gay.

Bastard.

The police car in front slowed as Hamer indicated. Then it disappeared. Johns followed cautiously. The entrance to the narrow gravel track was barely visible in the high bank of ferns. As they drove slowly along, Clare had the feeling that, even if Johns stopped the car, the overhanging fronds would continue to beat relentlessly at the side windows. The track widened just as it ended in a bowl overshadowed by a huge gorse break. Johns pulled up behind the patrol car and switched off both the ignition and PJ Harvey who had been singing *A Place called Home*. It might be your home, love, but it's not mine, thought Clare, as she got out of the car and looked around.

'He said his vehicle wouldn't be here as it's being serviced, ma'am,' called Hamer as he locked his patrol car. 'But he promised he'd be home.'

'And where's that?'

He pointed to where a path disappeared into a bank of high ferns and gorse.

'What vehicle does he drive, Kevin?' asked Johns.

'A Land Rover.'

Clare gave a cynical laugh. It had to be: Vine, Legge and

now this guy. Also Andy Melbury had told them something just before they left the station. As a result of his leaning-on the tyre dealer, Jigger Troy, one of the boy-racers had told Troy that he'd been in his car with a girl at the edge of the huge dark car park at about one in the morning on the date in question, and had spotted a vehicle drive in and park for a few minutes near to the footpath that lead through to the bus shelter where the message was sprayed. He was too far away to see anyone get in or out but he was adamant that the vehicle was… a Land Rover.

'What do you know about Yates?' Johns asked Hamer as they began to walk along the path. 'I don't know much apart from the fact that Dean Galpin was found guilty of kicking and beating him when he was an official observer at a hunt meeting for the League. Galpin's 140 hours community service and £100 fine seems pathetic.'

Hamer nodded his head. 'Yes, Matt. Dave Yates was annoyed about that. He felt hard done by.'

They seemed to have been walking up the path for ever and Clare was suddenly aware that she was becoming more and more uncomfortable with every stride. The crunch of their shoes on the white, quartz like, sands and gravels was seemingly becoming louder and louder, as was the relentless chirping of the large jewel-green crickets. Even the buzzing of insects was becoming amplified and the heavy motionless air was thick with annoying flies. Not ordinary flies – but huge, aggressive, alien looking things that –

'Stop, ma'am.'

It took Clare a moment or so to realise that the young policeman was not only clasping tight her left arm, but had also placed his other arm around her shoulders.

Hamer had applied the brakes.

She glanced down… and stopped breathing.

The snake was looking up at her with eyes that were

vertical slits, set below a head with a distinctive V, like a tattoo. After an eternity – it moved. Clare could feel Hamer pulling her back, but it had slipped to the side, its slither exaggerating the zigzag stripe along its brick-red back, just before it disappeared into the fern brake at the edge of the path.

Clare gasped, and gasped. Then she began to shake.

It still gave her nightmares. Lifting up the lid of the school desk and being faced by a large grass snake, its battered, bloody, head swaying from side to side. The dead snake had been fastened to the underside of the desk lid with a drawing pin and a short length of cotton. Unfortunately the bad memories didn't just end with recollections of the shock – there was the humiliation in front of her class mates which was worse… much worse.

She'd wet herself.

'Adder. It's the worse time of the year. The venom's stronger now than any time. Are you alright, ma'am?'

'Of course she's not alright, Kevin! Do you want to sit down, boss?' Johns was glaring at Hamer – who blushed.

'Oh, sorry ma'am, I'm stupid, do you –'

'Stop fussing the pair of you! I'm fine!'

The cottage was low, the tiny bedroom windows under the overhanging thatch looking like hooded eyes. The flint walls were unusual: the flint knapped from the nearby gravel beds was, unlike the black flint of the chalk, a strange iron-stained brownish colour. There was no garden as such, only a small fenced-off vegetable plot. Four small ponies were grazing the heather and purple moor grass that stretched away to the right.

'They're called heath-croppers, they keep the bracken and gorse down,' explained Hamer. 'Yates reintroduced them.

He's sort of gone native, reviving old heath crafts and so on. He even makes faggots out of furze – the gorse – for his fuel, just like they used to. It's hard work by all accounts. It's nasty spiky stuff. Anyway, someone in the pub said he was writing a book about it all.' Hamer took the sheet of paper that had been tucked behind the horseshoe nailed to the low weathered door. 'It says if he's not back, he's up at the Barrow – the old burial mound. I know where that is.'

Clare was looking around. 'This place is so isolated, what services has he got here, Kevin?'

'There's water but no electricity, though he has a generator and uses calor gas as well, I believe,' answered Hamer, who loosened his collar and took off his cap, as he turned to his left onto a barely discernible path that ran towards an area of undulating bracken-fringed ground.

Strange, a long branch, rather like a finger, on a solitary wind-twisted pine, seemed to Clare to be pointing the way.

The uneven ground they were moving into was man-made, relics of old sand and gravel workings, disused and left as wasteland.

Johns pointed to his left at an old wooden chalet set in a small stand of pine trees. 'Is that an old summerhouse?'

'Yes,' answered Hamer. 'I believe it belonged to a local wealthy family. It was abandoned for years apparently, but nowadays I think it's used by someone related to the family and –'

'Wow!' interrupted Johns. 'This is magic.'

'That's what's it's called, Matt – the Magic Pool,' said Hamer.

The pool appeared to change colour from green to an intense turquoise in seconds.

'I've read about these. Particles of clay suspended in the – Fucking hell!'

Johns stepped back with the other two as a figure lurched

out of the high bracken just in front of them. A figure wearing a long leather coat and leggings, goggles, and leather cap with side pieces like a medieval helmet, who was holding in one of his huge gauntlets… a vicious looking sickle.

Clare was looking out through the low cottage window at Hamer who was walking down the path that lead back to the cars. He turned and waved as the path disappeared into the high ferns.

She waved back.

'He's a good lad that Kevin – a very conscientious young copper.'

'Yes, he is indeed, Mr Yates.'

There was the clink of spoons and crockery as a tray was placed on a coffee table that appeared to have been made out of a large piece of driftwood.

'Here we are.'

'Thank you,' said Clare as she turned from the window.

He's just about a couple of inches taller than herself. On the slim side of well built. Mid to late forties? His clean shaven, weather beaten face, was really sharp featured. He had the trade-mark hollowed cheeks of the very ill, or the very fit – certainly the second in this case. Short hair. That cut, what do the French call it? Something *brosse*? Wonder what this one's background is?

'Tea?' Yates had turned his head towards Johns who was lost in a little world of wildlife books which occupied a large section of the bookcase.

'Oh, yes. Thank you.'

Yates looked sheepish as he poured the tea. 'I'm really sorry about earlier – I can't apologise enough.'

'No, as I said before, it's alright,' replied Clare.

'Yes, but I must have given you a real fright as I was

rushing back here in that ancient furze-cutters gear.'

'Well, you did look like,' Clare shot Johns one of her shut-up-looks – but it was too late, 'someone out of Mad Max.'

Yates smiled.

They are funny things, men, thought Clare, unlike women they seem to change age when they smile. He looked a lot older when he smiled. Simmonds? Talking Skull was different; he simply scared the shit out of everyone when he smiled. Matt and Kevin suddenly became twelve – no ten. And Rob Ellis when he bothered with that wide smile of his?

There was a creak as Yates swung back on his chair. He reached-out behind him and picked up an envelope from the top of the sideboard. 'Well, here we have it. 700 hours of Parliament's time, and what for – for this. I've had enough.'

Clare put down her cup and saucer as she looked at him. 'Your resignation letter?'

'Yes, although it didn't take up a great deal of my time, I'm sending back my monitor's badge back to the "League Against Cruel Sports".' He mimed apostrophes as he spoke. 'No more creeping around looking for badger baiters, fox cubbers, gamekeepers poisoning rare birds of prey. No more worrying about getting beaten and kicked, or shot in the arse with pellets. No more–'

'Looking for the drop pot men at work?'

'Drop–potting? I've not heard that term for a long while. It's was always very rare and I don't know of any round here.

Clare was watching him like a… like a bird of prey.

He was giving nothing away.

'Isn't it worth sticking with the new law for a bit? It's early days yet – despite what you said earlier,' suggested Johns.

Yates shook his head. 'There are 270 hunts. They're not going to disband – or change. They don't give a stuff. The Countryside Alliance spouted all that rubbish about job losses, putting down hounds, closing stables. Well, they're not going to.'

'But surely over time the law will have an effect?' persevered Johns.

'No, until the time a right wing Conservative majority rescinds the law, they will simply say that they were having a drag hunt and the dogs accidentally got a fox scent. The landowners will also make it more difficult for monitors to get on the land to get evidence – and your top brass are not exactly helping.'

Johns and Clare glanced across at each other. They were both aware that the Association of Chief Police Officers had said they will have difficulty in enforcing the law. There was something else about Clare's look. Johns nodded. Message received. He'd learned the hard way. Johns would not be saying anything else for a while… but she would.

'So, things are changing. Until now any violent action is by groups like the Animal Liberation Front –'

'ALF to their enemies… they haven't got any friends,' Yates interrupted.

'Yes, well, the action has tended to be towards laboratories, could that be broadened towards–'

Yates broke in again. 'Yes, I would never have thought so in the past, but now the sheer frustration of hunt saboteurs that despite a law so hard fought for, the hunts will just arrogantly carry on, and those bastards, the terrier men will still be around. You check your records; they're responsible for most of the violence at meets'

He fell silent for a moment or so, bringing his growing agitation in check. When he spoke again his voice was quieter. 'I realise that you must be aware, because I haven't asked you anything, that I know the purpose of your visit is to ask me about Dean Galpin. I've wished many things on Galpin since he attacked me – but being dead was not one of them. We all know it was probably a fluke accidental shot. They are not uncommon. A couple of months ago, a guy in Derbyshire tragically shot his fifteen year old son when they were out lamping. Anyway, I don't know one end of a gun from another.'

'Thank you – oh, before we carry on, may I use your loo?' asked Clare. She often used this request as an excuse to have a look around.

Yates pointed to a door at the far end of the sitting room. The toilet was at the end of a long wide corridor. A passageway lined with shelves piled high with climbing gear: ropes, helmets, chocks, carabiners and other hardware. Then on the shelf of boots and trainers, something caught her eye. She picked them up. They were an old pair of running shoes, slender with rubber studs.

Well, you're a long way from home.

They brought back memories of watching fell races near her uncle's farm in the Lakes. Most of the runners wore these Walsh's fell shoes produced locally. They made them the same for years in this bright red and green, which was how she'd recognised them so easily.

'You're a keen climber and runner,' commented Clare when she eventually came back into the room.

'Yes, climbing, walking and running. I'm a free-lance writer for outdoor magazines. The best commissions are those to recce and then write about climbing holidays and walking tours – there's some in those,' he pointed to some magazines on a shelf.

'This explains why you're difficult to track down. You're away a lot,' commented Johns.

Yates nodded. 'Yes, travelling around climbing and walking, and getting paid for doing it.' He smiled – and aged about ten years. 'It's a tough job, but someone's got to do it.'

'Do you go abroad a lot?' asked Johns.

'Yes.'

'Where to in particular?' Clare somehow knew what the answer would be. It seemed inevitable.

'Things have changed, years ago it was the Alps, but now it's Spain. It's cheap, the weather's great and there's lots of amazing routes in the Sierra Nevadas, the Picos, El Charro and the Pyrenees of course.'

Of course.

She smiled to herself – strange, it often happened in cases that a series of unlikely coincidences popped up in suspects. She chanced her arm. 'Seeing your old Walsh's fell shoes out there reminded me why we're really here. I need to see your fell runners' sack, Mr Yates.'

For a few seconds, Yates didn't move a muscle – then he suddenly got to his feet. He went out into the passageway. There was the sound of a cupboard being opened: he returned carrying a narrow dark blue rucksack with criss-cross compression straps. Bright yellow compression straps.

'You've been seen wearing that near to Full Moon Copse, Mr Yates. Perhaps you can give an explanation why?' said Johns.

'I've run past Full Moon Copse at dawn several times recently as it's on the way to Derriman Wood. I'm trying to get proof that one of the Winterstone Estates gamekeepers was putting down poison to kill birds of prey there.'

Clare was looking at Yates: remarkably he was as cool as the proverbial cucumber. He walked over to his desk and took out something from a drawer then came back and handed it to Clare. It was a hotel bill with a credit card slip stapled to it.

'On the morning that Galpin was shot I was eating an early breakfast at a London hotel before coming home. I'd had a League meeting the day before and was booked in at this hotel with other members.'

Clare looked at the credit card receipt. The date was

correct… and Yates had settled his bill at 7.45 am.

She could feel herself sinking lower in her chair.

Back to square one.

25

A heron standing in the shallows was peering down into the water. It looked old. Clare imagined it wearing little half-moon glasses. It took a half-hearted stab at something and missed, then shook its head. Hmm, I don't know… this used to be so easy.

Clare, while driving home from the station – Johns had dropped her by her car when they had returned from Yate's cottage – had, on a whim, turned onto the parking area at the edge of the nature reserve. She hadn't been down here since the visits to Nick Howarth, the pathologist, at the mortuary on the other side of the lake.

There was the slightest of ripples on the water. She looked at the carp fisherman who, with his two rods protruding out from under his fishing umbrella, looked like the rear-gunner of a Second World War bomber – and smiled at a memory. A thousand years ago, she used to go carp fishing with a boy called Martin, and she pestered her father into lending her his electronic bite alarm which buzzed loudly when a fish took the bait. Her father used it so that he could spend a lot of time dozing under his umbrella. She used it so that she could spend a lot of time under hers… snogging a boy called Martin.

A minute or two earlier, a small greenish yellow bird had perched briefly on an old branch at the edge of the reed beds near to the car. Chiffchaff? Willow Warbler? Her father had pointed out the difference when they were fishing but she'd forgotten.

Dad… two memories in a minute… must ask 'them' down sometime.

She turned the speakers up to the limit and the voice of Robert Johnson, and especially that haunting guitar, rebounded from every inch of the old GTI's interior, '*Come on in my kitchen – it's going to be rainy outdoors*.'

How did he do that? Long A and what? Clare held up her left hand and stretched her fingers out over several imaginary guitar frets. That triggered off another memory: that night at a blues club soon after she'd gone to university. She would never be a really good guitarist – she didn't naturally have the 'thumb' – but she'd practised a lot at that time. She'd picked up someone's guitar and was turning out a pretty fair rendition of *Smokey Mokes* – a tune that was difficult to play. When she'd finished she noticed this guy just staring and staring at her.

'What?' she'd said.

'You're a girl,' he'd said.

She and her dad: her fishing and guitar playing. But it wasn't as if he'd wished she was a boy. He'd been so disappointed when she gave up ballet lessons. It was inevitable really – she'd had all the co-ordination and poise of a baby giraffe.

She caught a glance of herself in the rear mirror – and nodded.

Yep, you look like shit.

Then she started thinking about the case again… about getting nowhere.

The lower pane of the sash window frames a view that is an artist's delight: a cock-eyed jumble of mansard and parapetted roofs of slate and tile, of diverse heights and ages, that somehow give the impression that they are about to tumble into the harbour. Closer to hand, in the quirky backs, there's a small brick tower that was once a fish smokery, some ramshackled old sail-making lofts and the disreputable White Dog Inn. Unlike the quayside pubs that are all fresh whitewash and dolled up-to-the-nines with hanging baskets, The White Dog, rather appropriately, lurks up a back alley as dingy as itself.

The top of an ancient crane marks the position of the tiny boatyard and the flight of steep steps up this slope are lined by a narrow metal track, along which ammunition was once hauled up from the quay to the old gun fort. The last piece of the palimpsest is as close as could be. The window sill of the flat is very wide. These thick walls, of what was the old cavalry barracks, were built ten years before Nelson gave the French navy what-for at Trafalgar – in a time when there was great fear of the possibility of the softening-up of this coast by cannonballs from Napoleon's ships, prior to an invasion.

Clare was leaning on the worn stone edge of the wide sill and her old National guitar with the battered steel resonator was resting against the wall alongside her. The bottleneck slide was on the windowsill, appropriately enough, next to the wine bottle and a glass. Clare picked up the glass carefully – she was still wearing long vicious looking finger picks on her right hand. She smiled at the thought that perhaps she should wear them on her next visit to the college in case she ran into that bitch of a secretary again. She scratched the air.

What was that again, Madame Whiplash?

Her thoughts were interrupted by a loud, unmistakable, knock on her door. Clare went down her hallway, turned the door handle – and stood to one side. Emma, wearing a black two-piece, white blouse and with her hair tied back, walked straight past her. Clare followed her into the lounge.

'Got any cat's piss?'

Clare, still wearing the guitar picks, pointed at the windowsill with a grotesquely long finger. Emma drank the nearly full glass, refilled it… then slugged that back as well.

'That hit-and-run prosecution?' asked Clare, as she moved towards the sideboard to get another glass.

Emma nodded.

'You don't often lose a case.'

'I fucked-up.'

'You do that even less.'

'Oh, you don't understand, I'll never hear the end of it for weeks in Testosterone Chambers. I have to be so much better. Oh, shit! I'm sorry, of all people to say that to. You understand – you're the same. Oh, I'm sorry… give us a hug,' said Emma, as she began to sob.

'What's that song about harbour lights called?' asked Emma.

Clare thought for a moment. 'Harbour Lights?'

They were leaning, shoulder to shoulder, against the sill. The sash had been pushed fully open – a habit from the now ditched three-a-week fag habit. But alongside the empty wine bottle, another banned substance had re-appeared… namely a gin bottle with the date line marker on it. When Clare had taken the gin from the sideboard, Emma had initially backed away and held her hands in the sign of the cross – but then said, 'the flesh is weak so I might as well succumb to the spirit'.

Emma had been going on, as usual, about Clare's social life – or rather ('You're like a bloody nun!') lack of one.

'What you were saying – it's not completely true.'

'What?' asked Emma.

'Me… I did. I did go out and throw myself at a man who was incredibly handsome, and–'

'And incredibly gay,' completed Emma.

'Yes, now that's a bit of a problem, I grant you, but the real problem – and I've given this a lot of thought – was that he was boring.'

Emma looked horrified. 'That Captain Gay Lovat was boring?'

'Guy Lovat. Yes, really fucking boring.'

'Oh, shit!' exclaimed Emma, as her elbows slipped as she started to laugh. She knocked a bottle and a glass onto the carpet. Both were empty. 'But not to worry, there'll be other fellers, some may not be boring… and some might not even be gay. You, like me, have advantages over most women. We have something a bit different.'

'What you mean?' said Clare, who in stark contrast to Emma, was beginning to experience some difficulty in forming complete sentences.

'Well for me,' said Emma, exaggerating her distinctive retroussé nose by pushing it up with a finger. 'This vorks lick a mignet – vile you hav those vierd eyes.'

'Thanks, very much… Pinocchio.'

'No, listen,' continued Emma with her nose back to as normal as it goes. 'Oh, God I despair of you! You've forgotten, forgotten, haven't you?

'Ouch!' said Claire, responding to Emma's finger prodding. 'Forgot what?'

'Oh, you silly cow! Forgotten that those eyes of yours – which you use as WMD's – if used properly could probably snap boxer-shorts elastic at twenty yards!' exclaimed Emma as she rooted around on the crowded windowsill for a bottle or glass that still had something in it. 'Though, talking about weapons-of-mass-destruction, how's Lloyd George?'

'Who?'

'The lecturer – that Welsh pain-in-the-arse.'

'Oh, him… him.'

Although in work the usual time the next morning, she was puzzled that the station seemed so quiet. Clare sipped her coffee, surprised that she had only a mild headache. She'd sobered up when she'd received a phone call from Matt Johns before seven. Poor Matt! He'd just heard that his father had suffered a suspected heart attack and he was about to drive home to Surrey. She'd told him to stay there as long as necessary.

The desk sergeant came into the CID office. 'Morning, ma'am, there was an incident yesterday afternoon and this form needs signing,' he said, as he detached the top sheet from the clip board he was holding. 'The Super is up at headquarters for another day… and you happen to be the most senior officer around at the moment.'

Alarm bells sounded in her head – then she realised what was going on. That's why it was quiet! People have buggered-off really early or are coming in later waiting until someone has been the patsy.

Clare pointed to the sheet. 'So, what is it?'

'It's an accident report, ma'am. You know Sergeant Tim Dodds?

She nodded. Dodds was an obnoxious, loud-mouthed, bully of a man. He had an unfriendly patrol car partner, who said very little. Collectively, they were referred to as Grimace and Vomit.

'Well, he slipped as he was going down the steps to the car park.'

'Was Dodds hurt?'

Stupid question.

'Ooh, yes.'

Was he deliberately trying to sound like that bulldog in those insurance commercials?

'Although there are only three steps, they can be tricky, especially when it's wet – although it was dry yesterday. Let's see,' he said as he looked at the sheet. 'Dodds's has got a broken nose, a badly cut lip and quite a lot of painful bruises.'

Clare knew the score. 'And the "unofficial" version of events?' She mimed inverted commas as she posed the question.

The desk sergeant gave her a little respectful nod – a sort of gunfighter's salute. 'Well, unofficially… there was a bit of a disagreement in the toilets between him and *someone* else.'

'Which resulted in Dodds receiving injuries compatible to those he might have received if he'd dived head first off those three low steps down to the car park?' interrupted Clare sharply.

'Yes, spot-on, ma'am.'

There was no way she was going to ask who *someone* was. She'd put money on it being Melbury, who was just about the only one around capable of tackling Dodds. Yes, bloody Andy had been a bit short tempered and rude recently as a result of his wife enforcing a strict diet on him. Clare herself, on one occasion, had told him to fuck-off to MacDonald's and apologise when he got back. Anyway, she'd find out.

She reached out and took the form. 'So, this is the "official" version you want me to sign as the most senior officer on duty on the Marie Celeste. Dodds of course has signed it?'

'Ooh, yes.'

He's doing it again.

'He came back in from A & E just before Vomit drove him home, ma'am.'

'And although those steps are not overlooked, you are of course not short of witnesses?'

He checked another sheet on his clip-board. 'Nine at the last count – though I'll whittle it down.'

Clare read and signed the form and passed it back. The sergeant thanked her and started walking to the door. He paused. 'Oh, ma'am, in the scuffle one of the toilet doors got damaged, so I gave Eva Braun a ring – you know, the traffic warden?'

Clare nodded dumbly.

God, what now?

'Well, Eva called in a couple of favours from Dibdens the joiners and Jolleys the decorators. They're both by the harbour and have a hell of a job parking their vans with all those double yellows down there. They did a nice job last night – free of charge. Dibdens's lads replaced the door and Geoff Jolley himself came up and gave it a quick drying undercoat and matched up the gloss. It was one of those British Standard colours. I think it's called–'

'Sergeant.'

'Yes, ma'am.'

'Piss-off.'

'Yes, ma'am.'

A second or so after he'd left and Clare had started muttering something about small rural police forces, he popped his head back round the door. 'Oh, ma'am, while they were at it, I got them to change and paint a door in the ladies' lavs that looked as if it had been booted-in. I don't suppose you know anything about that do you?'

He disappeared quickly – just before a copy of the Yellow Pages thudded against the glass panel of the door.

A few minutes later the door flew open.

This time the desk sergeant was stern faced and waving a piece of paper. 'It's *him* again.'

26

By the time, Clare – flying solo as Melbury and Karen were miles away – had pulled up with a screech of brakes, Rob Ellis was already at the bottom of the college steps.

'Morning, Stirling Moss,' he said as he opened the front passenger door of the Golf.

'Hello, Inspector.'

She hadn't noticed James Travers coming down the steps behind him. 'Dr Travers, I didn't know you'd be coming. Thanks.'

Travers threw the shoulder bag he was carrying onto the rear seat and clambered in after it. Ellis got in next to her, swinging his long legs into the car. He was also carrying something… a thermos flask.

'Don't turn your nose up. I always bring one in with me. And we could be in for a long morning,' he said, as he noticed her look. He pointed to the staff car park opposite. 'Oh, sure you don't want to go in the Volvo?'

'Positive,' exclaimed Clare, as she slammed into gear and then – with her accelerator foot as heavy as her brake foot had been – shot-off with another screech of tyres. 'I'm not going in that rust bucket.'

'It's brown paint. Anyway, who told you some people call it the Rust Bucket?'

'Guessed,' said Clare as she swung off onto the back lane past Vic's Garage, which she remembered from last time, as a short cut to the main road to the north. She heard Travers chuckling in the back. 'I really didn't expect to see you Dr Travers.'

'It's no problem, Inspector. I was in Rob's office when you rang.'

'Yes, that was a stroke of luck, Bix here has only just started to come in at odd times and – Christ, woman mind that – Shit!'

Clare ignored him.

'This it?' asked Ellis a moment or two later, as he picked up a folded sheet of paper that had been tucked into some CD sleeves.

Clare nodded. 'Yes, a muffled phone message said it was about the "killings", then quoted poetry – it's obvious where to go first.'

Ellis pushed his hair back, which immediately flopped forward again as he looked down and unfolded the sheet of paper.

From Barrows high
And twixt Sun and Moon

'What a mad bastard!' He held the piece of paper over his shoulder. 'Here you are, Bix.'

'Yes, I think you're right about the ridgeway, Inspector. Chalcombe Bumps should be the first call,' said Travers.

Clare had told Ellis what the message was when she'd phoned his office. He'd obviously told Travers while she was driving over. She'd twigged it straight away having used the internet a lot recently to learn about tumuli. The ones on the Bumps were Round Barrows, she'd also remembered from the last time she was on the heath, that PC Hamer had mentioned that a burial mound there – near to the Magic Pool – was actually called The Barrow.

She glanced in her rear view mirror. Travers was different from the last time she'd seen him. She'd not noticed before just how piercing, his ice-blue eyes were. Clare understood what Ellis had been on about when he'd said that the case had shaken Travers out of his lethargy – it had definitely given him some purpose.

The journey up the hairpin of the ridgeway and then along the stretch of straight downland road, apart from being punctuated by frequent mutterings from Clare's front seat passenger, passed relatively uneventfully. However a loud 'Fucking hell!' from Ellis, pinpointed the exact moment when the GTI hit the first pot hole after swinging onto the old drovers' road. Travers had been quiet. He broke his silence as Clare pulled up by the stile at the foot of Chalcombe Bumps.

'You two go up.'

Clare climbed over the stile first. Here we go again, she thought, 'it's déjà vu time all over again', Ellis Long-Legs Gump will be shooting-off like someone possessed. However, he didn't overtake. A minute or so later he was still a few paces behind her as she jogged up the steep slope.

Why? Yes, it's these tight jeans!

'Damn you,' she snapped as she glared over her shoulder. 'There are more important things at the moment than my arse!'

'Yes – like my sodding achilles, that's giving me gip.'

Oh, bollocks!

They reached the top in silence and headed straight for the stone post: the old Ramsden surveying post.

'Don't go too near,' ordered Clare.

'There's some new numbers in yellow at the top!' exclaimed Ellis. 'Ninety eight – that's it ninety eight!'

Clare used her mobile to take a photo and a call to the station as Ellis walked around the post. 'Anything else?'

'No.'

'Do you know Dr Travers's mobile number – it'll save time?'

Ellis, hair blowing out in the breeze, shook his head.

A few minutes later, after coming down the hill, they were peering over Travers shoulders looking down at the OS map that he'd placed on the car bonnet. It was the one he'd drawn lines on in the cartography room.

'Right, ninety eight from the Bumps – it'll be going east,' said Travers. He took a compass bearing and drew it on. The line ran parallel to the coast and crossed open fields.

'Now for the other one,' observed Ellis. 'As that crazy bastard puts it 'Twixt Sun and Moon' – and I think we know where that is.'

'I had a feeling about that intersection.' said Clare, looking at where Ellis had placed his finger.

'Yes, you did, Inspector. I remember you commenting on it when I drew the line that connected Full Moon Copse to the pub that used to be called The Sun.' added Travers.

'Yes, I had PC Hamer check but–'

'PC Hamer? Kevin?' interrupted Ellis.

'Yes, Kevin. He found nothing. Now, can we get there quickly?' Clare was anxious.

'Yes, there's a track down from the drovers' road to the coast road,' explained Ellis, tracing the route with his finger. 'It's steep and pretty well impossible to drive down… so it'll suit you to a tee.'

By the time he'd finished his sentence, Clare was already half-way into her driving seat. Travers folded up the map and within seconds they were all in the car and she was reversing down the short distance to the drovers' road. They drove quickly past the small secluded Romany camp of the Cooper family. No one spoke: Travers, popped-up in her rear view mirror every time they hit a bump, while Ellis was bracing himself with both hands on the dash.

Drama queen.

Then that thought took over her mind again. That *thought*. Why? Why all this rigmarole? Who is pulling our strings? And why? Why?

'What the hell's all this?' she exclaimed as she suddenly had to slow down.

'It's the Travellers – the hippy camp,' muttered Ellis.

It was larger than she had expected. Unlike the Romany camp, trailers and vans were spaced out and lining both sides of the track, and dogs, who were wandering around loose, were barking at their approach. Clare drove slowly past the first couple of trailers before hitting the steering wheel in frustration and shouting, 'Get out of the bloody way!!' Her remarks could have been directed at any one, or all, of the half dozen or so barking dogs and the individuals who were coming out of the trailers to see why the dogs were barking. She drove a little further and dogs and travellers seem to be cloning by the second.

'Sod this,' she said between gritted teeth and then startled Rob Ellis by suddenly leaning right across him, and with her arm resting heavily on his right thigh, she began rooting around in the glove compartment. She dragged out a lamp and lead, quickly plugged it in, and reaching out through her side window put the now flashing light on the roof – then, headlights on, she slapped a hand on the horn and a foot on the accelerator.

'Impressive,' said a rather dumbstruck Ellis a minute or so later, as he was looking in a rear view mirror at the mayhem behind them. Then he pointed at the roof, 'Is that sort of flashing legal?'

'It is if you're Motorway Maintenance… which was where it came from,' answered Clare, who even got in a sweet smile.

Five minutes later, they had turned off the drovers' road and Clare began picking her way down the steep track from the ridgeway. She tried to make up for lost time when she eventually joined the coast road.

'Slow down, let's get there in one piece – and you needn't glare at me like that.'

A few minutes later Travers spoke for the first time in ages. 'Watch out for a farm gate, just down the road. It's just before that very long straight bit that ends by the turning to Undercombe. We are nearly there'

'It's the third field in from the gate, isn't it Bix?' asked Ellis looking over his shoulder.

'Yes, it's nearly half a mile down the track.'

Clare pulled up, 'Damn! – the gate's padlocked. We'll have to run there'

Ellis jumped out, inspected the lock, vaulted over into the field, then going to the other end of the wide heavy looking farm gate, he flexed his knees, took a firm hold on one of the lower bars, and then, with a single movement, raised the gate hinges clear of the post spigots.

Clare shook her head.

Oh, God, now he's a weight lifter! What was that, a Clean and Jerk?

The tall lecturer, with his shoulders still hunched, then, by slowly backing into the field, walked open the gate. It looked heavy.

'It's alright, Inspector.' She could tell by his voice that Travers was leaning forward. 'No problem. Rob's a tough cookie. He used to be a crack climber – he could hang about by his fingertips like Spiderman apparently.'

Ellis, judging that he had forced open the gate wide enough, lowered it to the ground, gave that big smile of his, doffed a large imaginary feathered hat and with a bow and a great sweep of the arm, theatrically, waved her into the field.

Clever clogs.

He then pointed to the herd of cows at the far end of the

field and dragged the gate closed after Clare had driven through the gateway.

'Nice one, Rob,' congratulated Travers, as Ellis got back in the car.

As Clare began to drive along the track towards the next farm gate, she remembered his damaged tendon. 'Are you alright?'

'Yes… thanks.'

After crossing through two more fields, Clare pointed through the windscreen. 'Look! – there's something in yellow on that gate.'

Ellis jumped out almost before she'd stopped the car. 'Eighty three – it's eighty three!' he shouted over his shoulder.

'Right!' called back Travers, and Clare turning round on her seat could see him drawing a new line on his map. Travers seemed on a real high. She wondered if all this adrenaline rush was good for him. 'They intersect not far away… Tallington House!'

'I know that – it's on the way to the heath!' added Ellis who was leaning into the car to look. 'It's a lovely country house that's been turned into posh flats.'

After taking a photo with her phone and contacting the station, Clare drove back along the field track as fast as she could. Ellis jumped out and dragged the gate open again and after she'd driven through he closed it, and with some difficulty lifted it back on his hinges. Soon Clare was driving fast again on the coast road and then, after a mile or so, she turned, as directed, at a roundabout and headed inland. Where the road to the heath follows a wide valley to the east of the downs, there is a sequence of four humped backed bridges carrying it over a meandering chalk stream. The bridges normally act as a picturesque but pragmatic traffic calming device – but not today. Ellis, however, made no comment, on either the first, second or even the third occasion when the Golf returned to terra ferma. Clare glanced across.

Why's he not complaining? His Achilles? Was it that gate?

Clare drove slower over the last bridge.

A few minutes later, Travers leaned forward again. 'It's a quarter of a mile.'

The house was soon visible from the road and two ornate gate pillars clearly marked the entrance to the drive. Clare glanced around anxiously; the countryside was open, flat with just a few scattered clumps of woodland – no obvious overlooking hill to shoot from. Also there were no vehicles at the front entrance.

'We're first here – I'm surprised,' said Clare, raising her voice over the sound of tyres on gravel. The Golf crunched to a halt. There were some steps up to a large door at the front, the oldest looking part of the house, but the drive continued either side of the building around two elegant matching wings. Clare and Ellis reached the front door together. He banged – she pressed the intercom buzzer and pointed to the notice indicating that it was for Apartment 1 only and that 2 and 3 were the West and East Wings respectively and that 4 was at the rear of the house.

There was no answer though she thought she'd heard the buzz of a mobile phone. They waited a few seconds. 'You try the other side,' said Clare, as she began to run to the right of the building. She turned the corner just in time to see a woman with long red hair get into a large silver 4x4. 'Excuse me! Excuse me!' shouted Clare as the woman slammed the car door.

Then there was just a blinding flash and… and the last thing Clare remembered clearly, was that she was falling backwards.

27

Clare was staring out of the window at the reed beds and the lake. There were a few ducks nearby, just… well, sort of floating around. They looked plastic. She was sitting next to her detective superintendent in a room above the mortuary. There was a connecting door to Dr Nick Howarth's office – the pathologist who had carried out the autopsy on Galpin, and retrieved the bullet from the dog and now he'd had to deal with…

She shuddered at the thought.

Why hold the meeting here? Neutral ground? The dead less likely to eavesdrop?

She half-turned towards Detective Superintendent Paul Simmonds and he smiled. Well, at least Yorick gave his very best shot at one. Clare appreciated that. Opposite them across the table was Nick Howarth and alongside him sat a thickset bald-headed man. He hadn't been introduced. In fact no one had given their names. However she was certain that this grey-suit was from what the regional Special Branch guys refer to as MFI.

There were waiting for two people to join them.

She thought of that *moment* again – she had so many times – of the blast and being powered backwards. Then things were unclear: she dimly remembers Rob Ellis going ape-shit as he knelt over her. He'd travelled with her in the ambulance and had only left the hospital after it was decided that – as the bump on the back of her head reminded her now – that she'd got away with it. No fractured skull, no broken bones, and no stitches, just a slight concussion: it was a miracle. It was late before Ellis left, even though, she'd found out later, he had to be in Cambridge the next day to give a paper at a conference. Emma visited, and had flirted outrageously with a couple of young doctors. She had driven Clare home the next morning and, despite protestations, had fed her and stayed with her until the afternoon. Then Karen arrived, made a cup of tea and then left. She returned loaded with Tesco bags and said that with her new detective skills she'd deduced that the fridge contained 'the best part of fuck-all... and that out of date'. However, Clare had been relieved that the 'new detective skills', had not stretched to her being quizzed about why one bunch of flowers was larger than the others.

Then the door from the path lab corridor opened and two men walked in.

'Sorry, we're late,' said Captain Guy Lovat.

Lovat and his companion took their places at the table. Clare narrowed her eyes as she studied him. He glanced quickly across at her, and then looked away.

He knows, that I 'know'.

It's alright sunshine; you're secret's safe, she thought. She'd come to accept that it must be impossible to be openly gay in the forces... but she still wanted to kill him.

The captain and his companion, who was certainly also military, were in civilian clothes. Everyone, Lovat and Clare included, wore suits. The last time she'd seen him, he was all polished buttons in his dress uniform – and she was in high heels and wearing an evening dress.

Her grey eyes bored into him as the memory of her humiliation that night, swept away any sympathy she'd felt for him.

'Right, I'll start. The victim was Sonia Nichol. She was forty one years old. Single. We believe she lived alone.'

Simmonds, head down, was resting with both arms on the table, as if protecting the papers he was referring to. He looked up. 'Obviously, you're getting an incomplete picture from us at the moment – we're still trying to trace family.'

There was a pause before he leaned back in his chair. Her boss having, as arranged, passed the baton, Clare gave a little cough before speaking. 'Sonia Nichol, as far as we know at this stage, has been in this area for about four years. She bought the boutique called Number Seven – it's at that address in St Adhelm's Street in the town. She lived in the flat above the shop before purchasing an apartment at Tallington House – that's on the valley road to the heath. That was eighteen months ago. Well, it is an apartment in name only; it's really a wing of a country house.'

'Yes,' chipped in Simmonds. 'And that's where it immediately starts to get murky. Living over the shop one minute and then forking out thousands? We've not got far yet, have we?'

'No, sir. When we've checked up, we may find it's perfectly legit. She may have been left a legacy, for example. If cash was involved then we may have problems – especially down here.'

Grey Suit from MFI gave her a quizzical look.

She paused before continuing. 'Money tracing can be difficult at the best of times, but being only a half-day ferry ride from the Isles can really complicate things, especially cash movement. There are suitcase jobs. What you might call offshore banking at its most literal, really.'

This brought a smile from Nick Howarth. Grey Suit remained po-faced. Simmonds then suddenly turned towards him. 'Also, we've got absolutely nothing on file about her… What have you got?'

There was a long pause.

'Nothing,' said Grey Suit. 'Absolutely nothing.'

'We're all in the dark then.'

Clare glanced at Simmonds: Yorick's whole body language showed all too clearly that he thought the guy was telling porkies. He turned to the two army men on his right. 'Gentlemen?'

Lovat, with a barely perceptible sideways nod, deflected the question to his companion. There was a pause as the man took out a thin green folder from his brief case. Clare studied him. He looked about the same age as Lovat. Was he public school and Sandhurst as well?

'Well, you all know the gist of it – there's no doubt at all,' he began.

Not public school – not sure about the other.

'Staggering, isn't it,' he continued and looked around the table. 'It was a car bomb, and definitely a blast from the past this one – in more ways than one.'

Clare looked around the table, no one smiled.

'Firstly, this was a throw-back to the original use. It was a low-charge device aimed at assassination only and not, as now, a terrorist device used to impact on the surrounding area. A small package – magnetically held – was placed underneath the car. There's no need to wire into the ignition system, simply use some kind of rocker. The vehicle moving off will cause the rocker to connect and activate the detonator.'

Something here did not make sense but she was damned if she could work out what it was. Then another thought came into her a head… as it often did, in times like this.

'There's a grant going for a doctorate on Stevie Smith. I'm giving you first shout,' had offered her tutor. 'Oh, that would be brilliant!' she'd said. 'But I'm joining the police force.'

Wrong answer, she thought… as she always did, at times like this.

The Unnamed Soldier, after consulting his file, was off

again. 'One advantage we had was that there were clear leads as to where to start our enquiries.'

'If I may interrupt there,' said Simmonds. 'There is no doubt in our minds that the bomber and shooter are the same. The exact location of the second bearing on the bombing depended on previous information known.'

Clare nodded.

Then Lovat spoke for the first time. 'Firstly, because of connections between the Real IRA and the Basque terrorists, we have lots of links with the Guardia Civil and with GAT – the Spanish anti-terrorist organisation. As you know the shootings of both Galpin and the dog used very high grade Match ammunition, clearly identified as coming from a batch stolen, almost certainly by ETA, seven years ago from a military depot near Pamplona. During the same raid six specially modified C-75 sniper's rifles were also stolen. And, we can assume, because of the long range of the first shooting, that it came from one of the C-75's, as other sniper rifles in our sphere can't touch that distance. Now, rifles were not in ETA's *modus operandi* – the two recovered, according to the Spanish authorities, had been used for hunting.' Lovat, as soon as he had finished speaking, nodded to his companion.

Clare knew immediately that there was something else about explosives coming up, as this guy was clearly the bomb expert – perhaps it might clarify what was bothering her.

'The two rifles turned up in the Urola Lehoi, a small very isolated area in the northern Basque region. The community there is very traditional, very cut-off, very tightly-knit. One tradition is a pride in producing first class hunters. Boys are taught to shoot as soon as they are big enough to hold a rifle. Also…' Unnamed Soldier paused. 'Also, for a short period in the 1980's there was an ETA cell operating from the Urola Lehoi. What was strange was that it disappeared as quickly as it had appeared. Now, bomb assemblers leave signatures.

The ones they used had a peculiar quirk in the wiring, not seen before or since. Well, until that one at Tallington House. A lot is left behind after a low impact explosion. There's no doubt it was the same.'

There was a murmur in the room, and then Lovat cleared his throat. 'Now, about that rumour that an Englishman bought one of the guns and some ammunition – well, it's unlikely that he's our man here. It points to a Basque sharpshooter who also knows about bombs. There's an ETA ceasefire –'

'So, he's an ideal contract killer,' interrupted Simmonds. 'Only one problem here and that's the local knowledge incorporated in the messages left.'

Clare stared past Howarth and Grey Suit through the window at the huge reed beds. They were changing constantly: a strong shape-shifting wind was blowing from the south-west. Then it dawned on her. She turned towards the army side of the table. 'Sonia Nichol had only just got in the car when it blew up – and according to what you said the vehicle would have to be moving for the detonator to trigger.'

Unnamed Soldier nodded. 'Yes, you've spotted it. I was leaving our enigma until last. The timing mechanism was *different*. It used mobile phones. Someone pressed a button to set it off.'

Clare suddenly felt cold. Some bastard had been watching, waiting for the second that the red-haired women got into her vehicle… then pressed a button. She looked around. It was bizarre, everyone seemed so blasé yet we've got nowhere. Clare found herself speaking. 'So, to track down this mad man, who goes out of his way to make his executions as bizarre as possible, all we've got to do is to find a common motive in the killing of a man who fattened up fox cubs for hunting, the shooting of a small dog, and the blowing-up of a woman who sold frocks.'

Then she looked around the table and wished she'd kept her mouth shut.

Beam me up, Scotty.

28

Simmonds looked up from the papers on his desk. 'Sorry to keep you waiting.'

Clare turned on her chair. 'That's alright, sir.'

She had been looking at an old painting on the wall of a valley with a castle in the distance – it looked Victorian – while trying to remember part of *The Lady of Shallot*.

Willows whiten, aspen, something, something, something, *little breezes,* something, something, *by the river flowing down to Camelot.*

She'd never been a fan of Tennyson, anyway – but at least, for a minute or so, she had been distracted from thinking about *other things*.

'God knows how long that's been up there,' said Simmonds with a nod towards the painting. 'Now, let's see.' He tapped his finger on the desk-top as if making a bullet-point. 'The only witnesses were you and the two lecturers – and they're not going to say anything.'

No, I bet they're not! You could scare the shit out of anyone!

'The vehicle and *everything* was cleared quickly and quietly,' he said in a low voice.

Clare tensed.

Oh, that poor bloody woman.

Simmonds settled back in his chair and held his hands together. Somehow Clare knew he was going to make a 'statement' – she wasn't wrong.

'Cars do not usually explode if they catch fire. Now, Sonia

Nicol's store room in her shop was heated by calor-gas. That part of St Adhelms Street, with its fancy little shops, is too narrow for deliveries. We know that she had the gas canisters delivered to Tallington House and took a full one in and an empty back, when required. Leaking calor-gas would build up from the car well, as it is heavier than air. It can explode… and Sonia Nicol smoked.' He paused, unclasping his hands and rubbing the side of his face. 'All that is true, so the "Story", if we are forced, is that lighting a cigarette was the most likely cause of the explosion.'

Clare was holding it together. 'Have any relatives or friends come forward, sir?'

'Peculiarly – not a one. We are still checking on her background.'

'On a different point, sir. Who would believe the truth that a Basque terrorist was responsible?'

'You've got a point there. And we know that the Chronicle is not going to pry.'

Clare nodded. The Chronicle was the only newspaper in this quiet and fairly remote area. Unusual for a local paper it was a daily.

A couple of months ago a tip-off had lead to the arrest of the crew and 'cargo' of a boat putting in on the coast at night. A Chronicle reporter and photographer 'happened' to be in the area. It was some story. The arrest was made in an old smugglers' cove and the 'cargo' were illegal Chinese chefs, earmarked for take-aways, where the sons and daughters had their professional sights set much higher than working for the family.

Clare knew that Dodgson, the editor ('Eddie of the "Chronie" knows which side his bread is buttered' said Melbury) had sold the exclusive to the dailies – and made a packet for his paper.

It was not the first time something like that had happened.

As she got up to leave, Simmonds walked around his desk and placed a hand on her shoulder. 'Are you *really* alright, Clare?'

'Yes – well you know me, sir.'

'Yes… I think I do,' he said gently.

'You'd never guess would you?' said Karen.

Clare nodded. She'd parked, not at the front of Tallington House, but at the end of the east wing. The gravel drive gave nothing away. As Simmonds had said, *everything* had been cleared.

'I was in her shop the other day. She served me. Anyway, it would hardly be a case of mistaken identity what with that long red hair of hers, would it?' said Karen, who ironically was checking out her own long auburn hair in the vanity mirror. She tapped her mouth, as if rebuking an errant tongue. 'Oh, I'm sorry. Are you alright?'

'There's no need to pussy-foot around, I'm fine.'

There was a crunch of gravel as Melbury's car pulled up behind them. Clare noticed the concerned look on her big detective sergeant's face as he got into the car – as did Karen. 'There's no need to pussy-foot around, sarge. The boss is fine.'

'I am here, you know,' said Clare, turning and smiling at the young policewoman who'd been fussing around her like a mother hen since *it* had happened.

'That's good. Oh, I didn't speak to Matt yesterday, is there any news?'

'Well, his father's still making a good recovery, sarge, but his mother's not coping too well,' said Karen.

'When's his sister coming over from Canada?'

'Matt's still not sure, Andy. I've told him to stay until then. He's taking some leave,' added Clare.

'Good. Is that the copse that the SOCO's turned over?'

Clare and Karen turned to see where Melbury was pointing. There was a small clump of trees set in a ploughed field on the valley floor.

'Yes,' answered Clare. 'It's about the only cover around from where you can see where the 4X4 was parked.'

'But that's the weird thing,' said Melbury. 'I had a chat with a couple of the search team. They found no evidence of anyone being there – and they must be right because it would have been impossible to walk through that headland of grass and wild plants around the trees without leaving a trail. That few yards of set-aside, left unploughed for wild life, is really thick.'

Clare nodded.

Another sodding mystery! On top of everything else our killer's not only wandering around under Harry Potter's bloody invisibility cloak but leaving no footprints either.

'Anyway, Andy,' said Clare, who, beginning to feel uncomfortable, twisted in her seat – she still had some sore bruises. 'What have you found?'

'Nothing really, I've just talked to the gardener – who's also the odd-job man. He's only here part-time. The managing agents gave me his mobile number. I caught up with him at one of those big second homes at Undercombe.' The tone of his voice betrayed his feelings about second home owners. 'The guy said there's usually no one around apart from the old lady–'

'Mrs Donaldson,' interrupted Karen. 'I phoned her earlier. I'm going to see her in a minute. She said she was really too shocked to talk before'

'Well, the gardener could tell me nothing. He'd not seen anything, or anyone suspicious. I think I'll go round and have a chat at Tallington Farm,' he nodded vaguely east. 'Uniforms have been, but the farmer's a funny bugger who doesn't talk much. I know him vaguely. I might get something,' concluded Melbury, who, like Clare, was beginning to look uncomfortable – although in his case the causal factor was the disproportionate ratio between bulk and available space.

'So, Andy, you're going to the farm. Karen's off to see Mrs Donaldson, that's Apartment Two; the west wing. Apparently it's the mirror-image of this one.' Clare was looking at the dead woman's flat. 'Apartment One at the front has never been occupied – it's a tax-exile job. That leaves Apartment Four, which is the rear of the house. He's expecting me, is Mr...' she checked her note book. 'Isherwood.'

'Detective Inspector Morell? I'm Patrick Isherwood,' he said – Clare, speechless, nodded her head. 'Do come in.'

Clare was conscious of the sound of her shoes on the tiles of the elegant high hallway. She was also aware of the aroma of freshly ground coffee. The young man turned and smiled. 'Can I tempt you to drink while on duty?'

He showed her into the drawing room. It was like walking into a page from Homes & Gardens, but despite being in a most elegantly furnished room, Clare was immediately drawn to the view through the huge bow window: a black Porsche was parked on the gravel, and then a series of wide steps led down to lawns which sloped to a lake and parkland.

'Yes, it's lovely isn't it?' said Isherwood, as he placed the tray he was carrying on a table and joined her. 'It was a sort of 1840's Ground Force job apparently, based on a plan nicked from an old Capability Brown design book.'

Clare laughed as she turned to look at him. He was wearing dark jeans and a loose fitting white shirt. This place, that lake, *that* shirt, that TV production of *Pride and Prejudice*.

Yes, there are definite shades of Pemberley here.

'Darcy' Isherwood suddenly became very serious. 'Sorry,

that's really awful about poor Sonia. I know cars can catch fire and fuel tanks explode, but something like this is very rare isn't it?'

Clare nodded. She was pleased that it seems to be accepted that it was a horrific accident, also it was encouraging that he'd referred to the woman by her first name: he must have known her. Clare took the safe line that they were trying to trace family and close friends. Unfortunately he couldn't tell her very much, he and Sonia Nichol, he explained, just had the occasional chat when they met in the grounds, which was rare anyway. Isherwood worked in London – he said he was also abroad a great deal on business – so he didn't even get down here every weekend. He also said that, even if he was here, because of being at the rear of the building, he would not be aware of any visitors she might have had.

'So, I'm sorry I've not been much help,' he said, as they walked down the hallway as she was leaving.

'That's fine. Thank you for contacting us so quickly. You only got back last night didn't you?'

'Yes, the agents had left your number on my answer phone.' He opened the door. The sun had come out. 'I love it here, just hanging about really – I'm easily satisfied.'

Yes, bet you are.

'What do you do, if you don't mind me asking?'

'Don't laugh… I'm a merchant banker.' Then he tapped his head. 'I've just remembered something which might help to find people who knew her. Sonia was a keen rider. She used to ride with the hunt and things. Come to think of it, it was really surprising she gave it up, I'm sure she wasn't injured, or anything like that.'

'Do you know the name of the hunt?' inquired Clare in as off-hand a manner as she could.

'The local one, the Borne one – she also kept her horse at the stables there at, err… '

'Winterstone?'

'Yes, that's it.'

Dean Galpin, Frampton's dog, now her – they're all connected by the hunt!

Clare's head was buzzing.

'I hope you don't mind me saying but your hair looks great. It's very French – a sort of *coup sauvage* and–'

'What?'

'I like your hair style.'

'It wouldn't suit you,' she said – over sharply, her mind elsewhere.

Oh, you miserable bitch, Morell!

'I'm sorry,' she said, and gave him a smile… and a *look*.

Emma would have approved.

'So it's Sir Alan and Lady Charlotte next. What's the best way to Winterstone, Karen?' asked Clare loudly, as the Golf crunched its way down the gravel drive of Tallington House. In the space of a few minutes, Clare was thinking about Emma again: 'you stupid cow' she'd be saying if she knew Clare was going to see the Vines again.

'Right here, then before the heath, there's a road to the left that goes through the villages at the edge of the vale. This is a real lead this – all these connections. You know, boss, it'll be interesting to hear what Sir Sleezebag and Her Skinnyship have to say. It's unusual for anyone to give up a hunt – because it's so difficult to get in.'

'Yes, good point, Karen. Anyway, what did you get from Mrs Donaldson?' asked Clare as she reached the gates and turned onto the road.

'Oh, she was really nice; she's part of the family that owned the entire house before it was altered. Unfortunately she's old and doesn't get out much. And as her flat looks out over open countryside she didn't see anything. She heard the blast and didn't know anything until uniforms called to check if anyone was in the flats. She was a bit in shock but family came round straight away and she says she's alright now.'

'Did she know Sonia Nichol?'

'No, not really, they just had the odd chat when they met in the grounds – had a moan about the gardener and that sort of thing.'

They were quiet for a few minutes. It was the young detective constable who was picking out some of Clare's CD's from the door pocket, who broke the silence. 'Oh, that guy, that merchant banker… is he? Well, you know! Is he a–?' Karen broke off from rooting through the disks to make an obscene gesture… which she repeated several times.

Clare said nothing.

Karen waved a CD at her. 'What's this doing with all your blues stuff, boss?'

'That, detective constable, is an essential part of the woman cop's must-have pack. Don't you know nuffin?'

The road passed through a landscape that was a patchwork of small hedge-rowed fields, strung together by a sinew of river bank willows. A perfect backdrop for a Vaughan Williams Fantasia, or possibly something by Delius, but instead Gloria Gaynor belted out '*I will survive*', and she wasn't the only one.

It helped, it stopped Clare thinking about – for a few minutes at least – what would happen to this quiet peaceful area, if it got out that an assassin was going around shooting and blowing up people.

Ten minutes later, Clare, after turning onto the minor road that skirted the edge of the vale, pulled onto the verge just before the village of Winterstone to make a phone call.

'Well?' asked Karen, when she'd finished.

'Nothing new, they still haven't found anything on that

second mobile phone of Sonia Nichols.'

The remains of two mobile phones had been discovered at the scene of the explosion.

'Shit. If they could only get a trace on that mystery phone, we'd probably have all the answers.'

'I'm sure you're right, Karen,' agreed Clare, as she started the engine. 'I think we'll give Winterstone House a try first, rather than the stables.'

As they drove up to it, Clare thought the fine Elizabethan manor house looked particularly magnificent. There's something special about ridgeway stone in certain lights. The house was the colour of honey.

A young woman answered the door. 'Yes, can I help you?'
Spanish? Portuguese?

'Hello. Is Sir Alan or Lady Vine available?'

'No, I'm afraid not. May I ask who called?'

'We're from English Heritage. We'll call again.' said Clare – avoiding a phone call being made to the stables warning that the police were on their way.

The woman watched them as they got back in the car. Clare drove back down the drive and turned left at the road. The entrance to Winterstone Stables was, she remembered from her last visit, about two hundred yards away. As she was turning into the stable yard, she noticed that both Sir Alan and Lady Charlotte were down at the paddock watching a horse being exercised.

'That's nice and handy – two for the price of one.'

She pulled up alongside a Land Rover.
Is this one Vine's?

Three stable girls were leaning on a wall smoking. 'Is that sour-faced looking one in the middle, your old enemy from school?'

'Yes, boss, Sarah Diment, I'll do the honours,' answered Karen as she was getting out.

'Oh, look what the cat's dragged in. It's Karen Garland!'

Clare, leaving Karen to it, walked across the yard and down towards the paddock. Engrossed in watching the horse, the Vines, leaning on the paddock fence, didn't notice her approach. Emma's advice was racing through her head. She was going to be careful, these are powerful people.

'Hello.'

'Oh, hello!' said Vine as he swung round.

'Detective Inspector Morell,' said Lady Charlotte, pushing her hair back from her face, as she turned and straightened out her slim frame.

'Have you charged anyone?' asked Vine.

'No, I'm afraid not – oh, at the house, I said I was from English Heritage. I thought there was no need to unduly worry your staff.'

'Right,' he answered.

Clare found herself looking at the horse in the paddock. A grey. It was a magnificent beast.

'You ride?' Lady Charlotte made it sound more like a statement than a question.

'No… a little when young,' lied Clare. She hadn't ridden for about four years, but being brought up by her father, many of her school holidays were spent on her uncle's farm in the Lakes, and much of the time she was in the saddle. Memories… dear old Diamond, her pony that could cross fells like a mountain goat.

'Pity, you look as if you'd have a good seat.' Somehow Lady Charlotte made a compliment sound like an insult.

'I'm here because I hope you can help us with some information about a woman called Sonia Nichol.'

A look passed between them.

'Yes, we heard about it. An awful accident,' said Vine. 'But I don't see how we can help.'

'The problem we're having is trying to find contacts –

family, or close friends. I was told that she used to ride to hounds, and that she stabled her horse here.'

'I can understand that. She was something of a loner.' Lady Charlotte turned towards her husband and placed a hand on his arm. 'I can't think of anyone who really knew her. Can you, darling?'

He shook his head.

Clare decided to chance her arm, 'Why was she asked to leave the hunt?'

The Vines looked at each other: He nodded.

'It's a delicate matter, Detective Inspector,' said Lady Charlotte.

Clare was driving quickly back to town on the long straight road over the downs. They were close to a large hill fort, the great ditches and ramparts looking as formidable today as they must have to the centurions of Vespasian's Second Legion as they prepared to storm it, very nearly two millennia ago. Clare and Karen were unaware of surroundings: they had other things on their minds.

'Now are you sure, Karen?'

'Positive, boss. Absolutely positive.'

The Vines had told Clare that Sonia Nichol had been asked to leave the hunt, and the stables, because she had been sexually pestering some of the girls. The three stable girls had given the same explanation to Karen. They had said the woman was a 'raving lezzie'. Karen, however, was convinced that they were lying. She was positive that they had been told what to say.

'And you didn't let on?'

'No, boss, I'm certain they believed I swallowed all that bollocks.'

What the hell's going on?

Clare pulled into a lay-by and made a phone call. There was no reply so she sent a text.

'I'll try and see him again. It's a long shot, he might know something but just didn't like saying; he was her next door neighbour after all… Patrick Isherwood,' she said, answering Karen's look.

'Oh, the merchant–'

'Stop it, Karen.'

29

The Marine Hotel, a stylish 1930's building, had just re-opened after being closed for several months. It was lunchtime. It was quiet. The prices were sky high – presumably in an attempt to re-coup some of the over-budget costs of the expensive refurbishment.

Clare, in the otherwise deserted upstairs lounge, was sitting in a black leather sofa near to one of the huge, metal framed, curved windows. She was looking out. Close at hand was the old attractive part of the college campus, and beyond that, only looking west not east, there was a sweep of a view to rival that from the window table at Bellini's: the pier, along the curve of the esplanade buildings – one of the best Georgian townscapes in the kingdom – to the harbour mouth and the hill of the old gun fort near to where she lived.

Rob Ellis was at the bar getting drinks. He'd been waiting in the hotel entrance when she'd arrived a few minutes earlier. She was in hospital the last time she'd seen him; he'd had to leave town because he was taking part in a conference at Cambridge. That was five days ago.

Studying her reflection in the window, she touched her hair. It looked good. *Richard* had somehow fitted her in. It was a wonder how – his explanation, which went on the whole time she was in the salon, made it sound, that in comparison, the re-scheduling of the Last Night of the Proms to Christmas Eve, would, as she told Emma later, be 'a piece of piss'.

'Hello, Inspector Morell.'

'Oh!' She was startled – she hadn't heard anyone approach.

It was James Travers: Rob Ellis had mentioned that 'Bix' might 'pop in'. 'I'm sorry I made you jump, but I'm glad to see you looking – well, more than alright,' he said in a low voice.

Clare smiled.

It was strange. Here she was looking very different from the last time he'd seen her, when she was barely conscious and Travers himself had changed so much from when she'd first met him. His eyes were no longer sunk deep in his head and he'd lost that haunted look. In fact his eyes were now his most noticeable feature: they really were a piercing ice blue.

'I'm well, and you, Dr Travers?'

'It was obviously a shock. I was still by your car when I heard it. But everything is alright, and as I told Detective Superintendent Simmonds – he's very shrewd by the way – that if there is anything else and you think Rob and I can be of any assistance, then please do not hesitate to contact us.'

Weird? No hint that Yorick would have put the fear of God into him about keeping his mouth shut?

'Thank you.'

He looked out of the window. 'This is a great view.'

'Yes, I was just thinking that from here it looks as if the sea front is much the same as it was two hundred years ago.'

Travers smiled – he changed, he looked, well, suddenly enthusiastic. It was as if someone had flicked a switch. 'Spot on, Inspector!' He pointed out of the window. 'Can you see the part of the esplanade where that slipway is?'

'Yes, I know it.'

'Well, nothing has really changed from that time. It would be mid-morning when it would be packed, with ladies in empire waisted dresses and bonnets, and dragoons in gold-braided jackets from the barracks where you live.' He must have noticed her surprised look. 'Rob told me.'

Clare couldn't remember telling Rob Ellis about the flat.

'Then they would cheer as the horse-drawn royal bathing machine came past and into the sea.'

'George the Third?'

'Yes, Farmer George himself! And as he came down the steps into the water, the royal musicians, on a second larger machine, would strike up God Save the King. They'd do an encore when he came out.'

'What did they play while His Majesty was paddling about, Handel's Water Music?'

Clare thought he would never stop laughing. Eventually he did, and picked up his thread again. 'It's surprising how much some landscapes from that time have changed. Come and look over here!'

Before she could get to her feet, he was already most of the way towards the other end of the deserted lounge bar.

This window faced east, looking out to where the town bay ends at the low blue grey cliffs. Behind the curving beach and the coast road, there is a marsh of reed and bulrushes that swings round towards the nature reserve and the lake.

'Two hundred years ago, you'd have been looking at one of the best racecourses in the land. The grandstand was where that big patch of scrub is now. There were huge crowds and lots of betting, not just on the racing but on wrestling matches and prize-fighting.'

'Bare fist?'

'Yes, Inspector, Daniel Mendoza fought here.'

'Was he famous?'

'Well, let's just say, that on July 15th, 1789, the Times lead with a report of his previous night's fight. The second story was the Storming of the Bastille. He really invented boxing and used to beat sluggers much bigger than himself. Other things about him are fascinating.'

'Such as?'

'He founded a boxing academy. Lord Byron was a pupil.'

She knew that Randy George Gordon, despite his limp, was a good fencer and an even better boxer – now she knew why.

She didn't say anything.

Something was amusing Travers. 'We can blame Mendoza for a few things as well, and remember this is just about 1800.'

'What sort of things?'

'He organised the first bouncers, was the first to charge an entrance fee for sporting events and was the first celebrity to appear in panto.'

Clare laughed. She wasn't surprised his extra-mural lectures were well attended. 'Rob told me that you knew everything there was to know about this coast.'

Travers looked slightly embarrassed… and then thoughtful, as if something was on his mind. He glanced at his watch. 'Sorry, but I really have to go. Rob is slow getting served, I think they're completely disorganised here as they've only just re-opened. Now, remember, contact us, without hesitation.'

He leant towards her. He shook her hand – it was like getting it caught in a door. Well, that was different from the limp handshake the first time they met, she thought. Then, with a smile, he was gone.

Phew!

He was a strange man. She'd never seen him like that before. It was as if he'd suddenly been plugged into the mains – after he'd swallowed a handful of happy pills. Clare half-turned, but he was already, like a will-o-the-wisp, disappearing down the curved staircase with the beautiful glass brick wall.

She walked back to the sofa, sat down, and looked hard at her reflection in the window.

Yes, I wonder how his daughter died?

Did he find his partner after she'd committed suicide?

Where's this drink?

Her phone sounded. It was a text message from Patrick Isherwood. He would be back at Tallington House later today before returning to London tomorrow… then he was flying to Hong Kong for six weeks. Clare replied immediately, texting that she needed to speak to him 'about something'. She wanted to know if he could shed any light on Sonia Nichol being gay or not. She would meet him this evening.

'I hate those things.'

'Yes, I remember,' said Clare as she put her mobile away. She'd not heard Rob Ellis approach – the new carpets were thick. She looked up; he was standing between her and the window. She had not realised before quite how broad his shoulders were.

'Bix was in a real hurry. Here we are. Sorry, I've been so long, a few customers roll up at the same time and it's complete bloody chaos down there.' Ellis placed the orange juice and the coke on the glass table in front of her, then slumped down in the low armchair opposite and unwound his long legs. She looked across at him. He was wearing jeans and a nice blue shirt, with a thin sweater across his shoulders. He pushed his hair back; the way he was sitting with his head lowered drew attention to his high cheekbones. His hazel eyes were studying her over the top of them. 'Well, Detective Inspector Clare Morell. You look great. It suits you much better than that *Death of Ophelia* effect you were going for the last time I saw you.'

Clare laughed and took a sip of orange. 'I believe you had a visit from my Super.'

'Christ, yes! He's one scary looking bastard – he was alright though.'

Ellis looked as if he was about to say more but instead

picked up his coke. He took a sip then put the glass down. 'I asked him about you, about what happened. He said that with your track record I shouldn't bother about it. He didn't elaborate.'

Ellis had spoken quietly, seriously and Clare shivered. Yorick knew the part she'd played in the Langford Killings. The Langford Killings… that case was the reason why she was no longer in the Greater Manchester Police. She pulled herself together. 'How are you doing?' she asked gently.

'I'm fine.' Ellis gave a part-smile, and lowered his voice. 'Your boss offered counselling – but I think I can deal with it.' His face darkened. 'I've seen sudden death before.'

'Climbing?'

Ellis gave the slightest of nods.

'Dr Travers looked alright.'

'Bix seems alright. After all the personal shit he's had, perhaps it's… well, you know what I mean.'

'Does he live locally?'

'Well, sort-off. He's away a lot of the time, but he has a lovely old house in the hills above Haldon Cove – where we were at the pub the other day – I don't suppose he'll stay there, it's huge.'

'Also there must be painful memories, with both his daughter and his wife dead.'

'Isabelle was his partner, not his wife. I didn't know her – I only met her at college functions. Apparently it was her house. She was from a wealthy county family.'

Clare was just about to ask him about Travers's daughter's death, when she suddenly realised a couple of things, and smiled to herself behind her hand. Firstly, they had somehow managed not to spill the drinks all over each other – yet. Also, wonders will never cease, they'd not had a row – yet.

He noticed. 'What?'

She said nothing for a few seconds, then. 'I know we've

spoken on the phone, but thank you again for staying so late at the hospital and for the flowers, they were lovely… you shouldn't have been so extravagant.'

Ellis took a sip of his drink, then after he placed the glass down on the table, he stayed leaning forward towards her. He pushed his hair back. Clare noticed that the scar over his left eye seemed more pronounced than usual – his eyes intense. He seemed to be gearing himself to speak. 'I don't know what the fuck is going on, but as sure as hell it's not about shooting dogs. Simmonds *ordered* us to clam up completely.' He reached across and put his hand on hers. 'I've been worried sick about you… I've been thinking a lot about us…'

Clare had just come out of the warm cloakroom and was standing on the hotel steps: an unseasonably cold wind was blowing and she was fastening her jacket. It was beautifully cut, bought in a sale at Harvey Nicholls in Manchester. 'Wow! It's by You-Know-Who!' Emma had exclaimed when she'd fingered the label.

Now she was struggling to fasten the buttons on this expensive jacket designed by someone who ought to know better than to use these really fiddly coat fastenings. She'd succeeded in fastening two, then realised she was lop-sided. They were, of course, as difficult to unfasten as they were to fasten: a task made worse by the fact that her mind wasn't really concentrating fully on button-fastening.

Oh fuck what a mess!

She'd panicked and just started gabbling away up there in that bar, before saying that she would have to leave. God knows what he thought of her! He was going to ask her out, wasn't he? Ask her out! – God, that sounded so twee. But it was only a few days since they both could have been killed. The reason she was down here was because of a disastrous relationship started at a stressful time right in the middle of a case where four people were murdered. Clare had tried to ignore the feeling, to put it to the back of her mind, but she'd been aware for some time of the growing attraction between herself and Rob Ellis – even though they seemed a bit like a couple of magnetic hand grenades.

She cursed under her breath. Yes, it was too soon. That was shit timing, Welshman. And sod these buttons, the car's not far and –

A dog was looking at her.

A large dog.

A Wolfhound.

A familiar looking Wolfhound.

'Wyneb?'

The hound stared straight through her, turned, and padded-off.

'Same to you Fuck-Face!' she snapped.

Clare started to walk towards the car park. She hadn't got that right. Wyneb was the dog's name, which means 'Face'. She remembered that when Ellis swore at him in the pub garden he'd shouted 'Wyneb Cach'. *Cach* means shit. So it was Shit-Face.

Her Welsh grammar revision came to a sudden halt.

The woman was tall and slim. The *sort* that would look good in a bin bag – but ironically the *sort* that only ever seem to wear expensive, perfectly fitting clothes. This one looked as if she was in a photo shoot for Country Life. Chestnut brown hair cut so simply it must have cost a fortune, tight brown cords tucked into long boots and a short dark tweed cape. What are they called? Yes, a Dubliner cape. She looks so Irish anyway – even more so now as the Irish wolfhound starts to nuzzle against her legs. Of course, it's her dog! She's Ellis's friend who he was looking after the dog for.

Him, *him* and his friend, his Irish friend, were deep in

conversation. They were unaware of her approach.

'It's strange meeting you here. I must rush. I won't be late tonight, I promise,' said Ellis to the woman… who then reached up and kissed him on the cheek.

'Hello.'

Ellis swung round, 'Oh – this, this is –'

'Clare Morell.'

'Hi, I'm Mair Griffiths,' responded the woman, in a soft, but distinctive, Welsh accent.

Clare took a quick breath.

Damn! Of course – the dog's name. Well done, Miss Marple.

'Do you work at the college?' asked Clare.

'No… I'm at the hospital.' Mair Griffiths's shrewd green eyes were busy.

Clare straightened her back. Yes, go ahead Phony Irishwoman, she thought. Hair couldn't be better; great shoes bought on holiday in Rome, Diesel jeans *and* an expensive jacket, by 'You Know Who'.

Buttoned up… wrong.

Fuck.

'Mair's a paediatrician.'

They ignored him.

'I've not been here long, but Robert and I go back a long way,' said the woman, turning and smiling at the uncomfortable looking lecturer.

Oh, do you.

Clare forced a smile and pointed at the dog. 'I've met your Wolfhound before when *Robert* and I were having a drink. I even remember his name because *Robert* kept shouting it when he ran off. It's Wyneb Cach isn't it?'

She had the satisfaction of seeing the dog's ears drop, also the change in the woman, as she turned towards Ellis was amazing. Rob Ellis himself was looking at the ground – presumably praying for a miracle that a hole would suddenly open up, large enough for all of his six-foot-two to drop into.

Then, rather impressively regaining her composure, Mair Griffiths turned to Clare and smiled. 'You're obviously not at the college either. What do you do?'

'Clare's a–'

Ellis, in response to the double look, shut-up like a clam: lesser mortals would have dropped dead on the spot.

'I'm a police officer. *Robert* here is helping us with our enquiries,' answered Clare – leaving the other woman, the final cut… the *coup de gras.*

Her words came like ice. 'Oh, I do hope that he's not in any trouble.'

Clare drove straight home from the Marine Hotel. She quickly changed into her running gear – losing a couple of buttons off a ridiculously expensive jacket in the process. She left the flat and ran recklessly fast down the flight of steep steps that lead to the old harbour side. A few minutes later, after leaving the cosy cluster of quaint pubs and gift shops, she turned onto the esplanade and caught, full-face, the cold east wind that had been blowing for days. Just before Bellini's café, she went down onto the beach and running on the firm sand left between the tides and with streaming eyes, narrowed and almost hidden behind her cheek bones – she lengthened her stride and covered the whole curve of the beach, and back, faster than she'd ever done before.

30

The catch on the driver's door of the old GTI was getting worse. It took two very loud slams before it closed.

'You could have tried the doorbell – it works a treat.'

Clare swung round. Patrick Isherwood was standing in the doorway.

She laughed. 'I'm sorry!' she said and pointed to the Porsche. 'I apologise for parking my load of junk next to your car.'

'Oh, don't.' He'd joined her. 'It comes with the job. It's obscene isn't it? Damn nuisance in some ways as well, it's like a red rag to a bull.'

Clare nodded. Yes, she could see Grimace and Vomit blowing a gasket trying to book one of these. 'I hope I'm not too early.'

'No problem, I didn't have to go in to London. I met a client half way. I've been back some time.'

'Beautiful spot on a lovely evening,' said Clare, turning towards the lake.

'Yes, indeed. Shall we walk down there? There's a great view of the downs from the edge of the trees.'

'Thank you for seeing me,' said Clare, as they reached the steps to the lawn that sloped down to the lake. 'I'm really sorry to bother you just before you go away.'

'It's my pleasure, Inspector Morell. Anyway, I'm curious as to why you want to see me again'.

Clare took the line that the inquiry was solely concerned

with trying to locate Sonia Nichol's family, or close friends – which was true, as far as it went. She got round to it slowly. She explained that they were desperately following all leads. It was delicate, she said, but they had heard a rumour that Sonia Nichol was gay and perhaps, as her neighbour, he might know if she had a partner. If this was so, Clare, of course, understood perfectly why he'd not mentioned it on the first interview.

By this time they were standing on the edge of the lake. She turned towards him. Isherwood looked astonished, then he told her that, as far as he was concerned, the rumour couldn't be further from the truth. The young man then became embarrassed as he explained that after his first few weeks living here, he gave Sonia Nichol as wide a berth as possible – as she'd tried everything short of physical violence, in trying to get him into bed.

Clare smiled to herself.

Yes, her and how many more? Karen was right then: his lord and her ladyship were lying. So, why the hell was Sonia Nichol kicked out of the Borne Hunt?

They walked slowly back to the house. Clare felt better. She was glad to have put some distance between herself and the town… between her and Rob Ellis… and his Phony Irishwoman.

She was sitting on a sofa watching Isherwood who was looking out of the huge bay window. The light was fading. The sofa was low: she reached for the glass of wine he'd poured her. He turned away from the window, but instead of returning to the arm chair he surprised her by sitting close to her on the sofa.

'I don't want you to get the wrong idea about me, about what I said earlier about poor Sonia. She just wasn't my type.

The truth is, I like women a lot… especially at this very moment. There's something about your eyes that–'

'Shit!' Clare jumped to her feet having spilt most of a glass of red wine over her white blouse.

Isherwood picked up an open bottle of Chardonnay from the table – his other hand slipped round her waist. 'They do say, Detective Inspector, that treating red wine stain immediately with a *really thorough* soaking of white… can work wonders.'

Where are they? She was talking to herself as she looked everywhere. She lifted up and folded back, this and that. Oh, shit, is that the time! Where the fuck are they? What have I done? Stupid question – but how the hell did all that happen?

She was standing close to the window: something caught her eye. There, there through the trees, on the other side of the lake. It's him! He's coming back from a run! Running! He'd no right to be out running! He's stopped. He's pushing on a tree. Good, he's going to do his stretching. There may be time. Clare really didn't want to see him, really didn't want to see him. She grabbed her handbag and had one more glance around the bedroom, before going out onto the landing.

There was a full-length mirror at the top of the stairs. She looked like the equivalent of being dragged through a hedge, several times – which was about right. Well, it was three times to be precise. But at least the jacket looked alright, fastened, it covered up the lack of a blouse underneath.

She turned to go down the stairs. The stairs! Shit, the stairs! Oh, God, she'd remembered! She looked. They're still there.

She rushed down the wide staircase, her head throbbing – continually muttering 'Mistake! Mistake!' in time with every tread, and then, with barely a pause as she retrieved her knickers from the newel post, she ran down the hall and out of the door.

'Did you get anything from that merchant banker guy, boss?'

Fortunately DC Karen Garland was staring at her computer screen as she spoke.

'Err, yes,' answered Clare, struggling to gain some composure. 'Sonia Nicholl was definitely not gay.'

Karen punched the air. 'Yes! I knew those stable girls had been told to lie by his lord and ladyship.'

Karen said nothing more and Clare – although she was pretending to study some papers on her desk – realised she was being stared at. She looked across. The young policewoman had her head to one side. There was a frown on her face. 'Boss, why didn't you mention this when you came in?

Clare was saved by the bell – or rather by a knock on the door. The desk sergeant came in. 'There's a Mr Josh Legge to see you, ma'am. He said it's very urgent.'

'Bring him up.'

'Mr Legge is waiting in the courtyard. He's got this big dog with him. I've never seen one like it before; he said it was a Maring something-or-other.'

'Maremma,' corrected Karen. 'It's an Italian sheepdog.'

'Whatever. Anyway it's really nice looking.'

'Nice looking it may be, but it's got a hell of a bite,' said Clare.

'Takes one to know one, I suppose,' muttered the desk sergeant as he left.

Clare turned towards Karen. 'What?'

The young policewoman was struggling to straighten her face. 'Well, word got around that you chewed the sarge's balls off after he punched Grimace and dropped you in it when you had to sign that dodgy accident report.'

'Right, I wonder what Josh Legge wants?' said Clare out-loud, as she reached the door. She began walking towards the back stairs, glad to get out of the office. She was still shell-shocked after the events of the last twenty four hours. There was that weird meeting with Travers, followed by her panicky blustering when she'd left Ellis and then that bitchy playground encounter with the Griffiths woman. Yes, Rob Ellis is a bastard – trying to be a two-timer. And then to cap it all, she'd woken up in a strange bed this morning, after–. She caught her reflection in the glass and quickly looked away as she pushed open the outside door.

The Maremma rose from its haunches, shook itself, and then padded across the courtyard.

'Hello, Paulo,' said Clare as she rubbed his ears.

Josh Legge, was sitting on a bench. Clare and the dog walked over to him.

'Hello, how are you?' asked the shepherd as he got to his feet.

'I'm fine,' Clare put on a smile as they sat down and the dog curled round her legs like a huge white fur boot.

'Lal Cooper asked me – no, in fact told me – to come and see you personally, to say that she wants to see you, only you, as soon as possible.'

'Any idea what it's about?'

'No, but she says it's important. It's a puzzle to me this, I've never heard of Romanies offering to help the police before. You're not part-gypsy are you?'

'Of course not,' said Clare – as she took hold of his hand and turned it palm-up. 'Now, let's have a look.'

A piece of wattle fence acted as a gate across the narrow gap in the hedge. She could see three Romany caravans. Clare remembered the name; they were called vardos. Two women, one was very young, were sitting in front of the fire, which as always, she assumed, had the large blackened kettle hooked over it. The elder of the women – it was Lal Cooper – raised a hand in greeting. Clare responded and then barely needed to move the wattle-fencing in order to slip past.

As last time, the lurchers resting by the caravans, raised an eyelid at the most, but now even the puppy made no noise. It just came towards her, and as puppies do, rather than just wagging its tail, appeared to be wagging everything.

'*Sastimos,*' greeted Clare as she approached the women – using up about a fifth of her Romany in the process.

Lal Cooper laughed, '*Sastimos* – well you've wasted no time getting here *Rakli-Yak.*'

She remembered that. It's the 'Non-Romany woman with the eyes'.

'Watching you squeeze in like that, you're getting as thin as a stick, you and the fair woman, running like mountain hares. We've seen you.'

'Crystal ball?'

'Yes. Go up to the vardo,' said the Romany woman, pointing to the caravan just to Clare's left.

Clare walked up the steps of the caravan. There were wide sweeping views above the hedge row. She could follow the creamy white trail of the drovers' track almost as far as the main road and, to the south, the undulation of the ridgeway from Chalcombe Bumps to Drovers' Knoll and beyond. She laughed when she spotted, just inside the vardo door, a large ancient brass telescope.

As Clare came back down the steps, the Romany continued her teasing. 'I saw you with a long haired, longshanks as well. There was more than one storm going on when you were both on the Knoll.'

Ignoring the remark, Clare sat down on the empty stool

between the two women and turned to the young one. She was as pretty as the photograph she'd seen on her last visit, and was what? Sixteen? Seventeen at the most? 'You're Dora.'

'Yes, lady,' came the shy reply.

'I miss her,' said Lal Cooper. 'She's at her man's camp and away from all that stuff. And she's happy – well it's like that when you're just wed all–'

'*Shoska porada*,' said Clare, using up the rest of her Romany the wrong way round, though as it translated as 'tent pole erections', rather than 'erections like tent poles' – nothing was lost by the grammatical mistake. Lal laughed, Dora blushed – and Clare, immediately feeling really bad about being a smart-arse and embarrassing the young woman, apologised.

Lal poured some tea and for a minute or two, the three black-haired women, in a close half-circle, and looking like a covey of ravens, leant forward with their heads near together – supping tea from the mugs they were holding.

Clare, for the first time in days, felt her shoulders relaxing: there was a comforting, strangely homely feeling here that – then it came out of the blue.

'It's about Red Sonia, the dead woman,' said Dora, followed by hisses from the fire as Clare spluttered her tea.

Even if Clare had wanted to say something over the next few minutes, she would have had difficulties in getting a word in edgeways – she just sat there, clutching her mug, as the two other women explained what they'd heard on the Romany grapevine.

There were three small Romany camps on the ridgeway; the Coopers, the Farrs – where Dora now lived – and the Hughes. The Hughes' traditional camp was just above Tallington Farm, and they'd been told by the farmer that the police were asking questions following the death of the red haired woman at the House, who was killed when her big silver car caught fire. Dora said that she knew who it was as soon as she had heard, and after talking to her mother, Lal had got a message to Josh Legge to pass to Clare.

'How do you know this woman – this Red Sonia?' asked Clare, at a moment when both the other women had paused for breathe. Obviously, because of the nickname, it had to be red haired Sonia Nichol. But Red Sonia? It rang a bell.

'I was coming to that, miss. It was at the hippy camp. I'd heard her name mentioned, I don't think I was supposed to. She never came there, but I saw her once and that big silver car near where the track comes up from the road.'

Clare nodded. It must be the one she drove down with Ellis and James Travers. Sonia Nichol's 4x4 could have managed the steep track easily enough.

'What was she doing, Dora?'

'She was talking to the Shopkeepers, miss.'

'The Shopkeepers?'

Dora looked at Clare as if she was from a different planet. 'The men called the Shopkeepers; the ones who sell stuff from their vans – they also sell down in the town.'

'Drugs?'

'That's it, miss,' said Dora, with a smile. The sort of smile an adult gives a small child when they've done well.

'So, these "Shopkeepers" were buying drugs she'd brought up in her car?'

'Oh, no, she wouldn't do that! Someone else brought the gear up in a van.'

Shit! It's like Tesco's Home Deliveries.

'How often did this happen, Dora? Can you tell me anything about who came?'

'He came up quite a bit. I heard him called Neil: he had this old white van.'

'Was there anything unusual about the van?'

'Well, miss, he often had dogs in it. They barked like mad, but he wouldn't let them out because of the dogs at the camp.'

Clare blew out between her teeth. Neil Frampton the terrier man. *The case is all about drugs. It's fuck-all to do with Animal Rights.*

'More tea?' said Lal, as she gently touched Clare's arm. Clare nodded – her mind in overdrive. 'You pour it daughter. So, you see why we got our girl here away from there. There are bad people there. I told you about the drugs before – but no coppers have been bothering them. They shouldn't be here.'

Of course, that's really what this is about! That's why she's been told! The Travellers are a problem to the Romanies as well as to the farmers: Josh Legge himself has shot their dogs that were worrying his flock. Lal and others want police raids and that big camp broken up. Clare had been told by Simmonds not to go near the camp because the Drugs Squad were watching it. Lal and the others must have interpreted the lack of action as police lethargy or incompetence. So, she's using the death of Sonia Nichol to have another go and rightly expects a favour in return for the information.

'I'll see what I can do about them, Lal – I promise,' said Clare and then changed tack. 'Dean Galpin was at the camp quite a bit. Was he dealing drugs?'

'Oh no, miss. He probably got his straight from this Neil, as he knew him, and not from the Shopkeepers. Galpin used to sell ciggy tobacco.'

Right, part of the contraband tobacco shifting. So, why the hell was he shot? It makes no sense.

'Was he there for any other reason as well? He had a reputation for women.'

'Not there, miss! They live man and woman together, though…' the young woman fell silent.

'Though what, Dora?' asked Clare gently.

'Well, he did try once – when he were drunk. I stopped him.'

'How, he was a big strong man, Dora?'

The young woman pulled up the left sleeve of her shirt, uncovering a long leather wrist strap. She took something from it. There was a 'click': a second later Clare found herself looking at an open stiletto blade.

'I didn't see that,' said Clare, noticing at the same time that Lal Cooper was, surreptitiously, pulling down the cuff of her own left sleeve.

She remembered something from the mortuary, remembered that apart from the bullet wound to the heart, the puncture wound that Nick Howarth had pointed out, high up on the left leg of the dead man.

'Where?'

Dora Cooper patted her left thigh.

Clare drove in through the arched gateway and into the parade ground of the Old Barracks. She was glad to get home – or was until she saw an old Volvo estate.

How long has he been here?

She parked in her space, got out of the car and began walking towards it. Ellis had seen her; he was already out of the vehicle and arms folded, leaning against it before she was within twenty yards.

'What the fuck was going on yesterday?' he snapped, as she walked up to him.

'You tell me.'

'You were unbelievable with Mair. You didn't give me a chance!'

'A chance to say what exactly? Oh, here's my girlfriend. Oh, here's my lover – we go back a long way!'

'And if I did, or didn't, after the peculiar way you reacted in the bar, why the hell should you care anyway? I'll tell you something. I've known Mair, since, since forever. We grew up together – our mothers are best friends. Oh, yes, they did hope for us, and yes, we went out on a date when we were about fourteen and laughed – it seemed so silly. You see we're the brother and sister neither of us ever had.'

Clare felt as if she'd been hit in the stomach. How could she get it all so wrong, and then react by sleeping with someone who was in Primary Five when she was in university? Well, knowing her track record – easily.

She'd not seen him angry like this; Ellis, red faced and breathing heavily, paused for breath. Clare thought he was calming down a little.

Wrong.

'She adores that dog. She dotes on it. Now, because of you she thinks I let it run wild when I was supposed to be looking after it. We had a row last night. I think the last one we had was when we were about five when I pinched her sweets. Christ, woman! You know, I wished I'd have packed in helping you that time I was not only insulted but got fucking soaked – I could have caught double pneumonia or pleurisy and–'

'Don't exaggerate – typical man – I got as wet as you!' she shouted, as she hugged herself. 'No, wetter,' she added, remembering the embarrassment of being soaked through wearing a thin blouse, and an equally thin bra… and that was before being called butch.

31

Every fortnight, or so, The Lerret, the harbour side fish restaurant at the foot of the steep flight of steps that lead up to the Old Barracks – the flats where Clare and Emma live – tries out a new 'Special', at a sharp price.

Tonight was 'Special' night and the two women were here – as usual. They were sitting in the quiet corner – as usual. Clare, however, was anything but *usual*. She hadn't wanted to come, but Emma, who wasn't having that, had virtually dragged her here. Clare looked across the table at Bossy Boots who was flirting with a waiter. Emma, blond hair loose to her shoulders was looking fantastic after all the running they'd been doing. Clare had doubts about herself. The words of an aunt from when she was a skinny kid had come back to haunt her; 'You're looking like Little Orphan Annie.' – whoever Little Orphan Annie was, but she knew what her aunt meant.

The waiter, who was leaning over Emma's shoulder, was explaining tonight's menu. He'd been going on-and-on about chef's zero tolerance policy towards anyone serving unopened mussels and was now explaining chef's narrow asparagus-spear-cooking-window rule of fifteen seconds max, either side of perfect. Clare glared at the waiter, but he didn't notice because he was giving Emma's cleavage his undivided attention. He then began talking about the fondant potatoes, which apparently, apart from the occasional good shake of the pan, largely look after themselves. Oh, just fuck-off, thought Clare, but he didn't until an angry shout from the kitchens forced him to reluctantly drag himself away.

The main course, without fail, only ever travelled overland, all of the accurately measured distance – in old money – of sixteen yards and two feet from the harbour side mooring to the stove: appropriate for a fish restaurant named after an old local type of fishing boat. Today's fare was pan-fried sea bream. Nigel the chef inevitably made an appearance. He came over to chat and show-off his new sauce. 'Chervil and Armagnac,' he announced.

Nigel had once been sous-chef at a restaurant a couple of miles from Clare's old home in that posh northern borderland where the Cheshire Plain meets the Pennines – and where now, 'old' and 'new' money have at last something in common in that they both turn up their noses at those latest *arrivants*… footballers and their women. Just as Nigel was leaving their table he mouthed, 'What's up with her?' to Emma.

Clare noticed.

They were never in a hurry to close at The Lerret. Clare and Emma were alone in a deserted restaurant. A little earlier, Nigel had left the remains of the bottle of Armagnac on their table before going back to the kitchens to eat spaghetti bolognaise and drink beer with his staff.

Emma took a sip from her wineglass, which was half-full with brandy. 'I'd like a coffee with this,' she said after she'd put her glass down and looked across the empty tables to the open door to the kitchens – the source of chatter and laughter.

'Get your tits out again, then.'

Emma, who'd slipped on her jacket, looked across at Clare with a deadpan face. 'I don't know what you mean,' she said and then frowned. 'You're a miserable bitch tonight.'

Clare nodded and pointed to a large photograph of an

aristocratic looking woman on the wall. Nigel was an Elizabeth David disciple. In fact, one of tonight's sweets, they'd been told by the ogling waiter, was a *Crème Aux Fraises* from her *French Provincial Cooking*. 'There was an article in the paper the other day, about her; we have something in common.'

'You're a crap cook!'

'I'm not when I concentrate!' protested Clare. She leant back in her seat. 'No, it's that she was rubbish with guys as well.'

'I wasn't going to talk about it tonight, but the Hairy Celt had a point didn't he? What the hell was it to you anyway, seeing him with that Mair woman?' Emma paused as she reached across the table and prodded Clare in the arm, 'especially as you'd knocked him back about ten minutes earlier. I've thought for some time, when you've been going on about him. How does it go? – "This protesting cow doth moan too much".'

'Anyway, if I can get a word in, he has had his hair trimmed, and secondly, what do you mean?' said Clare as she tipped brandy into her glass.

'Well, think about it. You're always going on about him. You seem to fight every time you meet. I've not met him *yet,* but obviously you're both, in lots of different ways, a complete pain in the arse. You're perfect for each other. So –' Emma leaning forward, rested on her elbows, her hands cupping her chin. She lowered her voice, even though the place was deserted. 'So, this hesitancy you have, you're not like that in other things. And it's nothing to do with that fiasco with the Gay Hussar – it was something in the North, wasn't it? Look, girl, I'll make you a deal. You tell me everything – absolutely everything – and I won't pry. Now, I can't be fairer than that, can I?'

Clare nodded and took another sip of the pale Armagnac:

the brandy, with a tradition much older than Cognac, from the slopes of Gascony – ironically only seventy miles or so, from where the rifle, bullets and explosive, which were causing her so much trouble, came from. 'I was a senior officer on the Langford Killings investigation team,' she said quietly with her head lowered, before looking up at Emma. Emma had a hand over her mouth. 'Yes, the DIY Massacres as the gutter scribes called them. Four victims; the first killed with a Stanley knife, the second with a screwdriver, the third with a hammer, and the last with a spanner.'

Clare paused and gave a little reassuring smile as her friend reached across the table to take her hands. 'It's alright. I've not talked about it to anyone since I came down here, so it's probably a good thing.' She took a breath. 'Graham Styles was mad, but clever, and somehow he found out who was getting close to him. He made threats, and to add to the postman, the pensioner, the young mum, and the fifteen year old schoolgirl, there was nearly a fifth victim, a policewoman… me. Styles was in my house, holding a chisel – I got lucky with a kitchen stool.'

Emma looked horrified.

'That was kept quiet somehow because my superiors had made a cock-up of protecting me and I was in shock and didn't want to be in the limelight, anyway. The official report stated that he was arrested outside.'

Emma, her face drained of colour, looked thoughtful. 'I seem to remember that there was something about Styles being subject to some very heavy-handed policing, in that he looked as if he'd been really kicked and beaten up when he was charged.'

'I didn't call for back-up straight away,' said Clare quietly.

The kitchen of the Lerret was quieter now; most of the staff had gone home. But there was still no pressure on the two women to leave as Nigel lived in the flat above the restaurant. He'd brought out a pot of coffee for them. They'd been quiet for a while; then Clare spoke again.

'It was a hell of a time. One DI went off with stress and there was tremendous pressure on my DCI and me to get a result as the murder count went up. Jack and I started living in each other's pockets, sharing everything… including our beds. It got serious for me, but not for him – he dumped me eventually. Then a couple of months later his wife turns up at the station with three kids under five in tow and calls me out in front of everyone. I found out later that he'd been having it away with someone else, his wife had got suspicious, and so he told her about us thinking she would be more forgiving because he was under pressure at the time of the Longford case. She did, and blamed me and not him.'

'What a bastard! What happened?'

'Well the brass thought the sun shone out of his arse. He got the credit, though I'd made the key breakthrough. He's now a detective superintendent in the North East. A promotion to chief inspector was on the cards for me, but as I was by that time generally known as "The Home Wrecker", I had to get away. Putting distance between me and where it all happened has helped anyway. I had Acute Stress Reaction after the case, mainly headaches, but they are getting fewer and fewer and much less intense and…'

The last of the kitchen staff left and the two women got ready to leave so that Nigel could lock-up. Emma gave Clare a hug so tight that it was difficult to breathe, and then, as she broke away, she held Clare's hands and smiled. 'You're scared stiff of commitment, but you know that Young Darcy, the banker guy, who hit on you when you interviewed him–'

'He's in Hong Kong.'

'Well, you should be kicking yourself! Think about it – no strings. You should have seen him again and shagged him when you had the chance… What?'

Part Three

32

Clare turned towards the young policewoman, who, hair blowing in a strong onshore breeze, was alongside her. They were sitting on a bench, on the cliff top that rose up from the long beach that stretched down from the town. Karen's mobile rang. She looked at it.

'My mum,' she said apologetically. She got to her feet and walked a few yards away before she answered it. Clare looked down the coast at the headlands that cradled the bays and the little towns to the west. She remembered laughing when Rob Ellis had joked about Age-Concern rally team pensioners speeding-along in their motability scooters, down there along the Costa Geriatrica esplanades.

'Sorry, Mum. I have to go. See you later.' Karen switched off the phone and pointed. 'They're here, boss.'

Clare turned her head. A man and a woman, accompanied by a small dog, were approaching on the otherwise deserted coastal footpath. They were walking quickly. The man was wearing long lace-up boots, old jeans and a shabby parka: his T-shirt had 'Cyderdelic' printed on it. He was bearded and wore a beanie hat. Clare thought that DS Danny Breen of the Drug Squad looked a bit like Badly Drawn Boy.

The woman, also wearing a beanie, wore a nose ring, heavy combat trousers and a parka that was even filthier than the one worn by her companion. DC Rach McFadden was unusual for the Drugs Squad in three respects; she hadn't been in the force for long, she was an ex-bored research chemist – and, well, she was a she.

They were all meeting because Simmonds had authorised Clare to inform Breen about Sonia Nicol and Frampton's drug connections.

'Wotcha, ladies,' greeted Breen, exaggerating his Cockney. He sat down next to Karen. 'Thanks for the call, Clare. We really hadn't got a fucking clue about that Red Sonia and the Travellers – though we'd been around them for ages, sniffing about.'

'Smelling, more like,' observed Karen.

'Give us a cuddle, Karen.'

'Augh! Get off, Danny!'

'Can youse push up a wee bit?' asked Rach McFadden. The others shuffled along and the Glaswegian pulled the dog into her legs as she sat down. 'He's a whippet-cross.'

'What with, a floor mop?'

Breen gave Karen a smack across her knees. 'Don't, we're having enough trouble with him as it is. He's a picky eater.'

'What's his name?' asked Clare, leaning forward to speak to Rach McFadden at the other end of the bench.

'Raymond.'

Clare caught Karen's eye. They had perfected a straight faced routine recently, as despite themselves they had found it impossible not to keep winding Andy Melbury up. Except about his diet of course – there are some things you just don't joke about.

'Oh, I've just remembered what the sarge told me about the name Red Sonia,' said Karen. 'It was some fantasy film.'

'Yes, I remember that. The film star was a *big* girl.' Breen held his arms some distance in front of his chest. 'What?' he said looking at the women in turn… making his second, third and fourth bad moves.

'That's exactly what Andy said… and *did*,' said Karen, by way of explanation.

'Thanks for not going into the Travellers' camp mob-handed,' said Breen moving quickly on.

'Simmonds warned me off,' answered Clare, still leaning forward.

'Not that we've got in there. We'd almost certainly have got sussed quite quickly if we'd spent any time with them. Most of them know each other from a long while back. There's old Peace Convoy lot, even Battle of the Bean Field vets.'

'Battle-of-the-what?'

'Bean Field, it was about twenty years ago and not one of our finest moments. Check it on the web later, Karen,' said Clare – anxious to get on.

'So we just have a chat with some when they come into town on benefit day. They sometimes meet near the pier or at The White Dog,' said Breen.

Clare nodded. The White Dog was about the only pub that will serve them. Then she rubbed her neck. She was going to crick it with all this leaning forward and turning.

'Well,' said Breen. 'We're interested in them because they seem a good bet for a lead because of the type of gear that's coming in. They've got rules; anyone spiking-up gets the boot, coke's not their bag, but this triple-X THC skunk coming in is the business and –'

'What's THC?' Karen interrupted Breen in full flow.

'Tetrahydrocannibino,' stated ex-research chemist Rach McFadden as she stroked the dog.

'The correct technical term is Brain-Fucker – this is serious dope,' clarified Breen.

'Aye, it's nay soap-bar shite.'

'Also,' Breen said, picking up from where he was interrupted. 'There are large quantities of White Dove and Butterfly tabs being shipped-in.'

Clare leaning forward again, gave Karen a shut-up-look in

passing and caught Rach McFadden's eye. 'How do you read this, Rach?'

'Red Sonia's big fish feed must know we're looking for him – and not just us. He'll be scooting himself thinking he's next for the crem, assuming that someone really heavy wants to muscle in. You know Clare, I think the guy with the terriers–'

'Neil Frampton.'

'Aye, Frampton. He's yesterday's man. Big fish up the food chain probably won't replace Red Sonia – he'll concentrate on other channels, though it's no always easy.'

Breen was nodding his head. 'That's right, Rach, though it's possible that Frampton may have an idea where Red Sonia got the stuff. He might go looking. Most in his situation get used to the money, he might start getting desperate. We've got him watched since your call, Clare. We might be lucky in that he's not done this yet.'

Clare leaned forward again and turned her head. 'So, if this surveillance of Frampton goes OK, Danny, we can, hopefully, identify the next victim before our killer gets to him – and you can have a drugs result as well. But we'll leave it as your shout.'

'Fair enough. That's as much as we can do for now, so we'll be off,' said Breen. He touched Clare's arm. 'Are you alright? You look a bit under the –'

'I'm fine,' she said sharply.

As they drove back into town, Clare got that old sinking feeling. Drugs… so many times it's drugs. Karen, sensing her mood, fell quiet – even when they passed Queen Victoria's statue: her Majesty was today sporting a Girls Aloud cap at a very jaunty angle.

Clare was not amused either.

Because of road works she turned off onto the avenue that skirted the park. The children's play area had been re-vamped since Clare had last driven past: it was now all stainless steel and bright panels with ropes and complex climbing sections – like a mini SAS assault course. There was also a new finger post which said Teenage Area.

'What the hell's down there, Karen – special bins for their needles?' she said bitterly, as she pointed at it.

'Probably, boss. But they've also got a *special* free condom machine… there's GCSE revision questions on the packets.'

Clare laughed… then looked across at her young DC, who was now with her so much as Matt Johns was away.

'What?'

'Nothing, Karen.'

Thanks Karen, she thought.

I wonder if the ghosts of the harbour masters are with me now, on the upper floor of this abandoned building, looking down – just as they used to – from this jutting bay window to the mouth and both sides of this narrow harbour.

Are they watching the ships under sail, skilfully ease into their moorings? Are they deciding which ones need searching for contraband brandy and wine? Or which ones, when there is cholera in the Isles, or France, to quarantine? And are the younger ghosts fretting over why the steam packet mail is late? Or, getting anxious that the stevedores are too slow unloading the season's first tomatoes, new potatoes and daffodils, as other ships, with the same perishable cargo, are waiting in the bay?

Now, only local fishing boats are moored. But, I'm not interested. I'm looking across the water, to the other side of the harbour, at the alleyway between the fishing tackle shop and the small art gallery… that's the alley that leads to the White Dog.

Perhaps it will be tonight? As a boy I was taught to stay still for hours, eyes straining with concentration, when stalking a kill; so the last few nights sitting here, with a flask at my side, and night-binoculars on my lap, have been no hardship.

He is a creature of habit; when he comes into town in the evening he always parks that old transit of his in the old brewery square and cuts through to the White Dog. Is he in there now gaining Dutch courage? I'm positive he's been told in the past, never to go to the red-haired woman's supplier in any circumstances, but he will. He looked jittery enough after I'd shot his dog, let alone after I'd eliminated her… and he'll be missing the drug money.

There's someone coming out of the entry! Let's have a closer look. No, he's too tall…

It could be him. He's the right height and build. He's taking something out of his pocket. It's a tin, he opens it. He picks a ready-made roll up out of it, puts it in his mouth and searches for his matches. His face lights up as he strikes one.

It's him. It's the Terrier Man.

Why is he going that way? Ah, he's going into the Fryer Tuck. I've got time for a last drink from the flask, before I get ready to follow…

He's leaning on the railings opposite the fish and chip restaurant. He throws the occasional chip down into the water. Grey mullet cruise around the moorings over there. He looks around at a group of youngsters gathered around a bench a few yards away. They are trying to push chips into each other's hoods and are spraying each other with coke or something. Suddenly, he's moving; screwing up the chip paper, he drops it into a waste bin and now he's walking back along the harbour. It's almost exactly 11.00. He's walking fast. He's made up his mind and he knows exactly where he's going. He passes the entry to the White Dog and walks towards the bridge. I thought he would, it seems highly likely that Mr Big must be this side of the harbour where the clubs are, near to where the red haired woman's dress shop was.

He's getting closer to the bridge. Well, well, just seconds after he passes the Lerret restaurant, a figure appears from the shadows by the steep steps alongside, pauses, then follows. I think he's been tailed. The Terrier Man turns on to the bridge. Good, he's coming over this side. The tail is dropping back. Where's the next pick-up? The Terrier Man comes down the bridge steps and begins walking up this side of the harbour towards me, past two people who are watching a fisherman hose-down the deck of his crabber, under an arc cast by the streetlight. I don't think it's them. Yes, there. A figure has emerged from nowhere and follows carefully. The Terrier Man pauses and glances back. The tail has disappeared back into the shadows. He's a natural. The Terrier Man is coming past me now. He'll probably turn into the town soon. And here's the tail. That he is a she; a scruffy young woman dressed like a crusty. She's good. Too good, she's looking around – and up. I think I stepped back from the window in time. The Terrier Man disappears and the girl breaks into a jog. Another figure is running from the opposite direction. The Terrier Man has turned into the passageway called Monk's Way. It leads into a complex maze of little medieval alleyways called the Drongs which double back on themselves. There is only one way out, under an archway onto St Adhelms Street, where the clubs and busy pubs are.

And I can get there before him.

33

Clare, feeling tired and pissed-off in equal measure, was thinking how nice it would be to walk out of this CID office right now, get in her car, stop at the bakery half-way up the hill to her flat, and then, with the warm croissant (with lots of *proper* butter and *lashings* of jam) and a big cafetiere of coffee on the little table in front of her… curl up on the sofa with her old, well-thumbed copy of Jane Eyre.

She'd come back into the station last night when she'd had a call from Danny Breen telling her that the drugs squad were tailing Frampton as he'd gone into town. He'd kept her informed throughout about what was happening. He'd been furious when his team lost Frampton by the harbour. Frampton was next seen after midnight with a bruised face and a bloody nose. He was followed back to his transit van, and then he drove home. Breen came into the station at about one in the morning, where he and Clare had gone over things before deciding that there was nothing more they could do immediately.

Clare did not return to her flat until after two. It was now eight thirty and she was back here. DS Andy Melbury sat alongside her and DC Karen Garland opposite. They'd just had a call from the desk sergeant that DS Danny Breen, who was the senior drugs squad officer in this case, was on his way up.

Breen knocked on the door before coming in. Clare was surprised, and more than a little envious, that he didn't look at all like someone who, after a stressful night, had little sleep. He was all "bright eyed and bushy tailed" – well beard anyway, though somehow he'd found time to trim that, as well as wash his hair. He'd also ditched the crusty clothes and was wearing jeans, a plain black T-shirt and a bomber jacket. He looked really good and years younger. Instinct triggered Clare to glance at Karen… and sure enough, Little Miss Libido was giving Breen a thorough up-and-down going over.

Breen and the two women exchanged greetings. He sat down and he and Melbury nodded to each other.

Melbury then swung back on his chair, which responded with its usual creak. 'Where's Miss McCrusty then?

'Detective Constable Rachel McFadden is already out and about looking for more evidence.' replied Breen, frostily.

'Yes, well there'll be plenty of that, about how you and the rest of the Keystone fucking Cops lost Frampton, won't there?'

Clare had been trying to catch Melbury's eye but he was, deliberately she thought, leaning back and looking up at the ceiling.

'And you wouldn't have been suspicious following him? Even if dressed in a gingham frock and singing "Over the fucking rainbow", he'd still have twigged you as a copper!' snapped Breen.

'Right!!' shouted Clare as Melbury and Breen started getting to their feet. 'Both of you slap your cocks on the table *now* – then afterwards perhaps we can get on!' The two men, acting as if stuck by pins, sat down deflated, and Clare's sweep of a look also took in Karen who, slack-jawed, was speechless for once. Clare, shaking her head, wished she'd had a pound for every time she'd seen this behaviour between male cops from different sections: the rutting season lasts a full twelvemonth.

She decided to push on, pronto. 'Firstly, no one could have followed him through the Drongs – those alleyways are a nightmare. Two, CCTV has drawn a blank so far. That part of St Adhelms Street is really busy that time of night and odds are on him just crossing it, and then using the parallel back street that runs along the rear of the pubs and clubs which is poorly lit – but that's academic anyway as there's no CCTV on the back street. Agreed?'

She looked around. There was a trio of nodding heads.

'So, where do we think Neil Frampton was going to? What do you think, Karen?'

'Well, boss.' The young policewoman's hair fell around her face as she looked at her notes. 'In that stretch of St Adhelms Street near to where the Drongs come out, there are three pubs – the only really dodgy one's The Schooner – a couple of manky massage parlours and the Domino and the Cats Eyes clubs.'

'Thanks, Karen. Now, I think if we all had to put money on it being in one of those that Frampton, presumably trying to track down Sonia Nichol's supplier, got a slapping – it would be one of the night clubs. Clare looked around. She decided that the two big kids had been given enough sulking time. 'What do you think, Andy?'

'I definitely don't think it's the Cats Eyes,' said Melbury, punctuating his point by typically rocking precariously back in his chair.

Clare turned her head towards him. 'Go on.'

'Well, as you know the Cats Eyes is one of the many business interests of the Samways. They're an old local family: they've always been into something since the year dot. Their last big earner was selling electrical goods to the sailors working the East European fish factory ships that moored in the bay a few years ago. The sailors turned up with shopping lists and the Samways provided them in return for greenbacks. It was legit, sort of, as they always dealt in straight goods, bought cheap, nothing knocked-off. They're back to their old tricks now.'

'Like running that web of contraband tobacco?' asked Breen.

'Dead right, there's a family smuggling tradition after all. It's clever, the way it's run. There are a lot of family members and other locals involved and any under suspicion just lie low for a while.'

'So, why not drugs as well as tobacco?' asked Breen.

'The present Samways head of the family is called Uncle Joe. He's never had anything to do with the drugs trade; in fact he's always disliked it.'

'Yes that's true,' said Breen. 'It's never been easy for anyone dealing in the Cats Eyes club and recently my lot tell me that staff in the Cats Eyes now supervise the bogs and the rear of the premises at all times. There is also more CCTV. The place is now aggressively anti-drug. I'm damned if I know why.'

'I do.'

The other three looked at Melbury.

'I heard something recently when talking to someone who always seems to know what's going on in the town.'

Karen mouthed 'John Bellini' to Clare.

Melbury swung back on his chair again. 'The Samways are a big family. Uncle Joe has several brothers and sisters and they all have families. He's four sons but no daughters and he's always doted on his eldest niece. She's beautiful and clever. She went to Oxford; got a great job in the city of London... and now she's in rehab.'

Breen smacked his palm with a fist. 'So, that's why he's declared war. Thanks, for that, Andy.'

'That's, OK.'

Clare now felt something of a hypocrite. In the north, she

and a certain DI Janet Gregg, from a neighbouring nick – with never a hint of a ceasefire like this – always spectacularly got on each other's tits. Though, saying that, she thought, it *was* different… Jan Gregg was a first-rate bitch.

'What about the Domino Club, Danny?'

'Well, Clare, as you know it's owned by a Gavin Adams. He's forty seven and he's been down here for four years. I don't know if it's the real reason, but apparently he moved here because he's sailing mad. As far as the club is concerned, there's some pill-popping but nothing out of hand – he doesn't want to give me a reason for going in mob handed.'

'He has stayed as clean as a whistle since he's been local – I've found nothing on record,' added Karen.

'Yes, and he's something of a blank sheet before as well. He grew up in a comfortable north London family, trained as an accountant and eventually worked for an organisation that owned a casino and a couple of clubs. I can get nothing definite from my old Met contacts about them. If there was anything dodgy it was really well hidden, probably in offshore accounts… but there was a strong rumour.' Breen stopped and looked around the table.

It was Melbury who took up the baton. 'As he was an accountant and down here is a darn sight nearer the Islands where some of those bank accounts are likely to be, than London, the rumour was about money-laundering. Is that it Danny?'

'Half of it – it was money laundering of drugs money.'

Clare realised she was tapping her pen on the table.

Shit; she was turning into Yorick.

She cleared her throat, though it didn't need clearing. 'Let's assume that Adams has an ideal set-up here. He's supplying drugs and has the skill and contacts to launder the profits.'

'But surely, if Adams is the one, he must have figured out

that the death of Sonia Nicholl wasn't accidental? And, as Rach said, he must think he's next, mustn't he?'

Clare smiled. 'That's a good point, Karen. We need to find out if he's upped his personal security.'

'There's still something that makes no sense at all,' said Breen, scratching his head 'This killer of yours – unlike the Irish paramilitary groups, there's never been any evidence of ETA having any involvement with drugs.'

Clare and Breen were still sitting at the large office table, Karen was back at her desk tapping away at her keyboard, and Melbury was the other side of the room making coffees.

'So, you have no more interest in the Travellers' camp? asked Clare who was keen to settle that debt she owed Lal Cooper.

'No, Rach and I will hopefully be clean and tidy for a bit, though I don't always know what she's up to when she's following leads. Did you know that not long ago, she was dragged in here with a couple of foreign hookers?'

Clare laughed. 'Yes, it's gone down in station legend. She really looked the part. As you know, foreign working girls, even if not illegals, always take the precaution of not having any ID on them and usually make out they speak little English if cautioned. The two she was with are past masters at this. They usually work the corner by the garden centre and so the desk sergeant books them under the names of Russian Ivy and Dutch Iris. Rumour has it that when Rach tried to have a quiet word he couldn't understand her.'

Both Melbury and Karen looked round as Breen burst out laughing.

'Oh, there is something, Rach mentioned,' he said a few seconds later, then hesitated before he spoke again. 'She said it was certainly, with all the tension, her imagination running riot, but she had a weird feeling.'

'What sort of feeling?' asked Clare.

'A feeling that we were not the only ones watching Frampton.'

Karen's head jerked up as she looked over her screen and Melbury spilt some coffee as he swung round… a chair had crashed to the floor and Clare had jumped to her feet.

This coastline is showing a different face today. Well, in parts it is hardly showing one at all. There's a sea mist about. The location of the old naval base and the great gun fort that dominate the town, are from memory. It's quiet, sounds are muffled: the waves lapping at the base of the cliffs seem to be wearing kid gloves. There is barely a ripple on the water. It's slate grey. There's nothing much to see… apart from a ghost ship.

Anchored in the cove there is a two-masted sailing vessel – a brig. It's a training ship, but I can be forgiven the whimsy for calling it a ghost, because, by the greatest coincidence, on the morning of the last day of September, 1820, the brigantine Maria Crowther, lay at anchor in this same tiny cove. Two passengers had been rowed ashore. They spent an hour or so sitting on the small shingle beach and exploring the little caves of the cove before returning to ship. When the wind freshened, as it will later today, the captain, Captain Thomas Walsh, hurried the crew to make sail. Then, as the vessel crossed this bay, one of the two young men who had been ashore, opened up his copy of Shakespeare's Poems, and opposite A Lover's Complaint, penned a sonnet.

It was called 'Bright Star' and John Keats was never to write another poem… neither was he to set foot in England again. He was under the death sentence of consumption. He died in Rome, four months later.

There's the 'put-put' of an old lobster boat, as it comes out of the bank of sea mist. There is no mist onshore now. I have a clear view *down to the coastal footpath from up here…*

A sudden clatter of worn clutch plates and the grinding of tyres on loose gravel echoing up the slopes, breaks both tranquillity and atmosphere, as an old white transit swings into the quiet car park of the inn, that was once called… The Sun.

There's a moment's peace again – just a moment – before there's the yapping of dogs as three terriers race across the car park to where the coastal path starts to climb up this slope.

Thankfully, the Terrier Man is such a creature of habit. Same time, same place, every morning. He's walking slowly. Let's see up close through the scope. There is a bruise on the side of his face and sticking-plaster on his nose. I expected something like this. Thankfully he's only been given a warning, a 'don't ever come back, or else', warning – a serious beating and he wouldn't be here now. When I followed him to the back door of the Domino – I didn't hang around. Those tailing him could have been close. That woman was good.

He's breathing heavily even though he's only climbed a short distance up the path, but he's nearly level with the hawthorn bush. Close up, there's perspiration on his forehead. He's stopped. Well, he has been good. He led me to the Red Haired Woman and last night to Mr Big. And now, compliant to the end, he's stopped exactly at the spot where I shot his dog.

There is no need to alter the BD dial.

Check the compensator…

This long grass at the edge of this sycamore wood, high above the footpath, is wetter than last time – and some of the dew has transferred itself to the gun barrel.

I've just realised there's another strange coincidence: John Keats was twenty five when his death sentence was carried out.

Gentle, gentle, trigger squeeze.

Agur! Aoi!

The Terrier Man was twenty five as well.

34

Clare fell heavily against the shoulder of the police driver as he swung the car off the main road onto the narrow tree-lined lane: the lane that would end half a mile further, at the little cove and the car park... of the Galleon Inn.

'Oooh, shit!' came Karen's voice from behind her.

The traffic patrol car they were following had disappeared round the next corner, but they could still clearly hear the siren. That was not surprising; it seemed capable of shattering plate glass. This was the first time since leaving the station that Clare had not been staring at something that looked like a demented Christmas tree running amok. They'd followed as, flashing and hooting, it had bullied its way through the road works at the edge of town and then topped ninety on the straight stretch just after the Co-op Stop and Shop and the turning to Undercombe.

'I'm going to drop back a little, ma'am,' said the driver. 'Then hopefully, I'll have enough time to stop if Grimace and Vomit crash into something.'

'What?' Clare was pre-occupied.

When Frampton's dog had been shot, they'd thought that it was some animal-rights fanatic frightening him off, and later, when they knew about the drugs connection, they assumed it was someone putting the frighteners on him, on that score. But earlier, in the office, when Danny Breen mentioned that Rach McFadden thought that the police were not the only ones watching Frampton, Clare had jumped to her feet – convinced they'd got it all wrong. With Red Sonia dead, Frampton had been desperate enough, by last night, to go and find her supplier. Had he been followed by the killer as well as the drug squad? But had Frampton been followed before? After his dog was shot, had he lead the killer to Red Sonia?

Melbury had dashed out of the office with orders from Clare to bring Frampton in, but within ten minutes, before he had time to get to Sutton Cottages, there was a phone call about an incident at The Galleon Inn… again.

Clare's driver pulled into the pub car park close behind Grimace and Vomit. There was another police car already parked. Clare recognised it. It was the community policeman's, PC Hamer's.

'Good lad, Kevin,' said Karen, articulating Clare's thoughts.

The wheels had barely stopped crunching when she jumped out of the car and started running towards where the gravel ends and the narrow rough flinty track – the coastal footpath – starts to climb up the slopes alongside the cliffs. Clare turned her head back and shouted without stopping. 'Check the pub, Karen. And tell those two to organise vehicles here when they come.' She was pointing at the now silent, but still flashing, traffic patrol car.

'Yes, boss.'

She only had to run a short distance when she saw them. 'Christ!' she shouted. It was exactly the same place, by that hawthorn bush – the same place the dog was shot. There was a body, a policeman – it was Hamer – two men, and dogs, yapping dogs. One of the men was walking back down the path towards her. He was holding a struggling bundle of a terrier in his jacket. The man, Clare recognised him as the landlord, had blood on his hand.

'Little bastard bit me. I'll get him locked in the shed and

come back. Bloody nightmare this. Last time was nothing. I heard the dogs and came out then phoned your lot – Kevin's only just got here.' he said, glancing over his shoulder.

'Thank you, thank you.' It was mad. Hamer was trying to keep two, yapping, and hysterical terriers away from the body. A man was just watching. He seemed dazed. 'Who are you?'

'I help at the pub.'

'Well, get back there,' she snapped.

'Wait a minute.' PC Hamer, his young cheeks flushed bright red, had picked up one of the dogs and was gripping it firmly around the muzzle. 'Take this with you. Now, get hold of him here, tight, before I let go.'

The man did as he was told.

'Here's the cavalry, ma'am,' said Hamer, pointing down to the car park.

Clare had not heard the car arrive in all the commotion. The unmistakeable form of Andy Melbury, followed by two uniformed officers, was hurrying up the path. She looked at the body; the face was a mass of blood.

'That's Frampton,' exclaimed the big detective sergeant, when he was still yards away. 'We probably only missed him by ten minutes or so.'

Clare was looking up to the crest of the ridge… to the sycamores of Spring Top Wood. 'Kevin?' she was pointing.

Hamer turned. 'Yes, ma'am, I get it.'

'Kevin, you know where the dog was shot from last time – and the tree with the yellow symbol. Check, only don't go closer than you have to and guard the area.'

'Right away, ma'am.'

'You two with him!' she ordered the uniformed officers. 'And Hamer's in charge. Now go!'

'Ma'am.'

'Andy, get rid of this fucking dog!' Clare shouted as she

lashed out wildly with her foot at the remaining terrier as it tugged at the dead man's coat.

Her face, framed by heavy auburn hair, was porcelain white, and Burne-Jones, Rosetti, or any other of the Pre-Raphaelite brethren, would have beaten each other with sticks to have painted her. Clare had kept looking anxiously across at her, at Karen, who was gripping tightly the edge of the table she was leaning heavily against. The young policewoman, a post-mortem virgin, had volunteered to attend. 'Well, it's got to happen sometime, boss,' she'd said.

It's alright, Clare had told her. Everyone goes out and throws-up the first time. I did, said Clare. Everyone does.

Everyone except Karen.

'Sorry, that wasn't very pleasant,' said Nick Howarth as he replaced the sheet.

'Thanks, Dr Howarth,' said Clare.

Howarth was sitting on the opposite side of his office desk from the two policewomen who were sipping tea. He smiled at Karen, 'As Detective Inspector Morell will tell you, Detective Constable – the dry throat comes with the territory. You did brilliantly in there.' He picked up the sealed plastic bag containing a bullet. 'As you are no doubt expecting, it's bingo time again.' He looked at the two women over the top of his half-moons as he pointed to the ammunition. 'A special Match job – a 7.62x51 shell, it has the same limited code batch as the others. As far as I can tell it has the same striations, as the previous two. I'm sure it was fired from the same rifle. It will go to forensics and I'll contact *other* people.'

Clare nodded; he'd no need to spell it out – Howarth would be speaking to Guy Lovat. 'Are there any other observations – anything?'

'There is something. It's the accuracy. Just as the shot that killed Dean Galpin was as near to the perfect centre of the heart as possible; and how the hell he managed to even hit that little terrier, I don't know. This one, as far as I can ascertain – though the large calibre, as you saw, creates so much damage – hit Neil Frampton perfectly slap bang in the middle of the temple.'

35

Yesterday's curtain of sea mist had lifted completely. It was so clear, that Clare, looking right across the bay, could pick out the Old Barracks where she lived, on the skyline of the hill of the gun fort. Also yesterday's flat slate grey undercoat sea appeared to have been painted a bright blue gloss. The nearby coves, judging by their deeper colour, seem to have been given a couple of extra coats.

It appeared as if nothing out of the ordinary had happened here. Clare wondered how quickly things would change. Galpin's death had been accepted as probably being a tragic accident, the explosion had been covered up and the shooting of the dog largely ignored. But another man shot? Even though this was a quiet rural area, on the largely neglected border of two TV regions, where there were no 'stringers' – the independent journalists – and only the Chronicle, that would make no difference. Neither would the fact that the police – who only report one percent of the nation's crime to the press – would not be saying anything. It was inevitable, she thought.

Yes… the proverbial was about to hit the fan.

A police car, pulling into the Galleon car park, interrupted her thoughts. It drew up beside the one that was already there. Two policemen got out and began walking up the path. Clare assumed that they were going to relieve the two officers who were standing by the small taped-off area on the coastal foot path where Frampton was shot.

She was standing at the edge of Spring Rise Wood, close to where the killer had fired the shot that killed the terrier and yesterday's bullet that had executed Frampton. For execution it was. When Hamer and the other two policemen had reached here yesterday they found that the yellow tree symbol that had been sprayed on the trunk of a sycamore had an addition… a rope, with a noose. She looked around. It was strange to see, after yesterday's madness, the slow, surreal movements of the Scene of Crime officers, working in the cordoned-off area at the edge of the wood.

'Good morning, Detective Inspector Morell.'

Clare swung round. A short man with narrow rat-like features, wearing a white forensics suit, was standing behind her. It was the senior Scene of Crime officer. She often thought that when he had his hood pulled up, as he had now, it drew attention to his sharp features, and made him look as if he was in a production of Wind in the Willows.

'Oh, hello, Mr Johnson, have you found anything?' she asked hopefully.

'Well, no. And that's what I wanted to tell you about.'

Clare was puzzled.

He smiled. 'Sorry, that sounds silly. But that's it really. It's weird. We wouldn't expect much where he just sprays a message and possibly not a lot on the Bumps on that short turf. And there was very little here last time. But especially on a damp morning like yesterday, we would have expected more disturbance here,' he said indicating the long grass and scrub at the edge of the sycamore trees.

'Well you think he took the precaution of putting down a plastic sheet didn't you?'

'Yes, Detective Inspector. It's just that there's so little disturbance around, He must move like a cat. It's as if it's natural to him somehow. I'm sorry if that doesn't make sense.'

'Not at all, that's very useful,' said Clare. 'Thank you.'

They both looked around at the sound of a twig snapping. A young woman, carrying a white suit, was coming along the narrow woodland path. With her purple-streaked hair in bunches, a strappy black top, khaki cargos and Doc Martens, Clare thought that the girl looked as if she was about to join a Time Team dig rather than a murder scene investigation.

'Hello, Liz,' called Johnson.

The girl waved, walked over to the taped area, inside which three of her colleagues were working, put down her bag and quickly started getting into her suit.

Johnson, after making sure Clare had his mobile number, in case she wanted any more information, excused himself and re-joined his team. Clare made a brief call to Simmonds: Yorick liked being kept in the frame. Then she noticed two figures coming down the path. Yes, it's *him*, accompanied by a policeman.

'I'll leave you now, sir,' said the policeman before turning on his heels and disappearing back into the shadows cast by the dense sycamores.

Clare checked her watch. Spot on time. Well, that's the military for you, she thought. She was hoping he might be late – well, really she was hoping that he would not turn up at all. He'd insisted on the phone that he wanted to meet her here. There were some very important things about the case apparently.

Captain Guy Lovat was in civvies again, but not in the grey suit of that meeting in the morgue. He was wearing a leather jacket, jeans, and one of those expensive shirts that look fashionably worn-out from the first time they are put on. His hair had just the right degree of unruliness and as he smiled she was reminded of the competition that the women Identifit artists hold annually. The subject is always the same: 'The face you would like to wake up next to.' This one would have won hands down most years.

'Liz! Watch where you're bloody well going!!' came an angry shout from within the cordoned area.

Time Team Liz had obviously seen him coming as well.

'Join the Stupid Deluded Cows, love,' muttered Clare, narrowing her eyes as Lovat approached.

They were standing just outside the cordoned area at the edge of the wood. Lovat was nervous: he'd been jabbering in tongues – gun talk – for what seemed ages, going on about things like bi-pods and compensators and opti-scopes. He'd lost her, though it wasn't completely his fault. Clare, determined not to start on him, was diverting herself by flicking through a graphically-illustrated technical manual she was producing in her head, entitled: *A Thousand and One Ways of Removing Someone's Testicles*. Somewhat ironic that, she thought (as she paused before mentally turning over another page), because if she opened her mouth, she'd chew his balls off.

She eventually interrupted him after the rather predictable *Bolt Cutter Technique*, had come round for the second time. 'What exactly are you saying?'

He immediately looked startled but then relieved. A few minutes earlier, Clare had nodded when he'd said hello – but until now had said not a word.

'Sorry, it's that all the specialist rifle kit in the world, can't explain how Galpin was shot right in the centre of the heart in early morning light – granted it was calm – at over 1200 metres. Then, on a clear day, with a six knot breeze, he fired from here,' he said, then he pointed down the slopes to the two policeman and the taped-off patch they were guarding. 'And hit a dog down there. A terrier, one of the lively little ones they… I need to speak to you about something else.'

'Finish this stuff first. The dog was twelve inches high and weighed twelve pounds – small enough to go down a fox hole,' stated Clare coldly.

Lovat coloured and struggled to gain some composure. 'OK… and yesterday, he hit his target right in the centre of the temple. This is frightening. It's the best shooting I've ever seen. Who the hell is this guy?'

Clare told him what the Scene of Crime officer had said.

'Yes, he's likely to have been a hunter since he was a kid. Tell you something else as well.'

'What?'

'I re-checked with our Spanish contacts about that rumour that one of the stolen C-75 rifles stolen, almost certainly by ETA, had been acquired by an Englishman. They said they were told that "The Englishman" had one, not an Englishman. They said that it was unusual to get even that amount of information. Those particular Basque mountain people they say – their words not mine – are as tight lipped as a nun's whatsit.'

'You mean an individual, like The Jackal?'

'I suppose so, but we've not come across anyone with that name. Anyway, I have a strong feeling that these are not contract killings. Shots to the heart or head are the norm, but there's something else here.'

'In what way?'

'It's the precision. I don't know – it seems like some kind of ice-cold revenge somehow. I think it's personal. You should be looking for someone who knows his targets.'

'Not thinking of a career change are you?' she said reluctantly.

'Funny you should say that.'

They were standing by Lovat's car. He had talked, non-stop,

about the 'something else', the whole time they had walked along the path that snaked through the trees from the murder scene. He started by saying that he knew from the look she'd given him at that meeting in the morgue, that she'd seen right through him. Then he said sorry a lot. Sorry, about pretending to be straight because he needed a partner for that regimental ball. Sorry, about how he'd been living a lie about his homosexuality in the army environment in order to survive. And how *really sorry* he was for deceiving her.

She glared at him – he, sensibly, avoided eye contact.

You have no idea, Sunny Jim, she thought, remembering the humiliation and anger.

He eventually fell silent. It could have been worse. If he had said anything on the lines of 'she'd looked fabulous, and if only he wasn't…' then, she would, despite his military training, have hurt him before he could have defended himself.

Lovat opened the door of his BMW Z 3 and got in. 'So, I'm coming out. Well, no, I mean I'm coming out – then I'm coming out,' he gabbled.

'What the hell are you talking about?' It was the first time Clare had spoken for ages.

'I'm resigning my commission in a couple of months,' he said, as he gripped the steering wheel with both hands.

Clare, holding the edge of the door, looked down at him. 'What a waste, why are so many of you gay men so… Oh, fuck off,' she said, not unkindly, as she slammed the door.

He waved out of his window just before he disappeared around the corner, and then, as she could hear him driving quickly along the road that lead to the heath, she walked back to her car. Young men and their sports cars, she thought. Then her face darkened as the vision of an old Volvo estate came to mind, and as a result, her old long suffering GTI received yet another undeserved kick in a tyre.

Clare watched as John Bellini, as handsome and as well groomed as ever, placed a 'skimmed milk/no sugar' coffee in front of Andy Melbury. He then pointed to a minuscule biscuit on the saucer. 'Treat.'

Melbury theatrically lowered his head to a few inches above his cup to look… and then raised two-fingers as he straightened back up. On the saucer of Clare's usual latte there were, cruelly, two unordered chocolate biscuits. 'Tell the Inspector what you told me earlier.'

Clare had been driving back from Spring Rise Wood, when Melbury had rung and asked her to come straight here.

Bellini leant forward. 'They've gone crazy at the Domino Club since yesterday afternoon. All the security staff have been called in.'

'Thanks, John. Is there anything else?'

He leant forward even closer – subtle aftershave a little stronger, eyes a little darker, lips a little thicker…

'What do you think?'

He traced the line of a two or three day moustache with a finger.

'Ditch it. Why spoil perfection?' she said, somehow – under the guise of a throw-away line – managing to express what many women would agree were two true opinions.

Nice try, Valentino – but you're not my type.

The café door opened and two people came in.

'Now bugger-off *garcon* – and see to your customers,' muttered Melbury, as Bellini walked away. Then he pushed his cup and saucer to one side, and rested both elbows on the table. 'I made a couple of calls while I was waiting for you, boss. Gavin Adam's two kids are not at St John's School this morning. Apparently, Adam's wife, who's German, has suddenly got to go to her old home because her mother's ill and she's taking the children with her. It sounds like porkies – he wants them safe. Adams has driven them to Heathrow and then he's a day or two's business in London before coming back.'

'Wow! That's great,' was all Clare said – she knew better than ask how he knew.

Melbury's phone rang and he fished it out of his top pocket. 'Hi, Karen… yes… right… good… right… Well done my lovely! Oh, one more thing, have you put that poor frustrated young Kevin out of his misery yet? Language!!'

He laughed, switched off and looked at Clare. 'Adams has a big house on Grey Cliff. I asked Karen to have a drive past. I thought she'd be less conspicuous than one of the guys.'

'Karen, not conspicuous?'

'She said – her words not mine – that she'd tie her hair tight back and "wear something suitable", honest.'

'And she's not driving her brother's box of shit on wheels?' asked Clare, not entirely convinced.

'No, she's got a pool car… which would be marginally cleaner,' he teased. 'Anyway, there is a black beamer parked on the road outside with a couple of heavies in it – obviously Adam's is sending a clear message for anyone watching that they know and are ready for them.'

'Yes, Andy, the game's changed. The next intended victim already knows in advance that he is the next intended victim.'

'And leaves us twiddling our thumbs until Adams gets back?'

Clare nodded. She'd already thought of that… it would be a good time to honour a debt. Then she pointed to the miniature biscuit on Melbury's saucer. 'How is it going?'

He looked sheepish… but pleased. 'I lost three pounds last week. Annie the Fat Controller at Weight Watchers was chuffed for once.'

'That's brilliant! Just like the work you've done here this morning.'

He pointed at her saucer. 'Thanks. Can I have a chocolate

biscuit?'

    'No – it's not *that* brilliant.'

36

It was still very early, but the last of the night sky was fast disappearing into a series of purple streaks and the skyline of the ridgeway was backlit by a frieze of early sunlight. It looked a morning like many others on the coming of summer… but it was not. The usual early morning chorus of the downland – familiar to Clare from her gruelling runs with Emma – could not be heard. She couldn't hear the high chirruping of the early rising skylarks, nor the haunting call of the curlew on its way to the marshland. She wasn't even able to make out the bleating of sheep grazing nearby, or the inevitable moaning of cows echoing up from somewhere in the mist shrouded valley. All these sounds were being drowned out.

The Travellers were on the move.

Everywhere there was clattering and bustle as the vans were being loaded, and engines, with black smoke puffing from exhausts like smoke signals, coughed and spluttered into life. Some of them were already on their way. A transit with 'Dahl and Pitta Bread' painted on the side, trundled past, hitting the road to the lower division festivals rather earlier than planned. A couple of vehicles were having difficulty: three point turns were growing into five point ones. Any vehicle parked facing west had to turn around. There was only one way they were driving down the old drovers' road today – and that was east and the county boundary. Three squad cars barricaded the track to the west.

They had been blocking the road since late last evening when uniformed officers had gone into the camp and issued the Travellers with an ultimatum. They had exactly twelve hours to clear the camp completely, during which time there would be no vehicle inspections, no benefit checks – and no searches for drugs. There had been, as expected, some grumbling and anger from the Travellers, but Clare had insisted that they be told that nothing was negotiable and anyone, and their vehicles, still here after the deadline would be subject to rigorous scrutiny by all the agencies.

Clare was standing talking to Karen. They moved to the side as an ancient VW Camper crawled past, then both women swung round at the sound of a raised voice. Andy Melbury was explaining to an old hippy wearing a huge Rasta bonnet, that if he didn't want his dog to be on a permanent diet of milk sops, then he'd better lock him in his van quickly:

'Then get in yourself… and fuck off.'

Melbury was suddenly aware that Clare was looking at him. 'There's a good lad,' he concluded, with a pat on the shoulder.

Karen pointed to a small tumulus in a neighbouring field. Several people were standing on the top. There was also a man on a quad bike accompanied by a large white dog. 'I wonder who told the Gypsy Rent-A-Crowd and the Good Shepherd?' she asked, with a sly look at Clare.

'They probably saw it in a crystal ball, or read it in the cards, Detective Constable.'

Clare was smiling when one of the group, a woman who was watching through a telescope… raised an arm in salute.

'So, are we clear here? You are not in *any* circumstances to go near the Vines again. It would be easy to check that I was your neighbour and I'm not going to be compromised. Don't tell anyone, for your sake and the people who depend on them. You know you were right – so bury it. Agreed?'

Clare, who was sitting on the sofa clutching the neck of her guitar, nodded. The woman had, in seconds, changed like a chameleon – her features had sharpened, her eyes had become piercing and her voice had cut like a laser. Clare, who had heard that Emma Butler LLB could without warning suddenly become a 'really scary piece of work' in court, had just been on the receiving end of that experience at first hand… in her own lounge.

Emma had been explaining to Clare that she'd been worried that her friend ('You can be a head-strong bitch!') had not followed her previous advice about staying clear of the 'powerful, influential and potentially vicious, Sir John and Lady Vine,' who could seriously damage her career. So, she'd done some detective work herself, and as she was from a 'county family' – although from a different county – it had not been that difficult. It had been what Clare had suspected – the lesbian claim was a cover, it had been drugs. Emma had found out that a red-haired woman had been told to quietly leave the Winterbourne Hunt because she had been supplying cocaine at hunt parties she'd attended. The stable girls and the other members of staff had been given a party-line to stick to. There would be little chance of them leaking information to the contrary, not only because of fear of losing their jobs, but because, in many cases, the estate houses their families lived in were owned by the Vines. It had all been hushed up.

And now, Emma, has ordered her to bury it. Clare didn't like it, but had learned the hard way that some things, in this idyllic rural patch, are not what they seem. The tractor had long replaced the horse and plough… but the Lord and Lady of the Manor still ruled over their feudal domain.

'Right, now that's finished with, I'll order some food. Hungry?' Emma, phone in one hand and a take-away menu in the other, was leaning against the window sill.

Clare nodded – and prayed that she would never seriously cross Emma Butler. She knew that her friend could be ruthless, she realised that in the advice – though it was more of an *order* – as to what action to take when Mike Crick had made a complaint about her. She'd protested, 'I'd lost it! I was trying to throttle the fucker while he was having a slash! I didn't see anything!'

'It doesn't matter if it is fact or fiction. Peanut Dick will be finished. Trust me.'

And so it proved. Emma said afterwards that there was something sweet about an incompetent, bullying, misogynist – being shafted by a reference to his masculinity. Crick had moved to a new station straight away, and she'd recently heard a rumour that he had put in for early retirement.

'Emma's Law,' Christ! she thought – the bane of her life had disappeared, 'just like that'.

It was almost as if an author, rooting for her, had suddenly decided to write the character out of a book.

Clare still holding her guitar, watched as Emma – back to being 'Emma' again – take another slice of pizza.

'It's great this.'

'What?'

'Being able to *eat* – and not put on weight.' She illustrated her point by holding the pizza slice between her teeth, pulling up her T-shirt with one hand and patting her hard flat stomach with the other.

Clare nodded. She was tired. She'd been out at dawn at the Travellers' camp, and they'd just been on a run. It had not been far, but as always the two women had been competitive, and now they were getting very fit, they pushed each other harder than ever.

Emma pulled the faded T-shirt she was wearing down again.

'Be careful with that! And it's only for lends and not keeps. It's a collector's item.'

'Yes, I know – don't get your drawers in a knot!'

The T-shirt was special. It was one of the infamous Inspiral Carpet 'Cool as fuck' ones. Clare had worn it at the Hacienda during the 'Madchester' days of her youth.

'Oh, I've just remembered something else I'd been thinking about while doing your job as well as my own.' Emma, ignoring Clare's raised middle finger, carried on. 'It's that first one, the one who was shot in the heart – though apparently it would have been easier to hit him in the dick – who doesn't fit into the drugs thing. Well, if it's about him screwing young women, you should be looking for a father, an elder brother, or an uncle.'

'Yes,' answered Clare wearily.

'And talking about dicks, leads me nicely to you being a miserable cow these days. What about the scruffy long-haired Welshman?'

'He's not! He's had his hair trimmed and things.'

'Oh, and I wonder why that is!' mocked Emma – hands on hips. 'You, madam, need to let the past go, and both of you want your heads banging together. Well, that's not all you want banging together, then things might lighten up around here.'

'Emma!!'

Emma grabbed a tissue from the box on the coffee table, and waving it furiously, backed away to the window.

Clare yawned. She could barely keep her eyes open, in fact, as she sunk back into the sofa, she couldn't even do that.

Emma went into the bedroom and came back with a

throw. She carefully took away the guitar that was still resting against Clare's knees, and after placing the throw gently over the woman who had become her soul mate… crept out of the flat.

37

The Fiat Punto, just in front of her, turned off at the roundabout and drove into the campus. Clare followed it, and also tailed it into the visitors' car park… where it swung into the only vacant space. She was backing out slowly when there was a tap at her window. It was the gardener who'd kept an eye on the GTI when she had that puncture. What was his name? Yes, it was Jacko.

'Morning.'

She lowered her window. 'Hi, Jacko, I owe you a thank-you for when you looked after this load of junk until Vic collected it.'

'No problems. Any friend of Rob's is one of mine.'

Any friend of Rob's…

'Anyway, you can park near where I'm working if you like.' He pointed, with a strong weather-beaten arm, to his wheelbarrow and tools on a flowerbed about thirty yards away. Then he nodded towards the New Block. She remembered Rob Ellis had called it Saruman's Tower. 'Though things like clamping are a bit lax at the moment as the Vice Principal is off with stress – probably caused by him finding a sweet paper on a corridor, or discovering that the bog-rolls had been put on the wrong way round in the loos.'

She laughed, drove over to where he had indicated, and parked. She did not get out straight away.

The press vultures that had been circling had landed: Simmonds was making a statement this morning. He had talked to her about it. The gist was to be; that there were no suspects (true), that Galpin's death was now no longer regarded as a probable accident (untrue – they'd known that for ages), that both Galpin and Frampton had links with the local hunt (true), and Frampton's dog that had been shot was one that had been used in fox hunting (true).

When the press asked if it was likely that an animal rights fanatic was responsible, Simmonds would say, 'That all avenues were being pursued.' – and then hopefully, temporarily wave goodbye to the hacks as they scuttled-off to Winterstone Stables and the Borne Hunt.

That was the plan. There would be no mention of the explosion. He also told her to keep away as he would try and keep her out of it as long as possible. Her name could ring bells and her part in the Longford Killings re-emerge.

Bless you Yorick.

Clare got out of the car. No one here knew of the lecturers' connections to the case. Ellis had told Gill Doyle that they were helping with 'the spatial distributions' of some crimes. He had a point, he'd said, because if a geographer had been consulted early in the case, then it was likely that some of the Yorkshire Ripper's victims would still be walking around.

She began to walk slowly across the old part of the campus towards the wide flight of steps that lead up to the imposing doorway under the clock tower. There was something she really liked here: the building itself of warm local stone, with its narrow round-topped windows picked out in pinkish-red brick, and the groups of students sitting and chatting. It reminded her of the day she'd sat on the Spanish Steps in Rome.

A woman about her age, with long hair and carrying a large leather shoulder bag, began walking up the steps. The right sleeve of her velvet jacket was pulled up. She was wearing a wide silver bracelet. She said something to some students as she passed them. They laughed. She looks like an arts lecturer, thought Clare – and then the day she'd turned down a PhD came back to haunt her, as it always did when she came here. Could she jack in the force and complete one now and then teach? She had considerable savings from her grandmother's legacy, and if required, could do the long hair, big bag, bracelet thing. But then that warm seductive wishful thinking was replaced by the cold reality that she was too long in the tooth as a cop to be anything different. Anyway, even if she did, she'd probably get suspended within a week for putting some lippy eighteen year old knob-head in an arm lock and marching him out of the lecture room.

Clare, who was wearing a close-fitted trouser suit, walked up to the top of the steep steps, resisted turning and glaring at the group of lads she'd past who were sitting lower down, and pushed open the door. She knew her way through the twists and turns of the old corridors and soon reached the Geography Department. As she was passing the spiral staircase that lead up to the Map Room, someone called her name. She looked up – it was James Travers. He came down very quickly.

'Well, fancy meeting you here, Inspector.'

Clare smiled, and looking at him was surprised, just like she was the last time she'd seen him, in that he seemed different again. His ice cold blue eyes were even more piercing and he looked, well, younger. He was all so different than at their first meeting.

' Superintendent Simmonds has *spoken* to Rob and me.' He spoke quietly, although there was no one around. 'He told us that the last victim was the man with the terriers and also about that added noose on the tree symbol. The Superintendent also said we could possibly help again because whoever is behind this may lead us all a merry dance before he's finished – sorry I have to dash off.'

Clare, shaking her wrist after a vice-like handshake, looked in amazement as he disappeared around a corner – just like the last time they'd met, he suddenly had to 'dash off'.

'Christ, he's turning into the White Rabbit!' she said to herself.

As well as being puzzled by Travers, Clare was angry with Yorick. She knew that he had informed Travis and Rob Ellis about the shooting of Frampton, and appreciated that her governor had said he would take responsibility for the 'civilian help', really to make sure they kept their mouths shut. But why hadn't Yorick keep his own bloody mouth shut about her opinion that whoever was behind this would really try and spectacularly fuck with them at the finish?

She'd been walking down the corridor where the lecturers' rooms were situated as she'd been thinking… and all too soon found she was standing outside the door with Dr R Ellis on its nameplate.

She hesitated.

'What the hell am I doing here?' she muttered.

She knew that was not true. She knew before she came that Yorick had spoken to him about the case. The last time she'd seen Rob Ellis was when they'd stood by his car in the old Parade Ground outside her flats, when, if they weren't arguing, they were glaring at each other. The question was not why she was here… but what she was going to say. Clare took a deep breath and knocked. There was no answer. She knocked again.

'Detective Inspector Morell?'

She swung around.

Oh, no, it's Madame Whiplash!

But it wasn't. Gill Doyle was still all nails, tight pencil skirt and killer heels… but she was smiling. Smiling! 'Rob's out all day, I'm afraid. Sorry, are you alright?'

'I'm fine.'

'It must be worrying about that shooting.'

'Yes, indeed.'

'Anyway, I've just put the kettle on – come and have some tea.' She touched Clare's arm and Clare, grateful for no follow-up questions, but as much bemused as anything else by this unexpected cessation of hostilities, meekly followed her into the Geography Department office where a grey haired woman in her sixties was tapping at a keyboard.

'Detective Inspector Morell is having some tea with us, Grace,' explained Gill Doyle, as she led the way through another door.

It was a surprise. Clare found herself in an elegant room with a high ceiling dominated by three long, narrow windows with very low sills in a turret wall. They looked like a triptych of stained glass – a sequence of different coloured vistas from the green of the nature reserve marsh, through a middle view of greys and tans, where the great curve of the beach changed from pebbles to sand, to the blue of the bay.

'It's lovely, isn't it?' said Gill Doyle, reading her thoughts. 'Take a seat, the kettle's boiled; I'll only be a jiff.' She went into an alcove that had been converted into a small kitchen and a minute or two later placed a tray of tea things on the low table in front of Clare. 'Please help yourself, I'm just going to the loo,' she said nodding towards a door that lead off the alcove.

Clare had just poured herself a cup when a man, in his twenties, came through from the outer office. He looked, with his button-down shirt and mod suit, as if he was in a Jam tribute band; in fact she thought he looked a bit like a young Paul Weller… with a better haircut.

'Hi, I thought Gill was in here.'

'She won't be a moment or two.'

'I don't think we've met. Mark Dawson, English

Department,' he said with a friendly smile.

'Clare Morell.'

Gill Doyle came back into the room.

'Can I have a word?' he said gesturing towards the office. She nodded. He glanced towards Clare as he moved towards the door. 'What do you teach?'

'I don't – I'm in the police.'

'Wow… I'll have to behave myself then.'

Hello!! Clare clocked the look going between the Young Paul Weller and the considerably older Gill Doyle as he said this. The secretary then gave Clare an apologetic smile as they went out. A moment later the grey-haired woman Grace came in and sat down.

Clare could hear the secretary and the young man laughing as they left the office. She raised an eyebrow.

Grace gave a sly smile. 'I couldn't possibly comment.'

A few sips of tea later, Clare decided to chance her arm. 'It's funny; I got the impression that Gill and Dr Ellis–'

'That's understandable, but wrong,' interrupted Grace, as she poured herself a drink. 'She's always acted the mother hen as far as Rob is concerned; especially in the way she bats away our young Delilahs who want to do rather more to him that cut his hair. The thing is, he was rather fragile when he came here about four years ago.'

Clare, who'd been considering whether or not to be flattered by being thought of as a Young Delilah – pulled up sharp.

Fragile?

'Sorry, I must man the fort.'

Clare watched as the startlingly bean-spilling assistant got up, pick up her cup and saucer, and walk across to the door. She seemed to be amused by something. 'Gill and Rob indeed! It's no secret that Gill wouldn't be seen dead sleeping with anyone remotely old enough to be her husband.' Then

315

she left… leaving a drop-jawed policewoman alone in the room.

A fresh pot had been brewed and the secretary and Clare were sitting opposite each other.

'I'm sorry about earlier.'

'That's alright Miss Doyle, I'm not in a hurry,' replied Clare truthfully – she was in something of a limbo until Gavin Adams returned to town later today, or tomorrow, and she'd been told to stay away from the station.

'Gill – it's Gill.'

She picked up her tea and leaning back in her arm chair looked hard at Clare. 'It's a shame you missed Rob, it's been very noticeable how much he's changed, everyone's noticed the new smarter Dr Ellis, though recently–'

Clare stiffened. 'I've not seen him recently,' she blurted out, and then quickly changed the subject to stop the woman's fishing. 'I've just seen James Travers though, he looks really fit after all the difficulties he had.'

Gill dabbed her lipstick with a tissue. 'I knew Isabelle, Bix Travers's partner, very well.'

Clare was now all ears: this was the woman who'd committed suicide.

'We were boarders at Sherton School.'

Clare nodded. She's heard of the girls' public school in the north of the county. It was expensive.

The secretary read her thoughts. 'My family was not particularly wealthy. My father was an army major and posted abroad a great deal. Both sides of Isabelle's family were rich. Anyway, we were very close friends. She was brilliant when my ex walked. I wish I could have helped her more – but he was so difficult to live with.'

'In what way?'

'Well, Bix Travers is a driven man. Always has been. He'd get some idea in his head that would take over and make her life a misery. He's very clever and highly strung. He's had a breakdown in the past. He is a very strict Catholic. His early upbringing was very strange, he keeps it very quiet and I'm sure that's why he'd sometimes take-off for long periods... it's a pity he didn't after Hannah died. Though it was lucky he was away the year before when she had a problem – though he got to know of that eventually, well after the poor girl's death.'

Gill had spoken quickly and Clare could barely keep up with her. The woman really didn't like Travers and was taking the opportunity to get something off her chest.

'Was Hannah their daughter?'

Gill nodded and picked up her cup again.

'What happened to her?'

'She was at university in London – first year. It was just a tragic accident. Hannah was out with some friends on a Saturday night and it started raining heavily – well, as you know they never seem to wear coats – and as they were rushing down some steep steps she slipped and banged her head. That was all. It happened early in the evening. She'd only had a couple of drinks and... '

She choked on her words.

Clare nodded in understanding. From her flat, she'd often heard the clatter of high heels as hen parties went down the steps to the harbour. Yes, easily enough done.

Gill glanced at her watch. 'Oh, sorry. I have to go, Inspector.'

'Clare – it's Clare.'

38

DS Andy Melbury had been to the barbers. He'd explained to Clare that John Bellini, who sported a full head of hair, had told him that he'd read somewhere that the best solution for men who were losing theirs, was to have it cut short. He'd had it cut very short. Clare didn't think it suited him.

They were walking up St Adhelms Street. She caught a glimpse of their reflections in a shop window and smiled. The big detective sergeant looked like her minder. She thought, in the circumstances, that it was highly appropriate… as they were going to the Domino Club to rattle Gavin Adam's cage.

Melbury had told her that he'd heard that Adams – his wife and children now safe with his in-laws in Germany – had returned from London the previous night. St Adhelms Street, crowded and noisy in the evening, was deserted and quiet, until, just as they reached the club, the competing church clocks of St Edmunds and All Saints, began to strike ten. This process took some time to complete as All Saints had only struck five as St Edmonds finished its ten. Clare waited for silence before she pressed the intercom at the side of the Domino's heavy door.

'Hello. It's the police. We're expected,' she lied in a friendly tone.

'I'll just have to go and ask,' replied a voice – a surprisingly squeaky voice – hesitantly.

'I know who that is,' said Melbury, moving close to the intercom. 'Dennis?'

'Yes.'

'It's Sergeant Melbury. Open the bloody door, son – *now*.'

There was the sound of bolts being shot, the door opened and they went inside. Clare was surprised that Dennis, despite the voice, was built like a weight lifter. He carefully checked the door was closed and locked before leading the way along a wide corridor.

'Saw your missus the other day, Dennis. When's this one due?'

'In about a month, Mr Melbury.'

'How many will that be?'

'Five, Mr Melbury.'

'Well, lad, you'll be able to have your own team of bouncers soon.'

Clare spluttered into her sleeve. It was a lovely image: lots of little barrel chested kids tagging along behind Dennis.

The main bar and dance area, looked like so many Clare had seen before. They were always drab and dark when closed. A cleaner was mopping the floor. Three men – real heavies – were sitting in a corner playing cards. They stiffened. The atmosphere became suddenly tense.

Melbury turned towards Clare. 'Don't know those bastards,' he muttered quietly.

Dennis disappeared and a minute later, they heard someone coming down the open stairs to their right.

'Hello. I'm Gavin Adams.'

'Good Morning! I'm DI Morell and this is DS Melbury, my apologies, Mr Adams, for just calling in like this without warning.'

'That's alright,' he replied, after reacting badly to Clare's charming smile and second lie in a couple of minutes, with a momentary frown.

She thought that Gavin Adams didn't look much like an accountant. But then he didn't look like a club owner either.

He was lean and fit with slightly hollowed cheeks and a deep tan. He shook hands cautiously: Clare noticed his right wrist was heavily strapped.

He began to look uncomfortable and gestured to a door to their left. 'Come into the office.'

Adams, like most men when subject to assessment by DI Morell's eyes, especially for the first time – had acted true to form.

Danny Breen had been right in what he'd told her about Adams being a sailing fanatic. One wall of his office was covered in photographs of boats and the wall behind his desk was dominated by a large oil painting of an ocean going yacht. Adams noticed Andy Melbury studying it carefully.

'Yes, it's lovely isn't it? It shows Sir Thomas Lipton competing in the America's Cup.'

'He never won it though did he – though he tried five times.'

Adams looked surprised. 'You know about sailing then.'

Melbury turned and walked up to the wall with the photographs. 'Enough to know you race Flying Dutchmen. Which one's yours?'

Adams moved close to a large colourful photograph of several dinghies sailing close together. He pointed to the one with a bright red spinnaker with a black bar across it.

Melbury looked hard at the photo. '*The Tempest*. Nice name. It must be tough competing as this area's still a hot bed for the class isn't it?'

'Yes, indeed, Sergeant, there's a series of weekly races in the bay. Did you–'

Adams must have sensed Clare's boys-and-their-toys vibes. 'Oh, sorry, Detective Inspector, please take a seat. Now, what is this about?'

Clare sat down in front of his office desk. He sat opposite. Melbury, as she knew he would, remained standing. It was always good practice to leave the big guy looking down. 'Firstly, we believe you might be able to help us with something… and also we need to give you some information concerning your personal safety.'

She was looking at him carefully and noted the change in his expression.

Good, that's taken his mind off boats.

'What do you –? '

'Does the name Dean Galpin mean anything to you?', Clare interrupted.

'No.'

'Neil Frampton?'

Adams shook his head.

'Sonia Nicholl?'

'Oh, the woman who ran the boutique at the top of the street? She was killed recently when her car caught fire, wasn't she?'

Clare was playing it by the manual – no side tracking and keeping up the momentum. 'Did you know her?'

'Only by sight – well you could barely miss her with that long red hair and my wife bought clothes from her shop. What is this about?'

'Well, Mr Adams,' continued Clare – who was intent on throwing everything at him at once. 'Two men are dead as well as Sonia Nichol. Dean Galpin was shot then Neil Frampton was given a scare and we believe he lead the killer to Sonia Nichol. Her death wasn't an accident. Also we know Frampton was drug dealing… his supplier was Sonia Nichol.'

'I repeat – what's this got to do with me?'

Clare was fixing Adams like a hawk. He was keeping his cool. He was not looking directly at her. 'Just as Frampton was followed to where Sonia Nichol lived, we believe Frampton, after she was killed, was also trailed when he went looking for whoever supplied her – for who pulls the strings around here.'

'So, we were following him as well and lost him somewhere near your backdoor,' said Melbury, who'd decided to muscle in without a nod or a glance from his DI. 'We spotted him a bit later. He'd had a slapping – been warned off.' He moved forward, and hovering over Adams, pointed down. 'How'd you get that bad wrist?'

'If you continue on that line – I'll be phoning my solicitor.'

Clare, pleased with her sergeant's Even Badder Cop intervention into her Bad Cop routine, stared even harder at the man opposite. 'Yes, but you see Mr Adams, as Frampton has been shot, we think you already believe you're next.' She gestured towards the door. 'Why have all that muscle out there when you're closed, if not for personal protection?

'I've got nothing more to say,' said Adams as he raised himself from his chair.

'I have,' said Clare, getting to her feet and moving towards the door. 'Some advice... Check under your car before you get into it.'

Clare was smiling. So was Andy Melbury. In fact they were grinning at each other like Cheshire cats. They didn't speak, as St Adhelms Street was one of the town's narrow medieval thoroughfares where voices carried easily and they walked quickly down the short stretch of the street from the Domino Club to where it met the harbour.

'Yes!' Clare punched the air.

'Well, boss, he's the man. He's shitting himself and thinks it's a drugs war!' exclaimed Melbury, who she noticed was walking like ten men.

Ten very large men.

'Andy, how come you know so much about sailing?'

'Years ago I used to crew my brother's Firefly dinghy. I

couldn't now of course, as I'd sink the bloody thing,' he said with a laugh.

Clare felt better than she'd done for days, and this place, especially having just been in that dark club, was a good place as any to suddenly feel better. Where the street ends at the harbour side, everything seems different. The senses, like the vista itself, open up. There's suddenly the feeling of sea breeze on the pores of the skin; there's a blast of ozone through the sinuses, and ears have to cope with a sudden change from the sounds of the town, to the squawking of gulls and the 'put-put' chorus of boat engines. But it's the light on the water that's really special: the sudden intensity makes you blink.

Her mobile rang. She answered it and felt even better. Matt Johns was back. His father was recovering well from his heart attack, his mother was coping better and his sister was home from Canada. Johns's return had been expected, but not for a few more days. She told Melbury.

'Great! I've missed not having the clever, cheeky young bugger around. Don't tell him mind.'

They reached Melbury's car. It was parked on double yellow lines near a stack of lobster pots. He'd left a duster hanging from a sun-visor as a signal for Eva Braun the traffic warden, just in case she didn't recognise whose vehicle it was. Melbury laughed and then pretended to look under the car. 'That was one hell of a parting shot that, boss!'

Then he laughed again, so loud that a man walking his dog fifty yards away along the quayside looked around.

This was all very well, but Clare was not laughing: cold reality had returned.

Who the hell was going to blow up another car, or pull a trigger?

39

Clare, her mobile to her ear, was leaning over Matt Johns's shoulder. They were both looking intently at his computer screen when the CID office door flew open. She swung around – it was Simmonds.

'Is it him?'

'Yes… yes, sir,' answered Clare hesitantly. She'd been momentarily taken aback by Yorick's appearance, as the tall thin superintendent's usual pale cadaverous features were brightly flushed.

'We had a message a few minutes ago, sir,' added Johns, without taking his eyes off the screen. 'It said *"Finale – Keep Watching."* We're expecting another one.'

Simmonds came up to the desk. 'It looks like we were right, Clare, when we said that although there was no warning given before Frampton was shot, the mad bastard would have to do a whistle-and-bells job before he's finished. That's what I told our College guys. Have you contacted them?'

She shook her head. She'd never seen Yorick so animated – with the possible exception of the time when she'd been on the receiving end of a hairdryer bollocking. 'No, sir, they don't appear to be on campus. I've tried Travers's home, the line seems to be dead, and his mobile's switched off. There's also no answer from Ellis's home number. He doesn't have a mobile. The secretary at the College is trying to find them – sending e-mails as well.'

'Damn!' His face darkened: Simmonds looked around. 'And where the hell's Melbury and Garland?'

'Andy will be here in a minute. Karen has a day off.'

Johns momentarily looked up from his screen. 'I've texted her – I'm sure she'll come in.'

Simmonds gave a nod of approval, pulled up a chair, and sat down.

'Any coffee around here?'

'What the fuck does it say? I haven't got my glasses,' snapped Simmonds, on his feet and like the other two staring at the screen.

'It says *"First the House and Wood, then Sun and Moon make two – lastly posts by Ramsden West and East"* – followed by a *"Keep Watching"* instruction,' said Clare.

'Excuse me,' said Johns as he pulled open a desk drawer. He took out the ruler from a tray and then frantically began searching through the pens and pencils.

'What are you looking for, Matt?'

'A red pen, so that it will show up on that,' he said, nodding towards the Ordnance Survey map stuck on the notice board. It had the previous bearings and locations of all the other murders marked in black. 'Thanks, boss,' he said, taking the pen Clare had immediately spotted and was holding in her hand.

Johns rushed over to the map. 'The 'House' must be Tallington House, the 'Wood' is Spring Rise Wood, the 'Sun' is the Galleon Inn, the 'Moon' is Full Moon Copse, the –'

'What the hell are the Ramsden things?' interrupted Simmonds.

'They are old survey posts, sir,' answered Clare.

'One is on Chalcombe Bumps and the other on Drovers' Knoll,' said Johns as he completed marking the last two locations on the map with large red dots.

'There's something else!' exclaimed Clare who was now sitting in front of the computer. 'Right, *"209, 167, 212, 172, 175, 190"*. And a message, *"Look out for–'*

Johns took a compass out of his pocket – Clare knew he carried one with him all the time now. 'They must be bearings! Give them me one at a time, boss. I'll plot them in the order he gave us the locations.'

Clare did this and watched as Johns, using his compass, ruler and red felt tip, plotted the six lines. They intersected, as expected, in pairs.

'All three intersections are in the middle of the bay!' exclaimed Simmonds. 'It makes no sense – and that message at the end. What the fuck have colours got to do with anything?'

The CID office door nearly burst off its hinges: DS Andy Melbury had arrived. 'What've we got?'

Johns called over his shoulder. 'It's crazy, sarge. Three points making a sort of triangle in the bay and something at the end which says *"Look out for the Scarlet –'*

'And black,' completed Melbury, though there was no way he could have seen the computer screen.

The silhouette of a cormorant is moving quickly just above the surface. From high up here it looks like a fish with wings. Then the light changes suddenly and the bird disappears. It's strange when a cloud blacks out the sunlight – especially when the sea is choppy with white horses, as it is today – how the blue can immediately disappear. It's almost monochrome now: unlike close to hand where the yellow Samphire and dots of Red Campion fleck the dull green turf of this cliff top.

When senses are heightened, like mine are right now, then perhaps colours seem more intense? Also sounds and smells? That black-headed gull sounds as if it is squawking into a megaphone, and the pungent smell of rotting kelp that was thrown high up the beach by the last storm, is wafting up the cliff face.

They're getting closer. They are nearing the end of the second leg.

They have only one more to go.

I have only 'one more to go' as well.

From here it seems impossible that the tightly grouped dinghies don't keep colliding. With their white sails they look more like a flock of birds than a flotilla. Flotilla? I am sure its origin must be from 'flota' – the Spanish word for fleet. Hmm, funny that, the Armada, the most famous of all 'flotas', sailed into these waters and was given a rather warm welcome, just over there, to the south of the bay, by a sea captain named Drake.

Get ready; they are reaching the marker buoy for the last time *now. There is a flurry of activity with the leaders. Helmsmen and crew shift position as they tack around the buoy as tightly as they can. It is a huge advantage to be in front on the next leg, the fastest leg, where they will run with the wind. There are flashes of colour as they round the buoy and then the wind catches and fills out the spinnakers. The leader's sail is of yellow and blue, the second is white and green, and, the third… yes, and it's him.*

This third placed Flying Dutchman has just raised a scarlet red spinnaker with a black band.

Right – let's see.

Even close through the scope, the helmsman and his crew look very similar. They are both wearing black wet suits and yellow life jackets, with peaked caps pulled low over their brows. But the crewman is also wearing a trapeze harness and a bright blue neoprene medical support on his right arm.

Over a hundred and fifty years ago, along these shores, the cruisers of the Preventive Men intercepted, and sometimes fired at, smuggling vessels and confiscated the cargoes of contraband tobacco and brandy. Some of the brandy, if it had got through, would have been blended with opium to make laudanum… the 'crack' of its day. So, there's a tradition to maintain here – though I have a chance to go one better than the Customs men of old. Why bother catching a barrel load of dancing monkeys, when you can kill the organ grinder?

The helmsman is sitting on the shoreward side of the stern. Close up it can be seen that he is sitting quite still.

Well done, Mr Big – stay like that.

The great Victorian guns of the fort over there in the town could project a 300 pound shell over four miles, while three hundred years earlier the cannons of the tiny Tudor gun battery at the end of the ancient breakwater were hard pushed to fire a 6 pound cannonball a mile and a half.

It's not that range for me today… but close… just over the mile.

I know they expect a grand finale, the timing is perfect, and they must be really in a panic now…let's not disappoint.

So be it.

The helmsman is sitting slightly twisted – his body is turned more to the shore.

Perfect…

Check the marker range… good. The compensator needs adjusting… one… two… three… no, just two dots. There is a strap on the helmsman's jacket. Line the sight cross hairs on it… good. Breath in… breath out… breath in… hold the trigger… gentle, gentle squeeze.

Agur! Aoi!

It's done – it's all done.

Everything out there seems to be in slow motion, the scarlet and black spinnaker deflates as the helmsman slumps into the boat and the dinghy veers out of control, and other spinnakers – rather like surrendering flags – collapse as they mark the moment of impact as following vessels collide.

Apart from the two at the front, that is: the yellow and the blue, and the white and green, sail blithely on.

40

'Get out of the bloody way!' yelled Melbury out of the car window.

Clare, with the ex-Motorway Maintenance light flashing on top of the GTI, was driving through the town centre as quickly as she could. Not fast enough, however, for her detective sergeant, who wound up like a spring, momentarily broke-off from abusing other road users to offer some driving instruction.

'Go on! Go on! Get past him – there's bags of room!'

There wasn't of course.

'Shit, Andy!' Clare, as she swung back in, shot him a glare, but the big man had wisely turned his head and was staring out of his open passenger window.

However, once they'd got through the town, she was able to put her foot down along the old naval base road: past the sad line of now empty buildings; the closed shops and naval outfitters, and the once packed to the gunnels pubs – The Admiral Jellicoe and The Lord Nelson.

Melbury, when he'd burst into the CID office, had immediately recognised the three intersections on the OS map as the permanent triangular race course marked by buoys in the bay. He'd also remembered the photograph of Gavin Adams's dinghy with the red and black spinnaker.

They were off to the yacht club. There was a race on… well, there was more than one race on.

'Christ! Watch out for that van!'

'Oh, for God's sake – zip it, Andy!'

The truth is Clare was finding it impossible to concentrate solely on her driving. She had something on her mind about the message they'd received. It was that bit about the posts – about the Ramsden posts. It was so obscure. How the hell were they supposed to know what they were?

Unless the killer knew they knew.

A thought was taking shape… and she didn't like it.

She didn't like it one little bit.

Clare slowed as she drove alongside the high security fence of the yacht club which had relocated into part of the abandoned navy base. Ordered lines of yacht masts could be seen in the compound. As they were reaching the main gate, the barrier swung up. The gate man had seen and heard them coming. Well, with the flashing light and her hand on the horn, they would have been difficult to miss, she thought. Melbury gave the man a wave as Clare drove in. She drove past the car parking area and pulled up outside the main entrance of the lavish newly built club house. There were some steps at the side that led up to a viewing area on the roof. There were about twenty or thirty spectators up there. Clare noticed that most of them were now looking at her car and not out to sea. She turned to her big detective sergeant, but didn't need to say anything.

'Got it, boss,' he said as he jumped out and headed for the steps.

As she got out of the car and ran to the main door, her head was buzzing as connections between past incidents flashed through her mind. A security guard suddenly appeared and blocked her way. 'Oh! Police – it's an emergency.'

A large man, with an annoying smirk on his face – he didn't move. 'You can't leave your car there,' he said pointing at her still flashing GTI. 'The mayor's coming down later to present the prizes.'

Clare fished her ID out of her pocket and brandished it in his face. 'CID – now get out of the way, or I'll have you booked! And stop anyone else coming in, apart from police.' She pushed past him and moments later, a red-faced and out of breath Melbury, joined her in the deserted reception area. 'I've rung in, something has happened – the race's ended in a fucking shambles!'

They were just about to go through the door into the bar, when a man came out.

'Police,' they said in chorus.

The man, short and tubby, and wearing a blazer, looked astonished. 'You're quick! We've not long phoned the Coast Guard and Ambulance.'

'Has something happened to a Dutchman with a red and black spinnaker?' asked Melbury.

Blazer Man now looked completely bemused. 'Yes… the *Tempest*. We heard from the race referee on the observation boat. It may be a heart attack, or something.'

Clare and Melbury looked at each other.

Yes, or something.

Things, like the correct pieces of a jigsaw, were dropping into place in Clare's mind. She felt a growing anxiety. She knew she needed to be somewhere else – quick. 'Is it Gavin Adams?' inquired Clare.

The man turned to Melbury. 'Well, it's unusual but–'

Melbury stopped him. 'I'm Detective Sergeant Melbury, this is Detective Inspector Morell.'

'Oh, sorry… Inspector.' He was flustered as he looked at Clare. 'You see there's nothing in the club's racing rules that prohibit it, but it's unusual that –' His attention had been distracted by the sight of the security guard arguing with several people who were trying to get in.

'What's unusual?' demanded Clare, blocking his view: he looked like a rabbit caught in headlights. 'What's unusual, for

God's sake?

'It's very unusual that the helm and the crew change over from their usual positions for a race.'

The crowd of people standing by the landing stage of the yacht club fell silent as the two vessels approached: the race referee's observation boat was towing in the *Tempest*. As it got closer, it was possible to see a body slumped in the hull, the lowered sail part-covering it like a shroud and the black band of the collapsed spinnaker was draped over the bow as if in mourning. The crewman, with an arm support over his wet-suit, was standing up clutching the mast.

Clare was aware that Melbury kept glancing at her. He must be wondering why she was so distracted.

Then his mobile rang. 'Yes… right… thanks.' Melbury put his phone back in his pocket. 'Reinforcements are on their way and SOCO and the pathologist have been informed.'

Clare nodded. 'Who is it?'

'I think Doc Howarth is on call.'

'Good.'

She turned to the man wearing the blazer who was standing alongside them. 'Sorry, I don't know your–'

'Charles Baines – I'm the Commodore.'

'Well, Mr Baines, we need to use a large room like your bar, to take evidence from witnesses. And could you also gather the competitors there when they come in?' she said, pointing to the small fleet of boats sailing in at a respectful distance, like a cortege, behind the now, very close to shore, motor boat and Flying Dutchman.

'Of course, Inspector, this is dreadful, dreadful – I'll get on with it.'

Just as he turned to go, two policemen appeared.

'You were quick!' said Melbury.

One of them recognised Clare. 'Ma'am – we were only a few minutes away from here, when we had the call.'

Clare nodded. She was aware that Melbury was looking at her anxiously again. She was finding it difficult to concentrate on the situation here because all the thoughts in her head were converging, and converging. She made a decision and turned to the two policemen. 'You're under Sergeant Melbury's orders.'

Melbury looked astonished.

Clare took hold of his arm and turned him away from the other policemen. 'Andy, put that boat when it comes in under quarantine until SOCO and Nick Howarth get here. Then make sure that you get everyone into the bar who was sailing and take statements from them. Ask Mr Baines to make a list. You'll have enough help soon – phone if you need more.'

Melbury was left open-mouthed as Clare turned on her heels and ran back in the direction of her car.

Matt Johns looked around as a wild-haired Karen Garland rushed into the CID office.

'I know,' she said as she ran her hands through a bird's nest – making not one jot of difference. 'I usually get the auditioning for "Annie" cracks on the way in, but it's a shambles out there.'

Johns swivelled on his chair to face her. 'How much do you know?'

'Apart from you telling me to come back pronto as there'd been a new message, nothing until a minute ago when the desk sergeant told me that Clare and Andy had gone to the yacht club where someone's been shot, uniforms following and the Super has just charged off somewhere else.'

'Yes, and I've heard again from Andy – just a minute ago.' There was a worried look on the young detective's face.

'Apparently the boss is acting really strange.'

'In what way?'

'Well, Clare hardly said a word as they were driving there. Andy said she was really pre-occupied by something, and then, as soon as a squad car arrived, she left Andy in charge and pissed-off! She didn't tell him where she was going – nothing. She just told him he was in charge of getting the body onshore – everything!'

'That's unlike her! You've tried her mobile… of course you have,' said Karen, quickly back pedalling in response to the look on his face.

'No answer, I've left a message. Now, come and look at this,' He stood up and taking her arm, walked over to the OS map.

'The message coordinates gave these three points in the bay. It's the course they race on.'

Karen pointed to the nearest part of the coastline. 'So, assuming that there's been a shot from the land, it's likely to be from the headland above Haldon Cove and The Preventy Inn.'

'Got it in one. As well as the uniforms going to the yacht club, the Super himself – who was here when Andy first phoned – is leading the rest of the cavalry there.'

'I thought I heard sirens going down the coast road as I was coming in. What about Kevin?'

Johns nodded. PC Hamer could usually be relied upon to be the first on the scene to anything on his patch. 'I've tried him but he's miles away doing a Safe Cycling Course in a primary school.'

'What do we do now?' demanded Karen impatiently.

Johns who had started pacing up and down, stopped, and gave her a hopeless look. 'Well, just sit it out until we hear something, I suppose.'

41

Her phone rang again: she ignored it… again. She was driving as quickly as she could back into town from the yacht club.

Clare was finding it difficult to concentrate with all the flashbacks that were fighting each other as they surfaced from the depths of her mind – and then fitted in place like the pieces of a jigsaw.

'*Because of the way this killer thinks and the information left – these two College guys have made themselves pretty indispensable,*' had said Simmonds.

'*The daughter had a "problem",*' Gill Doyle had told her.

'*He asked me not to say anything about his problems,*' had said Ellis.

Then there was that meeting at that pub when he had that dog with him, she thought. After the time they'd argued when they were both soaked to the skin, she'd have been happy never to have seen Rob Ellis again, but Yorick had ordered her to. She remembered Rob saying that he'd been *persuaded* to meet as well.

Someone else, apart from Yorick, wanted Rob still to be involved in the case.

'Call yourself a fucking cop!' she shouted and hit the horn, more in frustration than as signal for the vehicles in front to get out of the way. There was – even though the roof light was still flashing – little chance of getting quickly through the narrow streets of the town centre.

But there was one bit that didn't make sense – where was the Basque connection?

When she reached the esplanade, she didn't turn up the road away from the coast which passed the police station, but drove fast past the pier and Queen Victoria's statue and turned off the tight roundabout into the college campus. Having managed not to catch the GTI's tyres this time, she pulled up by the clock tower steps and leaving the lights flashing, scattered a group of students as she took the steps two at a time. Clare ran down the corridors and rushed into the Geography Department Office.

Gill Doyle looked at her in amazement. 'I've just been trying to call you. What the hell's going on?'

'I'm not sure. Have you heard from Rob?' asked Clare anxiously.

'That's what I was trying to phone you about. Grace was in the corridor when –'

'What?' Clare had a tight hold of the other woman's arm.

'Rob was rushing down the corridor and nearly knocked her over. She said he was in a hell of a state. He said something like, "Sorry Grace – I've got to stop him – enough deaths." Then he rushed off.'

Clare was looking around.

'I've sent Grace to see if anybody in the department knows anything. Are you alright, Clare? You've gone white!'

'When was this?' asked Clare, ignoring Gill Doyle's observation.

'Well, it's a wonder you didn't see him drive off. You must have only just missed the Rust Bucket.'

'Where does Travers live, Gill? – I need to get there,' said Clare, at the same time as she was trying to breath.

'In an old house called The Grange. It's in the hills above Haldon Cove. You know where the Preventy Inn is? Why do you want to – God, you look awful.'

'I'm alright,' lied Clare – she'd realised that those cliffs were the nearest land point to take a shot at Adam's boat.'

'It's difficult to find the house if you don't know it – that's why I'm coming as well… And at the same time you can tell me what the hell's going on,' Gill added as she steered Clare towards the door.

Clare, the skin on her knuckles white as she gripped the steering wheel, swung round the campus roundabout. Neither woman spoke until they'd joined the coast road, and then Gill Doyle, looking anxious, raised her voice over the engine noise. 'Now, what's all this about?'

'In a minute, Gill.' Clare was struggling to keep it together, worried that Rob Ellis having somehow realised it was Travers, was now in danger simply because *he knows*.

Then she remembered something that Emma had said about Galpin. It was something on the lines that if he'd been shagging very young women, then they ought to be looking for an angry brother, an uncle… or a father. She'd thought for some time that Galpin was the key because he didn't fit with the drug dealing of the other victims and that just one break in connection with his death would have things falling into place.

'Gill, the girl Hannah, Travers's daughter, you said she had a *problem*. Was she pregnant?' Clare glanced across at her passenger who looked astonished at the question.

'How did you know? Isabelle confided in me and no one else… apart from telling *him*.'

'She had an abortion?'

'Yes, but –'

'Gill, tell me – it's critical. I need to know.' snapped Clare.

'Ok. She was so young, sixteen. Bix knew nothing about it at the time. It was during one of the times he was away –

sometimes he was away for ages. He didn't find out until after Hannah was dead. He was terrible about it. I told you he was strict Catholic. He blamed Isabelle. He made her life a misery when he should have been supporting her and look what happened… she killed herself. I hate him.'

'Did Hannah ride at Winterstone Stables?'

Clare glanced across again at Gill Doyle, who now looked completely dumbfounded. 'How did you work that out? Isabelle let something slip when we were drunk about someone at the stables. I've never breathed a word – well, I never knew a name anyway.'

'It was someone called Dean Galpin – the man who got shot at Full Moon Copse,' said Clare, trying desperately to be calm – trying desperately not to think of Rob Ellis.

'There was something else about Winterstone. Bix had got this stupid idea in his head that Hannah had become dependent on drugs and somehow the stables were to blame. He even thought that she may have been on drugs when she fell. It was all nonsense – she may have dabbled a little at parties like a lot of others, but nothing more. He was crazy.'

The last piece of the jigsaw!

Gill Doyle did not say anything more for a few seconds… then shouted. 'Oh, my God, you think Bix Travers is behind all this!'

'Yes, and there's been another shooting. Grace heard Rob say he was going to stop him. Somehow Rob must have realised as well. I'm worried sick about him,' admitted Clare, to herself as much as to Gill.

'You're not such a hard ass cop are you? said Gill as she touched Clare's arm. 'But I'm sure Bix Travers wouldn't harm Rob because of that weird upbringing of his, all that honour and loyalty to family and friends and companions crap, I'm sure.'

'What do you mean about Travers's *weird upbringing*,

Gill?'

As they drove east, Gill Doyle told Clare about James Travers. Sometimes she had to repeat herself, to make herself heard over the GTI's complaining tyres and engine, as Clare drove fast along the coast road into what was becoming very familiar territory. Firstly under the shadows of the ridgeway, with Chalcombe Bumps and Drovers' Knoll clear on the skyline, then past the Co-op Stop-and-Shop and Frampton's cottage before passing the gate that Rob Ellis had lifted off its hinges and the steep track that lead up to the Travellers' camp.

Clare swung off the road onto the tree lined lane that led to the Galleon Inn, but before the final steep descent down to the pub, turned left onto the narrow top road that skirted the edge of Spring Rise Wood. By the time that they were driving in the hills high above Haldon Cove and the Preventy Inn, where she'd met Rob Ellis and that dog – that fucking dog, she thought – she'd just about got the story that Gill Doyle was telling her about Travers, clear in her mind.

42

James Travers's public school accent, was just that, an accent he acquired at a public school from the age of thirteen... the year he first set foot in England.

He was raised by his mother, whose name was Maia Etuxa, and her close family in a village in the Pyrenees. She taught him English. He also spoke Spanish fluently, in addition to his first language, Euskera... the ancient, complex language of the Basque people. His family, like all the others in the isolated Basque mountain community where he was born and grew up, were highly conservative in their ways, religious and nationalistic. However, his family were special, in that his grandfather and uncles, were by tradition, all highly skilled hunters and mountain guides.

His father was an English travel writer of considerable private means who, while he was staying in the village writing a book on the area, had an affair with the pretty, English speaking village school teacher. As soon as he discovered she was pregnant, he quickly returned to his comfortable bachelor life in London and apart from forwarding a generous regular allowance had absolutely nothing to do with the boy's upbringing. However, when Maia, who died young, made a dying wish that the boy become an English gentleman, he came and took him to England and gave him his own name... James Travers. But he made no real attempt to get to know the boy, sending him immediately to board at public school. In fact the boy spent most of his vacations and free time hunting and tracking back home in his mountain community – something he kept up, in secret, to the present time.

James Travers Senior died when James Travers Junior was at Oxford. Travers, highly intelligent and articulate, had over the years gained a reputation as a cartographer and historian – in particular, as an expert on this particular stretch of coastline where he has lived for over twenty years. Travers has kept, throughout all his time in England, as a nickname, the name he was called as a boy in the mountain village in that remote part of the Pyrenees they call the Urola Urhoi.

Bix.

'He'd be surprised if he knew I was aware of all that,' said Gill Doyle when she had finished. 'He's very sensitive about his background. He never mentions it. People just assume he's English. Isabelle never talked about it either – it's just that we were so close that she told me in confidence. Slow down. It's a left turn in about a hundred yards.'

Clare only saw the gap in the huge wall-like bank of rhododendrons when she was nearly level with it. It was the start of a weed infested gravel driveway. A name plate with 'The Grange' written on it was almost completely obscured by a cluster of deep red rhododendron flowers. The drive lead up to a large, neglected looking, terrace garden.

'It was the Forbes's old house – Isabelle's family home. He's letting it go to rack and ruin.'

'No Rust Bucket,' observed Clare, as she pulled up outside the large elegant Edwardian villa.

'I doubt if Rob's parked round the back either, but we'll have a look in a minute.'

Gill was out of the car even quicker than Clare and was the first to the door. 'Bix? Bix?,' she shouted as she banged the door hard.

There was no answer, and Clare, peering through the nearest window, couldn't see anyone. 'Round the back,' she said as she set off running.

'Oh, shit!'

Clare looked back over her shoulder. Gill Doyle had lost a high-heel shoe.

Ellis's Volvo wasn't parked at the back of the house. The back door, as expected, was locked. There was a sash window over the sink in the kitchen. Clare looked around and then, kicking a brick free from a border edging, used it to smash the upper sash. She released the catch and after forcing up the lower window as far as it would go, struggled with some difficulty into the kitchen.

'The back door's deadlocked and I can't find a key. Hang on.'

Seconds later Clare shouted again. 'Front door's the same.'

'It's OK, Clare. I'll check the outbuildings while you look around.'

Clare ran through the house, only vaguely aware that it was untidy and dirty. She searched methodically, concentrating that she didn't miss a room, a wardrobe or large cupboard, anything, anywhere, which could contain a trussed-up – or worse – Rob Ellis.

There was no sign of him.

She looked for a telephone but could find only a couple of empty sockets.

Clare was climbing back out of the window when she heard the sound of splintering wood. She went around the corner of the house and was just in time to see Gill Doyle, while somehow still looking remarkably elegant, vigorously levering the padlock off an old garage door with a garden fork. 'There was nothing in the house. What are you doing?'

'Stupid question for a cop, I'm breaking and entering…

just like you. Oh, fuck!' Gill dropped the fork and looked at her left hand.

'Hurt yourself?'

'No, worse than that, I've broken a nail. Give me a hand to get this door open.'

They dragged open the door. It was dark. Clare unbolted the other half of the door and opened that as well. There was a car inside – an Audi.

'Travers's car here, so where is he?'

'I thought it might be. I was checking. You see he's got an old Land Rover as well.'

The right Land Rover at long last, thought Clare. 'Where do you think Travers could be?'

'He uses it when he goes to the old chalet Isabelle's family had on the heath. I bet he's there. It's near to a little lake called the Magic Pool.'

'I know it!' responded Clare as she was reaching for her mobile. 'I'll try just on the off-chance… no, nothing.'

'There's no reception from here to the heath. They say it's due to the military stuff at the army camp. What is it?'

Something had caught Clare's eye. On a shelf in the garage, with other paints, there was a tin with the distinctive Renault logo.

There were yellow paint stains on the lid.

Karen Garland had quickly become impatient with 'waiting' and was pacing up and down the CID office. 'This is killing me, Matt.'

'Yes, but I don't want to bother Andy again. He's got his hands full at the yacht club, and he's ordered us not to go over.'

'And the desk sergeant will come flying in,' said Karen, nodding towards the CID office door, 'if there's anything from the search team at Haldon Cove.'

Johns was looking at his mobile. 'Clare still isn't answering,' he said, stating the obvious.

'I bet she's gone looking for those lecturers.'

'Of course, I'm stupid, I should have thought of that!' Johns reached for his phone again. 'I've met Dr Ellis, but what was the other one called? I don't know him as I've been away.'

'Dr Travers, James Travers, though he's known as Bix. He's a well-known local historian apparently. He's a strange man, not surprising really I suppose, as he lost his partner and their daughter in–'

'What was that?' Johns had shot out of his seat. 'That name? That nickname?'

'Bix.'

'Christ! Come on!' he shouted as he grabbed his jacket from the back of his chair.

'Matt? Where are we going?'

'The College, Karen – Listen! – My dad often used to work at his company's office in Munich and we sometimes went with him. Well, he used to take me to the football and Bayern Munich had this brilliant French full back – his first name was Bixente. It was shortened to Bix!'

'He was French you say?'

'Yes, from the French side of the Pyrenees – but he's a Basque. I remember because ETA threatened him for not contributing to their revolutionary fund.'

Grace was startled , when two young people, a boyish looking man with short blond hair and a girl with a wild auburn mane, burst into the Geography Department office.

'Police,' they said.

'Goodness me, more of you!'

'More?' said Johns.

'I was coming back to the office, not very long ago, when I saw Inspector Morell and Gill Doyle, the department secretary, running down the corridor.'

'Do you know where they were going to?' demanded Karen – very abruptly.

Johns tried to catch her eye.

'No, but I think it is to do with Dr Ellis.'

'Why is that, please? Please, it's very important,' asked Johns, overcompensating for Karen's sharpness.

Grace then explained what Ellis and said.

Johns and Karen looked at each other – Karen nodded.

'Where does Dr Traver's live?'

Grace looked surprised at Johns's question. 'It's called The Grange. The phone seems to be dead and he's not answering his mobile – Dr Ellis doesn't have one. The house is difficult to find, it's on the old road in the hills above Haldon Cove.'

'Is that the one with the long stretch of rhododendrons?' asked Karen.

'Yes, my dear. And that's exactly where the house is.'

'Thanks! Come on Matt.'

'Sure you know?'

'Yes – stick with me, kid,' she replied, with a quick smile at Grace, as she pushed him towards the door.

'Oh stop!'

They turned and looked at Grace.

'Dr Travers spends a lot of time in an old chalet he has on the heath – it's by the Magic Pool.'

'Good, God,' muttered Johns.

The crunching of flinty gravel underfoot masked out all other sounds as Rob Ellis, pushing back long fern fronds as he went, ran up the narrow overgrown path towards the old wooden chalet that nestled in a small stand of stunted pines.

Then he saw him.

Travers was sitting by the lone gorse bush that was on the top of a small heather covered mound – one of the old barrows of the heath. Ellis moved up towards him.

'That's close enough, Rob.'

Ellis took no notice.

'I said that's close enough. Stop there!'

James Travers lifted up a rifle… Ellis stopped.

'What the hell is all this, Bix?'

'It's nearly at an end, Rob. That animal who raped my little girl was the first to go, that left the scum that turned her to drugs. The drugs killed her you know – when she fell, it was the drugs. The little turd that started it, who supplied drugs at the stables, I kept alive for as long as he was useful. He led me to that red-haired bitch that ran him. Then to the one at the top – the one who matters – the one who brings the poison into the county. But, Rob, I'm sorry; really sorry you had to be involved.'

Ellis didn't reply.

'Rob?'

There was still no response for a few seconds – then Ellis broke his silence. 'It was you? You used me, all along the bloody line, you used me,' yelled Ellis. 'The sob story that you weren't fit enough to be directly involved early on, insisting I say nothing about you, because you were still recovering – leaving me that newspaper and those old maps for me to contact the police. Yes, and making sure you convinced me to stay on the case when I wanted to walk away. What a stupid bastard I've been. You're off your fucking head. No! No! – Don't! Don't'! Please don't…'

43

Neither Clare nor Gill Doyle had spoken for a while. Both were deep in their own thoughts. It wasn't necessary for Gill to give directions because, once they'd left The Grange, the long straight road dropped down towards the heath and Clare put her foot down.

Gill was the one to break the silence. 'Let's hope Rob is –' She stopped short of the obvious.

'The stupid arsehole – why did he have to go off alone!' snapped Clare, as she hit the steering wheel with a fist. She felt the other woman touch her arm and turned to look at her.

'He does go on a lot about you.'

'Complaining I suppose,' said Clare defensively, feeling the colour in her cheeks.

'And how!' Gill laughed. 'But that's it you see. The way he's smartened up, especially having his hair trimmed. There's been no one, as far as I know, since he's been down here. You're good for him.'

So, that's why there's a cessation of hostilities?

Gill Doyle had paused, seemingly unsure how to phrase something. 'Rob was going to get married.'

'What happened?'

'She was killed. It was tragic.'

Somehow Clare knew. He'd seen death before, he'd said, including someone who was close. 'A climbing accident – Rob was there?'

'Yes.'

Clare braked hard as they joined the road that skirted the belt of conifers fringing the heath land. She knew where she was when she saw the MOD sign to the army camp.

'There's a turning along here somewhere, which gets you as near to the pool as you can with a car – Bix Travers uses his Land Rover to go cross-country.'

'I know where it is, Gill! A guy who lives in a cottage near there was briefly a suspect.'

True to her word, Clare remembered the almost hidden turning in a gap in a high bank of ferns. She drove along the sand and gravel track to the little amphitheatre of a parking area. She spotted it first. 'It's here!'

There was only one vehicle there. It was the Rust Bucket. Rob Ellis's unmistakeable old brown Volvo Estate. Within seconds Clare had jumped out of the GTI and was running up to where a narrow path disappeared into a wall of ferns and gorse.

'Oh, shit!'

She stopped and looked back. Gill Doyle was holding a foot.

'What?'

'Me and my stupid bloody shoes, I've twisted an ankle. Ouch!'

Clare came back.

'Damn, I feel so useless. Give me the car keys. I'll get to a phone somehow – take care.'

Clare seemed to have been running along the narrow path for an eternity. The sound of her shoes crunching into the flinty gravel being constantly interrupted as she paused to push long fronds of saw-edged ferns out of her way. And every time she did this, she seemed to anger yet another squadron of instantly airborne flies.

The ferns thinned a little and she was able to make out Dave Yates's cottage in the distance. Two ponies – heath croppers she remembered they were called – were grazing in front of it. Clare then began to look for the path that led towards the pool – the pool with the amazing blue water. She'd been walking down it with Hamer and Johns when a be-goggled Dave Yates, carrying a sickle and dressed head-to-toe in old gorse cutting gear had startled them – which had been the last thing she'd needed after having come face to face with an adder, ten minutes before.

This must be it!

She'd spotted a gap in the ferns that lead towards a huge yellow gorse break. But as she slowly found out, that was it – it lead deeper and deeper into the gorse. When she turned back, the gorse, that had seemed unusually benign as it drew her in, now caught and tore at her clothes.

The air, as so often on the heath, was stultifying, her throat was dry and then she ran into a cloud of gnats. Then she heard it; heard it over her coughing; heard it over the sound of her blood pumping; heard it over the buzz of insects, heard it over the amplified chirping of crickets… it was a voice… a man's voice! There was a gap in the gorse. She plunged through it and found herself on the path that led down to the pool.

That voice.

It was Rob Ellis's – and the great wave of relief that swept through her momentarily drained her of all energy.

Then she saw him.

Rob Ellis was shouting and waving his fist at someone. Then she spotted James Travers on a small hillock about forty yards away. She noticed he was holding something… it was a gun. Clare was now running fast and Ellis didn't notice her as she emerged from the cover of the ferns – he was too busy yelling at Travers:

'You're off your fucking head. No! No! Don't! Please don't!'

'No!' screamed Clare. Ellis turned just as she knocked him off his feet and together they rolled down a steep heather covered bank before falling into one of the small gravel hollows that pock-mark the heath.

'Christ, Clare! What the–'

'Thank God, you're alive!' Clare pushed herself up on an elbow, leant across... and kissed him. Then she got to her knees and a nonplussed Rob Ellis became even more nonplussed.

She hit him.

'You stupid, stupid man!' she shouted – then began hitting him again, really hard.

'Stop it!' Ellis grabbed her with both arms and pulled her to him. 'Clare! What's going on? Of course I'm alive – why shouldn't I be?'

'Grace at the College heard you say you were going to stop him,' she inclined her head in the Travers's direction. 'You were going to stop him killing again.'

Ellis, who was still holding her, twisted himself so that they were looking at each other. 'Look, I've only just discovered what a complete twat I've been. I've just found out how he used me – that he was the one who was doing all this. I came here because he sent me a message saying that he was going to end it. Saying it was all over. All finished. I was horrified, there'd been enough deaths in that family. Then the message went on and on about how he wanted to see me, to apologise for involving me but it was the only way, he said. I hadn't got a fucking clue until I got here. I thought he was just about to shoot himself when you came flying out of nowhere.'

'He's going to shoot himself?'

Ellis nodded.

'Oh, Rob, I'd got it all wrong.' Wrong or not she could feel the tension unwinding as she looked at him – held by him – and there were other feelings stirring that she'd been fighting off for some time.

Ellis let go of her – she didn't want him to – and crouching, looked out over the heather at the rim of the hollow.

'What's he doing?'

'Nothing, he's just standing there, holding that rifle.' Ellis was looking around. 'Anyway, where's the rest of your lot?'

Clare explained why she was alone.

'Right, so hopefully, Gill will be able to get to a phone. So we keep him talking, we keep him nice and calm,' he said, looking at her intently. 'OK?'

Clare nodded… then frowned. He'd made it sound more like an order than a suggestion. 'Who's the cop here?' she muttered.

'What?'

There was the sound of laughter: loud sardonic laughter. Clare, ignoring Ellis, cautiously raised herself and pushing some heather to one side looked out. Travers had put his rifle down. He was standing with his hands on his hips. 'Well, Detective Inspector Morell, seeing that rugby tackle it looks like you've got it wrong. Did you think I was going to shoot Rob, because he'd found out? You do seem to make a habit of making mistakes.'

She jumped to her feet. 'Fuck you, you arsehole!' she shouted.

Ellis hauled her back into the hollow. 'Well that's keeping him nice and calm.'

Travers laughed again. A different laugh. A laugh that merged on the hysterical.

'He's off his head,' said Ellis. 'He said the first guy he shot raped his daughter and the others he killed were responsible for turning her into a drug addict.'

'That's not really true, Rob – though he's responsible for

all the killings.'

Ellis pushed his hair away from his eyes and Clare thought that the scar over his left eye seemed more prominent than usual... or it could be that she was closer to him than usual. 'I'd no idea. He's a strange guy but this is unbelievable. In the past I've asked Gill Doyle. She really dislikes him and knows about him. She hasn't said why – she's loyal about some promise to his partner who was an old friend. Oh, what was her name?'

'Isabelle,' said Clare. Her mind buzzing. She was feeling stupid about the way Travers had used her – solving clues he himself had set. The sick, clever bastard, she thought.

'Inspector?' came Travers's raised voice. He'd rested the rifle against a gorse bush.

'That's good,' said Ellis – articulating Clare's thoughts as well as his own.

'Yes?' Clare called back.

'It's just a thought which you can treat as a final confessional if you like – before I join my Isabelle and Hannah. Is there anything you wish to know?'

Clare took a deep breath. Here was a chance to keep him talking. She glanced at Ellis, then narrowed her eyes at him, in response to the annoying, 'now don't fuck this up, woman' look he was giving her... he didn't blink.

She took her time before speaking – aware that she must raise her voice a little but not sound aggressive. 'Yes there are some questions. Why bother with the charade – all the yellow sign stuff – in the first place? You didn't need us. You tracked down everyone yourself.'

'It wasn't a game; I had to get slowly involved into a position where I could control you. It was practical – insurance in case I had problems following the trail. I had fewer than I thought. Frampton lead me like a lamb to slaughter, to that woman and to the Domino Club. It was also useful to know exactly what you were up to. And also I began to enjoy leading you around by the nose.'

Clare didn't rise to this, even though she realised that much of Travers's recent improved appearance and energy had, in part, been at her expense. Then she noticed he'd suddenly become edgy. He started pacing around the top of the barrow – but, at least he didn't pick up the rifle again.

'We were getting closer,' said Clare calmly. 'We knew about the Basque connection.'

'I'm impressed.'

'What the fuck's all this about?' grumbled Ellis – who then carried on mumbling about not been told anything.

'Shut up, Rob,' said Clare out of the side of her mouth. 'There is one question. Why go to the trouble of killing Sonia Nichol with that car bomb, instead of shooting her?'

'I wouldn't have shot, stabbed, bludgeoned or strangled a woman – that would be against the code I was brought up in. But it was permissible to get rid of her by other means.'

'How the hell did you do that – you were with us?' yelled Ellis. Clare looked at him. He was red with anger. She put a hand on his arm.

'It was easy enough. I had been putting her on edge with letters – which I told her to destroy immediately – for days. I'd convinced Sonia Nichol and Gavin Adams that some heavy drugs mob was about to make a move to take over their patch. The letter I sent the day before, told her to stay at home the following morning and when she heard three rings on her phone – she was to get away from Tallington House as quickly as she could, as her life was in danger. Ironic that, Inspector, don't you think? I used my cell phone, a simple pay-as-you go, when I was in your car, then I simply pressed a second mobile – the detonator – in my pocket when she got in that silver monster of a car. I needed to see her die.'

'You bastard – that's sick! And you could have killed Clare

here – she was lucky. I'll –' Ellis made to climb out of the hollow.

'No, Rob! No!' pleaded Clare as she pulled him back.

I'm so sorry, Rob – forgive me,' pleaded Travers. 'Now I've only got one thing to do.'

As they watched, he stood the rifle up on its butt and picked up a long thin length of metal.

Clare, knowing she had to do something quickly, ignored Ellis's obvious mutterings about Travers being about to press the trigger with the length of metal and shouted, 'What about Gavin Adams?'

'What about him? He's dead. He died at sea. It was *Agur! Aio*! – Good Bye! Like the others.' Travers laughed. 'Detective Superintendent Simmonds told us that there would be a grand gesture before it was over. I didn't want to disappoint him.'

'It's not easy to distinguish between the two men in a dinghy when they're sailing is it? said Clare, asking what turned out to be a rhetorical question. 'They wear identical dark blue wet suits, yellow life jackets, dark peaked caps – and invariably use shades.'

There was silence for a few seconds… though silence, with the continual buzzing of insects, is a relative term as far as the heath is concerned. Clare looked at Ellis and touched her lips. He nodded… and she was momentarily thrown by the fact that he'd just agreed to shut-up and not interfere.

'What are you getting at?' There was a cracked edge to Travers's voice.

'Gavin Adam's is very keen but he's not as good a helmsman as Simon Moore, the guy who crewed for him. Adams's boat, unusually so, was doing very well in the race, wasn't it?'

'Get to the point.' shouted Travers.

'Apparently there's nothing in the yacht club rules to

disallow it. To stop Gavin Adams, who's strapped up injured right arm and wrist prevented him from handling a tiller, doing what he did.' Clare paused, stalling for time. Then she raised her voice. 'Got it?… They changed places…. You shot the wrong man.'

'You're lying!!' screamed Travers.

'Think about it. One was wearing an arm support over his wet suit… the one you didn't shoot.'

Travers stood motionless for a second or so and then picked up his rifle. Ellis pulled Clare lower until they could just see over the rim of the hollow. 'Brilliant move that, Clare. You've certainly stopped him shooting himself, now he's probably going to shoot us instead before going looking for this Adams guy again!'

She suddenly felt drained: the little men with the hammers in her head had picked up the tempo; her throat felt like sandpaper, and she was uncomfortable. Her shirt – like everything else – was sticking to her. She took off her jacket and sat down. 'They'll know at the station soon. They'll be here soon and –'

Then she noticed it. It was looking at her. It was looking at her through vertical slits below a distinctive V on its head.

'What is it?' Ellis asked anxiously, looking at Clare, who deathly white, had begun to shake. Then he saw the snake. 'Oh… it's… I think it's a smooth snake. There are lots of them here – they're harmless.'

She knew he was lying: she'd recognised the adder's brick red body with its zigzag stripe. 'I've got to get out,' gasped Clare struggling to get to her feet.

'No.' Ellis was stopping her. 'Travers's will shoot. I'll, I'll get rid of it.' Ellis looking around found a stick.

It was a very short stick.

He held it out at arm's length and moved tentatively towards the snake.

Mistake.

'Oh, fuck – it's bitten me!' he shouted as the adder struck, and then slithered past him and Clare, with a scream, shot out of the safety of the gravel hollow.

'Clare, No!' He scrambled out after her and caught her ankle and as she fell there was a splatter of sand and flints in the bank behind them. Travers was standing on the lower slope of the barrow, the rifle was held at his hip. He'd missed. He must have been coming towards them. Ironically the man who could kill at a mile… had missed at thirty yards. Then he was looking not at them, but down at the gun. He was fiddling with it. There seemed to be something wrong and for a crucial few seconds, he was unaware that Rob Ellis was running towards him as fast as he could.

Clare got to her feet, 'Rob! No!'

Ellis's long legs almost made it.

Almost.

Travers saw Ellis when he was only a few strides away, and swung the rifle by the barrel. Clare screamed as Ellis fell and Travers turned the gun around and faced her. It was a moment that would haunt her for ever. That split second when she thought she was going to die and then the way, almost as if in slow motion, that Travers was powered sideways before he fell.

She was unaware, over the next few minutes, that a Jeep was approaching quickly down from the ridge: Clare was on her knees cradling Rob Ellis's head. 'Speak to me – speak to me!'

There was a crunch of gravel as the vehicle stopped. A soldier jumped out, rested his rifle against the vehicle and rushed over to Clare and Ellis. The driver, another soldier, got out and went over to where Travers was lying.

'He's dead,' said the driver. 'That was one hell of a shot, sir.'

'Thank, God,' replied Captain Guy Lovat, as he crouched and placed his arm around Clare's shoulders.

44

The Englishman, the young Basques of the village had called him, even though James Travers had been born there, been christened Bixente Etuxa there, had not stepped foot outside the area until he was thirteen – and had returned for long and frequent spells.

The last time he was in the village in the Urola Urhoi, he spent most of his time in the company of an uncle who had been an ETA member: a time spent in honing, on a newly acquired sniper rifle, the considerable marksman's skills he had developed as a boy – and learning about explosives.

Detective Superintendent Paul Simmonds always referred to it afterwards as *The Case of the Drop Pot Man*. He was delighted at the outcome, mainly because of the spin-off. Simmonds had immediately pulled in and, as he said, 'rattled an already shaken' Gavin Adams, turned over the Domino Club and Adams's home, and in co-operation with Danny Breen, not only closed down a drug business, but also opened a Pandora's Box on money-laundering links.

The Case of the Drop Pot Man, at the end, was in itself, well… simple. It had nothing to do with Animal Rights; really it had nothing to do with drugs either. It was just the case of a highly intelligent, unstable man – who had spent much of his adult life running back to a childhood cocoon – trying to offload his own inadequacies as a partner, and perhaps even more as a father, by blaming others for these shortcomings… and punishing them.

Clare was sitting in front of her dressing table mirror. She checked her make-up – again. She fiddled with her hair – again. It was a bit different but nice. *Richard* had managed to fit her in. It had, as usual, been difficult, apparently requiring a re-shuffling of all the bookings in his appointment book for the next eighteen months or so.

She got up and went to look at herself in the wardrobe door mirror. She'd put on a soft black velvet jacket with turn up sleeves over a white Muji blouse and her denim skirt. She'd been told she 'looked a million dollars' when she'd worn this outfit before – and that was without the advantage of the sling-back Jimmy Choos borrowed from Emma. The next time she looked in the mirror, she was wearing jeans and her favourite jacket, the linen one with the piped-edges. Hmm, it looked good. Dry cleaning had got rid of all the orange juice stain from the day she met Rob Ellis at The Preventy Inn. Clare found she was grinning at herself in the mirror, when she recalled him chasing Shit Face the Wolfhound, up and down the beach.

A few minutes later she was back again in front of the mirror, this time in her Harvey Nicks suit. She frowned. What the fuck's going on here? Who's writing this? As if the last few days had not been unreal enough… now she was in some 'chick-lit' novel!

Matt Johns and Karen Garland had driven to The Grange. Johns had climbed through the broken kitchen window and quickly went through the house, while Karen checked the forced-open garage and the back of the house. Within a few minutes they were back in the car and driving fast down the straight road that lead to the heath. Johns had immediately recognised the chalet that Grace had mentioned by the Magic Pool, from the day he was there with Clare and PC Kevin

Hamer. It was unlikely he would ever forget… because it was where Yates had loomed out like Mad Max.

When they reached the junction with the road that skirted the heath, there was, as expected, still no mobile signal. Johns, then – after discovering from Karen that the Bridge Inn was half-a-mile up the road – shrewdly turned north and not south. He made two phone calls from the pub. One to the station, and more importantly as it turned out, another to the nearby army camp. He spoke to Captain Guy Lovat before he spoke to the desk sergeant.

Soon after, they found Gill Doyle hobbling along the gravel track – her swollen ankle had been too much for the accelerator of Clare's car. Then they heard the sound of a low-flying helicopter overhead.

Clare had insisted on going in the army helicopter to the hospital with Rob Ellis. There was good news… and bad. The good news was that he only had a severely bruised shoulder from the rifle butt. The bad news was that – well, he had to be different as everyone at the College said – he'd reacted badly to the adder bite. Most reactions are mild, very occasionally there's a death. Clare was told that the last one in Britain was thirty years ago – which was of no comfort. Then he had side-effects from the anti-venom treatment. She'd refused to go home and sat with him. His fever broke in the early hours – and Clare fell asleep in a chair by his bed.

Later, Matt Johns and Karen Garland came to the hospital, and Clare nearly hugged the life out of both of them – though Karen insisted that the phone call to Lovat was all down to Matt's ('My BGF for life') quick thinking.

Then there was the sound of a whirlwind on the corridor… Emma had arrived.

Johns said afterwards that if only he had not had to go away, then 'Bix' Travers would have been exposed much earlier. Nobody was having any of it. His action had saved the lives of Clare and Ellis. Melbury ('I taught him all he knows.') went round the station like a proud uncle, and Simmond insisted that, 'The lad should go far – I'll make damned sure he does.'

The hospital corridor was quiet and Clare was cursing under her breath as she attempted to pick the stubborn Tesco price labels from the packs of grapes and strawberries she was holding. He'd sent her some lovely flowers and here she was bringing him some manky fruit! Everything had turned out into a rush. It shouldn't have been; it was a couple of hours since the phone call she'd made to this place, when she'd been told that Rob Ellis had recovered and was fussing to be discharged, but as a precaution he was being kept in another day.

She'd been ages getting ready. Her bedroom had clothes, including her favourite jacket and her Harvey Nicks suit, strewn all over the place and now here she was, standing outside a private room in the hospital wearing a velvet jacket, Muji blouse, denim skirt and Emma's Jimmy Choos. Clare was getting that feeling again, that this really wasn't happening. She'd once had a flatmate who used to change her knickers about every twenty minutes in case her boyfriend came round. That was possibly understandable – this had been ridiculous. She took a deep breath, tapped the door gently and part-opened it. 'Can I come in?'

'Yes… Hello, Meringue, wow! Glad to see you found your missing skirt.'

Rob Ellis was sitting up in bed. He gave her one of those broad smiles of his.

Clare closed the door behind her. 'You look great!' Yes, he really did, she thought – except for that rather hairy chest. He was broader across the shoulders than she'd ever imagined.

And surely that's more an eight pack than a six? He sat up further and the bed sheet slipped low on his slim waist and she was getting some strong feelings, that if they were to start one of their usual arguments – then she'd be ripping that off with her teeth.

Oh, say it woman.

'Look, Rob. I know we often –'

'Clare.'

'What?'

'Shut up. The answer to your question is a *yes* and a *really big yes* to the next one.'

She was sitting on the edge of the bed running a hand through his hair. 'I think I preferred it when it was long.'

'Oh, you perverse woman, I had it trimmed because of you.'

'You had it cut for me – augh!' she teased. 'Anyway, you're going grey.'

'That's not bloody surprising since I met you. Ouch! That hurt, it's my bad shoulder.'

'It's your other one that's got the bruise.'

'I forgot you were a cop. Anyway, there's a pattern here. You kissing first and hitting after. I think I'll have to slap you in handcuffs.'

'That can be arranged.'

He moved very close. 'Hmm, living up to your surname are we Mademoiselle Morell? Chanel No 5 bought in a posh city store before you came down here?'

'Close, Welshman. It's a Calvin Klein from Super Drug.'

But he'd got it right and she was having some mixed feelings here about a man recognising perfume. Though Chanel No 5, although not cheap, was common enough wasn't it?

Wasn't it?

They didn't speak for a moment or so. It was Ellis who broke the silence. 'Clare, stop looking at me with those, those things – those eyes of yours, like that.'

She placed her hands either side of his face. 'Oh, you mean like this.'

'For God's sake stop it woman or I'll be embarrassing myself here! Stop it, and I'll tell you a secret. Good. You remember when we were running up Drovers' Knoll, and you accused me of looking at your bum.'

'I'm a northern lass, remember – I said arse,' she replied in her best posh Cheshire accent. 'But don't remind me, I felt stupid. You'd hurt your Achilles tendon.'

'I hadn't, I lied. I was looking at your bum; it's a lovely, lovely... lovely bum.'

'Hey, cut that out!'

'Trust me – I'm a doctor. And this is a hospital.'

'No, it's that someone might come in. God, I... Stop it, Rob!'

He didn't and just like at The Preventy, her skirt started its disappearing act again, though this time the riding-up was manually assisted. Flustered, and in a battle, where one side – hers – was approaching surrender at the speed of light, she forced herself to move away from the edge of the bed.

'Clare?'

'Sorry, I'd better go' she stammered, though it was the last thing she wanted to do. 'I'll come back later.'

She'd reached the door before she turned round and looked back at the bed.

Oh, my God!

She just blurted it out. 'And you can cut out the PORADO SHOSKA while you're in here!'

'What?'

Clare turned away and reached for the door handle. 'Bye,'

she said weakly not trusting herself to turn round. 'Is there anything you want me to bring in later?'

'Yes, a bolt from B&Q for that door!'

She looked at the door handle – and then at the high backed chair in the corner. She caught her breath, then grabbed the chair, angled it and jammed it under the handle, but then, as she turned, felt incredibly nervous. Her fingers were shaking as she began to undo the buttons on her blouse. 'This'll just be normal hospital procedure,' she said, to try and break her tension.

He gave her that handsome smile of his, and a look from those hazel eyes. The only man's eyes she'd ever come across that could give 'the weird grey peepers' a run for their money. 'It needn't. We could always have a row first.'

'You bastard!' Clare laughed and then surprised him by moving quickly to the bed and kissing him on the neck.

'Christ!' he shouted, a minute or so later.

Clare, her head resting on his stomach, was looking up at him. She was holding a couple of chest hairs in her fingers. 'And the rest's coming off as well.'

'What, a few at a time, that's–'

He fell silent.

She'd turned her head away.

Acknowledgements

I would like to thank the members of the South Manchester Writers' Workshop and Writers' Inc for all their help through the first draft; thanks also to M.J. Hyland for introducing some rigour into my writing, John Mole for his cover illustration, and Helen Holden for her perceptive observations and proofreading. I am also indebted to Claire Askew for her invaluable advice on the final rewrite of the manuscript.

Thanks also to Mark Whitaker, who dealt so expertly with the technical side of putting the book together, and to Susan Singfield and Philip Caveney who since the beginning have, with Mark, given me so much encouragement and help.

A special thanks to my wife, Jean. Without her patience and understanding the work would never have been completed.

29156388R00216

Printed in Poland
by Amazon Fulfillment
Poland Sp. z o.o., Wrocław